FIVE PILLARS

MIRA'S JOURNEY

T.L.HUTCHINSON

Five Pillars: Mira's Journey

First edition. May, 2026.

DEDICATION

To:

Kat, Jillian, Ellie, Cisley, Katie, David, Emeric, and Bee

The best team that I could possibly ask for, this story wouldn't exist without you.

Thank you for being in my corner.

<3

TRIGGER WARNINGS

Chemical/biological warfare reference, unrestrained bioweapon/disease long term impacts explored, estranged father, dysfunctional family, anxiety, depression, war and all it's horrors, adoption, vomit, blood, gore, train crashes, food instability, housing instability, displacement, corruption, trafficking, sexual exploitation, car accident, grief, forced pregnancy mentions, being drugged, needles, classism, regicide, gun violence, racism, slavery, near drowning, open water (ocean), PTSD (care, fallout, reality, struggle, growth), doomerism rebuked (but present), death, and more.

Please take care of yourself <3

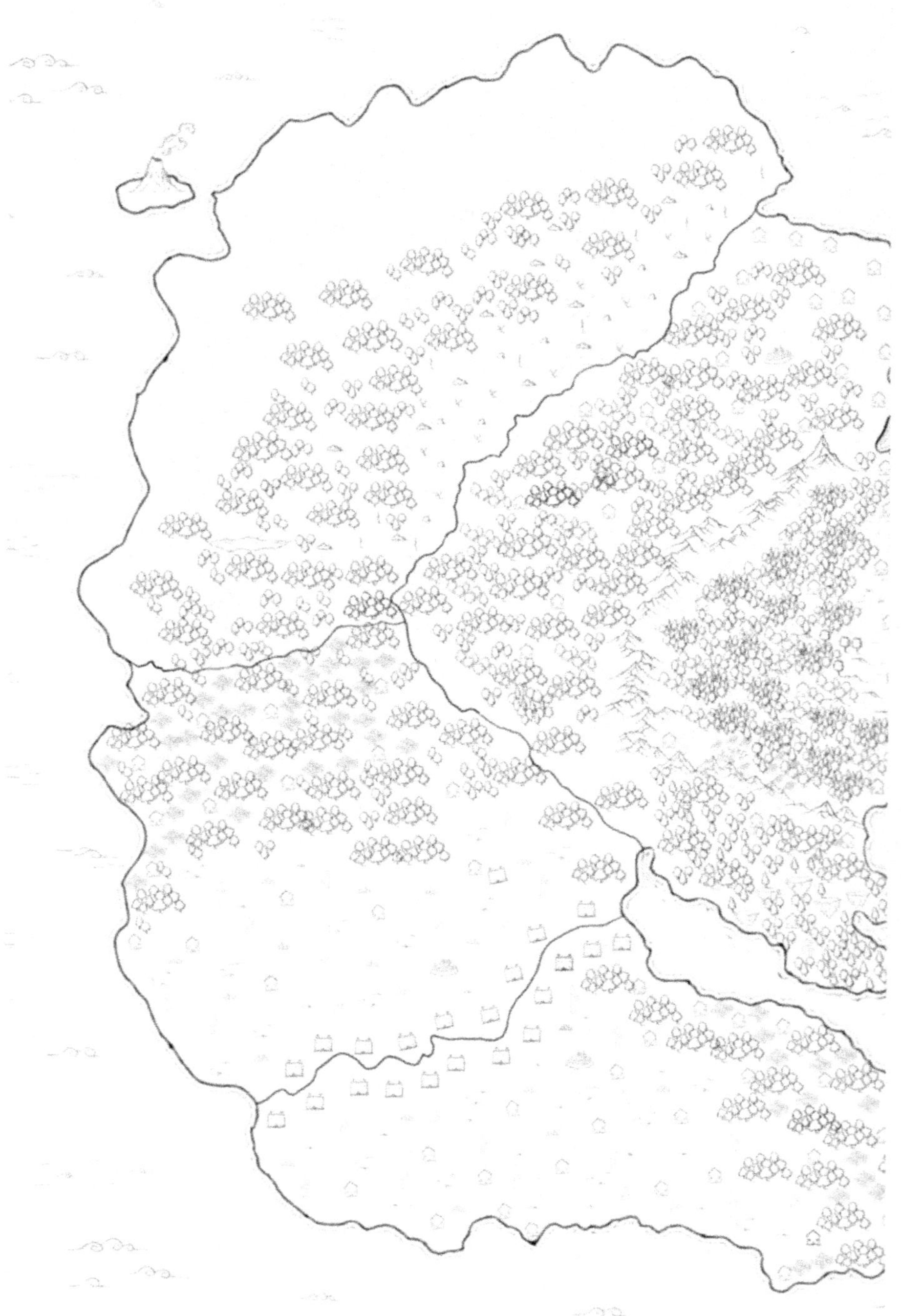

The Five Kingdoms

Donated by:

The Royal Library of Agrenon

1

"Hey, bitch, open the door." I knocked for the third time before I shoved open the large wooden doors and peered into the royal bedroom. Whisper had been in here when I went to bed, helping Saha work through some intentional loophole a certain icy asshole had left in a law, and I hadn't seen either of them all day. Now that evening had crept in, and this oh so special event was looming, I had to bother them.

The well-lit chamber had a bed tucked to one side, a large desk against the opposite wall, and a thick carpet that spilled across the room. Whisper was settled on her stomach surrounded by papers and scrolls, reading another she held open.

The last six months had been hard on me, mostly because she had grown so much. Instead of standing at the height of a toddler, she was now just a little taller than an average preteen. I had a sinking feeling I was going to look up to her when she was grown up. The light skittered from the places it touched her skin across the floor, painting bright pictures of gray-blue light where they lay.

"Hey, where's—"

She waved a hand at me, both getting my attention and cutting me off.

"Shh," she said, pointing to the chair at the desk. Looking closely, I could now see the all-too-familiar form of the Photomyran queen, Saha, sleeping like the dead. I slid into the room. "Don't you dare," she whispered as I crept closer to Saha, who had clearly passed out, the scroll she was reading still laying flat against the table, pinned down by her arms, which her head rested against.

I put my hands on the top of her chair.

"Oh my stars, Saha, the library is on fire!" I said, rocking her chair violently. She leaped up, terror in her eyes; terror that left the minute she saw me.

"Mira Hamilton, I'm gonna beat you within an inch of your life," she said, grabbing up a scroll and swinging it toward my head.

"Hey, watch it!" I said as she got me a few times, holding my hands up to protect my head from the soft roll of parchment.

"Serves you right," Whisper said, turning her attention back to her scroll.

"You take after your father far too much." I winced at the comment but she still gave me another firm smack on the head.

"You love it," I said.

"I do not."

"Yes, you do," Whisper interjected, moving down her scroll as Saha glared at her. She didn't pay the queen any mind.

Saha turned to me, finally setting down her makeshift weapon. "Why?" she asked.

I knew what she meant without the need for clarification.

"Something about you preaching to me about making sure I get enough sleep for today, then staying awake until who knows when just seems off to me. Something, something consequences of our actions or something like that." She didn't stop glaring at me the entire time I spoke.

"So you woke me up based on principle?"

"Yes, yes, I did," I said. "Also, I need to know if Graz is coming. You're announcing him as your heir and doing the whole 'I'm in charge again' thing, so like, is he gonna be there?"

"Oh, no, he's not. He's not quite ready for the world stage."

"Yeah, good call, considering he can't even look you in the eye."

Whisper had looked high and low for Saha's heir, but my uncle apparently thought it was a good idea to keep his enemies close. If it was Taryn or Graz, I would have expected it to be Taryn, with her unbridled confidence and bubbling personality, but no, Graz, with his crystalline blue eyes, and bright orange bloom, just like Saha's, was verified with a shattering accuracy. I didn't know how Whisper's DNA verification method worked, but she seemed completely certain it was him, and I had faith in her. Pair that with the fact that he had his mother's eyes and bloom and his legitimacy was hard to argue. The only problem was that he was everything a king shouldn't be. I knew better than to say that, though.

"We're working on it," Saha said, lifting her hand to her face to rub her eyes clear of sleep and stress. "What time is it?"

"It's midday, which is why I woke you up oh so gently," I started. "Brian and Tamaj are supposed to be at this thing. Did they come back last night?" I didn't want to ask, but needed to know. He was, after all, my father, who had released The Fever into the world, and she was the woman who had lied by omission about who my mother was.

"Yes, they're back. Still angry at them?"

"Meh."

"'Meh' means she's angry," Whisper said without looking up from her scrolls.

"Hush, you."

"Naw, you see, I promised The Two I'd be the biggest problem I could for you on their behalf, considering you still won't give them disguises, so I can't exactly 'hush'," she said, finally glaring up at me.

"Hey, they've already been kidnapped once, disguises just encourage them to run around outside, building who knows what—a life-sized replica of the titanic, a nuke, and whatever else their hearts desire."

"I could totally see them making a nuke if they had the information, but they don't,"

"What's a 'Titanic'?" Saha asked.

"A big boat that sank. Endering history stuff," I said before continuing with Whisper. "They're Echalon. Did you not read the Endering world history books and immediately start making bombs? They'd figure it out."

"They were small-scale replicas."

"One exploded."

"That one wasn't a nuke," she said.

I turned back to Saha. "Help me?"

She scoffed, tidying up her desk area.

"Looks like you're on your own," Whisper said, smirking that cheeky little grin up at me.

"If it's midday, can we make sure the guests have properly settled? They'll only be here for a few hours, but I want them to be very comfortable." Saha's ability to direct a conversation should never be underestimated.

"They're literally the kings, queens, or heirs to the other kingdoms, so I still don't understand why you want it to be pleasant, but I'll go check on them," I said.

"Thank you, Mira. And Whisper?" she said as I turned to head for the door.

"Yes?"

"Can you please ask The Two not to blow anything up tonight?"

"Fiiiine."

I couldn't help but smile.

"Oh, Mira?" I stopped at the door, looking back. "Don't forget they'll each have one Endering with them, and considering your uncle sent the invitations for your being crowned an heir, they are likely…ill informed."

"They're gonna hit on me, I know, but can you blame them? I'm gorgeous," I said, flipping my hair as I slid out of the room. I ran my fingers across the dress I wore, the same one I had worn the night the bond had snapped into place. A coy triumph rang up the now rope-like bond between myself and Anza and I turned on a dime just fast enough to see Anza freeze in place a few feet from me.

"What in the world do you think you're doing?"

"Scaring you?" he ventured, slowly pulling me into a hug, leaving plenty of room for me to pull back, to revoke the consent of the movement. I leaned into him, his hands at my waist as we swayed for a moment.

"Consider me terrified," I said, resting my head against his shoulder as we swayed. We didn't need many words, not now, I could feel him, every fluttering of emotion. Images and ideas flowed down the bond with reckless abandon, and we had even figured out how to push communication down the bond, though that had taken some work. I could imagine that for some people it could be aggravating, but not us. He had been holding back the entire way to the castle, but now, with the bond wide open and months behind us, he was so much more comfortable baring himself to me. He pushed an image down the bond of people filing into the ballroom, gentle and loving and soft.

"We need to go," he said through the bond.

"Fine, fine," I said out loud, lifting my head from his shoulder, his hand wrapped tightly in mine.

Together, we moved simply and quietly toward the ballroom, walking in step, side by side.

The day was already going to be an interesting day. Saha had let the leaders come here on Olaf's invitation. It was far too soon to send out other letters and cancel. There would have been an idea of inorganization, of weakness, in rescinding the letter. She wanted to kill any thought that Agrenon was anything but mighty in her reign. So I had to be pretty, and witty, and ready to show them I would bow to her, which I was fine with.

Being a princess, even if only for that handful of hours, had been daunting. It felt like the entire kingdom was on my shoulders, probably because that's what being a leader was supposed to feel like. Everything was on you.

We passed Graz's room, but I didn't dare knock, knowing he was actively avoiding everyone today. Taryn would be down in the ballroom, a new Queen's Guard, on her first official duty. Someone Saha could trust.

As we reached the top of the steps, I looked around the edges of the room, where the guards were usually posted for her, and caught sight of that boundless bubbling beauty. Her hair was pulled back into tight braids beneath her new green and white armor. A single diamond of orange at the top of the breastplate almost reminded me of a budding flower in its design.

Something wasn't right, though. Taryn was poised tightly in formation, doing everything she was supposed to, but her eyes weren't tracking the guests. No, they were locked on something. No, not something…some*one*. Something was wrong. *Very* wrong. The color had leached from her face, an obvious sign that a threat was present, one she recognized without instruction from her superior officers.

In fact, as I glanced about the room, all the Queen's Guard were looking at a single point. I tried to follow her gaze as I felt ice run through my veins, and there, in the center of the room, he stood. Eyes deep and fierce, his gaze met mine, his curly black hair pulled back out of his eyes as he smirked up at me. He was dressed in black with a dark red thread racing through his suit. The temperature of the air dropped and my knee ached at the cold as his formidable presence permeated the room.

"Oh, shit," I whispered as the queen of Korrewen leaned in to say something to him.

"Move, move!" Anza immediately turned me around and we

quickly rushed back toward the royal bedroom. I let his hand go just long enough to fling the doors open and step inside.

"We have a fucking problem," I said.

"It must be a massive problem considering you just barged right in," Saha said, deadpan.

"Olaf's here."

She finally looked up at me, eyes widening slightly as she looked us over.

"With Korrewen," Anza elaborated as Saha leaned back against her desk for support.

"He could try to assassinate her, " Whisper said quickly, sitting up on the carpet and looking to Saha, whose eyes shifted back and forth, as if analyzing pieces on a chessboard.

"The night he tore through your knee, did he see me?" Saha asked, looking at me. I shifted my weight, feeling the brace settled against my leg, a permanent reminder of that night, one that had haunted me in the weeks after he had nearly killed me. Now it was just a part of life.

"What?"

"Did he see me?"

I ran back over the events of that night in my mind again. The way he lashed out at me, how Tamaj and Anza and Whisper had been there, how he had left. How Saha had come after.

"No, I don't think he did. Why?" I watched a smile bloom over her face, touching every one of her features. With a shock, I realized why she was asking.

Olaf had thought he had successfully committed regicide.

"I have an idea."

2

"What if he just tries to kill me?"

"He won't. This is a formal event. He'd be declaring war. Breathe," Anza said.

"This plan is going to be the death of me."

"You've got this, Princess."

I flashed a playful glare at him, waiting for the doors to open as he rubbed my shoulders. When they opened, I had to be queen-like. If this was going to work, I had to act and portray every semblance of grace I had, which wasn't much.

Olaf knew Saha was dead. He was wrong, of course, but attempting regicide after betraying everyone in your entire family and all your friends in a desperate grab for power left plenty of room for loose ends. Pairing his betrayal with kidnapping, likely with the intent to murder Echalon children, meant Olaf was an immediate and imminent threat. Olaf wouldn't have shown up unless he had malicious intent, or maybe thought he still had leverage. This was going to be *delicious*.

"Is it weird that I'm nervous even pretending to be queen?"

"Not weird at all," Anza assured me. He was putting on a brave face, but the worry that laced through the bond was fierce. Our plan was dangerous.

But so was I. I had to remember that. I was dangerous. I sure as hell didn't feel dangerous in that moment though. My heart thudded in my chest, my mind raced a million miles a minute, and I'm pretty sure I was sweating in places that have no business being sweaty.

The fact of the matter was, I was about to face the man who had tried to kill me. The man who had tried to kill my children. The man I had trusted. And I couldn't just kill him.

Fuck.

The doors opened and I straightened my spine, cracking my neck before shaking my wrists, making sure that the bracelets were there.

"Breathe."

"Beauty and grace," I said.

"Breathing is more important," he countered. "Focus on you, on doing what you physically need to do. We've all got your back. I'm right here."

I nodded, taking a steadying breath, and stepped through the doors and out, lifting my head as all eyes turned toward me. They were expecting me. Olaf's invitations had been all about coming to see me declared his heir on the world stage, and I could already see Olaf talking to another Agregonian noble as if he owned the damn place. He was trying to weasel his way back in.

I felt myself turn toward him and had to correct my path, heading instead toward the stairs that led to the throne above everyone else. He seemed to see what I was going to do, though, and within moments, he sidestepped into my path.

"My lovely niece." Oh, we're going for niceties?

"My doting uncle," I said, flashing a smile at him. *Act cool, act cool.*

"How are you since I've been away?" he asked, a warning in his eyes telling me not to speak too freely.

"Just…smashing. I really would like to catch up, but I have a crown to settle," I said firmly.

"We really will have to talk about that sometime, considering it's my crown you've taken," he said as I sidestepped past him. His crown? It took everything in my power not to tell him exactly what I thought about *his* crown.

"We really will," I said, glaring at him over my shoulder as I ascended the stairs. *Don't fall, don't fall, he's going to look like such a fucking idiot in a minute, just don't fall.* I rose to the top of the stairs, stepping onto the landing. *Own the space. It's yours.* I took a breath, remembering Saha's instruction from moments ago and resting my hand on the banister. *Confidence. Emit confidence.* I turned to the throne before carefully walking along the banister until I was right in front of it, then spun to look out at the crowd.

Eyes turned upward, seeking me out as I rested my hands on the bannisters to either side of me. There was still chatter, so I lifted my hand as Saha had instructed. Olaf's eyebrows furrowed. He had recognized something familiar about how I moved. Good.

With eyes on me, I looked for Anza, searching the crowd. It wasn't long before I found him, mere feet from Olaf. He smirked, and an image of me standing on the balcony flashed in my mind, accompanied by the feeling of pride and validation.

"I'd bow to you, Queen Mira."

I almost scoffed at the thought.

"Not helping," I said back, but couldn't help the smile tugging at my lips. Movement to my right caught my attention; green with a hint of orange. Saha was ready. The crowd was quieting. It was showtime.

"These past few months have been treacherous in Agrenon; from plagues, to bandits, and everything in between, but that is no longer the reality." Pause. Breathe. "Many years ago, a Royal Endering, a man who has dared enter this court, tried to commit regicide." I locked my eyes on Olaf, his brow furrowing even more in confusion. I was outing him for what he had done, but he didn't know why. "*Tried,* being the key word. In the wake of his failed attempt, the only person who could have driven back the bandits, who could have silenced the plague, who could have saved this great nation, has returned." He went pale and I smothered my grin.

"Impossible," I barely heard him breathe.

"It is my honor to re-introduce to you all the elegant, gracious, ferocious, and all around transcendent true Queen of Agrenon. The Fire Tamer of the Middle Kingdom, the Wildflower of the North, The Queen Who Bowed, Queen Sahaveya Aurora Bloodthorne." I watched the color completely drain from his face as I spoke, every word leaving him paler and paler, until Saha strode out, her shoulders relaxed.

She looked like the epitome of elegance and grace. Her hair was woven into an intricate braid that was pinned up at the back of her head, framed by her orange floral bloom vine, a vine all Photomyran had that fell from their heads, though most had two where she had one. Multiple flowers spilled out atop the carefully crafted bun, and she held her chin high. Confidence. Emit Confidence. She had arranged her petals and bright green leaves into a billowing dress that fell to the floor, sleeveless and white against her flawless green skin. The burn scar up one side of her face was in clear view, worn like a badge of honor where her second floral bloom should have been. There was no gait to her step. She didn't walk, she glided.

Her movement looked effortless, but I knew better. This was the woman who had tripped over her own foot last week. She was far more careful than she let on.

Stopping a few feet from me, she waited as I took another nervous breath then turned to her completely and bowed as deeply as I could.

Stealing a glance out at the crowd, I was just in time to see Korrewen's queen turn her furious eyes to Olaf. I couldn't help but feel giddy as I stood back up, stepping back into the spot on the left side of the throne while Saha stepped forward, resting her arms on the banister to each side of her just as I had a few moments prior. Every single movement, down to how I walked, how I owned the throne area, even how I was to interact with the guests, was planned.

My only job at that point was to sit back and make sure no one tried to assassinate her. It was, in theory, the easy part.

"Imposter! Queen Saha is dead!" someone called out. My heart dropped. She had to kill that ideology. Now.

"You have quite the audacity to come into my court and declare me an imposter Amerette."

I looked to the person who had yelled. Amerette. Queen Amerette of Korrewen.

"Prove that you're Saha!" I knew better than to move. We had a code word. If she wanted my intervention, I would know. It was another person, though, who had found a chair a few yards away and stood on it.

"I can tell if she's really the queen."

I saw Saha's smirk.

"Prince Quaren," she said gently.

"Queen Saha called me something else once, the only time I met her before Agrenon's last Royal Endering took the throne. A name only myself, my father, and the real Queen Saha knew of."

I looked past her at the Maraung male. He was fit, wearing a cream coat with a purple sash draped over his shoulders. A tangle of dark hair was pulled back against his head. Did she remember? She had to remember.

"You were six, all those years ago. You've grown up quickly, Little Fish." His eyes of vibrant green softened at the name.

"It's her."

Olaf's eyes hadn't left her. I knew he could freeze every inch of her body with the wave of a hand, but he didn't dare. With all the guards, royals, and the three other Endering I had been avoiding, he would be dead before he left.

I spotted Brian there on the edges of the crowd, having avoided people by tucking himself away behind a pillar, watching with eyes alight with fear and fury, but not daring to move. He hadn't known about the plan, but Tamaj, who stood by his side, was no doubt quelling his worrisome fury as he glared at the brother who had left him in near solitary confinement for two decades.

Queen Saha was back, and there was nothing Olaf could do about it, but so was his brother, and I was practically giddy to watch his face as that revelation was made.

"I understand this may all be a shock to you," Saha started, "but I assure you, a crown is not needed to keep a steady hand on a kingdom. I would know." A few soft chuckles rang through the ballroom and she quieted them with a steady movement of her hand. "I must legally announce two things. First, Mira Hamilton, The Mountain of Agrenon and the Endering you all thought you were coming to see declared heir, is going to be my Royal Endering. I have vetted her and ensured that she does not share any of the same views or tendencies that her predecessor did, and I have in her the utmost amount of trust. Second, I must announce that I have had an heir. He was born back when my regency was stolen from me, and my enemy back then, thankfully, didn't have the sense to kill him, so Prince Grazham Bloodthorne stands ready to continue the legacy of Agrenon, should I fall."

More muttering, and more, angrier glares from Amerette. She was not at all trying to hide her fury.

"Welcome back, Your Majesty," Prince Quaren said, bowing slightly. She simply nodded her appreciation and turned her eyes back to Queen Amerette. They lingered on one another before Amerette looked away. Saha smiled softly and waved a hand at the musicians in the corner, a bright sound starting up as music cascaded throughout the room. She stepped backward, easeful, heading toward her throne without taking her eyes off the room.

Holy shit, did something actually go smoothly?

"Little to the left," I managed without moving my mouth, watching her make the fractional correction before settling onto her throne.

"Thank you."

"My pleasure."

"Did you see their faces?" Saha asked, meaning Amerrette and Olaf.

"He looked like he had seen a ghost," I said.

"Because he did."

"Bet he's kicking himself for letting Graz live," I said.

"For sure." Saha stopped speaking as she saw Taryn start up the stairs, her footfalls as soft as ever. I hadn't heard her approach. "Is there something wrong?"

"Queen Amerette…has asked to speak with you…directly," Taryn said, clearly a little nervous. Saha looked at me.

"Ready to face down a bitch and a traitor?" she asked as she stood.

"I was born ready."

"Good."

3

"My apologies for my lack of manners earlier. I was misinformed." There was no sincerity in Queen Amerette's eyes.

Poised on the end of the steps, I kept close to Saha. We had to keep this brief. The longer Olaf was this close, the more danger Saha was in.

"No hard feelings. It isn't every day a queen comes back from the dead, but I know the game you're trying to play, Amerette," she said before lowering her voice even more. "Let us make it perfectly clear that if he had stepped into this court alone, he would be dead. He is not here to protect you, my friend, *you* are protecting *him*."

Amerette's face fell as she turned to Olaf and I wedged myself between the queens, ensuring Olaf didn't have a clear shot at her. She was my charge. She was my queen. I was her shield and sword. I just had to play nice at this stupid event instead of ripping my uncle apart. I took her hand as she turned, reascending the stairs, making sure I led her carefully, helping her as she lost her balance once to ensure she didn't show it. As we got to the top, I looked back, meeting Olaf's eyes.

"I'm sure you'd like to catch up with your brother." *You know, the one you wrongfully imprisoned for nearly two decades?* "He's around here somewhere," I said, minding the words that actually came out before helping Saha back to her throne. He tore his eyes from mine, glancing about the room until they locked onto Brian's. He hadn't moved, but had been watching Olaf this entire time.

"You did well," Saha whispered as she settled into her seat. "With all of it."

"Yeah, I'm awesome," I whispered back, seeing the slight roll in her eyes, accompanied only by her slight smile on her lips.

"You think you're funny, hmm?"

"Of course I do," I said, spotting Taryn talking to another guard as they met her on the staircase. They were going to replace me at her side so I could mingle. I wanted to get to Anza, and I knew that playing nice with other royals and Endering would be necessary. I tried not to throw up in my mouth thinking about the overwhelming idea of stepping back down those stairs.

"Don't ruin your upper hand by vomiting on your dress," Anza said down the bond, the tension he was feeling still clear.

"I'm so happy my stomach's empty."

"Me too. I'm almost there. I'm trying to get to the stairs, but this crowd is thick."

"Take your time, no rush."

It was then that Taryn and the other guard got to Saha's side and I curtsied to Saha deeply.

"Don't stab anyone," she said, waving her hand toward me. We both knew it was just to appear as though I was beneath her to the guests. The other leaders couldn't think we were on the same level. They couldn't know she actually valued me as a person.

"No promises," I said as I rose, turning before she could protest, and I carefully stepped down the stairs, spotting Anza trying to step away from someone insisting upon a conversation with him. The irritation rang down the bond, but he didn't show it on his face.

"Hello."

I turned to the voice as I got to the bottom step. A man stood there, offering me a hand, his thick, curly, blond hair, pulled back as if he had run his hand through his hair too many times, a few stray strands settling around striking blue eyes. His skin was exceptionally pale, and his accent was familiar, too familiar, but I couldn't place it. He wasn't unattractive at all. He was dressed nicely in a simple black suit, the now familiar insignia of Legalia, a twisting golden snake that turned over on itself around a sword on a dark red background, on his shoulder.

"It's a pleasure to meet you, Mountain."

"And you…" I let the words linger as I took his hand, and realization flashed in those eyes.

"Nadder."

"Like a snake?"

"Um, yes." I looked for Anza, feeling jealousy flash down the bond. His eyes had found us. I shook Nadder's hand before quickly withdrawing my own. He pulled his hand back just as quickly, every inch of him tense, as if he didn't want to be in front of me.

"And for what reason do I have the pleasure of speaking with you?"

"Be nice." I sent down the bond to Anza.

"If he touches you again, he's dead."

"We talked about this."

"Doesn't mean I have to like it."

"I was just coming over to introduce myself. It's a lovely night for a queen to return."

"You can't kill him here, Mr. Jealousy."

"It really is, we're so blessed with her return."

"Never said it would be here," Anza said, and I had to fight to keep from rolling my eyes.

"Do you know if she has considered a treaty with Legalia yet? It would be quite favorful for her to have support in the southern seas."

"What kind of treaty are you talking about?" I asked, hesitating a moment before continuing. "One that would put a male Endering within her grasp?" He immediately went red. I knew what he was trying to do, and now he knew that I knew. "I don't think that's necessary, but I'll ask."

I stepped off the step, padding through the crowd toward Anza without another word. I wasn't going to pretend I didn't know what Nadder had wanted. Saha had already made it clear. I was, as far as they knew, an unpaired female Endering. This was their chance to get into Agrenon.

Before I could make it to Anza, another Endering male stepped in my way. His golden skin and dark hair complimented his face, his hooded eyes dark as his gaze met mine. I noticed his features were clearly of Chinese descent and quite attractive as well. He looked more healthy than Nadder. I opened my mouth to protest, but he spoke first.

"What a beautiful introduction you made with your queen."

"Now who has to be told not to kill someone?" Anza teased. He must have felt my irritation down the bond.

"Shush, you."

"Thank you, but I believe I'm needed elsewhere."

"If I could just get you a drink? I've heard all about Agrenon's delicious wines."

I leaned closer to him, feeling Anza's jealousy flare again, despite his attempt to carefully stifle it.

"I'd rather skewer myself with my own stones," I said before pretending to smooth out a nonexistent wrinkle on his shoulder and stepping around him, gliding to Anza's side.

"They're persistent."

"Quite. Got eyes on Olaf?" I asked as he offered me his arm. I linked mine with his as he nodded toward my uncle, who was trying to stick to his new queen while she spoke to my father. I watched my father regale the enemy queen, her laugh grating against my ears, before I heard a voice to my left.

"Unbearable, isn't she, Chispa?" I looked at the man standing beside me who hadn't been there a moment before. His thick, dark curls framed his entire face and he barely met my height, with tanned skin, which wasn't much lighter than mine. When had he gotten there? "So…bland. The façade is so clear on that one."

"And who are you?" Anza asked.

"Heartlock."

"Biena's Endering," I said simply, Anza shifting slightly beside me.

"Don't worry, young Maraung, I just have to *pretend* to be interested in your partner. Keeping up appearances and all."

"Oh, yeah?" I asked.

"Yes, though you are gorgeous, I don't swing your way," he said gently, flashing us both a look.

"Good to know," Anza said.

"Then why approach?" I asked. "Besides the fact that your leader wants you to?"

"For the fun of it, and because you all seem quite determined to not be doing what you're supposed to be."

"And what is it we're supposed to be doing?" I asked.

"Ah yes, it's a tricky thing, the thing that must be done. If it wasn't, it wouldn't be the thing that must be done."

"This guy is a little unsettling," Anza whispered.

"Being settled is a privilege that we do not have," Heartlock said.

"What are you talking about?" How could someone so small make such a big impression? What was all this nonsense?

"Everyone seems to be having a fabulous time," Anza said.

"Really? Where did your little ice bound traitor and his new queen run off to then?"

Anza and I looked up.

They were gone.

"Get close to your queen," Heartlock said in an almost sing-songy way, a knowing look in his eyes. Anza and I moved at once, spotting my father and Tamaj talking to some noble as we tried to get through the crowd. Brian tilted his head as I caught his eye, as if asking what was wrong.

"To Saha," I said quickly, and his eyes grew wide with understanding. Turning on his heel, he started up the staircase farthest from us, Tamaj quickly picking up that something was wrong as well.

Anza and I finally fought our way to the stairs through the throng of people and he reached for my hand, supporting me in case my brace gave out as we ran up the steps. A gasp rang out as the all-too-familiar sound of an arrow losing rang through the air. Taryn must have seen something. She moved, stepping in front of Saha as I pulled my warmth forward, sending up a wall of stone on the balcony to block them. An arrow vibrated from where it had bit into the rock, level with Taryn's side and Saha's head. A single red ribbon dangled from the end. Red. The color of Korrewen.

"Stop him!" Saha ordered as she stood, and I turned my attention to the man standing with a bow at the edge of the room. Before I could move, though, he drew a knife and pressed it to his throat. His blood spread across the floor before a single guard could touch him.

"What the hell was that?" I asked.

Saha answered as her eyes locked on that crimson ribbon dangling from the end of the arrow.

"An act of war."

4

"Move!" I hissed as we scattered. I wasn't sure where the other Endering rushed their leaders off to, but I rushed Saha toward the council room. I knew every hall and room of the castle, so it was only a matter of seconds before I slammed the door shut behind us, Anza, Brian, Taryn, and Tamaj watching the door as I slid the lock into place.

"Tamaj, where's Whisper?"

"Library, she's with Narin and The Two," she said, her mind brushing my own in a way not unlike the bond.

Narin was a force I was now familiar with, sweet on the outside but Saha's most trusted companion, known for her loyalty and ferocity. They were safe.

"Queen's Guard?"

"A half dozen with them alone. They're safe."

"They better be, if he's after them again."

"He's not after them," Saha said quietly.

"What?"

"If he was after them, he would have been more subtle. He would not have revealed himself at all, but he did. He wasn't after them. He was trying to finish what he started."

"That was a sloppy assassination attempt," Brian said quietly, almost plastering himself against the wall nearest the door.

"Well, he thought Saha was dead," Tamaj said.

"I've gotta check on the kids," I said quietly, trying to figure out how to lay eyes on them without leaving Saha. I had to defend them all, I had to, but I couldn't be in two places at once.

"I'll go," Anza said, pulling me to him to kiss me. *"Will you be alright near him alone?"* I knew he was talking about Brian.

"Be safe," I said after kissing him back. *"I have Taryn and Saha. I'll be alright until you get back. I'd rather be a little uncomfortable and know the kids are safe."*

He nodded his acknowledgement and Taryn went to the door with me. We guarded the only entrance as Anza slipped out into the hallway. Together, we closed the door firmly, and Taryn met my eyes, giving me a firm nod. She had the door. I went to Saha, who was wringing the fingers of one hand with her other.

"Hey, think, breathe," I said gently.

"Grazham?"

"The Queen's Guards would have gone right to him. This isn't their first rodeo," I said.

"I don't know what a rodeo is, but I'll take your word for it," Saha said very quietly. "What does he want? Besides me dead? There has to be an end to the means here."

"He wouldn't have been able to take the kingdom, not with Graz as your heir, unless he killed you both," Tamaj said.

"He didn't have access to Graz. He won't have access to him," I assured Saha, just for Brian's quiet voice to pipe up, a whisper in the adrenaline filled room.

"He might have been trying to invoke war with an untrained, unseasoned regent."

"A prince who would be a king too early," Tamaj said.

"He didn't know we found out about Graz," I said.

"Then an inexperienced Endering barely a queen." I would have been queen if Saha hadn't shown up and we hadn't found Graz.

My stomach flipped but I shoved the thought away. *"He wants to destabilize, but the question lingers: why?"* None of us had an answer for her.

It was then that Anza's voice washed into my mind from down the bond.

"The kids are all safe. Queen's Guard are everywhere. They're helping secure the other regents and leading them out of the castle safely so they can be sent on their way. Checking on Graz now."

"Please let him know he's not king quite yet. He's probably stressed."

"I can almost guarantee he's a mess. I'll let him know." I breathed a sigh of relief as a knock came at the door.

"Who is it?" Taryn asked, bracing herself against the door.

"Taryn, open this door." Titanys's voice rang through the wood and Taryn looked to Saha, who nodded, then quickly opened the door.

"Sorry, Sir, I–Um…"

"Were doing your job. Well done," Titanys, the head of the Agregonian military and a fast friend, said as he slid in, closing the door firmly behind him. Taryn visibly relaxed a little, stealing a look at me. I gave her a reassuring nod and she kept her post at the door.

"I really hope you have something for me, my friend," Saha said, still wringing her hands.

"Hey," Titanys said, and Saha finally looked from the table to him. "We're okay, everything's okay." I saw tears well in her eyes as he spoke, but she blinked them away as she took a ragged breath. "We searched the man's body. He was from Korrewen for sure. All the leaders from the other kingdoms are being escorted to their respective borders with a battalion each to ensure their safety," he explained.

"Not Korrewen, right?"

"No, Amerette and Olaf were spotted fleeing upon Barbarza toward Korrewen."

"Has the castle been searched?" Saha asked as Anza's voice came down from the bond.

"I've got eyes on Graz, he's alright, and very thankful he's not king."

"Yes, and I have personally searched your rooms and ensured there are no intruders," Titanys said.

"Grazham?" Saha asked.

"He's shaken but okay," Titanys said.

Taryn tried, and failed, to smother her small sigh of relief.

"Alright. Titanys, send out a battalion after them. Ensure they make it over the border. Once that's taken care of, we need to ensure our borders, especially along the Korrewen side, are secure," Saha said quietly. "Who knows what they've been doing the last few days?"

"Consider it done," he said, rubbing her back along the spot between her shoulders, a spot I had learned was where she held her stress. Her shoulders shifted as she relaxed a little.

"We don't have much military might right now. We might not be able to defend against Korrewen, especially not against multiple attacks if Biena or Legalia try their luck."

"It won't come to that. Let me work," Titanys assured, and she nodded. He patted her shoulder as he moved to the door. "Mira?" He didn't need to elaborate. I knew what he was asking.

"I've got her," I assured him, and he nodded without looking back at us before slipping out. "Let's get you to your rooms," I said gently, and Saha nodded. "Tamaj, can you check on the kids? Anza made sure they were alright and went to check on Graz."

"I'll stay with them. I've been wanting to tuck them into bed, but Mira…we need to talk."

"Not now," I said a little too firmly, and she lowered her head. She had still lied by omission about my mother, but we had bigger things to tend to at the moment as Taryn, Brian, and I stepped into the hallway, Saha stepping out behind us. Wordlessly, we navigated the space to her room. Six Queen's Guard stood outside, all at attention, but they relaxed a little when they saw us.

"Everything all clear?" Taryn asked.

"Oh yeah, all clear," Titans said as I opened the door to Saha's room, stepping in to take a quick look around myself. I trusted Titanys. He was fierce, and kind and loyal to a fault, but to ease my mind, to leave her here, I needed to see that her room was safe myself. As Titanys had said, her room was secure.

"Hey, you're set. I'll see you in the morning, right?" I asked as Saha slid into the room.

"Yeah, or at least you better," Saha said as I moved closer to the door, holding out my arms. She hugged me tightly. "Thank you."

"It was nothing."

"It wasn't nothing. You and Taryn saved me today."

"Kinda my job," I said, and she gave me another tight squeeze.

"Thank you anyway. Now, go, I'm sure you want to tend to your littles and meet up with Anza."

"Yeah," I said, nodding as we broke the hug. "Night."

"Night," she said as I stepped out of the room and closed the door behind me, turning to Taryn first.

"Go to Graz. We both know he needs to know you're alive."

"Thanks," she said, already backing up toward the door to Graz's suite of rooms. "And Mira?"

"Yeah?"

"Thank you."

"Yeah, yeah," I said, waving her away. She rolled her eyes and slipped into the dim light of the hall. Leaving me alone in the hallway with the guards and Brian. Damn it.

"*I might need you,*" I sent down the bond.

We had talked about my father in depth, and the impact he had on Agrenon. I still wasn't happy that Saha saw it fit to let him roam free out here, but being locked up for twenty years had apparently worn on him. He wasn't the man she had known, and she had not wanted to punish him too harshly. I had to convince Anza not to kill him on sight under the threat of being treasonous, and now we were effectively alone together.

"I'm coming."

"Mira, I—"

"I don't want to talk to you."

"But—"

"I don't care. I don't care about your reasons or your thoughts or where you stand on anything. I don't care if you're trying to apologise or connect. I don't care. I don't want to talk to you. The Fever you unleashed destroyed thousands of lives. Arlo's dead, Anza's family died before I came around, and so many more we don't know about. It took parents from their children, made good men and women into monsters, and ruined thousands of lives. You do not get to stand before me and say anything," I said firmly as he backed up a little.

"Tamaj isn't angry with me," he whispered.

"And you better be thankful for her good graces. She almost had her mate back, but you fucked around," I said, seeing Anza rush down the hallway behind him. I didn't need to continue, but I did need to keep them away from each other. "It's a miracle Saha tolerates you," I said before pushing past him to go to Anza, who quickly wrapped an arm around me.

"You alright?"

"Yeah."

"Lets go," he said, glaring daggers at the form of Brian in the hallway. I turned to look at him, his shoulders pulled in, elbows tucked into his side, as if trying to make himself small.

Part of me ached. I wanted to be supportive of him, wanted to comfort him, but that wasn't my place. He was lucky he wasn't sentenced to death. Lucky Saha was too merciful for her own good. Lucky she decided he had served his time.

Anza took my hand, ensuring he stayed between me and my father, and led me away, back toward our room.

"He didn't hurt you, right?"

"No, I just didn't want to be alone with him."

"Alright," he said as we moved. "I'll kill him if you want me to."

I smirked, knowing he was only half joking.

"Saha would have a problem with that."

"Contrary to popular belief, I'm not here for Saha."

"I know." I sighed. Even though he had joined the Queen's Guard and was actively training Graz, I knew that there would likely be a time when Anza and Brian spoke without me. I felt bad for him, Brian, because though I had been harsh, Anza would be far harsher. "Theres been enough killing today," I said as we moved toward the wing of the castle where our suite was, his hand sliding into mine as we slid into the simple space; four small square rooms settled with their entrances in each corner of a larger square room and a kitchenette set into the side wall to the right between two doors. Our bedroom was the closest to the front door, but I wasn't worried about getting to bed just yet.

Anza and I split up. He went to the room farthest from the door diagonally and I stepped to the left and quickly eased open the wooden door to peer inside. There were smatterings of maps on the walls and a workbench covered in components I couldn't make out in the low light, but tucked into bed was a small glittering form, the light of the window sending spiraling splashes of amber and gold throughout the room as she shifted under her blanket. I breathed a sigh of relief and stepped back into the main room, looking to Anza as he nodded, assuring me our little guy was alright as he moved to Whisper's room. I waited as he peeked in and watched his shoulders relax as he stepped back to my side.

"Tamaj is in Whisper's room. They're okay."

"Alright, alright," I said as he hooked his fingers into the belt loops at each of my hips. I rested my head on his shoulder and we swayed together for just a moment, breathing each other in before he took my hands and led me to our room.

"Sleep?"

"Sleep," he agreed. We quietly changed, washed away the dirt from the day, and settled into bed, slipping into a restless sleep.

We were going to war.

5

"Shh you're gonna wake them up." I opened my eyes to Anza stirring just slightly before I felt hard weight crash down on both of us.

"Incoming," I groaned, far too late, as Anza grumbled and rolled over, scooping up one of The Two and bundling them in a blanket without opening his eyes. From the flash of dark gray I spotted as he bundled the little one up, I knew it was our sweet boy.

"Oh no, I'll save you, Arlo!"

"Rania, the blanket is never ending, like the fabric of the universe! It is part of me and I am part of it!" Arlo declared.

"Too much philosophy," Anza grumbled as Rania scrambled haphazardly up to sit on his chest.

Her deep amber color sent spatterings of gold and orange across the floor as the sun spiraled through her, fragmenting like light on a disco ball or a crystal. Her round face almost made her look as innocent as any other child could be, but I knew better. The light of our lives, waking us up like demon hellspawn, Echalon weren't normal children. They could outthink you, out argue you, and run laps around you with ease. Rania could be sweet, and kind, and wonderful. She could also blow up the library, throw herself down a set of stairs just to scare the shit out of Narin, and stand toe to toe with experts in their field demanding information for her research without fear.

Arlo had no issue matching her in every horrifying, hilarious, and unfathomable way. Adorable and too smart for their own good, we wouldn't have it any other way.

"Not enough philosophy," she countered, and I snatched her off Anza's chest to hold her up in the air. She shrieked her joy, kicking her little feet with her precious little toes as I gently tossed her, catching her again.

"Are you missing your socks?"

"Socks are for the weak," Rania declared as I tossed her again.

"Socks are very important," Anza said, sitting up.

Arlo finally wiggled his way out of the blanket trap, his dark hair askew as he dramatically crawled to the edge of the bed, searching for his faux salvation as the door creaked a little farther open.

"I *told* them this was a bad idea," Whisper said as I stumbled to my feet, my knee threatening to give without my brace. I sat Rania down on the bed, helping Arlo to the floor as Rania hopped down herself.

"I think we'll live," Anza said.

"Are you sure?" Whisper asked as he got up.

"No," he said, and Whisper rolled her eyes, slipping back out of the room.

"Go get your sister," I encouraged, and The Two giggled, quickly chasing after Whisper.

"Mom!" Whisper groaned, and Anza chuckled as I closed the door.

We dressed quickly and slid into the main room. Rania and Arlo were now entertained with a small device they were crafting, Whisper reading quietly at the table at the far side of the room.

"Tamaj?" I asked.

"She snuck out already, asked me to ask you to meet her in the ballroom? I think she wants to talk about something."

I sighed as Anza rubbed my back a little.

"We should talk to her at least. It's Tamaj."

"Yeah, I missed her, and I wanna tell her about the cool shi-stuff, the cool stuff I learned," Whisper said, correcting herself as she saw Rania look up to her as she almost swore.

"Alright, we'll do breakfast, then we'll go talk to her," I said, moving toward the kitchen with Anza.

"What's the deal with you two anyway? You've been weird when I talk about her," Whisper said.

"It's complicated," I said.

"Then un-complicate it, jeeze," Whisper retorted and Anza snorted, failing to smother his laughter.

"As forward as ever," I said.

"Wouldn't have it any other way," Anza said, shaking his head and beginning to prepare ingredients as Arlo quickly abandoned his work to move to his side.

"I wanna help."

"Alright, bud," Anza said, helping Arlo up into a chair.

"Well," I started, deciding to elaborate for Whisper, "I'm not exactly happy with her. She didn't tell me Emai was my mom. We met her before we met you, and it would have been easy for her to say something, but she didn't," I explained.

"Yeah, if you don't go talk it out with her I might have to start being problematic," she said, shrugging.

"You're already problematic," I said as she gave me a sly smirk.

"Oh, Mother dearest," she almost sang. "You haven't seen problematic yet."

"Yeah, yeah," I said, giving Anza a look to see if he needed or wanted help, but he shook his head. I cleaned dishes as they worked, and only after everyone was done eating did we lead the children down to the ballroom, which had been turned into a dining hall for the time being.

Whisper rushed ahead of The Two to Tamaj, reaching up to hug her.

"Good morning, my sweet little Moonbeam!" Tamaj said, leaping up from her place at a table as Whisper hugged her, Tamaj's eyes meeting mine and Anza's.

"Hey, Tamaj," Anza said, stepping away from me to hug our friend as well.

"Don't you seem more confident Mr. Blush-a-Lot?"

"Hey!" Anza laughed, ruffling her hair as The Two each reached for my hand.

"You two met her last night, right?" I asked them.

"Yeah. Whisper said she's a friend," Rania replied.

"She is," I assured them.

"She had cool stories," Arlo prompted as Anza returned to my side, Whisper already talking Tamaj's ear off.

"Why don't you two come with me to the library? I think Mom and Tamaj have to talk about something," Anza said.

"Yeah!" they said together. Whisper took the hint, ending her ramble and hugging Tamaj again before following Anza and leaving Tamaj and I alone in the mostly empty room.

"Hey, um…"

"I'm so sorry." We had both tried to talk at once and we both stopped to hesitate before laughing awkwardly. *"I know I should have told you, but Emai asked me not to. She thought she might distract you if you knew."*

"Honestly, she was probably right, and she could have just said something herself, you know?"

"She wanted to, I know she did."

"You know her pretty well, huh?"

"Yes, and I've learned that even if I don't understand what she asks of me, that it's unwise to question her," Tamaj said, and I sighed. My mother was right there, but she could have explained and told me herself. Was it for the better that I hadn't known? I couldn't know now, but staying mad at Tamaj just to be mad didn't make sense.

"Alright, you're forgiven."

"Wait, just like that?"

"Just like that. I don't want to be mad at you, and you've been gone for months. Whisper misses you."

"Just Whisper, huh?" she teased.

"Fine, fine, I guess Anza and I probably missed you a little too," I conceded as she stepped forward. I moved toward her, hugging her tightly as she tucked her head against my back.

"How was your trip?" I sighed, relaxing a little as she stepped away from me, breaking our hug.

"Interesting, to say the least. We managed to get rid of The Fever across Agrenon, but I am concerned for your father." I tried to muffle my groan. *"You don't like him."*

"I'm angry at him for all the shit he caused."

"That's understandable and completely valid. He's made quite the mess of so many lives."

"So why are you worried about him?"

"The Brian I knew was confident, capable. He matched your mother. That man isn't much more than a ghost right now," she said, but as I opened my mouth to respond I heard footsteps behind me and turned. Saha was briskly walking toward us, a look of alarm on her face and Brian right behind her.

"What's wrong?" I asked, hoping he hadn't heard us.

"The....air? It's...spicy?" she said, as if trying to find the right words. " I don't know. Something isn't right, nothing's right."

"Hey, whoa, I'm sure there's an explanation," I said as Titanys slipped through the front door of the castle, a scout at his side.

"The air is spicy?" I asked him as he approached. The Photomyran scout nodded.

"I don't feel it, but many Photomyran mentioned it on my way in."

"It's not important," Saha said quietly. "You have something?"

"The battalion we sent after Amerette and Olaf was met with

Korrewen forces. They've already begun their invasion, last night, likely while you were holding the event. They thought they'd be facing either Mira or Graz, they didn't expect you,"

"How long before they're upon us?" Saha asked.

"That's…the strange thing. They're not coming to the castle." Titanys said.

"What?"

"We're not sure why. A small group is headed here, but they're not enough to be a real threat. The rest of the army is marching south."

"Why?"

"We don't know, but it would be unwise to let them get very far."

"Wait a minute, what is the only thing they could want in the south?" Whisper said, meeting Saha's eyes. I watched as all the color faded from Saha's features.

"The portal. They're trying to claim Agrenon's portal for their own. If Korrewen gets their hands on even two or three more Endering they would crush us at our best. Send who we can, I'll ride out as well. And we should take Graz; it's about time he sees what it is to be a leader," she said quietly, her eyes flicking back and forth on her invisible chess board again.

"We'll have to keep people close to him. We don't need him dying on us," Titanys said.

"Agreed," Saha said, her eyes flitting as she thought of the best person to stay near to her heir.

"Taryn's a good choice," I said before I could think. "If I hadn't pulled up the stone, that arrow would have hit her, not you."

Saha hesitated before nodding briskly. "Titanys, see to it that Taryn sticks close to the prince."

"Of course," he said as Saha turned her attention to me.

"Before we leave, I need a favor from you."

"Oh, jeeze. What is it?"

"It might be uncomfortable."

"Saha, what?"

"Olaf's journals indicate that he attempted to banish Emai."

"Hard emphasis on 'attempted.'" Tamaj chuckled, smirking at the information. I smothered a smile.

"Yeah, I remember seeing the mark at the back of her neck," I said, recalling the first time I met my mother.

"That may be a reason for her to stay away from the castle. She never did well on your side of the portal, the risk of a lifetime there might frighten her. We can undo this for her, we need all the help we can get after all. Whisper had found a banishment reversal spell hidden in one of the scrolls we were working on yesterday when you so gracefully woke me."

"Yeah?"

"It takes two Endering to perform."

"Oh," I said as I looked to Brian, who was clutching a scrap of paper.

"Please?" Saha asked, and I sighed, closing my eyes to compose myself for a moment.

"If I say no?"

"We'll have to find a way to do this without her." Saha would respect my choice, but even I knew my mother would be a massive asset in a war.

"Fine, I'll do it. What do I have to do?"

"It's pretty straightforward. The hardest part is the sigil."

I tried to ignore Brian, looking to Tamaj.

"Can you make sure the sigil looks right once it's made?"

Tamaj gave me a look of disapproval. *"I don't know a single thing about crafting magic, except how to not get blown up."*

"Great," I said before sending a message down the bond. *"I might need you up here, if the kids are in good hands? Bring Whisper?"*

Brian had taken the hint and stepped a few feet away, starting to work on the large, intricate piece, chalking it into the floor of the ballroom.

"Narin has them. I'm coming. What's wrong?"

"Saha wants me to do magic with Brian. It's for a good reason so I agreed, I just know magic can be tiring."

"Don't do anything without me there."

"I won't."

I waited, staying back as Titanys and the scout left to prepare to head out, Saha settling on a step, watching quietly. Tamaj tucked her feet under her, settling in like a cat might settle into a loaf shape as Anza appeared from the entrance to the library, Whisper on his heels. He came straight over to me as Whisper padded to Tamaj, looking over the sigil. I reached for his hand. He laced his fingers in mine without hesitation.

"You've got me?"

"I've got you, just give me a sec," he said, his eyes turning to Brian as he stepped away.

"Anza." He didn't stop until he was an inch from Brian's face. Brian didn't flinch, but steeled himself. I couldn't see him breathing. *"Restraint, please,"* I begged Anza.

"If a single thing happens that shouldn't with this spell, I will not hesitate."

"Why do you hesitate now? It's no secret you hate me."

"Anza," Saha said firmly.

"Because I've got people more worthy of my time. Beating your ass would just be, what is it you Endering say? The frosting on top?" They stared each other down for a moment before Brian lowered his eyes. "Not one thing." Anza stepped back, turning to face me as he returned to my side.

"Was that necessary?" Saha asked.

"You're lucky I didn't hit him."

I sighed, knowing he was being honest. His rage and hatred for Brian burned down the bond. I looked to Whisper.

"What do you think, Moonbeam? We're trying to get rid of a banishment spell."

"This is waaaaay more intricate than most of my books, it's gonna pack a punch. It'll remove a banishment spell for sure."

"Let's just get this over with," I said. "What do I do?"

"Take the place there." Brian gestured to a section of the sigil that was circular, as if designed to be a sitting spot. "Hands to the sides in the semi circles beside it." I moved to the position he asked of me, settling down with crossed legs in the spot as he did the same in a spot directly opposite me. "Magic can be a dangerous thing if you don't know what you're doing," he said quietly, almost as if he was talking to himself. "You can get hurt, or seriously killed."

"Like regular killed, but super serious."

"The most serious, dead, dead," he said, trying to smother a cracking smile. He knew I didn't like him.

"Seriously dead."

"Seriously," he said.

I hated that this back and forth was so easy.

"You know magic as well as Mom, don't you?" I asked, and he didn't look at me as he nodded.

"Only one of us needs to cast it. The second person, you, in this case, are just acting as a kind of magical recoil, so the brunt of the spell doesn't go to one person."

"So I realistically just have to sit here?"

"And be open. It'll sap quite a bit of energy, but if we don't do it this way—"

"Whoever is casting the spell will die."

"Probably. There's too much backlash in a spell of this magnitude for one person to handle."

"Alright, ready when you are," I said, knowing Anza wasn't more than a half step behind me now.

Brian nodded, settling his hands onto the sigil, and it only took a moment before the sigil flashed. I felt weight crash down on me, rushing energy spiraling from my fingertips, almost boundless, brilliant and pure.

Overall, the spell only lasted another moment, energy rising up between us in a pair of threads, one golden, and one silver, before it flashed again, the energy erupting outward, past us, and out into the world. The sigil faded to nothing but black smears on the floor.

"Done?" I asked.

"Done," Brian said.

"Great," I said before turning to look at Saha, my vision swimming as I tried to stay sitting upright. "Let's go to war."

6

Sil

"What the fuck!" Pain bit across my back as I leaned over the kitchen sink, the dish I was washing from my late breakfast slipping back down into the soapy water as the pain continued to burn, just as hot as it did *that* day. I couldn't catch my breath, my legs falling out from under me as shockwaves of pin-pricking pain rushed over me, through me. It rippled outward, over and over again, getting faster and faster. Was I dying? Was I going to die alone on this floor before I ever saw my granddaughter again?

Gradually, it slowed and I could breathe again, panting on the kitchen floor. I tried my legs, finding I could move them, and got up, rushing to the bathroom of the small cabin. The minute the mirror came into view, I turned and pulled down the neck of my shirt, revealing the source of the pain. The banishment mark, which had sat along the back of my neck, was gone.

"No fucking way." Had I seen that wrong? Was I dreaming again? I took my shirt off, turning to look again, only to find the familiar scars of the past, but no banishment mark. My heart stuttered before it leaped into my throat. Could I go? Was I finally forgiven? Would I be allowed to return? I put my shirt back on, steadying myself against the bathroom sink.

"Calm down. Calm down." I closed my eyes, trying to breathe deeply, but that face met me against the back of my eyelids, eyes as deep and beautifully blue as before.

Did I remember her correctly? Did my memory even do her justice after over twenty years? Her eyes, as crystalline as the clearest ocean, still looked back, her tears just as real as that day. The way her jaw sloped in that weak morning light. The hardened look in her eyes one of disapproval, of pain. I opened my eyes. Did *she* want me back? I needed to know.

"Just one more trip. Just one. If you can't go through this time, it's final. Really final," I said to myself quietly, as if the banishment could slide back into place if I spoke too loudly.

I moved to my office. The desk was still clean and clear, but it was the trunk in the corner I needed. I hadn't used what was in that trunk since that day, but I had a feeling I'd need it again and hadn't been able to bring myself to dispose of it. I felt like I was in a dream opening that trunk.

Slowly, I pulled my leathers out and dressed, tying the sunset-orange banner across my hips like a belt. The small saddle slid into place at the sheath built into the back of my leathers, adjusting for my slight size change, still as lightweight as ever. I sheathed the only remaining knife I had at my right hip. Slowly, I pulled out the goggles, sliding them over my head to rest at my neck, and took a breath. This was going to work. It had to.

Slowly, I moved back to the kitchen, fetching my boots from the small space near the door, sitting at the table to tie them before getting up and heading toward the back door. Each step made my stomach twist, the what ifs burning in my mind. What if it was a mistake? What if I tried the portal and it didn't work? What if she was there waiting for me? It made me feel sick, the betrayal in her eyes that day was still fresh nearly a quarter century later.

I stepped out of the house, closing the door behind me, and stepped down the back porch, heading directly out toward the portal. A portal I had gone to a thousand times over, tested and tried over and over again, foolishly hoping to go home. How many times had I hit my knees at the base of that portal, begging, praying to anything that would hear me, only to be left unanswered? Her fury had been insurmountable. Framed in those eyes, cold and hard and fierce. Do I even want to go back to her? That needy, frustrating, petulant, irritating, vile, desperate, needy, anger-inducing queen?

Yes.

Every inch of me screamed its need as the portal came into view. I stopped before it. I needed to make my way back to her. Every instance of trying, and trying, and trying only to fail came flooding back. I was facing either my salvation or my demise. Carefully, I stepped forward, taking my place between the arching stones.

Nothing.

I closed my eyes, feeling the tears well, before all at once, the feeling crashed over me, similar to a wave knocking me off my feet. The electric pin-pricking static ran through every inch of me. I stepped forward into a clearing in the woods I had known once, a lifetime ago. In the distance, among the trees, were small makeshift tents, but I couldn't focus on that.

This was a dream. It had to be.

I lifted my hands, burying them close to my chest, holding them just far enough away from my shirt to ensure my shirt wouldn't ignite if this was real. Then I reached. Down, deep, to that cavern within me that had been boarded up and shut off for more than two decades, to that extinguished wick within me, and I called it forward. The flame that had once rose and fell with each breath sparked to life in my hands as warmth simultaneously flooded me. The wick, not unlike that of a candle within me, lit again. Hot tears spilled from my eyes as I took a sobbing breath. The clouds broke and the light of day bathed the small clearing.

I was home.

7

Mira

"I'm coming!" I heard Whisper's voice as I stepped down the stairs outside the castle, following Brian, Saha, Graz, and Tamaj. Anza stuck to my side, troops flooding every inch of the space as they prepared for a war even our queen knew we couldn't win.

"You're not coming," I said, and her face dropped. A pack laden with supplies rested at her feet and she had dressed in her own formal pants and shirt. She had even gotten a pin, a twin of the one that sat at my shoulder, displaying the symbol of Agrenon, that small orange flower bud.

"Why not?" she said immediately. "I can't do anything to help you here!"

I opened my mouth to speak, but didn't need to.

"You're too important, Moonbeam," Anza said. "We worked so hard to keep you safe getting you here, we can't knowingly put you in danger."

"And I think Narin might have her hands full with The Two; she'll need your help."

"Ew, you're literally putting me on babysitting duty? I can fight."

"I know you can fight, but you shouldn't have to," Anza said.

"Just…promise me you'll stop him? This is gonna get bad if you don't. Like, bad."

"We'll give it our all," I said before Anza and I hugged her.

"Alright, I love you, Mom. Love you, Dad."

"Love you, too. "

"Love you, too."

"We'll be back," I said, knowing it was a promise I might not be able to keep.

"You better be," she said, giving me a stern look.

I kissed her forehead before turning to make our way to Tamaj several yards away, who had stopped and gently gestured for us to get on. Just like old times. Carefully, I climbed on, Anza settling in behind me, his fingers finding my belt loops.

"Theres no way on the face of either of our planets that she's not gonna try to sneak out with us." Anza said shaking his head.

"Oh no, for sure but I am just giving the tiniest illogical spark of hope that she dosen't do exactly the opposite of what we've asked her." I said, looking back to our daughter.

"Echalon do what they want." Tamaj laughed as I reached forward to pet her mane.

"Happy to see we've made up," Anza said quietly.

"You didn't seem as mad as I was."

"I wasn't, but I was mad for you."

"It was silly; I should have just told you," Tamaj said, her tail wagging.

"I'm going to put a special emphasis on the 'we made up' part," I said.

The six months had been good for her. She was stronger, no longer thin and weak. She kept up as everyone else settled on Barbarza mounts themselves. My dad was chatting with Graz, while Saha seemed to be speaking to the Barbarza she was on. Taryn just watched, looking about as Tamaj got to her side.

"Think we're ready?" I asked Taryn.

"No?" she said with a sharp laugh. "We can do this, right?"

"It'll be easy; we just find Olaf, whoop his ass, and get home by dinner. It'll be delicious."

"A rare treat," she said, smiling brightly at the idea.

I had a feeling deep in my bones that we would not be able to indulge in such a treat. This wasn't a journey across a nation with a half-starved Barbarza, a quirky and incredibly handsome Maraung, and a stab-happy Echalon. No, we had an army. We had a kingdom behind us. My father was here. Taryn and Anza had been teaching Graz how to really fight. Saha had been trying to teach him too. There was so much more that we had this time.

We left the City of Blood without fanfare.

Tamaj kept close to Saha's mount, a Barbarza from the military that I didn't recognize, and we headed south, along the eastern edge of Agrenon. The portal was on the right-hand side, but this path was one without thick mountains. Anza simply hadn't known it existed until one of Graz's many lessons Saha had us sit in on. We could skirt the mountains and head straight to the portal to defend it. We headed out toward the Shale Tree. Saha's plan was to go straight down from there, effectively avoiding the mountains. Once we hit the beach, we were to follow it almost completely to the portal.

Anza linked his fingers in my belt loop as we moved, Tamaj's brisk step matching that of Saha's mount. We sat in silence together, taking in the scenery, wondering how we had taken so long to get to the castle. Probably because every other second we were being blown up and chased down.

We passed through a village and I remembered which village it was as a familiar, sharp-eyed Photomyran looked over us as we passed from her spot at her tavern's door. I jerked my head toward the group, asking her to join us, but she shook her head and I let it be. She had asked me to forget she existed. So, I pushed her out of my mind as Anza spoke. It didn't feel like we were making great time, but Barbarza that weren't on the brink of death could move. We were covering a lot more ground.

"Do you think we're going to pass my village?" Anza asked,

resting his head on my shoulder. The bond rang with discomfort, which seemed to have multiple points of origin.

"Probably," I said. "You know he's not going to do anything to you; he wouldn't invoke my wrath."

"I know. I'm not afraid of him." There was almost a twinge of pain within him. Almost.

"You're a little afraid of him."

"Naw, him? No."

"Anza."

"Fractionally."

"My mother is literally the Reaper and you basically danced with her."

"Dancing and fighting are not the same thing, and she didn't bring an entire nation to its knees with a wave of her hand. Her power seems more confined to her being, his…his can reach out, fester and multiply and spread, without him."

"I guess that is pretty frightening to think about."

"What if he does it again? How fast can an illness jump from just one person to another?"

"I don't know, you'd have to ask him."

"I'm not asking him about anything."

I rested my head back against his shoulder. "Tremble-vine," I teased, having heard the phrase for a nervous person from Taryn.

"I am not, I'm just giving him a healthy amount of respect."

"And fear."

"Fractionally," he said again, smirking at me.

"Just a little baby fear."

"Exactly," he said. "And I don't know why, but his face looks so punchable."

"Did you feel that way about Olaf at first?"

"No."

"They're identical twins."

"Hush, you."

I laughed as he kissed my neck before he suddenly perked up, turning to look behind us at the other troops.

"What is it?" I asked, looking back.

"I thought I felt…hmm, must be nothing."

"It's never nothing," I said and he flashed me a look. He wasn't sure what he felt, but a plan was there in his eyes. Play along.

"I wonder if Whisper was right, if he really is going to the portal?" That fucking kid.

"Nah, it'll be fine. We could probably let him get to the portal, like what's the worst he could do with it?"

"No big deal?" I turned to see a Maraung, one of the few troops walking, not far from us. "It would be catastrophic!"

"And there she is," Anza said.

"Whisper." I hissed. She rolled her eyes as I made space for her on Tamaj, who just shook her head as Whisper begrudgingly climbed on.

"Children. Always doing exactly what you told them not to," she said.

"We are literally miles from the castle. What are you doing out here?" I asked as I pulled her up.

"Whatever I want. When has anything you've ever said stopped that?"

"She has a point," Anza grumbled.

"Hush," I said to him before opening my mouth to debate our daughter, but she cut me off.

"Olaf getting a hold of the portal would be terrible, catastrophic. No more Endering in, he could potentially double his ranks in who knows how much time? Endering kind of just wander through the fucking things if they don't know about them already, like come on it's more obvious than a fae trap."

"Alright, alright, we get it; it would be bad, terrible."

"And you still didn't want me to come along."

"We're sending you back to the castle," I said firmly.

"It would be better if you were safe," Anza backed me up.

"I'm not safe there any more than I am here, especially if you fail, and even if you tried to send me back, I'd outsmart whoever you sent to make sure I got there." I pursed my lips, looking out over the troops trudging across the plains of Agrenon, heading toward The Shale Tree. "I also want to see The Shale Tree again, and if we're going to end up going to Korrewen afterward, then we can find out if they really have Echalon trapped there."

"We probably are just going to beat them back into their borders and call it a day, we probably aren't even going to Korrewen." Anza said before Tamaj spoke.

"She's not wrong," Tamaj said. "Let her come. She knows magic and strategy; she'll be a great asset, even if we don't have to cross the border."

"Or a great ass," I grumbled, but she did have a point.

"Hey!" Whisper protested. "I'm the *greatest* ass."

"Sorry, the 'greatest' ass," I said, correcting myself. I could feel Anza withholding a chuckle. "Fine, you can stay, just stay out of the fighting for me? I don't need to lose a daughter."

"You have another one."

"I enjoy having two daughters," Anza said, reaching over me to ruffle her hair. She swatted his hand away and he pulled it back. They gave each other a look of fond irritation.

"Same," I said as Whisper rolled her eyes.

"Fine, no fighting unless I have to."

"Thank you," I said, hugging her as she wriggled.

"Ugh, you're welcome, Mom."

"I wonder if you two were this aggravating and moody as teenagers," Tamaj said.

"Probably."

"Oh, yeah," Anza said, nodding as Whisper leaned forward, putting her hands on Tamaj's shoulders as she paid attention to the movement forward.

"How much longer till we get to The Shale Tree?"

"Not much. It's a little easier to cover ground when I'm not about to collapse," Tamaj said happily.

"It must feel really great for your muscles to work again."

"You have no idea," she said as Saha and the Barbarza she was with stopped on a hill not far from us. I could feel the ripple of distress roll through the group before Anza slammed shut that small window that gave me access to his empathic ability down the bond.

"Anza?"

"Something's wrong," he said, his face falling as Tamaj picked up the pace. It was only a moment before we crested the hill and looked down upon The Shale Tree.

"Oh, no."

A swath of people were entangled in the wrath of The Fallen, The Shale Tree swaying slowly as small roots lashed out at them. It was a small group, but one large enough to rival the meager forces we had on hand. My stomach twisted thinking about those icy blue eyes. I was going to have to face him sooner rather than later, and that was as clear as the blood-red flags that rose to touch the sky.

"Korrewen's already here."

8

"They're too close to the castle. We need to move. Quickly," Saha said, looking at me.

"I need to get to the tree," Whisper said, and even though she was still disguised, her voice wasn't, and Saha snapped her head around to look at her.

"Who let you come along?"

"No one, I do what I want. If we go down there swords drawn, the tree's just gonna send The Fallen after us too. If I can get to it, I can help it see we're here to help it. I can show it the difference between the people down there and us."

"You literally just said you'd stay out of a fight," I said.

"If The Shale Tree weren't at risk, I would."

"Whisper," Anza warned.

"Come on, Dad, you know I have a thing with it."

"Yeah, the thing I remember wasn't exactly a picnic," Anza said, and I nodded in agreement, already feeling a sinking feeling in my gut. Could we survive another run-in with that catastrophic wave of dead Echalon?

"We don't have time to debate this," Saha said firmly. "You can do it?"

"I can, I promise," Whisper said as Saha looked back at us. I could feel irritation at Saha shooting down the bond as Anza's eyes bored into her. I wanted to smack her myself, but doubting Whisper's abilities never resulted in anything good. If she said she could do this, she could do this.

"Fine, but we stick to her like glue. We won't be next to you," I warned Saha.

Our daughter came first.

"Deal," Saha said, nodding her understanding as Brian on his Barbarza partner stepped up to her side. "You four, head to the tree itself. Brian, we'll take the fight to Korrewen's forces. Graz, Taryn, stay close."

"Can do," Taryn said, Graz shifting nervously in the saddle of his mount. This was their first actual battle. Espionage was a different game entirely, but he was about to brandish a sword against another living being. Part of me felt bad for him. The prior six months had been a lot, and he was sorely unprepared for what was about to happen.

"This is a sorry excuse for a plan," Graz grumbled, his voice but a whisper under his breath. He wasn't wrong. I held Whisper close against me as the group split, Tamaj rushing downward toward a space beneath the tree that had fewer of The Fallen.

"Get ready, we're going to push through," Tamaj said as we thundered closer to the smaller swath of The Fallen. Anza clung tighter to his sword, his cool steadiness a comfort as he took the left flank. I twisted my ax, readying myself to send out my bracelets if I needed to. I took a breath as Tamaj slammed into the group, pushing through. Their dead eyes turned to us as Anza and I together started to swing. I sliced one down, their hardened skin making it hard to toss them to the side.

"My haunches," Tamaj warned, and I pivoted, seeing a smaller dead-eyed Fallen clinging to her. I turned my axe to the side, hitting it hard with the pointed tip that sat opposite from the blade, sending it sprawling to the ground. Carefully, I sent out a bracelet, fanning it out into a thin shield to cover her haunches.

Another two Fallen fell away as Anza struck them down on her other side. There were so many. I glanced over to the others, catching a glimpse of Saha spearing her rapier through a Korrewen enemy; the elegant queen I had come to cherish was wrapped in the brutality of battle. She didn't hesitate to turn to the next, her form a red and green blur as she tore through him.

"Mira," Anza warned, and I turned my attention back to the task at hand, throwing up walls as high as I could to give us a better path forward. Whisper's eyes stayed locked on the tree.

Tamaj covered the distance quickly and we all scrambled off of her back. Back to back, we settled into a semi-circle around her as Whisper ran to a tree root. With a thudding sound, she slapped both hands down onto the root. The stones beneath us and around us roared with that fractured loneliness that was all too familiar. The ache of the tree faded a little as Whisper ran her fingers over the root. I turned my attention to The Fallen as they crashed against us like a wave. Anza held back three with a sword, swiftly kicking one's leg out from under it, forcing it to drop before driving his blade into another, no doubt dulling his steel with every swipe. Tamaj grabbed another Fallen by the leg, and turning, she threw her head, jaws closed around it still, using it as an extension of herself as she beat back a small group. I sent a bracelet to Whisper, crafting it into a thin shield as it flew. In my haste to keep her safe, I didn't notice the two fallen rushing me.

"Fuck," I hissed as they slammed into my side. I pushed back against them, taking one of their legs out. The second, who was much larger, pushed me back. I prepared to be overwhelmed. I prepared for its heavy body to crash down on mine. I was about to be ripped apart, to have to summon the stone beneath me to be able to survive, but The Fallen stopped before it could hurt me.

As I looked around, I realized they had all stopped. Every single fallen, both here and across the battlefield, had stopped in their tracks, unlike anything I'd ever seen before. A sea of empty shells, some broken and battered and barely functional, all ceasing their onslaught all at once.

"Got it," Whisper said as The Fallen before me stepped back, disengaging. We watched as each of the Fallen slowly turned their heads toward the larger battle. The hesitation only lasted a second before they all started to move as one. Whisper giggled as she pulled her hand from the tree root, clapping as the wave of Fallen rushed the Korrewen forces. "They're so *fucked*," she laughed as we gathered together, haphazardly climbing back onto Tamaj's back.

"What did you do?" I asked

"I might be able to talk to the tree," Whisper said, shrugging nonchalantly.

"When were you going to tell us about that?"

"I did the first time we got here, kinda. It took some figuring out."

"Well I'll say you figured it out!" Tamaj declared before whooping a howl into the air as we started heading back toward the main battle. The Fallen were everywhere, moving around us like a river parting around a rock as we rushed onward. It was only mere moments before we crashed into the remnants of Korrewen's forces.

I cleaved one of their heads off with my axe, swinging with all my might as I watched Taryn and Graz fight back to back. They were both bruised and slightly bloodied, but frozen, pressed together as The Fallen wove around them to leap up onto a Korrewen commander. The shells of Echalon moved as a sea, a hive, hell-bent on survival and bringing the Maraung to his knees. The fallen ripped him apart like bees honing in on a wasp threatening their hive as his screams sliced the air.

"Stay still," I called to the pair, knowing without a doubt this would be over soon. I had faith in The Fallen, I had faith in The Shale Tree, and most importantly, I had faith in my daughter. It only took seconds for The Fallen to rip every person with Korrewen's pin on their sleeve to pieces. As the last ones fell, a great rumbling rose from below as the tree shifted above, reaching its branches up and out. It adjusted a few of its roots, lifting them out of the ground to settle them into place once again. The Fallen spanned out, returning to their lumbering, peaceful state. Whisper looked back at me with the biggest smile on her face.

"What?"

"I think we just solved the whole almost extinct thing."

"How?" I asked, looking from her to the tree, which swayed with what seemed like purpose, reaching upward, toward the sunlight.

"It knows how to make Echalon. We all come from it, so the legends say. I told it we're almost all gone, and though it doesn't speak in words, it very much had the vibe of 'over my dead body'."

"It's making more Echalon?"

"Yup, gonna be a slow process, but it is."

"That's…incredible!"

"I'm scared, Mom. That's going to be a lot of kids. They're going to need help."

"They're going to be alright with you around. We'll figure it out, we always do. First, we have to make sure they have a world to step into when they get here," I said as Graz and Taryn scrambled back to their Barbarza partners.

"Yeah, we can do this, because we have to."

"That's right."

"Everything's going to be fine," Anza said as Graz and Taryn got to us. "Where's Saha?"

"I smell her," Tamaj said, starting through the crowd, heading farther out to where a majority of Agrenon's forces were congregating. Carefully, Tamaj sidestepped a few fallen Korrewen soldiers, vomit clinging to their clothing, boils having risen on their bodies. I felt a sickening feeling down the bond and reached over to hold Anza's free hand.

"Steady."

"Yeah, yeah," he said, trying to take a few breaths as we passed the mess, spotting Saha on her feet a few yards away, a soldier propped against her as she helped them to the medical tent.

"She's covered in blood," Graz said quietly.

"Something tells me it's not her blood," I said as they quickly followed Tamaj, his Barbarza partner staying close to us. Anza kept his attention on the prince instead of the mess we walked through.

"Hey, Sah!" I called as she passed the soldier off. Her face lit up as she saw we were all there.

"I am so happy you're alright! That worked better than I thought," she said, coming up to us. Graz turned his eyes away from her at her approach, but I held her gaze.

"Never doubt an Echalon," I said simply.

"I'm just phenomenal," Whisper said happily as Saha stole a glance at her son before looking back to me.

"I'm going to find Brian," Graz said quietly, slipping away quickly. Taryn shared a glance with Saha as well before she went after him.

"Do you find it weird that he can't even look at me?"

"You are literally covered in blood," I said, trying to cover for him.

"He's intimidated by you," Whisper said, clambering down to take her hand. "I've already told you this, you're scary."

"Maybe show him you make mistakes too?" Tamaj suggested.

"I don't think I've ever seen her make a mistake," Anza retorted.

"I make plenty of mistakes," Saha said, sighing deeply as she watched Graz slink away to my father a few yards away. My dad opened his arms in the offer of a hug and Graz dismounted and walked straight into it, hugging him tightly.

"It's strange, isn't it? Seeing your parent be so close to another child?" Saha asked, her voice almost lost amid the clamor of the battlefield. She wasn't wrong.

"Not as strange as watching your child be far more comfortable with another child's parent," I said, watching them still.

"I bet your father feels the same way."

"If Brian keeps his shit up, I'm going to lose my last meal," Anza grumbled, and Saha smirked.

"He is an…acquired taste," she said before sighing. "We can't worry about where we stand with those two right now. This was a very small number of Korrewen's forces."

"It was a distraction," Whisper said, almost confidently. Olaf was trying to slow us down. But why unless he wasn't at the portal yet? He had to have at least been close? He had likely days, weeks even to set up this attack. Yet he still had to slow us down. Did he know Whisper would figure it out? What did he need time for to set up an adequate defense? We would have known if he had tried this any sooner. No, there was something else, something gnawing at the back of my head like a rabid animal. This was no average border skirmish.

"We need to get to the portal."

9

"If Olaf thinks he can just take control of Agrenon's portal for Korrewen's use, he is sadly mistaken," Saha declared, adjusting her sword at her hip.

"I can't think of any other reason that he might be heading south and that was a pretty ample distraction" I said, settled on Tamaj's back right next to the Barbarza Saha sat upon, Tamaj and the other woman walking in step without hesitation, as if it was as easy as breathing.

"Which I thought of, helllooo," Whisper said.

"You aren't even supposed to be here." Saha huffed.

"What part of 'I do what I want' did you not understand?" Whisper retorted.

"The Shale Tree is an important piece of Echalon history. Marching toward it, and therefore the capital, might give him enough time to get forces in place to defend the new border," Anza said, getting us back on track.

"Someone's been paying attention in their classes," Titanys said from Saha's other side as we started south toward the portal.

"I might have picked up a few things hanging out in Graz's leadership classes," Anza said. "Gotta learn sometime."

"The hard way," Titanys teased gently.

"Yes, our favorite way to learn," I declared, getting a laugh out of him and Anza as Saha shook her head.

"It just doesn't make sense to me. What a petty reason to make such a big move," Whisper said. "There's something off about all of this, I just can't put my finger on it."

"You'll figure it out. You're a smart cookie," I said.

"I still don't know how a cookie can be smart, but I'll take it," she said, shrugging as I looked to Saha.

"Is the air still spicy?"

"Yeah…it hasn't gone away. In fact, it's getting worse."

"Still no ideas about it?" I asked, and she shook her head. "Whisper?"

"It's got me pretty stumped as to what it could be, exactly. I do know Photomyran are more in tune with the ebbs and flows of life. Electrical currents and energy that radiate through the world on a few different levels. They can even feel magic, even though wielding magic is of course bound to Endering. So maybe something big is happening? Or maybe you're just constipated?"

"I am not constipated," Saha grumbled, shaking her head as she sighed.

"Thats good, gotta stay regular. Don't worry, I'm on the case," Whisper assured us as I tried to hold back my smirk.

"Thank the stars," I said, gently tousling her hair. She groaned and gave me a glare.

"Easy, Moonbeam," Anza said firmly.

"I'm not a kid anymore," she grumbled.

"Teenagers," Anza said down the bond, and I nearly felt him roll his eyes as I smirked and let it go. She was trying to figure a lot out, and this was a lot of stress to put on her. Of course she'd be shorter than usual with me.

We had skirted past the Sky Fields and traveled south toward the eastern most coast of Agrenon where the land met the sea.

Whisper and Anza clung to me, keeping close as the trees started to crowd in on each other. We were getting close.

"What's that?" I heard Tamaj ask and I turned to where she was looking, only to spot a figure in the distance, tucked against a tree.

"That looks like a—" I started, only for Whisper to cut me off.

"Trap!" Whisper shrieked as Korrewen's forces crashed out of the treeline, separating us in a matter of seconds. Before I knew it, we were fully overwhelmed. I reached for Whisper, only to find the space empty as a foot soldier rushed me, knocking my legs out from under me before I realized what he was doing. Pain exploded at the back of my head as I hit the ground, desperately trying to get my bearings and find my daughter. The soldier lunged toward me, just for an Agregonian Barbarza I didn't recognise to grab him by his leg and drag him away.

I scrambled to my feet only to find Tamaj, Whisper, and Anza had been lost in the sea of bodies and fighting. I caught a glimpse of Tamaj, but my father was on her back now, charging into the enemy line, and I had to tear my eyes away to look across the field, finding Saha and Graz pinned back to back, Taryn driving her sword through a much larger Korrewen soldier as the queen and prince both fought for their lives. I caught him looking to her, searching for clues as to what the next right move was.

My attention was pulled from them as the sound of a bird of prey shrieked above me. I pivoted, barely missing the attack from the massive Maraung behind me, his gargantuan club smashing into the ground where I had just been standing.

Terror, raw and real and true rang down the bond. He didn't know where I was.

"I'm alright, are you?"

"For now. Where's Whisper?" I didn't answer, too busy dodging the Maraung's next attack,, only for a Photomyran to slip their arms under my own from behind, pinning them.

"Stab her through!" he shouted, and the Maraung drew a blade from a sheath at its hip.

I didn't hesitate to shape the dirt into two spikes below them both, driving it up through their bodies as quickly as I could, from their asses to their throats. Blood dribbled down the edges of the stone as I felt the Photomyran holding me go limp and watched the Maraung man take his last breath, sword slipping from his grasp.

I turned, looking for Whisper or Anza in the fray. I needed to find Whisper.

I speared another Maraung through as he tried to run at me, and ripped the ground out from under a group as they tried to pull down an Agregonian Barbarza who reared up, bringing his entire weight down on their shoulders. Even the three men couldn't handle that kind of power on their spines. I ducked past the Barbarza, trying to get my bearings, before I felt a foot at the back of my bad knee. I hit my knees before rolling to avoid what I only recognised as a flail as it crashed down next to my head.

I struggled to get to my feet, but my brace stuck for a moment. That was all it took for the Photomyran man with deep-green skin and blooms that resembled calla lilies to swing his flail down on me again. I pulled a slice of stone up over me, catching the flail and wrapping my stone over it before gaining my footing and rushing toward him, using my smaller form and speed to slam my axe into his side a few inches beneath his armpit. He shrieked, backhanding me off my feet again.

"You are gonna pay for that," he snarled, leaving his flail caught in my stones to pursue me. I got up, thankful that my brace seemed to hold, and fell into a defensive stance, keeping my feet wide to ensure I couldn't be knocked over. He stepped closer and I took a breath, reaching down with my mind. He took another step and I carefully lined up the shot. With a flick of my wrist, I sent another spike up through his body and into his brain. He wouldn't have even known what hit him, but as I tore my eyes from his body, dripping green blood down my stone, pain bloomed in my chest. I felt something rip into my body, through my middle. I looked down, expecting to see the blossoming red, to feel the shock start setting in, but there was no wound.

As the bond began to weaken, realization ripped my breath from my chest.

"Anza?" Silence. The agony raged on with no end in sight. My legs felt weak as shock and pain rippled down the bond.

"Anza!" I could feel my heartbeat in my ears as I tore quickly through another Korrewen soldier, spotting the familiar silhouette on the cold, hard ground, a sword still jutting through his chest.

At least four were dead, bodies scattered around him. He lifted a trembling hand, covered in blood and who knows what else, and weakly reached for the blade in his chest, trying to get it out. He struggled for breath, his messy brown hair stained with the crimson evidence of a head wound, those gilded eyes fixed upward on the sky between the branches of the trees.

I didn't think as I reached him, hitting my knees at his side.

"No, Anza, No."

"Too…many people."

"Don't talk, save your strength," I said.

"Find…her?" The bond grew weaker and the ground beneath him darkened, the dry soil drinking up his very life as it spilled out of him.

"I will. I've got you, I'll find her," I said, trying the healing sigil Whisper had taught me so long ago now. It didn't work. I couldn't focus. Even if it would work, would it even be enough for a wound this big?

"Love you. Live."

"Please, please," I begged, moving to cradle his head in my lap, resting my forehead on his. I could feel my sanity slipping as Anza's last breath brushed my ear.

Then someone shoved me out of the way.

Fury and grief rattled through me as I looked up ready to fight, ready to defend his body, but the rage immediately left me as I saw those slate-gray eyes.

The Reaper had come for us.

10

"Mom?"

"I think this is yours," she said, dumping Whisper, who was tucked under her arm, to the ground beside me. Her disguise had slipped and she hissed at Emai as she struggled to her feet before Emai pivoted, plunging her hands down onto Anza's chest, framing the wound.

"He's—"

"Still got brain activity, but we've gotta be quick. Now get this sword out!" she said.

I got to my feet, staggering back to Anza's side before grabbing the pommel and ripping the sword from his body. For a long moment, nothing happened, and she looked up to an empty space on the battlefield, her eyes locked on something I couldn't see.

"You cannot have him," she hissed before raising a fist and slamming it down on Anza's chest. Power leapt from the impact and she threw her head back, her scream cutting through the darkening forest as I watched the wound knit itself almost completely shut. I was unsure if the others on the battlefield were leaving us alone because of her or me, but there was a long moment; long and slow.

It felt like time had stopped.

The bond was nothing but a ghost within me as I watched, the remnants of his final breath whispering his love for me in my very soul.

Everything we had been through played out before me, from the first time he took a knee before me in an attempt to convince me he was not a threat to the time in that small sanctuary when I first noticed the beautiful gilded brown color of his eyes.

I remembered the feeling of him finding me in that cave after we had split up. He had come for me with fire in his eyes and vengeance in his heart.

The glittering of light in the early hours of morning as it bounced off the sharp shards of eggshells the morning The Two had hatched. The sheer panic that had raced down the bond when he realized what their arrival meant for us. The way he shoved that panic aside and lovingly, painstakingly, removed the razor-sharp pieces of crystalline egg from around our kids. The pure wonder that filled his gaze as he fawned over them once we were sure they were okay. The love that had filled that room had taken my breath away and nearly broken me with its power.

When The Two were infants, and exceptionally needy, he had stolen them away in the middle of the night more than once to sing to them and sway with one in each arm, reminding me of the way he had danced with Whisper in the tavern when we first met her. I remembered the rivaling colors of light as he danced them back to sleep.

He had always tried to keep up with Whisper's ramblings, especially when she got particularly heated, but eventually, he resorted to phrases like "You're the definition of gravity" and "Centrifugal force this that and the other thing." It had helped Whisper boil down her intellect. Being smart was wasted if you weren't understood, and he knew that. He was the reason she could articulate her meaning and she was losing that. She was losing him.

I remembered the first night he kissed me, face to face with the sudden realization that maybe, just maybe I could love him too, that there was more than just getting me to the castle and calling it. There was us.

All of it flashed before me and I wasn't sure I could remember how to breathe until sparking sounded in my chest again.

He took a sharp breath and I tried not to sob as I finally looked back to Whisper, who had covered her mouth with both hands.

"Hey, he's alright, he's alright," I said, my voice trembling as I reached out to pull Whisper into me, watching Anza blink hard. "We got him back."

"And we need to get him to a medic," Emai said, wiping away the blood that trickled from her nose.

"Is that...did I...?" Anza's voice cracked, his eyes still unfocused.

"Yup and yup, but we're getting up. Right now, up," I said, quickly moving to try to support him. Whisper grabbed the sword and my mom stood to his other side, helping hold him up, though she didn't seem so steady herself. A flash of brown flew through the air, fluttering, and I quickly recognised a bird that looked much like a falcon. Emai raised her hand as the bird carefully landed on her hand.

"Rivet...find Brian," she said before tossing the bird skyward. It gave a familiar call, one I had heard through the choking smoke more than six months ago, and flew off.

"It was you that night; that silhouette."

"You really think I was gonna leave you to finish that trip without at least trying to help?" she asked, meeting my eyes before we started forward, the chaos around us parting as we moved.

Whisper kept in front of us and Emai shifted Anza's weight to me as he tried to find his feet, lunging forward. It was then I noticed one of Korrewen's soldiers coming at us, but upon seeing who he was attacking, he tried to double back. Tried being the key word there. My mother snapped his neck.

"No smoke?"

"Not now. Too tight and too dark, I can't tell who's who," she said as she led the way forward.

The pressure of my straining brace against my knee blessedly lessened as Anza finally found his feet, a hand going to the remnants of his wound, and I breathed a sigh of relief. I didn't have time to question how he was still standing, however, as the sound of thundering feet was too much of a distraction and someone lost their last meal on their own shoes as they were cleaved apart by a well-timed sword strike, making room for Tamaj to leap in front of us, my father on her back, as the bird sounded above again.

"Em?" my dad said, his eyes locking on my mother, his face softening, no longer battle hardened.

"Reunion later, Lovey, get them out," my mom said, helping Anza to Tamaj's side.

"Oh, shit!" he said, jumping from her to pull a foldable cart from the back of her saddle and pop it open. "Put him here," he said, and I helped Anza move to the cart, barely making it before his legs gave out again. "I've got him," Brian said, and together, we worked to strap him in before helping Whisper into the saddle.

"I'm not going," Whisper said.

"Yes, you are," I argued.

"So are you," Emai said.

"What?" I said, turning to look at my mother.

"I just kept him alive, infection could still set in, a hundred things could go wrong, and someone needs to stay here to watch Saha and her little one's back. Help them get to a medic."

I wanted to argue, but Tamaj's mind met mine.

"Get on or so help me I will drag you in my jaws!"

I quickly settled into the space beside Anza, knowing full well she wasn't joking. Brian, in a move that seemed brazen for a man who had a hard time meeting my gaze, leaned down, grabbing my mother by the shirt and pulling her up to him, almost aggressively, to kiss her quickly. She kissed him back just as fiercely, clinging to his arms as if they had been waiting decades for that kiss.

"Go," my mom said. Tamaj didn't hesitate, turning toward what I assumed was a medical tent. *Where in the stars had that come from?*

"Don't die!" he tossed over a shoulder. My mother's only response was a resounding peal of laughter, as if he had just told the funniest joke, as she turned her sights onto some poor unknowing Barbarza not far from her.

I turned my attention back to Anza, whose eyes still weren't focused.

"Hey, stay with me."

"Cold," he said quietly, and I fought the cart's questionable stability to draw him closer to me, hoping to share some body heat.

"I know. We're almost there. You lost a lot of blood, but we're almost there," I assured him, rubbing my thumb against his cheek as I held his head in my lap.

"Um, Mom?" I turned at the sound of Whisper's voice, but looking from the side of the cart, I could barely see past Tamaj. It didn't matter though because the wall of soldiers standing in our way was hard to miss.

I shook my wrists, feeling my bracelets there, and reached out for that familiar warmth, catching the ground between us and ripping up a wall before cutting it down the middle and shoving both sides apart, making a path for Tamaj and the cart. We had done this before and she immediately raced along the pathway.

"Thank fuck," Brian said as we crashed through and toward the other side.

A large tent with Agrenon's symbol stood in the distance, haphazardly erected on the battlefield, surrounded by soldiers fighting to keep the enemy back as medics finished setting it up. Soldiers were already spilling in off the battlefield and as Tamaj scrambled to a stop, I leaped out of the cart, unfastening Anza and trying to help him out. Brian got off of Tamaj's back with Whisper and came to help me. Whisper moved to open the flap of the medical tent as we stumbled in.

Graz and Taryn were already there, and upon seeing us, the blood left both of their faces.

"Oh my stars! What happened?" Taryn asked.

"We got separated, he got overwhelmed by Korrewen," I explained as Taryn led us to a bed, where we carefully helped him lie down.

"Mira?"

"I'm right here."

"You need to back up," Brian said, gently resting a hand on my shoulder.

I couldn't even find it in me to snap at him through the sinking weight of my desperate worry for both Anza and Whisper.

"He needs me."

"He needs a doctor. Your daughter needs you."

I looked to Whisper, her face stricken with pain and fear as she looked across the dozens of wounded soldiers.

"I'm gonna make sure Whisper is okay. I'm just a few steps away if you need me, but the doctors need to get to you, alright?" I leaned down and placed a gentle kiss against Anza's blood-stained cheek.

"Go to her. Go," he said, and I studied his face, hoping it wouldn't be the last time I saw him alive, before I left his side and let the medics get to work on his wounds.

As I approached, Whisper reached her arms out and I hugged her close as she buried her head in my shoulder.

"Are you alright?" she asked.

"I'm fine, I'm fine," I soothed. "Dad will be too, he just needs a little rest."

"That wound, it…it was so bad."

"I know, but it's not anymore. Grandma Em saved us. You're alright, he's alright." I started rubbing her back and listened as she tried to regulate her breathing in an effort to calm down.

"That scary lady is my grandma?" she asked through shuddering breaths, and I laughed through the tears.

"In the flesh."

"She scooped me like I was a sack of grain," she fought out, trying to fight both a sob and a laugh.

"Yeah, she did a little bit, didn't she?" I looked up to Graz as her tears pattered onto my shoulder, rubbing her back as she continued to calm herself. "Where's Saha?" I asked quietly, and he shook his head.

"We got split up and *she* won't let me go anywhere to find her," he said, glaring at Taryn.

"Thank you, Taryn."

"Of course you're on her side!" Graz threw his hands up, frustrated, and took a breath, keeping calmer than I expected before he went to help comfort an incoming soldier.

I kept holding Whisper, rubbing her back and holding her close.

"He's doing better than I thought he would," Taryn said quietly.

"Good," I said as Brian started for the door, pulling his shoulders in as he tried to retreat to a far more welcoming battlefield.

"Em!" he said the minute he pushed the flap back, his shoulders slipping out of that hunched and fragile stance as soon as he saw her, but I saw the way my mother's eyes quickly looked him over. She had noticed.

"Look who I found," she said, letting the moment go for the time being, and a feeling of relief washed through me as Saha stepped in.

Whisper lifted her head to see what the commotion was and wriggled to be set down.

"Are you good?"

"I'm good," she said quietly, and I kissed her forehead before lowering her to her feet.

"I would have been dead if not for your wife," Saha said, moving to hug Brian, Emai bouncing in place as she waited for her turn.

As Saha pulled away, she all but tackled Brian, and for a long moment, they hugged each other, breaking it only to share a far more passionate kiss than the one they had mustered before. Tears ran down Brian's face, and carefully, lovingly, Emai wiped them away with her thumbs as she held his face in her hands.

"I've got you, Lovey."

"Thank the stars."

"Alright, you two, you can get a room later," Saha said, refocusing us all on the task at hand.

"We have to get to the portal. It's not that far away," I said, squeezing Whisper's hand to keep her close.

"We have to push past Korrewen's forces to get there. Emai, you're good at making people scatter."

"Our people are out there too. If I smoke up they'll be caught in the crossfire," she said, and Saha nodded with a sigh.

"We need a—" A roar filled the air from outside the tent, one that felt like it shook the very ground we walked on.

The day I met Tamaj flashed into my mind, heralded by the familiarity of the sound, and I rushed to get out of the tent with the others, my heart in my throat as I remembered fire and flirting with frostbite. Whisper kept close to me as we spilled out into the space between the battle and the medical tent, only to see a massive shape rush over the trees and a burst of fire.

"Are you fucking kidding me?" I looked at my parents and Brian carefully stepped forward, keeping my mother behind him.

"No control, that one," Emai said.

I looked at Saha, whose face showed nothing but fear. Raw, unbridled fear.

"Can anyone see her sash?" she asked, hushed, and quiet fell around us.

I looked back to the massive dragon who crashed through the trees on Korrewen's side, taking in its tangle of horns, its silver-blue scales, its long neck, its saddle. Wait, saddle?

There she was, settled on the saddle, her salt-and-pepper hair tousled with the wind. I had never seen so much joy on her face as she reached out, fire bursting from her hands as she took down a large Korrewen trebuchet.

My grandmother had returned. Had the spell to abolish banishments worked for her as well?

The wind caught against a sash tied at her waist, sunset orange against the silver scales of the dragon.

"She's with us," Saha whispered, seeing the orange sash, her hands resting just under her throat, as if she were physically holding herself together.

"Hey, she's the perfect distraction. We can get to the portal," I said quickly. Tamaj snorted as someone took the cart from her and I scrambled onto her back. Whisper came to my side.

"Not this time around, kiddo. I need you to stay with Dad, alright?" Her eyes filled with fear, but she nodded and backed up.

"I love you," she said quietly.

"I love you too, just stay safe," I said, and she nodded.

"Hey, please be careful," Brian said, my mom punching his shoulder.

"She'll be fine. She doesn't have to kill Olaf, just stop him," she said before looking to me. "We'll cover you."

"Right." I may not have *needed* to kill him, but I sure as hell was going to fucking kill him if I could.

"*Let's go,*" Tamaj said, starting off immediately.

I turned for one last look at my family, both blood and chosen, and spotted Saha quietly watching Sil as she tore into Korrewen's forces, a look of awe I'd never seen her express blanketing her face, before focusing forward on the task at hand.

I saw Sil turn to spot us as we left the medical tent, so I stood in Tamaj's saddle, pumping my fist into the air, trying to show Sil that I saw her, that I was alive. Even after all the shit she failed to teach me, she at least deserved that much.

She lifted her own fist in acknowledgment, smiling.

I turned to the wall of people, reaching out to craft a path just like I had earlier, spiking several Korrewen soldiers through as Tamaj ran. Approaching a thicker wall of people, I pulled a slab of dirt up, crafting a path over their heads that Tamaj quickly took, charging toward the portal as quickly as we could. A massive Barbarza almost slammed into us, but another wedged itself between us at the last moment.

Brian, wielding a sword, cut down its legs as the frame of another not far to my left came into view, my mother on its back, looking over the battlefield, the wind ripping through her locks as she kept our left clear; both of them dangerous and all too ready to leap into the fray.

As promised, they were covering us.

The fighting thinned and Tamaj and I ran headfirst into the only clear spot on the battlefield. I had no idea why it wasn't better protected, but I knew the portal was there.

"I smell someone," Tamaj said.

"Olaf?"

"No, not Olaf," she said, looking about as we approached the portal, slowing to a stop. The clearing was empty except for a woman who settled at the edge of the portal. Her long stick straight brown hair hung over her shoulders, her brown eyes alive with wild sharpness as she focused on weaving a sigil into existence complex and intricate, weaving magic I didn't recognise around the base of the portal. What the hell is she doing? Regardless, it couldn't have been good.

Five spots settled throughout the sigil, four with bodies tied tightly in place, framed only as silhouettes as far as I could see. The woman sat, hands pinned to the sigil as she smirked.

I dismounted Tamaj and reached down for my warmth, but

before I could move, a voice rang out. From everywhere. From her. Resounding throughout the space as my muscles locked up. I couldn't move an inch as that beautiful voice sang long, even, elegant notes. Tamaj couldn't move either. I stood there, watching, unable to move an inch as a thin white thread sprouted forth from the ground, rising toward the sky.

I wanted to scream, to use my power, to lash out at her, to stop her, but I couldn't. I was trapped in place, as if entranced by a siren. It wasn't until I saw my mother's figure that I knew there would be solace.

As my mother crashed into her, sending her sprawling and returning control of my body to me, the thread touched the clouds above. She looked up as my mother and her mount wedged themselves between us.

"You're too late." She barely got the words out before a blast radiated outward, fierce, crackling like electricity, knocking us all onto the ground. My head was already swimming with pain, and by the time I looked up, the woman was gone and that frail arch of stone was just fragments scattered about the ground.

I got to my feet, hearing Tamaj go to my mother to help her and the other Barbarza up, and stepped forward, past the bodies, past the sigil now burned black into the space where the portal had stood, stepping carefully through the space that should have pulled me back to Earth. It should have been able to take me back home, should have been activated as I stepped into it, but nothing happened.

Agrenon's portal was gone.

11

Korrewen's soldiers fled quickly, retreating toward the border faster than I expected as Tamaj carried me back toward the medical tent.

Saha was still where we had left her, staring out at the great expanse of dragon that tucked itself into the ground, letting my grandmother off of its back.

I headed to the medical tent, hoping and praying for Anza to still be alright. As I rushed in, I found him sitting on his cot, a nurse still settling dressing into place.

"I'm fine."

"You're not fine," Whisper argued, and Anza met my eyes before taking a deep breath.

"There you are."

"I'm okay."

"Did you stop him?" Whisper asked, and I felt my shoulders grow heavy. I couldn't look at her, but kept my eyes locked on Anza.

"We tried. We tried…" I said as he tried to get up, but failed. I moved to his side instead, hugging him and tugging Whisper into the embrace when she stepped up to us.

"It's alright, there are other portals in the other kingdoms," she said quietly.

"He wasn't even there, he sent some woman."

"That's very much like him, always sending someone else to do the dirty work." I looked up at Saha's words. She still looked dazed, as if something had shaken her.

"Are you alri—"

"Sahaveya!"

Saha went rigid as a stone as the temperature of the room crept upward by several degrees before turning briskly on her heel to face Sil, who then looked to my parents—no, to my mother, who I hadn't noticed came in behind me.

"Emai."

Brian stepped forward and between them, and the glare on my mother's face made it clear that she was not the one he was protecting.

"Sil." Emai nearly spat her name.

"We're not doing this here," Brian said firmly, and Saha seemed to snap out of it.

"Em, it's not worth it," she said, lifting her chin and squaring her shoulders. I knew that face. It was devoid of emotion and she only ever wore it at court. I had only known her a few months, but it was my job to read her like a book, to know her inside and out. She was putting on a front. "It's a pleasure to see you again, Wildfire."

"And you, *your majesty*." It was Sil's turn to spit words that shouldn't be insults out like they were weapons.

Realization dawned on me as my throat tightened; Saha was the one who had banished her.

"It is wonderful to see that you're still loyal to me after all these years."

"Oh, don't flatter yourself." Sil started turning to put her back to us, but not before giving Anza a firm glare. I moved to keep him and Whisper behind me as I felt confusion rise from down the bond. "I came for Agrenon, Saha, not for you." She stormed out as Anza took my hand, his confusion turning to understanding.

"What's her deal?" I asked, looking to him.

"It's…not us."

"What do you mean?"

"She's feeling a lot, all at once." He nodded in the direction Sil had just exited and I caught sight of Saha, who was still unmoving from the place she'd stood since Sil stormed out.

"Great," I said flatly.

"She can be quite the problem," my mom said, coming to our side, Brian hanging closer to Saha and shooting me an apologetic glance.

"Wonderful," I said before turning my attention back to Whisper and Anza. "Whisper's right, you're in no condition to be getting up and moving around."

"I need to talk to someone."

"Who do you need to talk to so badly that you're willing to risk your health?" I asked firmly.

"Yeah, don't forget I am still strong enough to knock you out," Whisper reminded him, her tone unwavering.

"I like this one," Mom said, reaching out to ruffle Whisper's hair, but it wasn't enough of a distraction to keep me from noticing the way Anza's eyes flitted to my father then back to me, pleading. I immediately knew he wanted to speak with him.

"Why?" I asked Anza.

"It's…I just…I want to clear things up," Anza said.

"That's quite the sudden change of heart," I said.

"Death will do that. Come," Emai said, gently taking my hand before addressing Anza. "I'll send him over."

"I can stay here. If Brian has anything to say, he can say it in front of me."

"Come," my mom said again, leading me away. Whisper reached for my hand in solidarity.

"But—"

"No buts."

"Haha, *butt*." Whisper giggled as we reached Saha's side, where my mother looked at my father and jerked her head toward where Anza sat waiting for him. He scrunched his face in confusion and Em just rolled her eyes and jerked her head toward him again before gently resting a hand on Saha's shoulder.

"Breathe, she'll get over herself eventually," Emai told Saha, but I couldn't bring myself to pay them any attention beyond that with all my focus on the bond.

We were far enough away that I couldn't hear what they were saying, but I could feel how nervous Anza was. I stole a glance over my shoulder, watching them as Anza watched the floor, my dad still staring at me as if watching over me from afar. The conversation only lasted a few minutes before my dad patted Anza's back and stood. They exchanged a few more words before my dad nodded and turned, briskly walking to join me near Saha, then leaning in to whisper in my mother's ear in a language I didn't understand. Anza's nervousness was still there, but it was…different.

"All good?"

"Yeah, I just had to talk to him about something. Everything's okay."

"You're nervous," I pressed.

"It's just stress from the day, I'm alright."

I surveyed the bond, checking for a lie, and there was a twinge of a bad feeling there, the tiniest deception. What was he up to? Was Brian an ass to him? I might have forgiven him, but there was no forgetting Arlo's disemboweled corpse not far from where we were that very moment.

What did they talk about?

"We need to get moving the first moment we can," Saha said quietly, snapping me out of my thought spiral.

"The night is creeping in and these people need help," Emai

said, gesturing to the other wounded soldiers in the tent around us.

"Can you help them tonight?" Saha asked, and Emai nodded.

"It'll be slow. Bringing Anza back from the brink wasn't easy."

"Alright, do what you can and we'll head out in the morning," Saha said, still quiet, as if not quite present.

"To where?" I asked, drawing Saha's gaze to me.

"We can't go to Biena, Legalia, or Eynon; they'd see it as an invasion. I'm sending out a warning to them to let them know what may be coming."

"Thats it? We just warn them?" I asked.

"And then we go home," she confirmed.

"They just decimated the only lifeline Agrenon has to any construct of power and you want to go *home?*" I asked.

"We do not have the funds or the men for this."

"And you think the people of Agrenon will just…what? Be told that there won't be any more Endering, that they will be totally vulnerable if we perish and they'll be cool with it?" I asked and she bit her lip, staring blankly at me as she mulled over what I had said.

"Careful, Mira," Brian warned.

"Hush, you. Mom's right," Whisper pipped up. "They just dealt a massive blow to us, changed life in Agrenon fundamentally. If framed properly, we could rally troops and have them meet us at the pass of Sharvene and continue on. The people problem isn't that there aren't people to fight, many left Agrenon's army when Olaf took power, it's that they don't have a reason to. This is their reason," she said.

"And your insistence on the matter has absolutely nothing to do with the fact that you've read my journals and know there is likely a group of Echalon being held hostage by Korrewen in order to harvest their hearts so they may continue to control their very powerful Endering?" Saha said without missing a beat.

"We'd both be naïve to say I have no such bias," Whisper retorted, and for a moment, they sat in silence.

"Titanys," Saha finally said, "see if we can...drum up some support."

"Thank you," I started, but Saha shook her head.

"We go as far as the pass. That is the border. If we are not met with more troops, we turn back," she said just as firmly and I knew there was no argument to be had. She had compromised when she didn't have to. That was more than enough. We were going to the border with Korrewen.

"There are at least two Endering in Korrewen, and I didn't see Tank out here," Emai said quietly.

"I hope she's alright," Brian said, my mom nodding.

"Who's Tank?" I asked

"Someone I knew a long time ago. She's a force to be reckoned with and very, *very* difficult to wrangle," Emai said, flashing me a sly smirk.

"So we send word to the other kingdoms, go to the pass, hope we have more troops, and go to Korrewen from there?" I said, knowing that Whisper had always secretly wanted to know if more of her people were actually being held in Korrewen.

"Or go home from there," Saha said firmly.

"Right," I said begrudgingly.

"You're missing a step."

"Which is?"

"We pray the other kingdoms listen to reason, unlike you," she added quietly, and I rolled my eyes before turning to hug Whisper tighter for a moment.

"Hey, stay with your dad, okay? I'm gonna find Graz and Taryn," I said, kissing her head.

Usually, she would fight back against such a brazen display of affection, but she didn't, she just hugged me tighter, then quickly slipped over to Anza.

I slid out of the tent, leaving Saha with my parents as I wove my way through the crowd to find the two Photomyran together, sitting close to each other around a nearby fire and holding hands.

"Is Saha coming?" Graz asked quickly, almost pulling his hand from Taryn's, but I shook my head, spotting Sil stroking her dragon's muzzle as it nuzzled her head.

"You two really need to stop hiding from her. She's gonna find out eventually."

"*I'm* not hiding," Taryn said quietly.

"I just...don't want her to say no," Graz said quietly. "Forgiveness and not permission or something."

"I think she's got bigger problems right now," I said, sitting on a stool near them. "And she loves Taryn."

"As a Queen's Guard," Graz said quietly.

"You two were blushing at each other far before she came back. If she has a problem with it, I'll kick her ass myself," I said jokingly and Graz sighed.

"That'd be treason."

"Probably, but she would totally deserve it."

"Yeah...I don't know."

"I can't tell you what to do, but I can tell you that if she finds out you've been sneaking into each other's rooms"—they blushed, looking away from me—"she's not exactly going to be thrilled," I said, looking up as the last of the light crept away from the sky. It had been a long fucking day.

"Mom?" I turned to find Whisper standing there.

"What is it?"

"I wanna show you something, if that's alright?" She held out a hand to me.

"Remember what I said," I told them, getting up and taking her hand.

"What is it, Moonbeam?"

"This way," she said, leading me away from camp.

"Whisper, where are we going?" The night was sinking in and fireflies lit the path through the woods that some animal must have carved as she led the way to a small clearing.

"You'll see."

As the clearing came into view, there was nothing but grasses, fireflies, and Anza, standing in the center waiting for me. Whisper led me to him.

"What exactly is this?" I asked him as he held a hand out for me. I took it and Whisper dropped the other one, then slipped into the darkness. His nervousness was almost palpable on my tongue, those gilded eyes meeting mine as somewhere in the forest a violin began to play, soft and quiet, a beautiful melody rising into the night.

"What's all this?"

"Just dance with me?"

"You should be in bed. You nearly died today."

"Please?" He trailed his hand up my arm, guiding my wrist up around his neck, and I let him lead me in a dance.

My heart began to race as realization crashed against me, my brain frantically scrambling to recall the steps that Sil had taught me as he led me in motion. I knew this dance. Sil had drilled it into me, what it meant and the finality of it. The people of the Otherworld proposed and married all in the same moment.

Shit.

"Are you sure you want to do this?" I asked. "I could ruin you."

"I'm sure."

"But—"

"Listen to me. I love you, I have for so long, and I don't want to become a star in that sky without you knowing that down to your bones, and if that means being ruined, then I beg of you, ruin me."

My throat felt suddenly dry as he spun me around in the familiar and simple number. I couldn't speak, the music rising and rising and rising as he danced with me there, our breaths rising and falling as one. He set me up to spin me, but my feet felt like lead. We were walking toward our deaths, and there was no one I'd rather walk into that star-studded sky with than him.

He spun me out away from him, and as my fingers left his, I turned a final turn before coming to a stop, looking directly at him down on one knee, head bowed, both hands out to the side.

He was already mine. I knew that. But there was something else to this, something eternal and final and fierce to such a simple gesture. He was giving all of himself to me. Every flaw, every vulnerability, every thought. We were partners already. He was asking me to be his mate, completely united in every way that mattered, and I had no idea how to accept it.

Thankfully, Tamaj's mind met mine.

"If you intend to accept, get on your knees before him."

I moved to do so, my whole body shaking as I settled before him.

"Take his face in your hands."

I reached up, touching his jawline, watching as he lifted his eyes to meet mine

"Repeat after me: as you give, so do I."

"As you give, so do I."

He rose from his position to take my face in his hands, moving as carefully as always as he pulled me into a kiss. We knew it was just us, together, he and I. We had felt one another in every way possible, calling him my mate had never mattered because he had always been that; my other half. But we were facing the biggest threat to our lives, and I, just as he seemed to, did not want to do this with any question from any person, especially not Sil, as to what we meant to each other.

We pulled apart just long enough for him to produce two necklaces from his pocket; our symbols of union, like rings we humans used back home. Like the feathered earring Tamaj still wore. He carefully rested one over my head and around my neck. A single small stone, round and worried through sat upon it, brown with flecks of gold, reminiscent of his eyes, was woven into the artfully knotted necklace. I took the other from him, noting the same intricate weaving with a slate-gray stone instead. To anyone else, these would just be silly necklaces, but to us, we were carrying our mate with us. I slid the necklace over his neck, sealing our union as he leaned in to kiss me again.

He was my husband. My mate. My.

12

Someone, I assumed Taryn, had the foresight to set up a tent away from the others for the night. It was still close enough to the rest of camp to ensure that if there was danger we could come to them, or they could come help us if we were in danger, but Anza and I were not worried about potentially being harmed as he led the way to the tent. We barely got it zipped closed behind us before we started on each other's clothes.

"My mate," he said quietly, the bond alight with euphoria.

"My mate," I said back, meeting his crashing kiss as he slid my pants off, carefully and masterfully undoing my brace as I leaned into him.

Someone had tried to make the space cozy, with furs and soft lights, but I didn't take much notice. I was too distracted as I tore off his shirt, my hands finding his chest. He took a sharp intake of breath as I reached for his pants, his hands finding their way to my shirt. Within seconds, we were naked together and he lifted me up, laying me on my back against the furs. His hands ventured up along my arms, grabbing my wrists and positioning them above my head before he started to inch downward, planting kisses as he moved. Down my jawline, down my neck, across my breasts, down my stomach to my thigh, only letting my hands go when he had gotten too far down to hold them in place.

"Anza." I was breathless with anticipation by the time he settled his face between my thighs. His hands moving to keep my legs apart as he steadily began to devour me, a hand gliding up along my stomach as he worked.

"Fuck," I gasped, wondering how he could breathe down there.

"Believe me, it would be an honor to die by your thighs." I couldn't help the laugh that trembled out of my throat as he wound me tighter, moving to loop his arms underneath my legs, pulling me to him, getting better leverage, the bond singing with delight as my pleasure must have been crashing into him.

"Almost," I warned.

He kept going and I couldn't help but buck my hips, arching my back, grabbing hold of a blanket and throwing my head back as raw pleasure bubbled over, a cry I tried and failed to muffle slipping between my lips. It wasn't until I finished that he came up for air, kissing up my other thigh as I panted. He quickly wiped his dripping wet face with a blanket before moving back up my body, planting kisses as he moved.

I shivered, carefully turning over as he moved. He didn't stop me, just kept moving, fitting behind me as I got to my hands and knees, his left leg framing my own to ensure it didn't slip as he positioned himself at the edge of my being.

"My mate," he whispered, pressing forward.

"All yours," I groaned, rocking back as he slid into me, his hand pressed over mine, fingers wrapping in mine as he pressed his face into my shoulders, biting at my skin as he started to thrust, jolting me forward with each movement. A groan slid from both of us, his own pleasure a perfect harmony to mine as it swirled around us.

"Mira," he moaned against my skin as he buried himself fully into me, winding that need again.

"Yes, my mate, yes." I moaned in return, dropping my head

as he responded to my desire, adjusting his pacing without needing to be asked. I couldn't help the noises escaping me with every thrust. The bond and our bodies trembled with our pleasure, his lacing its way through me, compounding on one another to bring us both to the brink as he buried himself deep inside me.

"You're doing so well." He shifted his weight as he spoke, still supporting me as he reached for my hips, guiding my legs open a little farther. I obliged, giving him more leverage and better access as he tightened that need again, bringing my hips back as he thrusted forward into me. It was easy to fall into such a rhythm with him, every inch of me shaking as, together, our euphoria bubbled over, raw, unbridled pleasure spilling over us he buried himself fully into me. Finishing together, we groaned as one, his hands still wrapped over mine.

"Please, again, I'm begging you," I whispered as he pulled himself from me.

Turning to face him, I noticed through the bond that he wasn't finished either.

"Again, hmm?" he asked as I pushed him back into a sitting position.

"Please, please," I fought out between quick, sharp kisses as I crawled into his lap, settling my legs to either side of him, framing myself over him.

"You have been quite a good girl," he whispered, guiding me down onto him, feeling him press his way into me once again.

My breath caught in my throat as I rested my head against his shoulder. He nuzzled my neck, leading me to lift my head and meet his kiss, sharp and hungry, as we began our dance all over again. The tempo was more erotic now, more sensual. He gave where I took and I returned the favor, prolonging my peak for the sake of his pleasure until we were both nearly mad with arousal. My hand tangled in his hair as he moved, holding me tightly to him, soft groans escaping as I ground my hips against his, bringing him into me as deeply as I could.

"You're doing this on purpose," I panted. I could feel it, wrapped in that raw, unbridled pleasure, his coy triumph.

"I have no idea what you mean." *Lies.* I rested my hands on his shoulders, lifting myself to guide myself to him before he kissed me again, guiding my hands away from his shoulders, holding my wrists tightly to keep me from going too fast. "Greedy girl."

"Anza," I groaned as he slowly started to pick up the pace.

I met his gaze, staring into the depths of him as he drove me slowly closer to that euphoria. I relished in the love I could see shining there, the desire burning brightly in the dim light of the moon filtering through the canvas walls, in the primal need I could feel roaring through the bond.

"I've got you."

"And I you," I said, running my hands up his chest as he thrusted, his pleasure walking the same fine line mine was.

"Safe," he moaned.

"Safer," I groaned. "Safer together."

The slide of his palms along my skin set my flesh ablaze, the greedy dance of his fingers along every curve of my body sending jolts of pleasure to my very soul. Never in my life had I felt more cherished, more desired, more loved, and as his hands settled back on my hips and he began to lead me into a more frenzied rhythm, something inside of me snapped, my mind going fuzzy and my body taking on a life of its own.

"Yes, faster," I begged, my body rocking against his.

He suddenly lurched forward, moving us as one so I was flat on my back but never breaking the connection between us. His hands quickly slid back to mine, our fingers intertwining once more.

I quickly wrapped my legs around his middle so he couldn't pull out too far as he grunted, thrusting into me much harder this time, jostling my body with every thrust as he quickly but masterfully balanced our pleasure. Each short quick grunt drove me mad, and it was only a matter of moments before I threw my head back as my body tightened down on him. He pressed himself into me firmly again, his own pleasure spilling into me as he finished as deeply as my body would let him go.

I kept my legs wrapped around him, not wanting him to leave me as he rained sweet kisses on my neck, both of us panting, his legs trembling.

"Mmm, you are going to have to let go eventually," he said, moving his hands to brush a lock of hair from my face, and I grumbled, but let go, allowing him to slide from me.

He pulled me close, tucking me under his arm and pressing his front to my back. I turned my head just enough to meet his kiss before spotting the bloom of red beneath his bandages.

"Hey," I said, sitting up and resting a hand on his chest.

"Oops," he said.

"Don't 'oops' me," I said, quickly drawing a healing sigil, feeling the magic weave its way from me into him as I focused. "I'm sorry. We should have been more careful."

"Hey, don't do that. I wouldn't have changed a thing about what just happened, even if it killed me." I couldn't help the heat that rushed to my face as I lightly slapped his arm, his dark humor covering up the twinge of fear at his own mortality. "I'm alright."

"You better be," I said, leaning up to steal a kiss from him.

Carefully, I ran my hands over his bandages, unwrapping them to check on his wound, and he didn't stop me. It had stopped bleeding, but the splice where the sword had been was still fresh, though it was far shallower than it had been originally. It would scar for sure.

"I'm alright, I promise."

"I almost lost you. I thought getting the eggs to the castle was hard...but this..." I said, shaking my head before digging around inside to find the small triage kit in our tent.

I carefully bandaged him in the comfortable silence, allowing the reality of everything we've gone through to settle around us.

It was only once I finished that he drew me close and spoke again.

"You didn't lose me, I'm right here," he said, pulling my hair over my shoulder to work at the tangles. I rested my head on his shoulder, marveling in the feeling of his fingers working at my messy mane before I gently pressed him back against the furs.

"We should rest."

"Yeah, we should," he said, kissing me again as I settled down beside him, a hand on his chest.

"Rest easy, Stone-Slinger," he whispered, kissing my temple.

"I'll try, Beetle-Brain," I said, snuggling close to my mate as sleep slowly took us.

13

"About damn time you got up!" I heard Sil, but ignored her as Anza's anger pricked down the bond.

"Easy," I said as we finished getting our breakfast.

"What, are you not going to talk to me?"

"Sil, I'm just fucking tired right now, alright? Give me a minute to eat," I said, trying to keep myself from snapping at her.

"Fine," she said before whisking her own half-eaten plate away and storming over to her dragon.

"I really don't like her."

"Yeah, me either, but there would have been a lot more death if she hadn't shown up when she did."

"Still, she didn't teach you magic, or tell you about Emai," Anza said.

"Thanks for the reminder." I sighed. I didn't want to get into a fight with her, not this morning. I knew that things were going to eventually take a turn for the worse though. It was only a matter of time before she demanded we talk.

"Soooo, how'd you sleep?" Taryn's voice snapped me back to reality and I couldn't help the immediate flush that came over my face.

"Pretty good, thanks to you," Anza responded.

"My pleasure. Us girls gotta stick together," she said, giving me a wink, which must have made my face go even more red as we sat on the makeshift stools around a collapsable table.

Graz pretended to be very interested in his meal.

"At least Emai is steering clear of Sil," I said, turning to Tamaj as she settled beside me.

My parents were in the midst of a food fight with their breakfast. Whisper sat near them, carefully dodging their attacks on one another as she tried to smother a smirk. At least they weren't all pissy and demanding like a certain Wildfire.

"Are they always like that?" I asked Tamaj and she nodded.

"Those two never left that puppy love phase, but after living most of their lives separated against their will, who could blame them?"

"I guess you have a point."

It was cute, watching the two of them eat together for the first time in my life. It had only been a few months since I had believed them both to be dead, yet there they were, launching eggs at each other for shits and giggles.

"It is nice to see Brian returning to himself, even if it's just in small ways," Tamaj said as I spotted Sil watching them in my periphery, unsure if her pursed lips and fierce eyes were disdain or some twisted form of relief.

"My love?" I asked.

"Yes?" Anza said, gathering more food on his fork.

"How does Sil feel about my parents?"

"Hmm…" he said, popping the food into his mouth to chew. He didn't respond until he swallowed.

"She's pretty mixed up there emotionally, a lot going on; anger, fear, resentment, guilt, frustration, but she's smothering all of it."

"You can't tell what's Saha related and what's related to my parents, can you?"

"Nope, just that she's an emotional mess. Sorry," he said, gently taking one of my hands to kiss at my knuckles. "Now eat, please? We both need to be able to not die out here." I rolled my eyes but turned my attention to my food. We ate peacefully, rose to tend to our plates, distracted when I heard the heightened arguing.

"You don't get to order me around like I'm your Royal Endering again, not after what you did. Hindsight is a bitch, isn't it?"

I looked up, seeing Sil mere inches from Saha's face.

"Hey, hey!" I said, but neither of them turned to look at me.

"I'm not trying to order you to do anything, I was just asking if—"

"No, the answer's no," Sil snarled.

I shook my head. I could see the waves of heat rolling off her, even some of Saha's petals shied from her, so I threw a wall of stone up between them.

"Enough," I said firmly.

"And where, exactly, do you get off telling me anything?" Sil snapped.

I guess we're doing this now.

"Ohhhh, wrong move." I heard Whisper nearly laugh, but I was already moving, storming over to her.

"I get off telling you everything from where to shit to when to eat and everything in between because I am Royal Endering of Agrenon. I'm in charge after Saha and Graz, not you. You don't get to just storm back in here like you didn't completely ignore magic and its weight on this world and act like you're high and mighty when you didn't even tell me my mom's fucking name. You are very seriously out of line and I *highly* suggest you pipe the fuck down and figure out where the hell you misplaced your manners and tact."

"And if I don't?" she challenged.

"It'll be an earth and fire slug fest, and last time I checked, kicking dirt over a fire is a great way to smother it," I snarled, stepping closer to get in her face. She didn't look away, both of us holding our ground until I felt a little pat on my shoulder and Brian wedged himself between us.

"That was a threat."

"Come now, this isn't necessary," he started gently.

"Oh, look, you do have a brain," I hissed over Brian, completely ignoring him.

"Mira," Brian prompted.

"She started it."

"And I'm finishing it. Please, go check on Saha."

"Yup," I said, but didn't break from Sil's gaze. I wasn't the little kid she raised. Not anymore.

"Mom, go back to your friend over there?" I heard Sil audibly growl, but she broke the staring contest and went back to her dragon.

"What is her fucking deal?" I hissed.

"You're in her spot, for one. One of her kids has gone rogue, the other's actual death incarnate, and she's mad about all of it. She'll live. Go to Saha."

I nodded, turning to drop the wall only to find Saha gone.

It didn't take long to pad to her tent. Stepping into the doorway, I saw her startle, and she sighed seeing it was me.

"You good?"

"Yeah, I think so."

"She didn't burn you, right?" I asked, and Saha shook her head before hesitating and gently urging me closer with a single wave of her hand. I approached and she dropped her voice quickly.

"I am unsure if we can trust her. We don't know how long Olaf's army was near the portal or if he was there when she came through. She could be compromised."

"You think she'd take Olaf's side?"

"I don't know," she said honestly and took a breath. "I don't want to push her away, I just...I don't know what to do with her."

"Our best bet, honestly, is to keep you and Graz away from her the best we can, or at least keep you separate."

"She has a dragon. If she wanted to burn us alive, she would have already."

"Then if she's on Olaf's side, she's spying."

"Badly."

"Very badly," I agreed. "We'll figure it out. Are you sure you're okay?"

Saha nodded but swallowed hard. It was then that a silhouette came to the door.

"Who is it?"

"Scout Jervan. I have a report."

I watched as she visibly collected herself before responding, "Come on in, Jervan."

I stepped to the side as the scout entered the tent. He was clearly weary and tired, but the Maraung man was quick to enter regardless.

"Your Grace," he said, giving a small bow. "Most of Korrewen's soldiers retreated toward the pass of Sharvene."

"Excellent. We'll pursue them. Can you send Titanys to me?"

"Of course."

"Thank you," Saha said, giving him a nod to let him know he was dismissed. He slipped away quickly.

"Are we really going to invade Korrewen?"

"We are, and I'm going to send word of Olaf's plans to the other three kingdoms tonight. We cannot let him succeed," Saha said. "I trust you'll stay near to Graz and I, in case Sil…well…"

"You don't have to say it, I've got you."

"Alright, go get ready?"

"Yeah, I'll be back in no time."

"Thanks," Saha said as I slipped out of the tent and went to prepare.

In a flurry of packing and movement, Agrenon's army was setting out toward Korrewen.

I kept close to Saha, Graz staying close to me as well on his own Barbarza partner. Anza kept him distracted with conversation while Whisper slept tucked against my front, head resting on my shoulder, like she had when she was younger. Safe in her mothers arms. My mother stuck to my right, on the edge of the group, keeping her eyes outward, tension in her shoulders as Brian rubbed at them. Every now and then they'd drift close enough for me to catch snippets of Brian's attempts to comfort her.

"This time's different" and "It's okay, you're safe" and "I'm right here, I'm not going anywhere."

Emai didn't respond often and something felt off; she was distant and distracted.

Sil took up a spot at the rear, on a Barbarza partner who seemed to be just as no nonsense as she was. Every once in a while, I'd catch a glimpse of the distant silhouette of a dragon, unsure whether to be comforted or concerned that her fiery friend was keeping up with us.

"How long will it take to get to Korrewen?" I asked Tamaj.

"Not long enough," my mother whispered, Tamaj moving to nudge her knee.

"We've got you," she said before turning her attention back to me. *"Just hang tight for me? We'll probably need to stop to rest, and get to the pass tomorrow."*

"Can do," I said, Whisper stirring slightly before snuggling close to me again.

I held her as we slogged on, trying to keep my attention on the delicate balancing act of not letting anyone get too close to each other. Graz couldn't get too close to Saha, Sil had to stay away from them both, Anza had to keep from Brian, Emai had to stay away from Sil. It was exhausting. I constantly asked Tamaj to adjust, and many times she had to physically place herself between people to keep the volatile tension to a minimum. At least I wasn't in this alone.

By the time we stopped and settled in for the night, I felt

exhausted. But after dinner, quietly, a hand found my shoulder and I looked up at my mother.

"Can I steal you away for a moment?"

"Is everything alright?"

"Yeah, nothing scary, I just want to talk." I nodded, Whisper asleep in a small tent of her own near the one Anza and I had just finished setting up. I looked to him.

"Go on," he gently nudged. *"I think it'll be good for you"*

I rolled my eyes before letting my mother take my hand and lead me away from the group. We walked about far enough away where we could see the campfire's smoke rolling upwards, but almost lost visual of the tents, to make sure we couldn't be heard, a thick rolling purple fog all around us, before I spoke again.

"Not too far alright? I've gotta stick near Whisp—" I didn't expect the hug that stopped the sentence in my throat. It took a moment for my shock to pass before I tightly hugged her back. We stood there for the longest time, just hugging one another, before she spoke.

"I'm so sorry."

"I'm not mad at you."

"I should have gone back to Earth for you."

"If you had, you wouldn't have been able to come back here. You were banished."

"It wasn't selfish. I need you to know that I wanted to be there with you."

"What was it?"

"I was trying to help get Saha back, trying to…build you a better world."

"You succeeded."

"No, I didn't."

"Hey," I said, finally pulling back, wiping the tears that were brimming in her eyes. "Yes, you did. Saha's back. And sure, it's not everything you wanted, but that means we can build a better world *together*. What an adventure that will be."

"Yeah?"

"Yeah…you've been off lately, is there something else you want to tell me?" She hesitated, tearing her eyes from mine. "I won't be mad, you don't have to tell me if you don't want to."

"I just…I was an Endering of Korrewen before…and going back? I don't want to go back."

"You don't have to."

"I'm not just letting you go there without me."

"I have Sil and Brian." She winced a little.

"That isn't confidence inspiring."

"Which one isn't confidence inspiring?"

"Both. Sil is, well, Sil. And Brian's…not the same."

"I'm pretty scrappy. You don't have to come," I said, trying to gently give her an out. She was off, in every fathomable way. This wasn't the coy, teasing woman who had vaguely threatened our lives in the mountains. What had happened to her in Korrewen?

"I missed out on your whole life already, I'm not missing out on another single second if I can help it," she said firmly. "You'll be there, and so will your father, I can make it through anything with you two."

"That sounds a little more like that creepy mountain woman I met a few months back."

"Sorry I scared you so much back then."

"Honestly, it was probably me just being paranoid. I couldn't even tell you how many people had tried to kill us by then."

"Well, I'm just glad you're not scared of me now."

"Me too," I said.

"I've got this."

"*We've* got this," I corrected, and she nodded, sighing her relief as I hugged her again.

"I don't want to give Sil any credit, but she didn't totally screw you up."

I laughed, pulling out of the hug. "Whats the deal with you two anyway?"

"She thinks I corrupted her perfect little angel baby."

"Did you?" I asked, and she tried to smother a smile.

"Maybe," she said, a hint of light returning to her eyes as she grinned at me.

The sound of metal on stone shattered the moment and we both spun toward it, only for fear to rush through me as we looked up at the towering metal form above us.

"Run!" I managed, but we were already moving, running as fast as we could together to get out of the rushing metal tower coming down on us. I knew we weren't going to make it, but I didn't expect my mother, ahead of me, to turn back and wrap herself around me, pulling me to the ground and forcing her body between me and the tower of metal. I threw my hands up, summoning stone forward as I landed on my back, barely catching what I could now recognise as a train car just above our forms.

"Mira?"

"I'm fine, are you alright?"

"Yeah, I'm good."

I pushed up on the train car, giving us both enough space to scramble out from under it as the sound of metal against rocks and trees rang out in the woods not far from camp. The rest of the train was grinding to a halt nearby, as if it had materialized from the fog.

"A train, a fucking train."

"There aren't any trains in the Otherworld."

"There are now."

14

"Mira, where are you?" Anza asked down the bond.

"I'm okay, did it hit the camp?" I responded, feeling my heart slamming in my chest, my mother's hand intertwining in mine as if trying to settle me.

"No...what is 'it'?"

I had no idea how to respond to him. How could I explain this? How had this even happened?

Slowly, we approached the train, my mother a step ahead of me. She dropped my hand as we started to search for an entrance to one of the cars.

"What if there are people inside?" I asked.

"What if there aren't?" she asked in return.

I wasn't sure which terrified me more: a ghost train dumped in the middle of The Otherworld, or a derailed train with people just trying to live their lives dumped into The Otherworld, but there *could* be injured people on board and I couldn't just stand around doing nothing about it.

As we got to the cars, I ran my fingers along one, feeling the sweet hum of something deeper within it, but pushed it aside. I reached up, resting my hands on the edge of the top of the train-car, using a little boost from my stones below, and inched to the side until I found a door.

"I've got a way in," I said, and my mother gave me a reassuring nod.

"I'm right behind you," she said before I molded my bracelets into the crack of the door and forced it open. I carefully crafted steps for us to use and stepped up toward the doors, my mother on my heels. The metal of the train clanged as we walked the few steps to the now-open door.

"I'll go first," she said, gently resting a hand on my shoulder.

"I can go," I said, and she swallowed hard before speaking again.

"Please?"

I met her eyes, which were brimming with tears, her face deadly calm, as if she knew something I didn't.

"Okay, okay," I said, nodding before she quickly dropped into the darkness. Silence stretched for a moment before I heard her voice again.

"Clear."

I dropped through the door and into the darkness.

"Mom?" I asked into the darkness, not seeing her at first as my eyes adjusted. The creaking of metal on metal as the train shifted slightly put me on edge as I started forward, still unable to see my mother. Something crashed down on my shoulder and I whirled, meeting those familiar slate-gray eyes.

"Sorry, sorry."

"You scared the piss out of me!" I said sternly.

"You knew I was down here." She chuckled, smirking as she teased me gently.

"Yeah, but who knows what else could be down here?"

"Like what?"

"Like…a spider person with backwards joints or something," I said, her eyes glittering as her smile finally reached them.

"The Mountain trembles, hmm?" she said, looking me over and crossing her arms.

"No," I protested.

"Yeah."

"Nope."

"Oh yes you did, you're going to try to tell me you're not shaking in your boots?"

"Did not," I said, punching her shoulder playfully as she snickered before leading the way into the darker parts of the train. I kept close, following her carefully.

As we moved from car to car, stepping over shattered glass and broken metal pieces, I thanked the stars that there were no remains. No one was on board.

"Not even a conductor?" Emai asked as we finally got to the front car.

"Some trains are automated now. Looks like it might have been a passenger train, late at night. We're still lucky there were no passengers," I said quietly before I heard Anza's voice down the bond.

"Whisper refuses to wait for you, says it's important. We're coming to you."

"That is a terrible idea."

"You and I both know wrangling her is, well—"

"Impossible," I finished and sighed before looking to my mother. "We need to get back to the surface. Whisper's got a theory."

"Of course she does, she's an Echalon," Emai said. "I only get really worried when she's stumped."

I couldn't help but smirk as she led the way back toward the door we had slipped through. A deep creaking noise sounded as we stepped from one car to the next and she stole a look back at me.

"Is something wrong?"

"Run."

"Mom?"

"Run!" I rushed past her, running for the door, glancing back at her to see her glance behind her into the darkness, where something I couldn't see must have lingered. As soon as I touched the edge of the car beneath the door we had opened, the metallic noise erupted from behind us.

"Up!" I didn't hesitate to pull the earth up through one of the train windows and to our feet, launching us up into the sky.

I saw it and reacted all at once. A second train, crushing into the first one, running it through right where we had been a few moments before. I felt her cling to me as I pulled my bracelets from my wrists and threw up the thickest wall I could muster for us. Even then, I felt the impact all the way up my stone pillar as it started to crumble beneath me.

"No!" I managed to fight out as I clung to my mother, turning one of my bracelets into a flat plane, like a shield, before I slipped it underneath us, catching us before we plummeted. My head started to pound as I kept us there, midair, as the second train ground to a halt.

"Mira, you have to go down."

"I don't know how."

"Think. *Think*. You know."

She was right, I knew. The space between my sternum felt hot, but slowly, I lowered my stone, and therefore us, to the ground.

"Get up," she said as we rolled off of my flattened bracelet and onto the ground.

"You first," I insisted.

"No. I'll fight you on this," Emai said firmly and I rolled my eyes, trying to get my pounding head under control. "Did you just roll your eyes at me?"

"Call it a right of passage, Mom," I said, rubbing the bridge of my nose.

"I like it when you call me that."

"Good, get used to it," I said before trying to sit up.

"Anza, there's another one, everyone alright?" I asked

"Yes. We felt it. What the fuck is going on?"

"Hopefully Whisper knows," I said as I spotted the fluttering of light signaling their approach

"Don't get too close to the trains!"

"I see it, I see it," Whisper said, irritated, as I ensured my mom could sit up as well. She twisted her wrist as if it ached but didn't say anything.

"You're not hurt, right?"

"No, no, just strained it a little. I'm fine," Emai said, Whisper rushing toward us more quickly than I cared for.

"Please, for the love of the stars, slow down," Anza said, trying to slow her down from a few paces behind her.

"Speed up!" Whisper tossed over her shoulder before she stopped a few yards from the train.

"Dad said you had a theory," I called to her.

"Yeah, and if I'm right, and I think I am, this is gonna suck."

"Well, spit it out."

"This thing, it's of your world, right?"

"It is," Emai said, nodding as she sat on the ground, trying to get her bearings.

"Well, if it's here, there's a chance that losing portals is thinning the veil that keeps the worlds divided, your world may be leaking into ours," Whisper said.

"How big of a chance?" I asked.

"Not a small one."

"And every portal that falls…" Anza said quietly.

"Will only make it worse," Whisper confirmed. "I'm willing to bet my heart that it's not a one way thing either. The worlds are probably leaking into each other. The portals act like pillars, keeping the worlds suspended apart, and they're collapsing."

"The people of Earth didn't know about The Otherworld, Endering keep it a secret back on Earth to prevent the governments from trying to enter and meddle with this world," Emai said.

"Right," I agreed. It was the first lesson Sil taught me: tell no one.

"The key word is didn't," Whisper said. "The Otherworld has got to be leaking onto Earth, too."

"He's doing this on purpose. He knew this would happen," I said.

"That does seem the most likely theory we have, and if the people of Earth didn't know about us—" Whisper said, but I cut her off.

"There is no way in either world that they don't know now."

"And who knows what devastation we're about to face, what consequences there will be, even if we win," she said, shaking as she looked from me to Anza to Emai.

I could feel her feelings through Anza's empathic ability. She was spiraling. We were vulnerable to all sorts of horrible things from Earth's side.

Even if we were to win, I might not be able to save them.

15

"We have to figure out how it got here and minimize the impact. We have to."

"We can't just delete a train from existence. It will take months to clean up, even with magic, and we don't have any leads on how it even got here. We should be thankful it wasn't near any villages," I said. I knew I had to curb her spiraling, it was going to distract her as we rode up to the pass behind Saha. I caught the glimpse of a mass of men and women in battle gear out of the corner of my eyes. Several battalions waited for her, Titans, and I. Agrenon had answered their queen's call for aid. We were going to Korrewen, I could see it in Saha's eyes as she glanced back at me to give me a nod. We were doing this.

"The ecological devastation of a leak between worlds is—" Whisper started again.

"Whisper, focus," I said, trying to get her to pay attention to the next leg of our journey. She was spiraling, but she was right. "Saha sent word to the other kingdoms. All we can do is secure Korrewen and prepare to help the others if they need it."

"The end of the world should supersede politics," she hissed at me.

"If we just invade another kingdom in an attempt to stop

Olaf, the forces of that kingdom will instead be trained on us, ensuring we're fighting a war with two different nations when we can barely handle this one," Saha said from her spot a few feet ahead of us and to our left.

Anza shifted a little behind me as Whisper grumbled and turned to look at the pass of Sharvene, a towering slab of mountain that was split down the middle, a thin winding path, just large enough that carts could pass side by side, wove through it.

This was the only easy way over the mountains to Korrewen, especially while moving a whole army.

"I know," Whisper said, and I didn't need empathic abilities to feel her frustration from where I sat. It only took a moment before she spoke again. "There are anchors along the side of the pass farther up, likely for tripwires. It looks like they're within range of the flags and likely rigged to go off upon being touched," she started, reviewing the entrance to the pass. "There are multiple charges set along the edges as well, and throughout the pass. This is going to be slow going, but I can disable them as we go."

"Without getting blown up?" I asked as she moved to get off of my stone Barbarzas back.

"Well, yes. I'm good at getting blown up, but it would be nice if you were right there in case I do need cover," she said, and I nodded, slipping off the Barbarza and moving to follow behind her.

"If we keep the flags down, that should stop the higher up ones from triggering all together," she instructed, stepping up to a small spattering of dirt. "Mom, can you feel them? If you feel out this space, you should be able to see the empty spaces where they are."

"I'll try." I reached out with my power, and sure enough, there were masses of space, about the size of a Frisbee each, tucked under the dirt. Barely. "Should I lift them up?"

She bit her lip looking over the pass again. "Maybe try one

farther out? We don't know if the trigger is on top or bottom for these, and don't want to activate it."

"Alright," I said, ready to slam a wall up in the pass if we needed it. Not throwing the switches was going to be the hard part. Fast movements and the element of surprise were how I had usually used my power, now I had to be careful?

I took a breath, reminded myself my mom was watching, and remembered the last time I had seen her before she had saved Anza, how she taught me about being careful and precise, and reached out to the farthest mine I could sense. Carefully, I pushed up, and it rose up out of the dirt. Everyone flinched, expecting an explosion, but it didn't go off.

"Looks like the trigger is probably on the top," Whisper said, and I nodded, throwing up a wall along the front of our forces before carefully raising each one up.

There were thirty seven. None went off.

Carefully, I lowered the wall and Whisper padded forward. I followed her, Anza scanning the cliffs as she disengaged the first mine. After she disengaged it, she met my eyes for what felt like too long before she slowly slid the disarmed mine into her pack.

"Whisper…"

"You saw nothing."

"Whisper," I warned again.

"I need it," she grumbled.

"It's not going to blow up?"

"No. I know what I'm doing," she said, rolling her eyes, and I sighed, knowing it was pointless to argue. If she said it was safe, it was safe.

I looked back and waved Saha forward. Slowly, our forces started to creep through the pass, disarming mines along the way, Whisper tucking them into her bag whenever she thought I wasn't watching.

I spotted my parents atop Tamaj, my mother sitting rigid, fear in her eyes as my father rubbed her back.

"It's alright, it's not forever. Agrenon is always your home.

We won't let anything happen," I heard. His constant reassurances seemed to be helping but her eyes flicked to me. I held her gaze and took a deep, slow breath before letting it out. She mirrored me and nodded. I was here. We were okay.

Carefully, we picked through the pass, leaving Agrenon behind as we slid into Korrewen. Sil kept close to us, as did Anza.

"Hey, Dad, are there any cool stories about how this place was made?" Whisper asked.

"He's not your dad," Sil growled, keeping her eyes on the ridges.

"And you're not a grumpy, bitter, tactless, old woman who needs to get laid," Whisper retorted without missing a beat.

"I really like your little one, very spunky," Emai called back to us as Sil prepared to respond.

"We found her like that!" I called back, and Emai threw her head back, laughing at Sil's disgusted face.

"I do actually have a cool story, *daughter* of mine," Anza said, glaring right back at Sil as I urged the stone Barbarza between all of us and her. Sil closed her mouth, turning her attention back to the ridges as Anza told a story about how a great god with the power of creating stone had apparently carved out the mountains.

I paid more attention to whether or not our daughter was about to be blown up and keeping a count of how many mines she was sneaking into her bag.

I knew she asked to help keep her nerves down. She was handling bombs, after all, and the wrong shiver of fear could end with both of us being blown up.

We methodically crept forward, cold starting to inch into our bodies as we moved, but we weren't as cold as I thought we'd be. Sil didn't shiver at all. But it wasn't until we dispatched the last one that she fell in line with me as I searched to ensure there weren't more.

"What is your problem? I sent you in here all full of hope,

now Arlo is AWOL and even you're treating me like I'm a burden," she grumbled as we walked.

I felt Anza's fury roar down the bond and shushed him.

"Well, firstly, Arlo is dead." I saw her flinch. "He died the first night we were here, actually, because your son is a manipulative, cruel jackass who doesn't care about others. And I am not talking about Brian," I said.

"He's...gone?"

"Yes," I said, firmly meeting her softening-but-still-fiery gaze. "If I had known magic, it would have been way easier to get to the castle. If I had known about my parents, I would have recognized my own fucking mother the first time I saw her, and maybe, just maybe, I would have put a couple puzzle pieces together before I got to the castle and not after, oh, I don't know, an entire plague being attributed to your other son?"

"I taught you how to survive."

"Yeah. Yeah, you did, and for that, I'm thankful, but you seem to think that *wasn't* the bare fucking minimum," I said firmly, helping Whisper up to Anza before I climbed on as well, picking up the pace to get back to Saha's side. Sil was right behind me.

"Hey, I was talking to—"

The sound of a sword unsheathing interrupted her as I turned to see Anza rest the point of his sword at her throat, her hand a mere inch from my wrist.

"Clearly, the conversation is over."

If Sil had laser eyes, she would have killed him, but she stepped back as we continued forward.

"Try not to be too hard on her," Saha said quietly as we got to her side, Anza sheathing his sword.

"Why?" I asked, turning my eyes up toward the ridge.

"She's used to being where you are. She's finding her place again, it'll just take some time."

"Her place is on her knees, groveling and begging for forgiveness."

"That's a bit harsh," Saha said.

"Not harsh enough," Anza said as Whisper nodded.

"You're taking her side an awful lot for someone who saw it fit to banish her," I said, and Saha fell silent, her eyes locked on the back of her Barbarza partner's neck.

"That was a mistake."

"Yeah?" I asked.

She didn't look up. "Yeah."

"Ambush," Titanys whispered, picking up the pace to get near Saha and I.

Saha nodded as he fell back again. I wanted to tell Sil I didn't trust her, but most of the army was moving through the long and dangerous pass. This wasn't a time to be petty.

"Give them a surprise?" Saha asked me.

"Just don't set off the charges in the walls," Whisper added.

"What's she going to do, throw a rock at them?" I heard Sil mumble.

She had seen me in the field. She knew what my power was, but she did not know its breadth. She did not know how Saha and I had been working on my range. Nor did she know just how creative I could be. I slipped off my stone Barbarza and stepped forward, just as I had before, as if looking for more mines, and shook my wrists, feeling my bracelets there.

"Oh, Mother, that's right, you haven't been properly introduced," Brian said, his voice coy. His shoulders still carried such weight, but his eyes danced with light as I turned my attention to my task.

I could almost feel his pride from where I stood as I reached deep, not searching for any specific movement or stone, feeling instead where the ground was pressed in, where the dirt shifted as people moved up on those cliff faces. I reached out, just like I had on that mountain. I knew where they were. At least a dozen, if not more, but there were too many to spike through. I needed smaller, more precise targets. Finesse.

"Bow before the power of The Mountain of Agrenon."

I dug deep, drawing a section of stone beneath myself before shoving my power, and myself, skyward with great force. Drawing me up in a single moment until I was eye level with the cliff faces. Maraung, Barbarza, and Photomyran faces looked out, fear in their eyes as, in a single second, I sent out dozens of small stones, sharpening them, forcing them through multiple skulls at the same time. Every single person almost simultaneously dropped. And with them, a trigger hit the ground.

"Oh no." Three beeps. That's all it took before I realized what was about to happen and slammed two sections of stone out at an angle, crafting a roof over the army below as the detonators went off.

Whisper was down there. Anza was down there. Saha and my parents and Sil and Graz and Taryn and Tamaj and Titanys; they were all down there.

Crumbling stone rattled down the sides of the cliff as dust filled the air. I looked down to find the earthen debris caught on the slabs of stone I had pulled forth from the ground. Carefully, I pulled away the debris, returning it to its spot on the cliff faces, solidifying it into place before I pulled the makeshift roof away to hear a clear, loud voice declare, "That's my wife!"

"Idiot," I teased down the bond.

"Yeah, but I'm your idiot," he said back, delighted as I commanded the pillar I stood on down, settling onto the ground again as Saha, who had slipped off her Barbarza partner's back, stepped forward to hug me.

"Well done, Mountain."

"Piece of cake," I said as, together, we went back to the Barbarza.

I clambered up next to Anza, pulling up Whisper and tucking her close. Tamaj kept close to me, my parents on her back, my mother still tense and looking quickly over the terrain. I reached over, resting my hand on hers.

"I'm right here," I said. "So is Brian."

She nodded, looking at me and swallowing hard, steadying

her breathing. What could make her, of all people, so terrified? So out of sorts?

I tried not to think about it as we slid into the forest, tucking into the other side of the mountain range. It took some time to set up camp that night. Between Sil, my mother, and Saha all trying to avoid each other, and Graz and Taryn trying to keep out of Saha's sight, it took much longer than expected.

Finally, we all settled around a fire, my dad rubbing my mothers back between her shoulder blades, Whisper sitting between Graz and Taryn working on a project as they ate. Sil glowered at me from her spot across the fire and I looped my arm in Anza's, using my other hand to eat.

"You're making her mad."

"Good."

"I don't tell you enough that I love you." He laughed down the bond and I smirked as Tamaj lay down behind us.

"Try not to antagonize Sil. We don't know where her loyalties lie and Olaf was very likely at the portal when she came in. They were very close," she warned us, and I gave a curt nod before a sound erupted from the box Whisper was working on. Music. An upbeat song I didn't recognise.

"Whoa, it works!" she said happily.

There was only a heartbeat of silence, the song the only thing interrupting the heavy stillness of the night, before Brian stood and offered my mother a hand. She smiled and took it.

"Guys," Sil warned, but that didn't stop them from beginning to dance, the tension vanishing from both their shoulders. Saha looked up to Sil as Graz and Taryn got up, sneaking away to a shadowy spot behind Saha to dance as well. Whisper bounced up to us and grabbed both mine and Anza's hands.

"Up, come on!" she said, pulling us over onto the makeshift dance floor.

I rolled my eyes but Anza's hand found my empty one and we slid to our feet. Anza picked her up, which he almost couldn't do now, and we leaned against each other, starting to sway to the song.

Saha and Sil didn't move.

"What is it going to take for those two to get their heads out of their asses?"

"No idea. Hopefully they just talk it out soon."

"Yeah, before someone dies." I sighed as he spoke, but turned my attention to my parents as their laughter rose up around us.

"Brian, put me down!" He had slung my mother over his shoulder and trudged over to Tamaj.

"Have you seen my wife? I swear I can hear her—"

"Brian!"

"It's almost like she's right here," Tamaj laughed as my mom patted my father's arm.

"Curse you, Tamaj," Emai laughed, Tamaj's tail wagging as Brian made his way to us.

"Have you two seen my wife?"

"Sorry," I laughed, shaking my head. Anza held his tongue, letting them have this moment.

"Save me!" My mom laughed as he turned.

"She doesn't actually want to be saved," Anza clarified.

"So weird, I could have sworn she was right here," my dad said before padding off toward their tent with her.

"Brian, I swear by the stars!" She laughed as they vanished into the swath of tents. The silence stretched on for a while before I looked into Anza's eyes.

"What are you thinking about?" he asked.

"I've tried to imagine my parents and the way they loved each other hundreds of times, but I never expected that I'd get to see it," I said, swallowing hard. I blinked to fight back the threat of tears.

"They're dorks and I love it," Whisper said, resting her head against Anza's shoulder, her eyes heavy with the stress of the day.

"Agreed," Anza laughed. "Even if I do want to strangle one of them."

"It's...it's just..." I couldn't find the words for it but Anza could.

"It's a beautiful realization. Closure for all the time you wondered what they could be like," he said quietly.

"Yeah."

"I can feel it, how watching them heals you," he said quietly.

He wasn't wrong. I could feel myself knit together a little more the longer I thought about their bubbly, goofy, delighted relationship.

Whisper fell asleep against Anza and I rested my head against his.

"I have *parents.*"

I hadn't allowed myself to think too much about them on our journey to the castle. I hadn't put a lot of thought into them until I found Brian and found out who my mother was. Then it was just a big question mark, of why they would do what they did, act how they did, but now I got it. Seeing them together made it easier to love them as the parents I never got to have, even if Brian was still not someone I'd actively choose to be around.

"Parents who are probably going to have to put their tent a little farther away tonight."

"Eww, Anza, no." I slapped his shoulder gently and smirked. He just laughed and I shook my head at him. "You're terrible," I said before looking to Sil and Saha, both still sitting in their places, staring into the fire.

"I know," he said.

"At least they don't hate each other like those two."

"Hate and...something else are very closely related emotions."

"Does it start with an *L*?" I asked, looking up at him again, meeting those gilded eyes.

"It does."

16

My heart ached and my stomach twisted itself into knots seeing the state of the people of Korrowen.

Before I stepped foot in this star forsaken kingdom, I had thought only of sharp-toothed children and angry men and women who were ready to rip apart my kingdom. It wasn't until we were almost at the castle that I even saw the first sign of life as we passed through a town.

Up to that point, I had only caught whispers of shadows in the trees. Our scouts had reported that they were not threats, just people who had been displaced from their homes, half-starved and terrified, abandoned by those they had trusted to protect them, all but spirits from the dozens of empty towns we had come across on our journey.

Hollowed homes with none of their usual comforts in their rotting frames had been abandoned for the forest.

A mother, cradling her child close, both of them underweight and malnourished, was the only person we actually came face to face with. Her eyes looked sunken in, betraying her fear and pain.

"Slowly," Saha said as Graz, behind her, slipped from his Barbarza partner and padded to her, offering her some of his rations. She took them, Taryn watching for danger as he returned to the formation.

"Why should he move slowly?" I asked, looking over the mother.

"Many people here are not used to kindness leaving them suspicious of intent, and often swift motions are mistaken as dangerous for them," she explained and I sighed, looking back at the mother, sadness running through the bond from both sides, and leaned back into Anza.

"She said they left—the king and queen. They're taxed heavily if they have a house to call home. They send people to take all they have, people who often do horrible things to them. They can't get enough coin to put food in their children's mouths, so they take to the woods. You can't steal from, assault, and use those you can't catch," Graz said as he returned to our side.

"I can't imagine they can grow food easily in those conditions," I said.

"No, I can't imagine they can," Saha agreed, her voice somber and soft.

"She also said that the army has marched elsewhere. I can't imagine that they wouldn't leave *someone* behind for us to fight though," Graz said.

"Unless Olaf has convinced the king and queen to move the army en masse elsewhere. Or..." Saha said quietly.

"Surely we can do something?" I asked, cutting her off.

She nodded. "I have let Korrewen get away with harming my family and my kingdom for far too long. We have made little truces and deals so their leaders could stay in power in order to keep peace between kingdoms. I will no longer do such a thing," she said.

"This trip isn't just to establish if their portal is also cut off," I said, and she nodded.

"It's an invasion of a kingdom long overdue for aid," she said quietly.

Hope sparked in my chest. Maybe, just maybe, we could do some good for these people.

Saha was still very tense, her eyes flitting from space to space, as if searching for threats.

"What is it?"

"We haven't met any resistance since the pass, like Graz said. He's right, that is…unusual," she said quietly.

"Maybe they're all at the castle preparing to defend it?" I proposed.

"Maybe…" Something was unnerving her. There was something more here, something she was picking up on that I was missing, but what was it?

I glanced back, seeing Sil farther back in the formation. Though I couldn't be sure, she was suspiciously close to Graz.

"Do you still think she's a danger?" I asked Saha.

"Sil?"

"Yeah."

"No? Yes? I don't know." Her voice hardened.

"Have you two talked or anything?"

"Leave it alone, Mira" she said firmly before urging us to keep going.

We thundered toward the castle, unhindered as we moved. I felt Anza hold me tighter to him, determined to keep me close as we approached Korrewen's capital city. Saha didn't slow until the walls were well into view.

"Whisper?"

"Yupper?"

"What are the chances this is a trap?" she asked, gesturing at the barren, empty landscape before us. The gates to the city were wide open and there wasn't a single guard in sight.

"If we were going to meet resistance, we should have by now, for sure," Whisper said. "But the gates are open and I have yet to see any movement. They're either hidden, waiting for us, or gone."

Saha nodded. We had come to the same conclusion.

"They can't be gone," Saha said before looking at me.

"When we get in range of your ability, can we get a sweep of the city?"

"Yeah, it's made of stone?"

"It is," she said as we continued forward.

Carefully, I took the lead, watching the edges of the city walls.

It took only moments for me to get in range and, reaching my power outward, I could sense the world within the walls. Houses rose in small groups beyond me. Most stood firm, but there wasn't a single shifting motion in the city. If there were people there, they weren't even shifting their weight into the dirt. There was no compression, no push or pull of stone. Even breathing sometimes caused micro-shifting in your footing, a change I had learned to focus on in the last few months. I could say with near certainty that there wasn't even a single living person within those walls, let alone an entire army.

"I think it's empty." Saha shook her head as I spoke, biting her lip. "There aren't even compressions from people moving in the dirt. I've got nothing,"

"We do have a dragon. He could totally check it out, right?" Whisper asked, looking at each of us as if we'd lost our minds. We had a giant fire-breathing recon beast, we might as well use him. Sil rolled her eyes as Saha looked to her, but her whistle rose through the air and her dragon descended almost instantly, brushing over the treetops and heading for the still-towering doors. We watched it circle once, then twice, before Sil shook her head.

"He says there is nothing."

"And how does he feel about that? He is more experienced than any of us," Saha said, eyes still locked on the open entrance.

"He's nervous."

"A nervous dragon?" Whisper nearly laughed at the absurdity as Sil nodded.

"That's really not good," Emai said as Saha wordlessly urged us forward.

I could see the tension trembling through my mother's shoulders with every step we took. The slow, gradual, methodical process of moving into the city was one that pained her. When we walked through the gates, Brian whispering more comforts into her ear, there was no ambush. There wasn't a soul in sight. My power still did not pick up a single thing. The entire city had been abandoned.

Griosghortha landed on a large, stone building, which, thankfully, did not crumble under his weight as we started quietly through the city, toward the castle at its heart.

The dark castle was eerily beautiful, standing against the mixing grays and browns of the sky and trees. Made of cut stones that had been pulled from the ground centuries ago, two towers soared upward at each corner, connected by walkways in the sky, supported by eroding, but once grand stone supports. Windows, carved into the stone and pieced together like puzzle pieces, bolted up each of the towers, giving plenty of potential advantage to archers, but none took to their posts. Sweeping wings embossed in the stone beneath each opening swept out and upward, as if embracing the dark, empty spaces. The arched entrance was filled with two massive doors, one barely standing on its hinges.

Even at a distance I could see the fresh fissures from what appeared to be ice sticking out of a few places in the windows and doors, sending small fragments of the walls clattering to the ground.

Carefully, Saha led the way up the stairs and into the castle.

I had to cover my mouth. The stench was horrific, putrid and sickeningly sweet, akin to rancid meat, and my stomach twisted.

Saha lifted a hand, silently commanding the bulk of our forces to wait outside as she covered her face with her other hand.

As we stepped around the precariously hung door, the castle

opened up into a ballroom, brown stone floors spilling out before us to nearly black stone walls. Small nooks held snuffed lanterns at eye level, and above, reaching up the remainder of the wall and to the ceiling, were stone carvings of what I could only assume had been Endering. A man with wings of night tucked against a painted startlit backdrop; a woman with fists full of crumbling stone at each side of her; and a small girl with swirling smoke tendrils rushing out from her body were the only ones of note I could make out before I spotted the source of the putrid smell of rot.

Lying at the base of the towering throne, were the bodies of a Maruang man and a woman. A king I did not recognise, a giant slit up his stomach, limp on the ground. The woman though, I recognised her in an instant. Her throat slit, terror still trapped on her face as she lay lifeless in a pool of her own blood.

"Amerette," Saha said, slipping from her mount as she rested her hand on her sword's hilt.

Olaf had successfully committed regicide. The reason we had met no resistance was suddenly and abundantly clear. He had learned from his mistake with Saha and finished what he started here.

He was moving on to another kingdom and had taken all the resources he could muster. He had abandoned Korrewen.

"Spread out, search for survivors. They had at least three Endering here," Saha commanded. "Em?"

My mother didn't respond, eyes locked on the form of the dead regents.

"Emai."

Finally, my mother looked to Saha, swallowing hard, her panic obvious in the way her eyes darted around the room.

"Ye-yeah?"

"Are you up to going down into the dungeon or no? No pressure. I know being here again is hard."

I looked to the depiction of the child, smoke and death strewn around her.

My mother had been an Endering of Korrewen before she became an Endering of Agrenon. She knew these walls.

"I can do it. If Tank is down there, she might rage if someone else goes instead…Mira, would you come with me?"

"Of course," I said immediately, but I bit my lip, shifting my weight slightly as Graz passed me a torch, Sil wordlessly lighting it.

"Every wall down there should be stone. It's just like the mountain. You won't be trapped, you'll be surrounded by opportunity," Anza said down the bond as I carefully slid off the stone Barbarza and dropped to the floor. I nodded to him as I reached for my mother's hand.

"Lead the way?" I asked.

"Want me to come down with you?" Brian asked, but Mom shook her head.

"Just…watch out for them?" Em said, nodding to the others. "I can't worry about them and everyone down there," she said quietly.

"I'll make sure they're still here when you get back," he assured her. "You know what to do if you change your mind."

Emai nodded and started leading me toward a passage I hadn't noticed until we were right up on it. I could feel her heartbeat in my hand as we began to descend the stairs.

"I'm right here," I said as her breathing picked up, each step forced and fierce. "You're alright, we're alright."

"The things they did to us here…"

"We're not here for that, we're here for Tank." Whoever that was. "And for the others. We're here to get them out," I said, and she shivered but nodded, steeling herself before leading us forward.

The dungeon came much faster than I expected, and with it, another blast of sickeningly sweet rancid meat rushed my nose, twisting my stomach. My mother held my hand tighter before reaching for the torch, I let her take it, and she placed it in a nook in the wall I hadn't seen in the darkness. The smell of something chemical flared and flame darted from the torch down a thin path along the top of the dungeon, contained in a set-in grate, it was just enough to light the space. In the low light I could see a burnt out torch nearby. Carefully, I swapped it out for my torch, leaving the used one on the ground.

"That smell…it's—" I started.

"No!" She cut me off, letting my hand go and almost vanishing into the darkness before us as she ran toward the first open cell. I followed her closely, hoping she wouldn't find what we both knew she would.

The first cell harbored a man, his unmoving body limp against the floor. As dark as the night itself, his dark brown eyes were glazed over, gone. There was a pool of blood beneath him from a wound I couldn't see. On his back, two scraps of what looked to have been feathers protruded from between his shoulder blades, but there was little more than a bare, broken joint jutting from where I assumed wings should be.

"Mom?" She didn't hear me, abandoning the cell to go to the next.

I felt my heart drop to my stomach, knowing what we'd find.

My heart sank when the full extent of it came into view; a woman's body, arms bound taught to the wall in chains, eyes glazed over, a single stab wound to her heart.

"No, no, no."

I tried to reach for her but she slapped my hands away, slipping into the cell to hug the lifeless body. This must have been Tank. I felt my blood turn to ice as my mother, someone who has flashed a toothy grin in the face of danger, who taunted infected Hazzal to come play, who teased the Wildfire and commanded Death itself, wailed her anguish into existence.

Who had this been to her? How had they known one another before she came to Agrenon? How had they been separated? A soft noise in another cell made me look over just in time to see a single feather flutter to the ground. I moved to check the cell, giving my mother a moment of privacy in her mourning, and found a bundle of feathers in the corner. I kept my eyes on it, watching for movement, before seeing a subtle shift. Breathing.

"Mom!? Did Tank have a—"

I didn't get to finish my sentence before he moved, a dagger clutched in his fist.

He couldn't have been more than fourteen. His skin was dark, his thick hair an afro, unkempt and framing eyes, which were alive with a fire that I recognized as the blaze of someone's soul fighting for its very survival.

It was crystal clear that, as far as he was concerned, I was a threat.

17

"Whoa, whoa, whoa!" I said, dodging three frightfully quick attacks before the dagger finally slid across my cheek. Evasion wasn't going to be an option here, he was too quick. I couldn't hurt him though. The fear in his eyes was so clear. I stepped back again, feeling my own blood start to well in the shallow wound before Emai sprang from the darkness, tears still staining her cheeks as she pinned him to a cell door.

"That's enough" she said firmly as he twisted, trying to bite her. "Eh! What did I just say!" He stopped, meeting her eyes, fear still very much alive there. It was a long few seconds of eye contact before my mother spoke again. "Are you hurt?"

"Y-yeah." He shuddered.

"Alright, I'm gonna fix you up, if you'll let me, and I'll let you keep the knife because I know you're scared, but we're not going to hurt you. We can help, if you let us, but that means no stabbing. Can we agree to that?"

"You have storm eyes," he said.

"That's what she used to call me, Storm Eyes." The silence hung for a moment as something passed between them, an understanding I couldn't fathom, before he nodded.

"Deal."

She let him go, resting a hand on his shoulder just long enough to heal what I could now see was a deep slash along his ribs. After she finished, he shied from us, pulling close the two masses of feathers on his back as if they were a shield.

"Is there anyone else down here?"

"No."

"Okay," she said, wiping her tears from her cheeks. "We're gonna go up, and you're not going to stab anyone. This is Mira, my daughter, and I'm Emai."

"Sorry."

"You don't have anything to be sorry about," I said. "My best friendships have all started with me almost getting stabbed."

"That happens to you a lot?" he asked.

"Yeah, more than it should. What's your name?"

"Abronoma, but most call me Abry."

"That's…very fitting. Let's get you outta here, Abry," Emai said, focusing her anguish on getting him out.

Was she thinking about the last time she had climbed those stairs? The last time she saw that place? How many times had his feet brushed the edges of the places she had walked before him? I pushed the thought out of my mind as we ascended to the top.

"Ope, she's back," Saha announced as we got to the top, her eyes scanning us as if expecting there to be more than just Abronoma. She locked eyes with my mother, who shook her head. My dad immediately took a few steps closer, but stopped when Abronoma's hand tightened on his blade and he hid behind my mom.

"Hey, it's alright. That's not the same man," I started as I realized who he thought it was. "I know they look a lot alike, but that's just because they're twins. This one's way nicer. Usually," I said to him, hoping he wouldn't try to start stabbing again.

He looked at me, a little unsure, but peered past me to Brian, who managed a soft smile that didn't touch his eyes. I was terrified for a heartbeat, worried that this scared young kid was going to make a terrible choice, but they held each other's gaze for what felt like millennia before Abronoma nodded and they broke eye contact. Brian didn't hesitate to go to my mother, who hugged him tightly, speaking quickly in Twi to him, something I didn't quite understand, and he nodded.

Someone else had caught Abronoma's eye.

"Mom, I haven't found anything yet about—" Whisper started.

"How did you get out?" Abronoma asked, eyes brightening as he stood a little taller. I didn't realize what he meant until Whisper spoke again, her mind working far faster than mine.

"I came with her," she said, pointing to me. "You know where the Echalon here are, don't you?" she asked, but he was already nodding, pointing to a door with a large lock on the other side of the room. Whisper immediately headed toward the door.

"The key is around the king's neck," Abronoma said quietly as I moved to follow her, reaching out to tear the single metal key from the mangled monarch's body. I wiped the blood off and passed it to her as I reached her side at the door.

"Hey, what might be on the other side of this might not be pretty," I warned.

"I'm ready," she said firmly before taking a breath, reaching up, and unlocking the door.

We slid inside together, bracing ourselves in the low light of the sconces lighting the small, cramped room. On each side, there were cells lining the hallway. I swallowed hard, looking into the cell on my left and finding six Echalon women of varying ages tucked into a corner together.

Echalon could live hundreds of years. How long had they been there?

Each looked at me with a measured fear and uncertainty, but when their eyes trailed to Whisper, understanding bloomed. Still, they did not move.

I turned to look to my right, where four Echalon men, also of varying ages, sat together, though not as closely as the women, watching us, afraid and hopeful. Each of them was dressed in scraps of clothes.

"Are you going to let us out?" The youngest of the women asked.

I looked to Whisper, who already had tears rushing down her face. She was smart enough to know what had happened here. Smart enough to know what had happened to these people, whether they had wanted to partake or not. She nodded, moving to the women's cell.

"We're gonna get you out of here," she loosed through a sob. None of them moved, shocked in place, until the same woman spoke again.

"There is a cell in the back to the left of the bedroom. They keep the children and eggs in there."

"On it," I said as Whisper looked to me. She quickly unlocked the cages before passing me the key.

I moved down the hall, unlocking the bedroom as I passed, before stopping before the cell the woman had indicated. Four children sat there in a circle, a few games settled in the corner, and six eggs sat on shelves with different tags on them. I could see, even from where I stood, that the tags had names on them. Parentage labels.

I could barely contain my fury as I unlocked the cage, the kids shying from me, but thankfully, it was only a moment before Whisper was there at my side again.

"Come on, let's go to the others," she said to them, and with nothing more than that suggestion, they left with her.

"I need help in here. Bring empty bags. There are eggs," I said down the bond.

"Hang on, I'm coming," Anza said back.

He was at my side before I'd had time to even process what we'd found, several empty packs in his hands, crusted with gemstones and jewels. He had taken them from the king and queen's closet.

"Perfect," I said as he passed me one. I carefully grabbed hold of two eggs and tucked them into the bag I had. He reached out to take it, passing me another before filling the third bag with the last two as I filled the second.

"Where did Whisper take them?"

"They're in the main room. Saha's trying to settle them and Whisper's figuring out what to do. They can't exactly come with us," he said, and I nodded as he led the way out of that horrible place toward the main room.

I didn't know what I expected, but they were all sitting together now, children reunited with parents, fear and worry and hope in their eyes as Whisper and Saha talked.

Anza and I approached, but I couldn't take my eyes off of Whisper as she cleared the tears from her cheeks again. Anza carefully worked to get the eggs back to their mothers, gently assuring each of them that their plight was over. A few didn't want to take them, but their fathers stepped forward instead and it was only moments before each of the children and eggs were settled with the group and Whisper came to my side.

"Hey. I'm so sorry, Moonbeam."

"We got them out, that's the first step. We're gonna send them back to Agrenon with a note for The Two. I want them to check something for me. They should be able to handle them, and they shouldn't have a hard time getting there with the battalion Saha assigned to them," she said quietly.

"Are you alright?" I asked, and she shook her head, but didn't meet my gaze. I opened my arms slightly, offering a hug but she shook her head again.

"I don't really want to talk about it, we just have to get them out of here," she said, her voice breaking.

"Okay, are you going with them?" Part of me hoped she would, they would need guidance, but I knew her answer before she spoke.

"No, Rania and Arlo should have this covered. I'm not letting you two ding dongs get in too deep," she said as Anza got to her side.

"Is Abronoma going with them?"

"I think he's too scared to leave Grandma Em's side," Whisper said as I looked for them, spotting the small winged boy a mere foot from my mom.

"I just hope he's going to be alright, knowing what we're facing," I said quietly.

"I think he will be. There's a…tentative curiosity there. He's scared, but I don't think the fear has him so stuck he can't think. It'd be good for him to see some of the world. Who knows how much they've let him see," she said quietly, Anza's hand finding mine.

"We did well here. *You* did well here."When Olaf shows up unexpectedly under the guise of being an Endering of Korrewen Mira isn't quite sure what he's up to. Until a ruse comes to light that could destroy both Earth and The Otherworld, sending all those she loves to the edge of death itself in more ways than one.

With worlds hanging in the balance Mira and her newfound family and friends must fight with everything they have to stop him. But as the other kingdoms, and Endering, get involved the line between friends and foes gets blurrier by the minute and Mira is left wondering what exactly she's fighting for.

"I just wish we didn't have to 'do well' at all," I said, looking from Abronoma to the group of Echalon and back again. "Did you guys find the portal?"

"Yeah, it's gone, just like we thought. They probably took this one out first before going to Agrenon's, but Saha doesn't know where Olaf may have gone," Anza explained, leading me back toward the others as Whisper introduced the Echalon to the captain of the battalion that would take them to the castle.

"If a single one of them dies, there will be more than your blood on my hands" Whisper said, and I tried to ignore the firm way she was beating into the battalion's leaders just how important these people were as I got closer to the group.

"Biena is closest, but that's the easiest target. He might avoid it if he thinks that's where we would look for him first," Saha was saying as I came up.

"And the least likely target?"

"Eynon. They're technically an island continent, but they have a much more ferocious military. Even Olaf would know he couldn't survive it alone."

"Unless it was a stealth mission," Abronoma said quietly.

"Grio says your bird is coming back," Sil said flatly to Emai.

"Rivet? Already? He shouldn't be back for ages," she said, leading the way to the steps of the castle. Sure enough, the small falcon descended to my mother's outstretched hand not long after we stopped on the steps, a note tied to his leg.

Emai removed it, the bird lighting upon her shoulder and settling into her locks as she looked over the sealed note before turning and passing it to Saha. I noticed Biena's emblem pressed into the seal that held it closed. She opened it quickly, tears slipping down her face as she devoured the message.

"What is it?"

"He tricked us. He got ahold of some of Biena's Endering and he used them to trick us. They're asking for help." Her breath was shaky as she took in the note and the weight the small slip of paper held. "He's already there."

18

"I was so foolish! I should have just taken us to Biena. Why did we wait?"

"Easy, Sah. The scout said they retreated into Korrewen. You were working with the information you had. That's all we could do," I said, trying to calm her as we got ready to leave quickly despite Whisper's 'I told you so' look as we packed.

The trek to Biena would take a few days. A few days they probably didn't have. He had put distance between us and the army he had gathered in Korrewen's forces. What had he promised them if they fought for him? Freedom? Food? Safety? Any positive change might be enough for people in such a dire state.

"If I had known he had gotten his hands on Biena's other male Endering I would have been more careful. I know what their powers are, why didn't I take it into account? It was so short sighted of me—"

"Stop it," I said a little more firmly than was maybe necessary. "Beating yourself up won't help us now. Focus on what we do next."

Even I knew we were probably going to be too late to make a difference as we packed and prepped, my parents leading the

Echalon down to the battalion that would take them to Agrenon with Whisper following them down the front steps of the castle. Abronoma had stopped at the top of the stairs, Anza still by my side as always, while Graz and Taryn helped arrange for a swift burial of the two Endering in the dungeon and Amerette and her fallen king.

"You all right?" Whisper asked, looking back at Abronoma.

"I've never…been this far before," he said, looking back to the doors we had just stepped through before turning back to Whisper. A breeze buffeted his thin form and he flinched. "What was that?"

"The wind?" Whisper started back up the stairs and I watched Emai take a step after her, only for my father to catch her elbow.

"Does it do that a lot out here?"

"Yeah, it does," Whisper said.

"It feels…right?" Abronoma said as Whisper ascended a few more stairs.

"Open your wings a little? It might feel really good…"

He pursed his lips, looking her over before slowly opening his trembling wings. They were cramped and thin, but it was clear someone had told him how to care for them based on how clean they were. The wind rushed through them, sending a shiver up his spine, and his wings trembled, every feather moving.

"That was…"

"Good?" Whisper asked when he couldn't finish the sentence. He nodded, slowly folding his wings again. "This world can be a cold and scary place, but there are wonderful, beautiful things everywhere," she said, reaching her hand to beckon him. He stepped down a step. "I know you're not used to this, but we're here, and we won't hurt you." He stepped down a few more. "And I think you are amazing to have survived what you have, but there is so much more out here than that."

Whisper reached the bottom, stepping onto the grass. "Ever felt grass before?"

"No," Abronoma said before finally taking her still-outstretched hand. I glimpsed my mom patting at my father's shoulder, eyes alight as her smile broke across her face.

"I know," my dad said gently, moving to hold her closer at the hip as Whisper guided the barefoot boy to the grass.

Abronoma closed his eyes, exhaling a deep, heavy breath, as if he had been holding it his whole life and could finally breathe.

"It tickles a little. Does the ground always feel so…calm?"

"Yeah, that's your dysregulated nervous system. You'll get used to it."

"What's a dysregulated nervous system?"

"I am soooo glad you asked! So, you see, sometimes—"

"Should we save him?" I asked Anza as she led him back toward Emai, knowing Whisper would happily trail on for as long as he let her.

"No, no, he's very curious. If he starts getting annoyed, I'll stop her."

"Promise?

"Promise. Besides, he's distracting her from her doom and gloom."

"Yeah, you're not wrong there," I said.

"We need to head out," Saha said quietly, and I looked back over the army for a moment before flagging down Whisper with the wave of a hand. She returned to my side, Abry sticking to my mothers side as we convened in the courtyard prepared to head out.

We were ready. I gave the signal, knowing we were about to be divided; some were going back to Agrenon, others were staying here to stabilize Korrewen, and we were going to Biena.

I couldn't stop thinking of Heartlock as I summoned the stone Barbarza beneath Anza and I, helping Whisper up. Heartlock had slyly advised me to stay close to Saha. What would be happening now if she had been killed? Tamaj kept close, knowing that Abronoma seemed to find Emai and Whisper comforting, and though my father stayed at a cautious distance, he smiled a soft smile as Abronoma and Whisper talked.

We headed south west, starting at a steady pace to ensure everyone had enough power to keep going until well after nightfall.

Keeping the mountains to our left we picked our way through towns of ghost houses. Rot threatened to toss every wooden structure to the ground, and any homes made with stone stood crumbling on their foundations. Tiny eyes peeked through window slats before skittering back into the darkness, and the few people I caught glimpses of as they scrambled away from the battalion were malnourished and terrified. Most watched warily where they thought we couldn't see them.

"Why do they do that?" I asked Saha as we slipped past one of those small communities.

"They're afraid. Of the tax collector, and of change. Suffering is normal for them. Today is the last day they suffer, they just don't know it yet," she explained as we continued on.

"How do you know so much about Korrewen?"

"You should always do your best to know your greatest enemy," she started. "I'll send word back to Agrenon and we'll start sharing resources across the border. I don't want to make a big deal about it, but for now at least, Korrewen is Agregonian," she said firmly.

We kept going well until nightfall, with no one to stop us before the sun sank below the horizon. We settled carefully in one of those small ghost towns, building a fire pit in the center and setting up guards along the perimeter.

The smell of cooking food lured out a handful of children who had stayed hidden in the homes. Their approach was slow, but one was a little more bold than the others, darting forward to steal a bread roll.

"No need to steal what is freely given," Emai said, offering another roll. They moved together, as if prepared to scatter if one of them was snatched up. I ladled stew in a few extra bowls as the children quickly double fisted bread, shaking as they realized they would be fed and unharmed. They remained near the outskirts of the group, even after I passed them the bowls of stew, and Whisper wandered over to sit with them, undisguised. I kept an eye on them all as they ate until their bellies were full.

"You're safe, at least for tonight," Whisper said, and I smiled at the little ones as she stayed close to them. They pulled out small trinkets that reminded me of fidget toys, their eyes still untrusting, but slowly, they let their guards down.

Saha didn't join us, choosing instead to tuck into her tent with her bundles of papers and war strategies, preparing for the inevitable onslaught that would come in Biena.

"Emai?" Abronoma asked my mother.

"Hmm?" she said, and he leaned close to her, whispering something in her ear that only she could hear. "Oh, of course my dear, sit," she said, gesturing for him to sit in front of her before fetching a small bag she had with her. She was soon deftly brushing out his unkept hair, sectioning it off to prepare it for braids as Brian passed a bowl to Abry.

"Is that fufu?" he asked her, as if not believing what he saw.

"It is."

Tears welled in his eyes as he enthusiastically grabbed a piece, tossed it up, caught it, flattened it, and scooped up a piece of the thick stew, popping it all in his mouth. Almost rolling his eyes with delight at what must have been the most delicious fufu he'd had in his life as my mother tended his thick, tight curls.

Whisper tucked her radio close and settled in to eat near Abry and I tried to push away the tension in the back of my head. We were walking directly toward the demise of the world. *Both* of my worlds. Whisper had made it incredibly clear that there was no path that didn't lead to devastation; entire ecosystems collapsing, species going extinct, an onslaught of illness so fierce it would level entire villages…and that was just the beginning. There was probably so much more that she knew could happen that she had not yet shared with us. Saha, and Taryn, and Graz, and Narin, and Titanys would all get so sick, and who knew what would happen to Tamaj and her people, or Whisper and the Echalon now coming forth from the Shale Tree. Anza would get sick. My husband. My mate.

There wasn't an outcome where the worlds fell together and people didn't perish in mass. I couldn't lose them.

My mother's laughter pulled me out of the spiral and I turned to her, finding her and Brian engaged in a half-hearted thumb war with one hand. Even Abronoma held back a giggle.

"*Opposable authority,*" Tamaj laughed.

"Oh, I'm gonna get you!" Brian declared.

"Oh, no you're not!"

I couldn't help but smirk at Anza's hand sliding into mine.

"Welcome back from your doom-cation."

"Yeah, thanks."

"We're going to be alright. We have you, after all, and them," he said gently, nodding to my parents.

"They are pretty great, even if they're incredibly cheesy."

"Why don't we…sneak away for a bit, ease those fears? I think some of the empty cabins were set up for sleeping tonight?"

I thought about it for a moment before I nodded, quickly finishing the last of my meal before letting him help me up and lead me away from the group toward a cabin just far enough away to be considered private.

19

The minute the door of the cabin closed, he pinned me back against a wall. My tongue slipped into his mouth as his kiss crashed against me, hands feverishly working at my pants as I tore away his shirt. We needed this distraction. *I* needed this distraction.

"Anza..."

"Mira." He groaned into my mouth as I unfastened my brace, stepping out of my pants and leaving them together in a heap, but as he made a move to bury his hand between my legs, I pivoted, twisting him around to pin him against the wall instead.

"Ah-ah, we're not going to be greedy today," I said, carefully leaning on my good leg to ensure I didn't fall before reaching to untie the orange cloth attached to his pants showing his allegiance to Agrenon.

"Oh, I think you forgot who's in charge here," he growled, spinning us until he was back in control, then lifting me up with a hand as his pants slid to the floor.

"Hmm, have I?" I asked, feeling him harden against me as he nuzzled my throat. I arched my hips into him, his trembling need blazing down the bond. "Looks like I might be in charge tonight."

"We both know that's not true," he growled as I slid back to my feet. I pivoted him again, pinning him back against the wall.

"What about now?" I asked, seeing the surprise in his eyes.

"I'll let you think you're in control, for now, but what exactly do you plan on doing with all this…'power'?" he asked as I reached up to drape the cloth over his shoulders.

"Anything you'll let me," I said, kissing him deeply as his hands found my waist. I pulled him farther away from the wall with each kiss, drawing him over to the short table where I pushed him back until he sat on it. I clambered onto him, tucking myself against him as he groaned before lowering myself to him, feeling him tucked between my legs, on the verge of pressing him into me. He leaned back on his arms to give me the leverage I would need and I lowered myself, sliding him into me as he leaned his head back, groaning.

"Fuck…"

"There we go," I said before moving again, rising up on my knees before sliding back down. I moved slowly, feeling his pleasure compound with mine, rising like a tide.

"Why?" he asked, laying all the way back as I buried him fully within me, slowly, methodically, carefully taking everything I needed from him.

"Just a little payback for the tent," I whispered, rocking forward and back again.

"I'm at your mercy."

I leaned forward, pressing my body to his as I kissed up his jaw to his ear before whispering to him, "I am not known to be merciful."

I kissed him deeply, taking the cloth from his shoulders to blindfold him before sitting up slowly. His hands cupped my thighs as I rose and fell on him, his hips bucking into me with each movement.

"When you're done torturing me, I'm going to use this blindfold to remind you why I'm in charge." He shuddered through a moan.

"Oh, really?" I asked, rocking back against him again. I could feel him trembling with the effort to not take me, like a conqueror, like I wanted to be conquered. Oh, did I want to be conquered, but it was my turn.

"Mmm," he purred, holding my hips to him as he shifted quickly beneath me, quickening the pace.

"Oh, what did you call me?" I asked as he thrust again. "Greedy?"

"Damn it, Mira," he growled before shifting his weight, moving to get up. I tried to press my hands into his shoulders to stop him, but couldn't. I couldn't help but giggle as he held me firmly to him, still inside me as he turned on a heel, pinning me to the table beneath him. It groaned beneath our weight as he reached up to remove the blindfold and toss it toward the bed.

"Take me," I begged, knowing exactly who was in charge now. He thrusted into me firmly, both my whole body and the table shaking as he buried himself inside me, his hand moving up to tangle in my hair.

"I am going to show you"— he grunted as he thrust into me again, sending me back against the table and drawing a feral cry of pleasure from the depths of my soul—"what worship looks like."

I shuddered as he quickened the pace again. The table wasn't going to last much longer, but euphoria bubbled over his hand, still tangled in my hair as he slid out of me before picking me up.

"That wasn't so hard, was it?" he said before throwing me down onto the bed, snatching up the cloth I had used as a blindfold before using his body to pin me down at the hips.

"And what exactly are you going to do with that?" I asked before he gathered my wrists in his hands. I bucked against him as he tied my hands together, using one hand to hold them back against the bed.

"There, now you'll be a little easier to manage," he said

before running his free hand down my body. He let my wrists go, but only long enough to grab at my thighs, hoisting me against him before sliding back into me. I tried to reach for him, to grab at him, but his hand pinned my wrists right back down.

"I don't think so," he said as he thrust again.

"Oh, fuck," I groaned, arching into his next thrust as he wound me tighter, my body careening toward sweet release. I couldn't help the sounds he drove from me with each movement as he pressed his lips against my neck. I tilted my head, giving him better access as he growled into my ear.

"I've got you now. You're not going anywhere."

"Please, please," I begged as he buried himself within me before pushing me with his body toward the bedframe. It only took a moment for him to tie my wrists to the headboard, freeing up his hands. He started thrusting short firm thrusts as he guided my legs as far apart as he could. I could feel him deep within me as his hands slid back up my body, caressing every inch of me, cradling my hips, gliding up my stomach, caressing my breasts as his thrusts grew more fierce. His mouth found my neck and he bit me again, settling his hands just above my shoulders to minimize my rocking as he threw himself headlong into getting as deep as he could.

"I've got you," he said, dragging kisses along my jaw with every movement.

"Almost there!" I cried as I tightened down on him. He groaned, shoving himself farther into me than I thought possible, his hands holding me firmly in place as we came together.

"That's my good girl." It took a moment to catch my breath as he pulled himself from me. He untied me carefully and I scooted toward him, letting him pull me to him before I turned to kiss him. "Love you, Stone-Slinger."

"I love you too, Beetle-Brain. Sleep?" I asked him, and he nodded, pulling a blanket over us.

"Sleep."

"I'll try."

We settled in and I stared at the wall for what felt like an eternity, trying not to worry about what tomorrow may bring.

20

The light filtering through the windows is what woke us the next morning, but I buried my head under Anza's arm and sighed.

"Still haven't beaten that sun, huh?"

"One day," I said, my legs trembling as I tried to get them to move.

"Easy, Stone-Slinger," he said as I pushed myself upright, sitting up and holding me closer, gently kissing my neck.

"Saha's gonna be pissed if we don't get our shit together. It looks like it's late," I said.

"She's still a little distracted with Sil. We could probably buy ourselves some time."

"You're not wrong," I said as he held me, his hands working downward, massaging the tension out of my legs, moving carefully to make them ache a little less.

"Any better?" he asked as he finished massaging them.

I nodded. "Thank you, Beetle-Brain," I said, kissing him gently.

He pulled back to speak. "Any day, any time, Stone-Slinger," he said, kissing me again before helping me to my feet. We carefully got dressed and slipped out of the cabin, him leading me toward camp through the fog of early morning billowing all around us.

"Oh, there they are," I heard Brian say and couldn't help but blush. "You two might want to eat while you can. Sah is trying to leave. The fog is making her crabby."

I rolled my eyes as he passed us the plates. Anza shoved down the irritation that spiked when Brian approached and we ate quickly, trying to stay out of sight before we slipped over to the group. Whisper sat with Abronoma, whose hair was now tucked into neat braids of different widths. My mom was half asleep on Tamaj's back as Brian joined her, encouraging her to lean back against him.

"Rest, Lovey."

"Hair always takes so…" And she was asleep, leaning back against him.

He held her gently around the waist and for a moment I wondered if that was how Anza looked at me, only for his hand to find mine.

I pulled up the stone Barbarza as Abronoma clambered onto Tamaj with my parents, clinging to Brian and testing his wings. Whisper climbed up with Anza and I spotted Sil suspiciously close to Saha, but not so much so that there was danger. Graz was settled on a Barbarza only a yard or two away from her, Taryn keeping close to him.

We moved, the fog closing around us, swallowing us up as we continued more south than southwest now. I tried not to think about the fog as we passed toadstools, but it was so easy to get lost in the way it spun and swirled. It felt familiar and set me on edge.

"You alright?" Anza asked.

"Yeah, just nervous I guess. Have you ever been to Biena?"

"When I met you I had barely been beyond the Sky Fields. I only knew how to get to the castle because I'd seen it on maps," he admitted and I swatted at his knee.

"You could have gotten us killed!"

"But I didn't," he laughed, kissing the side of my head.

"Um, guys?" Whisper asked and I turned forward, only to be met with an impenetrable wall of fog. There were no silhouettes of Saha or Sil, my parents weren't there, it was only me, Anza, Whisper, and the fog. I kept moving the Barbarza forward, feeling even more unsettled.

"Guys?!"

"Mom, do you recognize this fog?" It wasn't until Whisper spoke that realization crashed into me. I clung to her, panic rising in me. I can't do this again. I can't.

"Stay behind me, I've got you."

"They're going to be searching for each other," I said, my voice strangled and strained as I settled the stone Barbarza to the floor, guiding Whisper with me behind him.

"And what do you do when you search for one another?" Whisper prompted.

"You call out their names." The words had barely left my lips before the onslaught of voices rattled me as I remembered when Anza had let my name slip. Whisper had to save me last time. The twisting creatures of that day still haunted my nightmares, but I can't let them swallow me now. I clung to Whisper, unsure what I should do, but as I looked down to her, I found it was only a branch in my hands. I dropped it, Anza turning to look as the panic rose in me. Where did she go?

"Sah!" My grandmother's shriek filled the air, wrapped in anguish and longing.

"Em? Emai?" Abronoma sounded like he had been crying, scared and alone.

"My Always!?" My dad's voice, did he know not to call for her by name?

"Always!" My mother cried somewhere in the mist, but her voice was laced with anguish. As if it had already gotten her.

"Mira, what a pleasant surprise." I knew that voice. It was the same one that haunted my nightmares from our journey to the castle. Anza shifted in front of me. The feeling of my skin burning returned like a ghost of a memory as the fae materialized beside us. Anza kept himself between us.

"There's a dagger set in a sheath against my back; its handle is along my spine, get it." His voice was like cold death in my head, but I stayed behind him, clinging to his shirt, tearing my eyes from the being as I carefully moved to grasp the hilt of that blade.

"Why not your sword?"

"And what do you expect to do?" the being asked Anza, reaching up toward his face.

"I do not consent to you touching me, or my mate," Anza said firmly.

"Remember those classes Graz took?"

"The ones he asked you to sit in on? I thought those were just leadership classes."

"Right, well, one was about the creatures of Agrenon. Normal swords won't work on them, they need to be made of—"

"Iron," I thought down the bond, feeling the slightly warmed metal tingle in my grasp.

"We have a clever one here, don't we?" the Fae said. "You're the one who gave me her name the first time."

"A rare weapon, from a well-prepared prince, so what happened last time never happens again," Anza said down the bond.

"Not a mistake I'm making again," I said.

"No, but you are still here," he said, stepping within an inch of Anza. I felt the bond numb before panic rose. I didn't hesitate slipping from behind Anza to plunge the iron knife into the Fae's neck.

"You bitch," it shrieked, a blast of fog rushing in, threatening to tear Anza and I apart, but his hands found my cheeks, the fear fading as he clung to me, the smoke around us starting to twist and writhe. I spotted the shapes—Arlo, dying bandits—and Anza buried my head into his shoulder.

"Don't look. I've got you."

"You're seeing things too?"

He didn't answer, but I reached up, guiding his head to my shoulder as well. We clung to one another. Whisper was out there somewhere. She was a smart girl. I knew she would be alright, especially if she found Abronoma.

It wasn't long though before a noise shrieked through the cold fog, a familiar noise. I lifted my head, the spilling figures gone, as if the fae had abandoned us here. There, in the depths of the fog, were two round lights, barreling toward us. The blare of a horn. The revving of an engine.

"What is that?" Anza asked.

"Car!" I pulled him to the side, the side mirror of the gray-green Subaru bashing into my arm before swerving and slamming into a tree. Agony ripped through me and I snatched my arm close to my chest.

"What the fuck is a car?" Anza asked, looking out at several other pairs of headlights.

"Something you don't want to get hit by," I said, clinging to my arm before slamming up a wall around us.

I could hear them swerving, smashing into trees. Horns blared and metal twisted. Were the others alright? Were these people alright? The veil between our worlds was getting thinner.

My arm screamed with pain as I held on to Anza.

It almost sounded like the cars weren't going to stop coming in, but after a moment, there was silence, just long enough for the Fae to reach up over my wall.

"Silly little Endering. I can't wait until we're loosed back upon Earth, we'll—"

A knife plunged through his throat as my brain registered a flash of green; Graz pulling him back off the brink of the wall. I dropped the wall as he dropped the disintegrating body to the ground. He was spattered in blood, but held out a hand to us, panting heavily.

"I found your Moonbeam. We've been pulling people from the fog. Come on."

I clung close to Anza, who reached for Graz, taking his hand and pulling him into a tight hug.

"You are a sight for sore eyes, my friend."

"Don't mention it, lets just get out of this creepy fucking place," Graz said, smirking.

We let him lead us through the twisting gnarled remnants of cars and trees. I peeked into them, finding that several were empty now, but many still contained bodies, limp and dead.

I kept close to him and Anza, thinking back to the day we had met him.

He'd been so shy, quiet, reserved, but fierce in the defense of what he believed. He hadn't had the gall to look me in the eye for months. He strode through this forest with confidence though, leading us toward safety. Leading us.

For the first time, I thought of what it might look like to see him as king, though I knew I would never live long enough to see him reign. Photomyra lived hundreds of years, and Saha wasn't exactly old by their standards.

Still, Anza and I kept close.

I cradled my arm as the fog started to lift, the silhouettes of people starting to slide into view.

"Oh no," I heard, seeing my dad heading toward us.

"Are you two alright? You look like you've seen a ghost. What happened to your arm?"

"Car," I managed to get out.

"A car?" he asked. "The leaks are getting worse." It wasn't a question, but I nodded.

"Is…The Reaper around?" Anza asked, still unsure about using names. My father nodded.

"Over here," he said as Graz started to walk away. "Hey, Graz?"

"Yeah?"

"Thank you."

"A prince has gotta do what a prince has gotta do," he said, shrugging as he walked over to a seat Taryn was sitting beside.

My father led us quickly toward my mother, who was sitting with Saha and Tamaj.

"Are you guys alright?" I asked.

"What the hell happened to your arm?" my mom said, leaping to her feet and rushing to me.

"Car."

"What's a car?" Saha asked.

"A motorized vehicle. They serve as a transportation device for people and things, but they're large, metal, and incredibly quick. It clipped my arm."

"Which is broken. Wonderful," my mom said, settling a hand on my arm. The familiar tingle rushed through me, and I had the passing thought of how far we had come from me being terrified of her power.

"I really don't know what I'd do without you, Mom," I said as I flexed my now-healed arm.

"Probably keel over," she said, hugging me and ruffling my hair.

"Dad! Mom!" I tore my eyes from my mother to see Whisper leading Abronoma toward the group. Anza and I moved together, rushing to her, and I pulled Abronoma in too as we hugged them tightly.

"I thought we lost you two," I said.

"No chance with this one," Anza said, jerking his head at Whisper.

"She is pretty amazing," Abronoma said quietly.

As I looked over the group, I took note that the sea of an army wasn't far beyond them and allowed myself to feel some relief that they were all here. Even Sil sat in the group, eyes distant, as if thinking on something.

"I'm gonna go talk to her," I said.

"Mira, is that a good idea?" Anza said gently.

"Probably not, but you heard her, that scream. I know she's made some big and stupid mistakes, but I have to make sure she's alright," I said as he nodded.

I planted a kiss on the top of Whisper's head and moved to stand in front of my grandmother.

"Hey." She flinched as I spoke, looking up at me.

"Oh, hey."

"Can I sit?" I asked, gesturing toward the spot next to her. She nodded and I lowered myself to her side. "Are you okay?"

"No."

"Wanna talk about it?"

"Why would you want to talk about it?" she asked, her voice as hollow and empty as the fog had been.

"Because even though you've fucked up, like, a lot, I still give a shit about you."

"Terrible choice, really." We both laughed, looking out at the others in a moment of comfortable silence.

"You had a reason right?"

"For?"

"Not telling me about them. Not teaching me magic."

"Yes."

"It's not cause you hate them?"

"I don't hate them," she said.

"They seem to think otherwise," I said as she sighed.

"I worry about them. Brian would follow Emai off the edge of the world, and Emai is reckless enough to jump, just for the experience." I wanted to argue, but I remembered how she had taunted the infected Hazzal the first time we met. Sil was right. Some moments they were careful and measured, and others they were the opposite; loose cannons shot into the night, unsure if there was even a target to aim for. They had the potential for recklessness, but they seemed to know when it wasn't a good idea.

"You're afraid of losing them," I said, realizing that she might be so harsh because she actually gave a fuck.

"Them, and you."

"You're not gonna lose me."

She gave me a tight-lipped smile. "Damn straight I'm not."

"And what about Saha?"

Her face grew harder.

"What about her?"

"Nothing."

Clearly, it was a *pick your battles* kind of moment, and I knew a battle I couldn't win when I saw one.

21

I could feel the difference in the ground as the earth shifted from rocky and rugged to a more sandy texture as we stepped over the border with Biena. Emai slowly breathed out as we left Korrewen and the pains of her past behind.

"See? We're alright," my dad said, rubbing her shoulders.

"Yeah…" she said, nodding as I noticed Korrewen's thicker, spruce-like forests had gradually given way to a sprawling savannah with thin brown grasses and a spattering of scraggly trees.

It wasn't long before a small group of soldiers briskly rode up alongside us.

"Your Majesty," a Photomyran man greeted.

He looked different than Saha, physically larger, his floral bloom resting low on the back of his head, small, soft spines sticking out along his arms and legs, peeking out between the spaces in his armor. He looked like a cactus.

As the Barbarza he was on stepped forward, I saw Tamaj perk up. He looked familiar, deep russet fur, and those eyes…I remembered those eyes. For a moment I was haunted by the ghosts of my first night in Agrenon. Haunted by a familiar form rushing to me. Demanding that I get on his back as Hazzal cackled in the brush.

"Baden?"

"Mom!" he said happily as they made their way to each other. Both the Photomyra and my parents slid from their backs as they got to each other, giving them space.

Arlo. He looked like Arlo. I could see it in his hair and how he bounced, in the perk of his ears and the way his tail swished. Had he known when he left to head to Earth she had been with child? Had he ever gotten to meet them?

"What in the sake of the stars are you doing all the way out here?" Tamaj asked

"I heard there was a commotion at the border, people scared, something happening with the stars. I came to help where I could and this group needed help to find you fumbling tremble vines," he said, tail wagging happily before his eyes met Saha's. *"Oh, pardon me, Your Majesty, I've forgotten my manners."* He dipped into a bow, which Saha waved away with a single hand.

"It's good to see you, Baden."

"It's good to see you too," he said happily before the Photomyran man whispered something in Baden's ear. *"I can show them the way, you go."*

"Go?" Saha asked

"Korrewen's forces have laid siege to the castle and half their army moves toward Legalia. Though our kingdoms have never been friends, this problem involves all of us."

"You're going to warn them?"

"Yes," he said as another of the party helped him up onto another Barbarza's back. Biena and Legalia had been at war for decades, with scrappily drawn truces lasting just long enough to raise a new generation of soldiers. They were always at each other's throats for water, food, land and so much more, but not for this. "You'll have to go with Baden as a guide to the castle."

"I'm sure he's more than capable enough," Saha said as

Baden danced into place beside Tamaj, light on his feet, alive with energy as the man nodded his farewell, heading off toward Legalia with the rest of his group.

"Where is your sister?" Tamaj asked as we started toward Biena's castle.

"Helping refugees on one of the border towns. We're supposed to meet up back at the castle, though honestly, she's probably halfway there by now. Back to the castle, I mean."

"She takes after her mother," Saha said, smirking.

"Even I wasn't as fast as her at her age," Tamaj retorted and Baden rolled his eyes before glimpsing me.

"Is that a stone Barbarza?"

"Yeah, my power is pretty much just rocks," I said, shrugging.

"Looks…uncomfortable."

"It gets a little sore, but I can't imagine it's any worse than any other."

Baden fell back to our side, Saha settling on my other side.

"You could…" He nodded to his back and I felt my heart drop.

"Come on, Mira, he doesn't bite," Tamaj said, shaking her head and snorting at my ridiculousness.

"Yeah, if you're cool with it," I said as Whisper reached for him. I helped her on his back as we slowed, sending my stone Barbarza into the ground before Anza and I climbed on Baden's back. There was so much power in every movement he made, his steps were more brisk, swifter than Tamaj's even. I had to remind myself that she was my mother's age and Baden was likely around my age. I had never truly worked with a Barbarza in their prime.

"See? Much better." He laughed happily as he led us forward, and even that reminded me of Arlo.

"Yeah, yeah," I said, reaching forward to ruffle a patch of his mane, trying not to think back to the last time I was seated on his father's back. I didn't expect the rush of emotions to wash over me, but I clung tightly to the saddle anyway, feeling Anza steady me as I rode them out.

"He's not him. It's alright, I'm right here."

"I know," I said down the bond, trying to slow my breathing to match his.

It only took a moment, just long enough for Saha and my parents to fall in on each side of us, before I could settle my breathing and focus on the remnants of the savannah and the blazing sand dunes in the distance. The cold of Korrewen seemed a distant memory as Baden led us forward toward the castle, the heat starting to blaze from above.

Abronoma lifted his wings, spanning them outward to both soak up the sun and create shade for himself and my parents. Water was quickly passed from person to person as we left the shelter of the trees. I kept an eye on Saha, seeing her visibly wilt before turning to look for Graz and Taryn who passed water between the two. I noticed quickly that most of the other Photomyran were having a hard time, but they kept pressing forward, drinking deeply as we moved. We had to make sure we stopped to fill our water soon. I couldn't help but think of the cacti-like Photomyran and how he had appeared far better suited to withstand the heat.

I felt Baden turn to look behind us, noticing the struggling members of our troops before picking up the pace.

"There's a stopping point not too far ahead. We can rest and get water there and keep moving at night," he said.

"Awesome, thank you," I said, reaching forward to run my hands through his mane. It wasn't long until a structure rose from the dunes, massive and made of sand-colored stone. The only reason I could pick it out so easily was the sound it made as we approached, steady and resonant, like salvation in an otherwise endless sea.

"There!" I said, pointing to where the building's shadow fell.

Baden led us to the small oasis built there. Dozens of stations to fill water canteens were settled behind the building and

Photomyran piled off Barbarza to the heavy stone bowls settled beneath each spout. Baden, Anza, Whisper, and I kept close to Saha as we escorted her to a nearby basin. My parents helped Abronoma before Mom came to check in with me. We didn't need words. A single glance, a soft hand of reassurance; we were alright, we were safe.

"I hope you don't think we're replacing you with him," she said quietly, glancing back to where Dad was filling a canteen with Abronoma.

"What? No, he needs someone and he trusts you." I saw the relief flood her stormy eyes and pulled her into a hug. It wasn't until she pulled back that I saw her relief storm over in disgust. I pivoted, seeing Sil pass Saha without a glance, following Graz and Taryn.

"Easy, we're all tired."

"Of her bullshit," Emai grumbled before giving me a quick kiss to the head.

"Go," I said, nodding my head toward Abronoma and Brian. She gave me a tight-lipped smile and left my side as I moved to fill my canteen beside Saha.

"Sil's keeping close to your heir," I said, feeling the prickling irritation down the bond. Saha blinked her understanding. We still didn't know how dedicated Sil was to Agrenon. She could easily be targeting Graz.

"Flag down your father?" Saha asked, knowing she wanted to keep Brian close to Graz. They trusted each other, and Brian could see through Sil's bullshit better than most, even just to mediate. I felt my irritation pricking up though. I didn't want to rely on Brian to wrangle Sil. I couldn't trust him. Putting Emai in charge of her, though, was asking for a fight. I could tell just by the way they glared at each other.

I gave the smallest nod, stepping aside before feeling Anza's hands on my hips, gentle and assuring, trying to pull me back from my spiraling thoughts. Giving Sil a babysitter was the right choice. Even if it was Brian.

"Why so prickly?" I asked him down the bond.

"You're one to talk."

"Oh, hush," I retorted, and I could hear his laughter down the bond.

"I'm just tired, and they're not making this easier. The hatred between Em and Sil and the tension between Sil and Saha just…it's just a little much," he said, trying to keep his temper from flaring. How long could he last before he gave them a piece of his mind? How long could *I* last before I gave them a piece of mine?

"Just try not to kick the nazzir hole?" I asked, trying not to let the goosebumps roll over me as I remembered the dark hole the giant worm had yanked me into what felt like a lifetime ago. We hadn't wanted to stir the beasts beneath the floating islands any more than we wanted to stir up trouble with people with code names like The Reaper, Wildfire, and Ghost Queen. *We* couldn't add to the powderkeg of emotions any more than we already had. Anymore than I already had.

"You too."

"I'm not starting anything at all, promise me you won't either?"

"I'll try," he said, and I gave him a quick kiss before I moved toward my parents, Abronoma helping to fill another canteen.

"Hey, Captain Violin?"

"Alas, a proper code name! Whatcha need kiddo?"

"Sah needs you. I think she's worried about Sil being too close to Graz and Taryn."

"You mean Graz."

"Yeah. Do you think she knows they're…" I let the sentence hang.

"Oh, no, and she's so distracted I don't think she'll notice anything any time soon," he said quietly. "But I'll head over to them now. Honestly, it's probably a good idea to have someone between her and Sah, anyway."

"And me," Emai added.

"I didn't say—"

"Didn't have to, Lovey," she said, giving him a sly smile. "I still have to get her back for letting me be a ghost to our daughter."

"That might have to wait until after we save the worlds."

"Fine. We should get some rest though."

"My shoulders hurt," Abronoma said quietly.

"Probably from holding up your wings so long, huh Abry?" Emai asked.

"Yeah, probably."

"Do you think your wings would work, like, in the air?" I asked and he shrugged.

"Whisper and I talked about it. Maybe? My bones would have to be pretty light though, and even if I could fly, I need to get used to flapping them first."

"Well, holding them out like that will probably help your stamina and strength, but don't overdo it, alright?" I said gently.

He nodded, turning his eyes to the blazing sky as I walked back to Saha's side.

"Is Abry alright?" Whisper asked before taking a deep drink from her canteen.

"Oh, you're calling him Abry too now?"

"He's a friend, and he likes Abry, so fight me," she said.

"I'd lose," I said, though we both knew that probably wasn't the case.

"Yeah you would," she said as I looked out over the group.

Tamaj lay near Baden in the shade, everyone drinking deeply and filling their canteens. Whisper's hand found mine, Anza looping a finger into my belt loop.

"You don't know how far Biena is, do you?" I asked him.

"No, no idea," he said as Saha stepped closer to my side.

"We'll wait here until nightfall and head out then. We should, if we keep a swift pace, reach Biena by morning."

"Thats not too bad."

"I just hope they can hold out."

"What do we know about Biena's Endering?"

"They have four—"

"Four?" *Four* Endering.

"Yes. It's an exceptional amount. They rival us in numbers, but thankfully, they're not our enemies this time."

"Right," Anza said.

"You've met Heartlock."

"He was…off-putting," Anza said and I nodded.

"That's Heartlock for you. There's also Perception, and two more that they did not introduce. When asked why, it was said that their powers were at a 'low level'."

"What the hell does that mean?" I said, immediately feeling anger rise up. No person or power should be thought of in such a way.

"It means they won't send them onto a battlefield, in the hopes of being able to maintain an Endering population…"

They were keeping them for breeding.

"That makes me sick," I growled, my stomach twisting as I looked out over the sand dunes so I wasn't glaring at her.

Saha sighed. "If I had the resources, I'd wage wars for every Endering."

I could hear Sil snort from here but my father said something hushed, calming her temper.

"But you don't," I said, and she nodded, wringing her hands.

"We should rest while we can. The portal is in the heart of Biena's castle. We'll need to fight through Olaf's siege to get to it."

"Right," I said, leading Anza and Whisper closer to the others.

Baden nodded against his flank as he and Tamaj settled in a way that let us lean against them. Abry was tucked between my parents, facing my father's back, his wings spread out over them, draping like a blanket. My mother lay on her side facing him, humming to settle him to sleep.

As I settled beside Baden, Whisper tucking against me, I couldn't help but think of how they would have been amazing parents to me, had Olaf not gotten involved. He had taken so much. My parents. My childhood. He had even stolen my children. And now he was trying to take the whole damn world. This beautiful, chaotic, wonderful, wild, dangerous, gorgeous world.

Over my dead body.

22

We kept a steady pace through the night. The cold sent shivers down my spine as Whisper and Abry talked about the stars. Looking up at them, it was clear something was wrong, constellations that were familiar for the wrong reasons shone back at me; The Little Dipper, Orion's Belt. They flickered in and out of sight as I tried not to think about the atrocities that had likely already started, focusing instead on watching Sil. She had struck up a conversation with Graz and Taryn, and though I couldn't hear it, the three of them seemed to ease into it. I kept my eyes on them until dawn came, the silhouette of a castle in the distance revealed in the weak morning light.

Along with the massive army settled around its outskirts.

"Alright, here's the plan," Saha started as she drew us all to a stop. "They don't seem to have gotten to the portal room yet, but that can change at any point. We're going to attack swiftly at the area in front of the front gate and push our way in. From there, I want Sil, Brian, and Mira to defend the portal room while Emai and I find Olaf and his cohorts."

"I'm gonna rip him apart for what he's doing," my mother snarled.

Sil shifted slightly, but Brian stayed between them.

"Abronoma and Whisper should stay near Brian and Mira; Anza, you work best at Mira's side; Tamaj, Baden, I need your size to help us push through the front."

"Got it," Tamaj said.

"This is going to be awesome," Baden said, dancing on his feet. I stole a look at his pelt again. Where Tamaj's was worn with age and marked with long-faded signs of battle, his wasn't. He had never seen battle before.

"No, it isn't," Sil said firmly. "Fights like this are anything but." Slowly, everyone, even my mother, nodded. Even Abronoma had a better chance than Baden. We would need to watch out for him.

"Don't you think it would be a better idea to have Mira build a bridge over the Korrewen forces? If we worked quickly enough we could—"

"That's a wonderful idea, Whisper, but Mira has always had a hard time holding sand long term. It takes much more effort and it is just not feasible for her to hold it that long."

"But—"

"No, we have a plan," Sah said gently. "I know you believe in your mom, I do too, she's done amazing things, but all power has limits."

"Let it go," I said, resting my hand on Whisper's shoulder, and she nodded but crossed her arms.

Carefully, we fell in line as Saha inched us closer to the siege. We managed to get about a hundred yards away before someone shouted from atop a dune. With the draw of her sword, Saha led us forward, shouting a single word.

"Charge!"

Baden surged forward, Tamaj at his side, and I could feel Anza behind me, sword drawn, ready, breathing deep, that determination within him undermining the kernel of fear settled deep in the bond. I took a breath, holding Whisper to me as I brandished my axe, watching the edge of the siege rush toward us with every one of Baden's strides.

He crashed into a spear tip, the top shattering as it slid into his shoulder. I reached out, hooking the jagged end in my hand and throwing it back as he balked, Anza cutting down a Korrewen soldier as I reached to pull the piece from Baden's chest.

I didn't need to be able to feel his emotions. The experience was sobering enough.

I quickly wove a healing sigil against the wound as he pressed forward, not at all hesitating as he drove his teeth into the throat of an enemy soldier. I turned just in time to see a spear tip at my flank, Whisper grabbing it to pull the wielder in close, slashing at his throat as he fell away. Blood hit the ground.

I couldn't see the others, but before I knew it, Baden yelped and we were pitched to the sand. We couldn't be on the ground, there were enemies everywhere.

We were on our feet in a flash, Anza, Whisper, and Baden not far from each other. Anza fought away the person responsible for the thick gash now gleaming with fresh blood on Baden's leg. Whisper had somehow managed to remount him and clung to his back, a sea of people between us.

"Anza!"

"I'm alright!" he said as they got onto Baden's back. I felt a hand on my shoulder and turned to see my mother's stormy eyes.

"Mira?!" Anza said.

"Keep those two safe, I've got her. Go!" my mom shouted at him, pulling me up onto her mount. I clung to her as tightly as I could as we barreled forward until he was lost in the swell of the battle. The last time I lost sight of him, he nearly died.

"What if he…" I asked quietly as I clung to her.

"He won't."

"How do you know?"

"I'll explain later. We'll see him inside," she said as we

barreled forward. People actively dodged out of her way and I caught snippets of fear leaving people as we passed.

"The Reaper."

"Run."

"Doomed."

"Can we tr—"

"This better work," I said, clinging tightly to her as we raced to the steps. I looked back, catching a glimpse of Anza and Whisper on Baden's back, not far behind us now, as my mother cut through the crowd.

Saha's plan was simple: fight forward, get to the portal, defend it, kill the icy murderous traitor.

Chaos erupted all around us as Agrenon's army battled fiercely, pulling the attention of the majority of soldiers as we reached the doors—doors which were already open. We didn't stop, rushing inside and into the tightly packed fighting. Swords would be useless in here.

"Thank you Zizah, go!" Emai said to the Barbarza as we slid off, and Zizah bolted back out into the fray, her plate armor keeping her safe as my mother and I lunged at the nearest pair of enemy soldiers, already pinning down a smaller Agregonian soldier. I pulled mine back by the shoulder, the confusion still in her eyes as I buried my axe into her neck while my mother drew a dagger and quickly plunged it into an eye socket. Both bodies dropped, almost simultaneously, but the crowd was so thick we were being backed against a door. We needed space.

I tried the handle and it fell open just as I caught sight of a man moving toward us, murderous intent clear in the set of his jaw and the hatred blazing in his eyes. We backed into the room but before I knew it, an arm went around my throat. Someone was holding me back against them with one arm, a syringe in the other. I grabbed their spare hand before they could jab me, but Emai, with a person behind her and another slipping into the room, wasn't so lucky.

"No!" I managed to strangle out, trying to pull up my power, trying to stop them, as the syringe slid in and they hit the plunger. My mother backhanded one so hard it sent him sprawling before her body started to go limp.

"There you go, there you go."

I could feel the one I was fighting with press the needle close to me and I focused all my energy on trying to avoid it, my vision starting to blur as the man lay my mother down, leaning over her, dangerously close.

"Look at you. The Reaper. Not so scary anymore."

"Thirty seconds," my mom coughed out, her eyes dilated, body limp. I wasn't sure who she was speaking to.

"Oh, yeah?" Silence. "How about we wait that thirty seconds, just for you?" I fought against that syringe hand, feeling him have to soften his hold on my neck to try to get the syringe in. I could breathe a little better as the seconds ticked by. Nothing. "See? You're useless. You don't even have your powers." He laughed and the sound of it curdled my stomach.

"I don't *need* them." In an instant, she was up, eyes still dilated, but her target was clear. He had expected her to be limp, useless. As had I. I hadn't been able to move when I had last been jabbed, but she slid her dagger into the spot beneath his breastbone at an upward angle, sneering at him as he dropped.

I took the opportunity to drop my legs out from under me as the terror set into the man trying to harm me, sliding out of his loosened grip, and pivoted. Still holding his syringe hand, I pushed it forward, into his own neck, and hit the plunger. He dropped. I turned back around to find my mother pinning the second man against a wall with her blade in his throat. Her body was trembling, but he gasped his last gasp, blood spilling down her arm as she tore his throat out.

"Mom?" She pivoted, blade up, until her eyes met me.

"Mira, I need, I need…" She held her arm out and I went to her, letting her lean on me.

"Easy, easy."

"They, they…" She trailed off, her other hand reaching for the puncture wound where they had jabbed her with her dagger still in hand. I snatched it from her as her hand moved so she didn't accidentally stab herself.

"How are you still on your feet?"

"T-toler-tolerance." She had done this before, and for a split second I couldn't help but remember her reaction to realizing I had been jabbed when we first met.

"Can you fight?"

She nodded, shifting her weight to stand on her own, and I gave her her dagger back.

"I need Brian."

"I'll get you to him, just stay close, alright?"

"Alright," she said, still trembling, but she gripped her dagger tighter before giving me a nod to let me know she was ready.

We slipped back out into the fray and I quietly prayed to who or whatever would listen that she would make it through. As we stepped out of the small room though, a series of explosions sounded throughout the space, making the roof groan and the ground tremble.

"What was that?" Emai asked as I got a feeling of triumph and pride down the bond.

"Whisper," I said as we started toward the stairs. At least those mines were coming in handy.

The fighting had thinned, bodies nearly covering the floor as we ascended a staircase. I had no idea where the portal room was, and my mom was too busy looking for potential enemies, ready to pounce. We needed help. But the sight at the top of the stairs made it clear where all the enemies had gone. Graz stood, sword drawn, dripping in blood, pivoting to lash down two people as another tried to approach. Raw fury burned in his eyes as he slaughtered the third; quick, agile, fast on his feet.

The small platform was littered with bodies, and at his feet, choking on her own blood, an arrow in her neck, hand still tightly wrapped around her sword, lay a far-too-familiar Photo-myran woman. The petals of her floral bloom blended in with the hot, green blood all around her as her eyes looked to us, begging us to help, more blood bubbling out of her mouth.

"Taryn!"

23

"Graz! Graz!" I threw the stone of the floor up through the few remaining enemies, dropping their bodies as he turned to me, sword lifted. I grabbed his wrist, meeting his eyes, and the moment hung as he, trembling, snapped out of his rampage.

"Taryn's—"

"I know."

"She's—"

"I know, we need somewhere safe to take her."

"The door to the portal room," he said, looking back to the door behind us.

"Has it been breached?"

"No," he said as we moved together. He lowered his sword before sheathing it and we lifted Taryn. I grabbed her knees and he slid his hands under her arms as Emai opened the door and we rushed in.

"Can't you heal her?" Graz asked, his voice trembling with anger.

"No."

"What use are you if you can't do the one thing we need you for?" he snapped, fire in his eyes.

"Graz. She can't right now," I said more firmly, and he glared at me as we lay Taryn down.

The room was round, with depictions of different Endering towering up in painted slivers toward the cresting top. A single step rose to a round platform in the middle where a familiar stone arch stood, humming with power. It was still standing.

I looked down at Taryn, her blood leaving pale green spatters across the floor as she started to shake, colder than usual to the touch.

"We have to do something. We have to, please, please," Graz sobbed, the firmness in his eyes dying, faltering with desperation, and I could hear people coming in as I pressed my hand to the arrow wound at Taryn's throat.

"What happened?" I didn't look up at Saha's voice as Graz clung to Taryn, holding her hand tightly with one hand, the other tangled in his hair as he rocked, desperately clinging to hope. I pulled the arrow out, swiftly drawing a healing sigil in her spilling wound. Was it enough? Had she lost too much blood? "Her leg…"

I looked to where Saha gestured as she settled beside Graz, rubbing his back as she set down a medical kit. I reached to the gash ripping up her leg that I hadn't seen and quickly healed that over too. Hopefully, just enough to keep her alive.

"She almost died," Graz sobbed, Taryn's eyes distant as she swallowed. I wasn't sure she could hear us anymore.

"It's alright," Saha said gently. "Mira has her."

"She might still die," he choked out as Saha rubbed his back, reaching up to wipe his tears away.

"I know, I know, I'm so sorry," Saha said as I tried to focus on Taryn, taking the medical kit and quickly cleaning and bandaging the shallowly healed wounds.

"I tried to keep them away from her."

"You did such a good job."

"It wasn't enough."

"She knows you did all you could," Saha said, looking from

me to Emai. I looked up at my mother, her face frozen in anguish as she watched, helpless, her power torn from her.

"She got jabbed," I said quietly to Saha, who pursed her lips, carefully trying to calm Graz as he became incoherent in his anguish.

It was only a moment before I remembered other people were there and looked up to see my dad coming in. He immediately rushed toward my mom, pulling her focus away as they crumbled into each other. Anza was hot on his tail, ushering Whisper and Abronoma in, unscathed.

"Thank the stars," he said, spotting me, but he grew pale when his eyes found Taryn.

"She's alive," I said, and he nodded.

"We need Emai to be able to get Taryn back on her feet," Saha said quietly. "The inside of the castle is clear. The king and one of his Endering are on their way here so we can work together to stabilize the outside of the castle walls and break apart the siege," Saha said to me, gently. "We stay here until Emai is alright. She's too valuable for us to try to find Olaf or his cohorts without her." She was right, of course.

"Where's Sil?"

"Here." I looked toward the door as she slipped in. A handful of Agrenon's Queen's Guard stood watch outside the door. My grandmother was spattered in blood and soot, but I couldn't see any wounds on her. "I have Grio being the biggest problem he can be outside. He's pulling a good portion of the attention."

"Good. Those soldiers likely haven't ever seen a dragon before," Brian said quietly, still cradling my mother as she shook against him.

"We wouldn't have been able to clear out most of that lower area if it weren't for these two pulling that distraction," Anza said, nodding to Whisper and Abry as he settled beside me, checking Taryn over for more wounds.

"Yeah?" I asked, and the two nodded.

"We're an unstoppable force," Abry said, smirking. I noted

the boost in his confidence and how Whisper nodded enthusias-tically.

"Good job. Now, we hold out," I said, looking to Saha as Graz buried his head in her shoulder. It was the first time I had ever seen him go to her like that. Usually, it was my father he went to when he needed someone. Tears streaked down her face as she held him, breathing steadily as she tried to contain her emotion for his sake. Taryn is one of her Queen's Guard; a rookie, but a ferocious defender of hers. She had grown to enjoy her company, and now she lay on the brink of death before them.

I turned my attention back to Taryn again.

"Nothing you missed," Anza said down the bond and I nodded, grabbing a cloth and wetting it with my canteen before carefully wiping the blood away.

Slowly, a settled tension came over the room as we all found spots to sit on the edge of the portal's dais, waiting for Biena's king. I knew it would take time before they were confident enough to move him, so I settled my bag under Taryn's head, her breathing short and pained as my dad whispered things in Twi to my mother, helping her stay calm, encouraging her to drink. How long did it take for a body to metabolize one dose?

It felt like an eternity before anything happened, but the fluttering of noise rang out as a shifting cloud slid through the doors, crafted of dozens of dark-brown creatures smaller than a baseball. It took me a moment to realize what they were.

"Bats?" I asked, and they rebounded, leaving the way they had come.

It was only a few more moments before a Queen's Guard called in, "King Meyal and one of his Endering are here."

Saha rose from her place next to Graz, and Anza reached for him, redirecting him toward putting his energy into Taryn as Saha rubbed his back once more and moved to greet the king.

"You really are a sight for sore eyes Sahaveya," he said as he stepped in.

His hair was grayer than even Sil's and his beard fell past his waist. Beady eyes, piercing and almost the same shade of gray as his beard, quickly scanned the room, analyzing the current situation and taking stock of any potential threats. His hands remained hidden in the ends of his smoke-singed gray shirt and his belt was far too tight around his middle.

The Endering that stood at his side was a much smaller man, thin, with light brown skin almost glowing with warm undertones. His pitch-black hair was tousled by the dark wrap of cloth he had over his eyes, obscuring them and the curving gray brown ears that poked up. He kept his hands neatly folded in front of him, his shoulders slumped inward, face turned downward as if looking at the floor. He wore well-crafted light-brown fabrics woven with yellow thread and stayed just behind King Meyal.

"It's nice to see you too," she said, stepping forward as he offered an embrace. A moment hung as they stepped apart where he looked over the room again, *really* looking at my parents, me, Sil.

"Your Endering have forgotten their manners," he said as his own gave a quick bow. Sil tensed, tearing her eyes from him as my father glared in his direction, still cradling my mother. I shifted my feet, preparing to stand before Saha spoke.

"We could just leave."

The king flinched, looking her over, trying to judge if she was serious. That soft face of kindness was gone, the mask, cool and calculated, had been drawn. Even Sil stepped a little closer to Brian and Emai, watching Saha with what looked like confusion and shock.

"No, no, I guess, considering what they've been through, it's forgiveable." He was not in a position to deny help on such silly grounds.

"That's what I thought," Saha said firmly before looking to his Endering. "It's a pleasure to meet you. Your name?"

"Bats," he said, quickly and quietly. The way he said it, his voice, so quiet, made me think that this was a code name, like

The Mountain or Plague. This was one of the Endering Saha didn't know about. He had not been at the feast.

"Let me guess, that shroud of creatures was you?" she asked.

He managed a nod.

"Paired with the light sensitivity as a downside, it's impossible to use out here in the desert though, only really useful at night," King Meyal grumbled. I saw Saha purse her lips, her petals twitching. Agitation.

"I'm sure he's plenty helpful," Saha said gently before shifting gears. "Our biggest problem right now is that we don't know where the leader of this attack is. Is it possible to use your power inside?" Saha asked Bats.

"Of course you can," King Meyal barked, and I saw her petals curl before she turned to face the king completely.

"I assure you, I was not asking you," she hissed.

"He's *my* Endering," the king growled as Sil stepped forward to rest a hand on Saha's shoulder. Upon the touch, I saw her temper cool.

"Of course, I forget myself," she said, stepping back. Silence hung heavy in the room for a few moments before the king turned to Bats.

"Recon inside, tell me if there is anyone hiding within the castle walls," he commanded, and Bats nodded before erupting into a mass of bats and sliding out the still-open doorway, scattering in different directions.

"That is so cool," Anza said quietly, and for a moment, I could feel a twinge of jealousy down the bond before he quickly smothered it.

"Once we find Korrewen's Endering, we can dispatch them and end this. If permitted to do so, of course?" Saha said, looking the king over. Meyal nodded.

"From there, we'll need support in taking back Biena's outer wall and, if we're successful, a support ring outside the city until tomorrow to ensure there isn't an attack in the night," Meyal said.

"That can be arranged," Saha said simply, and he nodded.

I looked over to find Brian leading Emai over to Taryn. Graz was still a mess, trembling as he tried to stay quiet. As my mother tried to heal Taryn, I saw relief wash over him as Taryn's wounds stitched fully together and she tried to sit up.

He hugged her tightly and she hugged him back.

"I'm alright, I'm alright," Taryn said as my father comforted my mother.

"See? You made it. She's alright. You're alright." My mom nodded, sighing her relief into him as the fluttering of wings and the soft squeaks of bats rose.

Bats had returned.

His form materialized quickly as the bats settled close to Meyal, his large ears twitching.

"Speak for all to hear, boy."

I had to suppress a growl. Even Anza's anger pricked down the bond. I had to gently remind myself who the real enemy was.

"A majority of the fighting within the castle walls is concluding as I speak. There are a handful of people within the castle who seem to be hiding from the fighting, likely injured, but a group is making their way to the roof. They're setting up directly above us."

I felt my heart tense.

"Whisper, do you think you need to be at the portal to destroy it?" I asked quickly.

"Not if they make the correct adjustments in the sigils. You have to be within proximity of it, but…"

I looked toward the doorway, feeling eyes on me, my heart aching as I spotted him there. His tousled, dark hair in his face, those ice-blue eyes looking in at me, his hand up, level, ready. How had he gotten so close?

Before I could open my mouth to warn anyone, a sheet of ice spilled into the room. My parents covered each other, reaching for Whisper and Abry as they did. Abry covered Whisper with his wings, both ducking to shy from the blast, and I pulled up a stone slab to cover Anza and myself as Graz shielded Taryn.

Saha moved to shield Sil.

And Sil's scream rang out as the spike of ice tore through Saha's middle.

"I'm sorry," Sil whispered as she slowly inched Saha to the ground as the icicle vanished into the wound, slipping back to a liquid state.

"Not your fault," Saha said through spilling blood and rushed breaths, trying to cradle Sil's face as she quickly faded away.

"I'm gonna fucking kill him," my mother snarled.

"No, go to her," I said firmly, and she growled but nodded. She knew I was right. Saha needed her more.

"I'm so sorry," Sil said again, holding her up, cradling her head as my mother went to Saha's side. "Tell me you can fix this. Tell me you can fix this, Em."

"I'm gonna try, but I'm weak from the jab and…this is a lot."

It was hard not to look at the torn open hole in Saha's stomach. I had thought Taryn was bad, but I couldn't even see Saha's spine. He had torn clear through.

"Dad, stay with them, protect them. Anza, you and I—"

"I'm with you," Anza said. I didn't know where King Meyal or Bats had gone, but they were no longer present. What a coward.

I slipped out of the room and looked for any sign of where Olaf had gone, seeing him steal his way up a set of stairs to the left. I could hear the ruffle of wings and heavier footsteps behind me.

"Don't you two dare!" I said.

"And who's gonna stop us? Not you if you want to catch him," Whisper challenged.

She was right. We didn't have time to argue.

Anza and I rushed up the stairs after Olaf, Whisper and Abry hot on our heels as he led us up a winding tower. As we got to the top, I felt my stomach twist when I locked eyes on the group. Olaf wasn't there.

Two Maraung, a Barbarza, and a Photomyran leapt at us and I instantly realized what this was: an ambush.

A flash of glass plummeted toward me as I caught a Maurang man's hand. He was much bigger than me and easily lifted me up off the ground to slam me back again. I reeled as the air rushed out of my lungs, focusing on keeping that syringe from my neck as the Photomyran pulled Abry by a leg, arms struggling to keep himself up. The Barbarza had pinned Anza against a pillar, and even though Anza's sword bit deep, he wasn't looking at the Barbarza's snapping jaws. I turned to follow his gaze to Whisper, pinned down by the other Maraung, a gash already in the side of her face. He held up a chisel, aiming for her chest.

"Don't!" I shrieked as the Maraung pinning me down tried to shove forward, tried to jab me. I twisted my head to the side, narrowly avoiding the needle before looking back, catching a flash of green hit the ground before Abry turned his attention to Whisper.

Rushing forward like a sliver of night, he shoved his shoulder into the Maurang's side, grabbed him around the middle, and shoved. As the Maraung slammed into the barrier at the edge of the stone banister that led around the top of the space, it gave way, the stone crumbling as both the Maraung and Abry slid toward the edge. Abry tried to pull back, digging his feet in as he approached, but the Maurang grabbed him, pulling him over the edge with him. I saw a glimpse of fingers as Abry reached, trying to save himself with the edge of the crumbled wall, a flash of fear in those brown eyes. He missed.

"No!" I screamed as the Maraung tried to stab me again, shifting his weight back to get better leverage. I threw myself forward, surprising him, and twisted the syringe out of his hand before stabbing him in the eye as Anza's sword slid through the

Barbarza's leg, leaving him yelping on the brown stone as we got to our feet just in time to hear the sickening thud.

Silence hung, our enemies bleeding out and Whisper finally sitting up to turn to look at where Abry had fallen.

"Is he…?" I couldn't help the terror inside me as Anza fought to smother his own fear. He had saved her. Without thinking, without stopping, he had saved her.

Then he screamed. He screamed a scream of fear which quickly transformed.

I moved, rushing to the edge of the tower just in time to see that flash of night rise, caught on a hot puff of wind, wings extended, braids dancing in the hot breeze, the warm undertones of his skin alight with the sun's rays as he raised a fist into the air and screamed with all he was.

"Whoooooo!"

For the first time, Abronoma flew.

24

"I fucking knew it!" Whisper screamed back, raising a fist as I helped her to her feet.

Anza stood back, a hand on his hips as we watched Abry rise, only to see him turn the look of terror on his face as he started to flap.

"He doesn't know how to land," Anza said quickly. "Hey, here! Aim here!" Anza patted at his chest as Abry started to glide down, trying to flap to slow his descent. Aiming both feet for Anza's chest. It only took a few heartbeats before Anza knelt slightly and Abry's feet touched his chest, using his hands, he shifted them downward onto each hip as he crouched low, trying to support Abry with a hand on the back as he landed. Anza stumbled back a few feet from the force, but kept the stance, slowing Abronoma completely.

"Did you see it? Did you see me?!" he asked, jumping down from Anza's legs before bouncing on his toes. Anza righted himself as Whisper scooped up Abry around the waist.

"Of course we did! You were brilliant!"

"The sky looks good on you," I said as Whisper spun him. It was then that I noticed that the fear and terror he had initially been draped in when we met him was gone.

"Your parents would be so proud," Anza said gently as Whisper let him down from the spinning hug.

"Yeah?" Abry asked

"Yeah," Anza agreed, gently patting his back. "Gotta work on that landing thing though."

Abronoma was practically bouncing, full of joy and light as we searched for any possible route Olaf may have taken to escape, only to find nothing.

He had been here. He had tried to kill Saha. He may have even succeeded.

Quickly, we went back to the portal room, slipping past the Queen's Guard. I surveyed the room. Graz and Taryn both looked pale, watching as my parents and Sil clung to Saha. Her leaves and petals were crumpled, her eyes glossy, and for a moment, I thought her chest might not be moving. But after a few thudding heartbeats, it rose and fell quickly.

"Brian?" I asked, and he looked back at us.

"It's going better than it looks," he assured gently, but as he turned back to Saha, Anza caught my eye and shook his head. It was a lie. I looked to Graz.

"Hey…" He didn't respond, eyes locked on his mother "Hey!" His eyes snapped to me.

"Sorry, sorry I just…I just thought she was…untouchable, you know?"

"She's just as able to die as any of us," I said, nodding. "We need to know what to do next. Olaf got away, no sign of him, and she's not exactly in a spot to be making calls," I said gently and he started nodding.

"We follow the plan, we press back what's left of the siege and settle around the castle to ensure there are no further attacks."

"Alright, you know what happens if—" I didn't finish the question and nodded to Saha.

"Yeah, I know," he said quietly, and for a moment, it looked like his shoulders were straining under the weight he was being threatened with.

"She'll be alright," I said, rubbing a shoulder before starting to gather the others.

Sil, Graz, and Taryn stayed with my parents by Saha's side as we left. Together, I led them back toward the fighting to see that Grio had taken out more than two thirds of the enemy forces. We needed to establish a medical tent and get people settled.

The sun threatened to sink below the horizon, but as Royal Endering, it was my job to see this through. Carefully, I got everyone to work, and by the time the night fell, we had a well-established buffer between us and any remaining troops. The medical tent was packed to the brim, and as I got Saha's tent set up, I turned to see my parents carrying a gurney down, using both hands. My queen was covered in a blanket, but alive as they moved her into the tent.

"What's it looking like?" I asked Graz as he and Taryn passed, hand in hand.

"Not good. Your mom is pretty good at focusing on the most important damage, the spine, blood vessels, etcetera, but I don't think she has much more juice left in her," he said as I peeked through the curtain. I could already see my mother was heavily relying on my dad for support. He held her upright, respectfully, whispering into her ear as she focused on Saha.

"She's probably just trying to get her to a point where she'd survive if medics were to take over," I said and Taryn nodded.

"I think so."

"And how are you doing?" I asked her as her free hand moved to caress the spot at her neck that was now healed over.

"About as well as you can hope," she said quietly and I nodded.

"Right," I said. "Well, we're not going to be much help tonight. Let them do all they can," I urged, quietly gesturing for them to go to their own tent. "I've arranged for dinner for you guys. Try to get some rest, you've been through it."

"I wish we just had a sliver of good news," Graz said quietly.

"We kept the portal up. Oh, and Abry flew today."

"He did?" Taryn asked. "That's amazing!"

"Yeah, he's a pretty cool kid," I said, looking over to where Abry and Whisper were putting up one of the few remaining tents.

"Go on," I said, nodding to Whisper and Abry. Graz and Taryn didn't hesitate to start their way.

"So I heard you finally got to use those wings of yours," Graz started before a soft squeak rose in the coming dark. I turned, seeing a bat clinging to the outside of the tent.

"You weren't much help in there," I said, and it fluttered away. I followed it, just in time to see it join the others as Bats materialized on the edge of the space our tent was set up on.

"Sorry," he said quietly. "Had to get him outta there."

"I get it, don't be sorry, just be sure to let him know Saha might die because of him."

"He probably won't care."

"Yeah, I got that vibe from him," I said, and together, we sighed.

"I'll tell him," Bats said.

"Thanks."

"Can I ask you a question?"

"Yeah."

"Um, Saha seemed to be…more lenient than His Majesty and I was wondering if that was a…well, um…"

"You're wondering if that was genuine?"

"Yeah," he said quietly.

"I have a feeling that Saha has had to learn the hard way about how you do and don't treat people. It was genuine, and she's lying in there right now because she protected her Endering."

"They do consider us precious…"

"Yeah, but our leaders are very different," I said.

"Are they?"

"Yeah, they are. What happens if you try to make a break for Agrenon?"

"The sun would be quite a bitch to fight. I can't navigate well in the day, and even if I could, I couldn't leave her."

"Her?"

"Her," he said. "She doesn't get to…use her power."

"So you're trapped here in one way or another?"

"Yeah, and if I got caught, well, I'd never see the night sky again."

"I'm so sorry."

"Yeah, me too. Other kingdoms have it worse. Don't think that they don't."

"Doesn't mean *you* don't have it bad."

"Don't worry about us, worry about your queen, and what happens if that prince becomes a king," he said gently.

"Can I ask you a question before you go?"

"Sure."

"What's your real name? It can't be Bats, right?"

Even with his eyes hidden, I could see the sadness on his face.

"I should go." He was gone before I could open my mouth to protest.

I sighed, shaking my head, and returned to camp just in time to see my dad swish out of Saha's tent, holding my unconscious mother in his arms. I could see her chest rising and falling, but the small bead of blood at her nose made it clear that she had overstretched her healing ability. My dad didn't see me though, too concerned with moving her to their own tent. I knew she was in good hands by the concern written all over his face.

Carefully, I crept closer to Saha's tent, hoping to see she was fine, but on my approach, I heard a voice and stopped, my hand on the flap of the door, unopened.

"It was my fault. I shouldn't have—" Sil started.

"No, no it was mine, if I had made a different choice, maybe we wouldn't be here right now," Saha retorted.

"But if I hadnt…I could have stopped this."

"You just said it yourself, they're your boys, you can't."

"I just, I just hope you can forgive me," Sil said.

"I hope we can forgive each other," Saha said before silence hung.

"Together?" Sil asked.

"Together," Saha answered.

I couldn't help but smirk. *That's* what it meant.

I left them alone, slipping away toward the tent I shared with Anza to find him waiting up outside for me.

"There you are."

"Here I am," I said as he stood to hold me tightly.

"You did so well today," I said, kissing his neck.

"So did you." He lifted my chin with a finger to give me a proper kiss. "Let's get some food and rest. Tomorrow's going to be hard if we're asked to head out," he muttered before kissing me again.

"Dang, you're not wrong," I said and sighed.

"I have dinner in here," he said, and I caught the scent of meat and fufu and vegetables.

"You are the best mate anyone could ask for," I said, leaning up to kiss him again

"Damn straight," he said, smirking before leading me inside with his hand in mine. My muscles screamed with the effort of the day as we settled into our meals, and it wasn't long before we laid down, tucked against one another, sweet sleep descending over us.

———————————

The ground shook as sound blasted past us, crumbling rock and shuddering stone, and my eyes flew open, the tent coming down on us as the blast rang past, all too familiar. Anza and I scrambled to our feet and out the doorway of the half-fallen tent to see that the top of Biena's dome, where the portal had been, had burst outward, sending rubble across our campsite. Even from here, I could see the small platform the portal had been on. It was gone.

Screams rose up all around us as the rubble crashed over our troops, taking out dozens of tents and campfires. Anza and I looked to each other.

"Whisper and Abry," I said firmly as he nodded, and we wordlessly split up.

I ran, desperate to find my parents' tent, knowing that Whisper and Abry would have separate, smaller tents near them, nearest the two most dangerous and realized Endering I knew. They had to be alright. They had to be.

I dodged around a massive boulder that sat on a crushed tent and froze at the sight of the person lying beneath it. A gray-spattered Barbarza with a single beaded feathered earring, she turned to me, reaching for me with her jaws.

"I can hear him, he waited for me," she said, her voice a whisper in my mind.

"Tamaj?" She didn't respond. "Tamaj!"

"Tell me you can heal her. Tell me she'll be alright." Baden's voice hit my mind in a flourish of desperation as I hit my knees, trying to find a pulse on Tamaj's neck. Her eyes were already glazing over, blood spilling slowly from her mangled maw. I tried a healing sigil, but nothing happened. I couldn't even see how bad the damage was beneath the boulder that pinned her down, the tatters of the tent folding over against her frame, but I could see from the sway of the rock that everything was crushed from her shoulder down. If I moved it, she'd bleed out, but if I didn't, she couldn't breathe, even if I *could* get her out. *"Mira!"*

"I've gotta get my mom. Stay here!" I said to him, unsure what to do or if there was enough time, if she was rested enough to save Tamaj, and ran for her tent. Before I could reach it though, I felt my feet slide out from under me as something slid into my shoulder. I looked up, expecting to see a person as the white-hot fire leaped into my veins, but there was nothing there, an invisible entity. I couldn't even see the syringe.

I screamed as they started to pull me away, my vision tunneling until darkness descended.

25

The familiar feeling of dead weight was one I hoped to never be reacquainted with, but as I regained consciousness, I found myself staring at the walls of a tent. Instead of brown or orange or green, the canvas walls were red; as red as spilled blood.

"Easy Chispa." I felt water touch my tongue and realized how thirsty I was as I looked over to see Heartlock. Was he an ally? He had warned us about the assassination attempt on Saha, and as I looked down, it was hard to miss the chain that wrapped tightly around his foot. I drank.

I reached for the bond, hoping to tip off Anza, only to find it was pulsing, as if partially interrupted. Spikes of emotion—fury, confusion, distress, anguish—rattled down the bond before it would quiet completely.

Heartlock gently pulled the canteen away.

"Where..." I couldn't get the question out, but I didn't need to.

"Korrewen's camp," he said quietly.

"Was I—"

"No one hurt you beyond kidnapping you." I sighed my relief and tried my hands, only to feel cloth and some sort of binding. "He put gloves on you to prevent you from playing with rocks. We're both bound." His voice was quick, to the point; very different from when I last saw him. "No matter what he tells you, you must not believe in him. It is the only way."

"What do you—" He pressed a finger to his lips and I let the question die as I heard footsteps approach. He dropped his hand before Olaf came in.

Heartlock looked up as Olaf entered, holding the canteen tighter.

"Looks like our new friend is awake."

"Barely, but I don't think that will contain her disdain," Heartlock said.

"Let her hate me, she won't by the time I'm done."

I could barely see the Endering behind him. He looked almost familiar with his thick, golden hair, pale skin, and those blue eyes. Healthy muscle supported his frame, which was almost shocking since every other Endering I had met had at least appeared slightly undernourished. Had I seen him before? Why couldn't I place him?

"Taking away her brace would be an effective means of control," Olaf said, gesturing to my leg.

"Bad," Heartlock said, capping the canteen before starting to play with a few small wooden blocks carved into crude statues, moving a few pieces, like he was trying to visualize something bigger than us.

"Why?" Olaf prompted.

I didn't trust my tongue to form coherent sentences, but maybe I could learn something here. Heartlock looked like he was thinking for a moment before he just nodded firmly.

"Bad. Terrible, even. Atrocious consequences."

Olaf growled but didn't move to confiscate my brace as Heartlock fiddled with a few of his wooden pieces.

"You said we needed her," Olaf said.

"I did," Heartlock confirmed.

"For?"

"I'm not sure yet."

"If you don't want me to—"

"Remember my downside," Heartlock sang, and Olaf huffed, leaving just as quickly as he had come.

"You really gotta stop pulling his strings," the blond-haired man said.

"He pulls our strings, Percy, I'm just returning the favor."

"Just don't pull the wrong string."

"Do I ever?"

Percy's eyes softened and he sighed. "No, I suppose you don't."

"Stay alive?"

"You too," Percy said as he slid out, following Olaf.

"Gonna…kill him."

"Hmm. No, you won't, technically, but you *will* be the reason he takes his last breath," Heartlock said, his voice hushed as he shrugged.

"Good enough," I fought out as the heavy feeling in my limbs began to lift.

"How many—"

"One dose. You sleep like a log." We couldn't be too far from Agrenon's camp if it was only one dose. An hour? Two? Six? How long? Then it came back to me, the body I had seen before I was taken.

"Tamaj?"

"She's…not here anymore. I'm sorry."

I felt my throat grow tight as I tried to stifle a sob and blink away tears. I couldn't let them see I was hurting.

Heartlock left his pieces, coming back to my side, and placed a single hand on my back. He rubbed my back gently as I tried to smother the noises trying to force their way out.

Tamaj. Bright, sarcastic, steadfast Tamaj. Brave and strong and fierce Tamaj. How many times had I thought I had lost her the first time we traveled together? How long had I been angry with her for not telling me about my mom? Wasted time I could have been telling her how amazing she was. How thankful I was for her. Now she was gone, because I set her tent up there. I set up her tent there. She was gone because he was trying to ruin everything. Her low-toned growl of warning, her warm and bright laugh, the way she loved Whisper and the The Two. Gone. She had been just as there for them as Anza and I while Brian was recovering. She doted on them, told them stories, inspired their wonder, and now, with a single spell and a rock tossed wrong, she was dead.

I couldn't see, couldn't breathe, couldn't think.

Heartlock kept rubbing my back.

"She'll be with him," he said quietly. "It was quick, she couldn't have felt it."

"Shouldn't h-h-have been her," I sobbed, curling tightly toward him, shaking as I felt my body slowly returning control to me.

"I'm sorry, there was no path where she did not fall," he said, still rubbing my back.

My tears fell on the pad of brown cloth I was lying on, shaking as he tried to comfort me. They soaked into the cloth as I tried to think of a way I could have saved her. Had she been dead already when I found her and Baden? I wasn't able to find a pulse. My head ached, my shoulders shaking as I sobbed until I couldn't cry anymore.

Heartlock brushed away the last of my tears and offered me more water, which I drank, and he helped me sit upright.

"I wish I could do more," he said. But he couldn't, neither of us could. Tamaj was dead.

"Does he have anyone else?" I asked, my voice cracking.

"No." He lowered his voice before continuing, "He was looking for your Moonbeam but could not find her."

He was after Whisper again.

"Why?"

"An Echalon heart is a hell of a bargaining tool when you're trying to get access to a portal. If a ruler doesn't know what he's up to, a heart for a day at the portal is an amazing deal." I tugged on my bonds just to find that I was somehow bound to the ground through the mat. I wasn't going anywhere. "Shhh," he said, and I stopped with my questions just as Olaf stormed back in.

"Why do you think we have you here?"

"Because you're a self-centered douche who would sacrifice his own friends and family to get ahead?" I snarled, seeing him flex a bandaged hand. When did he get hurt? His long sleeves had been hiding it, but I could see the edge of the burn peeking through his wrappings. "What's the matter? Mommy dearest get ahold of you?"

"You leave her out of this or so help me, I'll—"

Oh, I had hit a nerve.

"What? You'll what? Kill Tamaj? Ope, already did that! But you failed at every other attempt at homicide you've made in the last few days. Both Sil and Saha are alive and well. You may have taken three of five portals, but mark my words, when they come to get me, you'll have led them right to your camp," I snarled, and he threw his head back laughing at me.

"You might be right about my shortcomings, but you're wrong about one thing, Mira. They're not coming to save you," he snarled right back.

"Of course they are. Anza wouldn't leave me here."

"No, but Saha would, and as their queen, she could command him to stay,"

"No, she wouldn't. I'm her Royal Endering."

"And she's a queen. She has people to think of, people to put to rest, and she's still trying to cook up a way to stop yours truly. Believe me, writing off one Endering as missing in action is far easier for her than you realize.You and Emai lean far to heavily on Saha's good graces, the Exit Clause, the kindness in her eyes, it's all a guise to make you think you have a way out. Em keeps coming back, you both keep forgiving her again and again." What did the Exit Clause have to do with this? Saha had solidified it, a pathway out of serving the kingdom for any Endering, into law herself, she wouldn't revoke it. I opened my mouth to protest, but he continued. "You don't matter to her. I get that you think she's this wonderful queen, that you think she is all good and righteous and kind, but look around you. Who does she send into battle first? Who does she strategically place where the fighting is thickest? Who does she put in harm's way every single time a problem comes up? Famine, drought, sickness, economic collapse; an Endering is the solution," he said, sending my mind spinning. He was wrong, he had to be wrong. "She's using you to fix her problems, just like the other leaders. She's just better at making you think she's not."

And with that, he left again.

"Anza?" I asked down the bond. *"Can you hear me?"*

"He can't hear you. There's too much distance," Heartlock whispered. "Don't tell him about the bond."

"Your power, you can see the future?"

"I just see the truth, about what is and what will be."

"You know what's going to happen?"

"No, I know what could happen, and I try to make choices and help others make choices that are good. Bad choices lead to different paths."

"And that's why you told him taking my brace was bad?"

"No, I told him taking a tool you need to get around is bad because it's a cunt move, and he's a bit of a cunt. Also, you're going to need to be able to use that leg to run eventually," he said, smirking.

"You're a pretty cool guy, you know that?" I couldn't help the ghost of a smile pulling at my lips.

"I know."

"Why does he have you tied up?"

"Percy….doesn't really…like what we're doing."

"You two are together?"

"We want to be, but kingdoms kind of frown on pairings that don't result in biological children."

"This was your out."

"Unfortunately. Sometimes paths and decisions converge into one option. We're chasing that option with all that we have."

"And what do I have to do with it?"

"If I told you, it'd ruin it."

I sighed and nodded. "Is…is he right about Saha?"

"Foggy. I can't say."

"Are you lying to me like you lied to him about my brace?"

He didn't look me in the eye, but shrugged.

I sighed and shifted my weight to lean back against the wall behind me. Closing my eyes, I reached for the bond, trying to send that I was alive down it. Trying to calm myself enough to think. What would Whisper do in this situation? I needed to find a way to escape, and figure out what direction Agrenon's camp was from here.

I looked out, seeing night settling as I felt the last of the jab wear off and resigned myself to one fact: tonight, I would mourn and sleep. Tomorrow, I would be the biggest problem I possibly could.

26

"Are you ready for a tour?"

I groaned and turned my back to Olaf, hearing Heartlock snicker from his spot on the other side of the tent.

"Naw, I'm pretty comfy right here. I'm just gonna wait for Anza to come serve you your own ass on a silver platter." I yawned and Olaf sighed, reaching down to unfasten my bindings from whatever held me down, trying to pull me to my feet. I let myself stay limp against him.

"Mira, this is childish. Stand up."

"My legs just don't seem to be working. Huh. What a shame."

"This is gonna be great!" Heartlock cackled, wiping tears from his eyes as he tried to smother his laugh. It was at this point Olaf lifted me up over a shoulder.

"You're going to be difficult, aren't you?" he grumbled.

"What in the world would give you that idea?" I could feel now that none of my bracelets were beneath the gloves he had put on me while I was asleep. He had disarmed me. My downside kept me from using my power unless I was touching a stone. My bracelets, even my necklace from Anza, were all secure pathways to my power. My necklace still hung at my neck, just with a cloth tied around it now. "Aww, you do have a heart…somewhere." I said, surprised he had let me keep my symbol of union.

He sighed as we exited the tent.

"Good luck with that one!" Heartlock called after us and I gave him a wink. I had to be stone. I couldn't let him know he had shaken me. I couldn't let him see to the pain I had lingering in my chest. I couldn't let him see he had broken me.

"What are you thinking about, exactly?" he asked.

"Oh, nothing that matters." I couldn't let him know he made a mistake. That rock could be my ticket out of here. "Why are you showing me around anyway?"

"Call it an olive branch."

"Your olive branches suck." He wanted me to be his friend. His ally. That wasn't going to happen, but maybe if I played along I could get an opportunity.

Frustration bolted down the bond, and then anger; an anger I had never known Anza to have, even in our first journey. I didn't let the torrent touch my features as he slung me off his shoulder and into another tent, where someone had prepared a very nice dinner and set two plates.

"Are you going to behave long enough to eat?"

"Only if you let me feed myself."

He pursed his lips.

"Come on, I can't start trusting you if you don't trust me too," I said.

"Don't try to fool me. You and I both know that the moment you get hold of a stone, you're going to try to kill me."

"Unless you give me a reason not to." *Don't believe him*, that's what Heartlock had said. Don't believe him.

"Fine," he grumbled, moving to unfasten my hands. I still didn't see anything stone, but he retied them in front anyway.

"Really?" I asked.

"You're lucky you're getting that," he retorted.

"What do you want me for anyway? Heartlock said I was important."

"Yes, but I can't completely trust he's not lying to me." *No shit.* "So I guess we get to hang out until the reason for your importance becomes clear."

"Yay. That's just…so thrilling."

"Your sarcasm was always your best trait."

"And your traitorous tendencies were yours," I retorted, picking up a fork and stabbing some meat through. I braced myself for what I was about to say. I had to say this with a straight face, even if it burned me up inside. "Was killing Tamaj worth it, Snowset?" He flinched and his jaw cracked as he clenched his teeth. "She was your friend, right? Seems to be a shitty way to treat a friend." I popped the meat into my mouth.

"She was…a necessary sacrifice."

"That's rich." I laughed, swallowing the food as he picked at his plate. *Keep your face settled, don't let your pain show.* "You know, I did always wonder something else. What exactly did you have on my dad to make him send out a plague that could level a nation?"

He hesitated just long enough to look me over before meeting my eyes.

"You."

"Me?"

"You were an infant, and fathers will burn the world for their daughters."

"So you took advantage of him for your own personal gain? Threatened to come for me?"

"My mother wouldn't have suspected a thing. Infants die all the time."

"That's really fucked up."

"You know they were my friends, right? Tamaj and Arlo? Brian is my *brother*. A choice like that isn't exactly easy to make."

"Yeah, it's down right *impossible*. For anyone with a shred of dignity, anyway."

"The only reason someone would make a choice like that is if they felt there was no other way."

"Heartlock tell you that?"

"No. And I couldn't have known those decisions would lead to Arlo and Tamaj's deaths," he said firmly.

"But you did know you were going to kill *someone*, that people would die," I said, and his face fell.

"Yes, I did."

"Then why do any of this shit at all? What do you have to gain from destroying the portals?"

"I'm sure you've noticed how Endering are treated."

"I have."

"And you can just sit by and let it happen?"

"What other choice is there?"

"To change it," he said simply. "I wanted to change it. That's why I stole away the Echalon that night. I could have bribed three of five kingdoms, and I was in control of the fourth. The fifth would have fallen easily to a unified army."

"You were trying to take over the world to…save us?"

"Free us, but that didn't work," he said, no longer looking at me. "So I figured if I cannot have the kingdoms, I will bring them to their knees."

"By throwing the worlds together."

"I'm sure your little Echalon has told you about dozens of potential consequences for this."

"She has."

"Has she told you what it means for Endering?"

"No."

"It means we will have a catastrophic increase in numbers," he said simply. "There are thousands of Endering on Earth that don't know who they are or what their birthright is, and once the worlds fall together…"

"They'll get powers."

"And they'll want to know why."

"That's really fucked up."

"What part, exactly?"

"The part where you're willing to throw away two entire planets' ecosystems and threaten people's lives just to get to this little end goal of yours."

"Have you seen the other Endering here? How they're treated? Have you *really* seen it?"

"Yeah, and while it sucks, destroying the worlds isn't the path to saving them. You're just condemning everyone else."

"I knew you wouldn't understand." He sighed before waving a hand. Percy sighed as he stepped in and picked me up, flinging me over yet another shoulder. "Maybe you'll get it when you realize Saha's not coming," Olaf said as I tried to fight against Percy.

"Come on, don't make this harder than it already is," he said, sighing as he carried me out of the tent. I tried to swing leg down toward his groin but he caught it with a free hand.

"Sorry, I promised myself I'd be a problem today," I said, trying to dig my elbows into his back. If I could just get free, I could get a hold of the rock on my necklace.

"Cut that out," he grumbled as we slid back into the tent Heartlock was in and he set me down.

"Well, that was fun!" Heartlock said, clapping happily.

"Don't worry, I didn't believe him," I said as Percy retied me to the link on the ground.

"I didn't say don't believe him, I said don't believe *in* him," Heartlock said, and for a moment, my stomach pitched sideways. What did he mean? Why couldn't he just tell me? Did that mean that what he said about Saha being the same as the others was true? It couldn't be. I knew Saha, she saved Sil, she tried to do all she could for her Endering. I bit my lip as Percy moved toward the door of the tent. "Green light," Heartlock said as he left, and Percy nodded, letting the tent close behind him.

"What does 'green light' mean?"

"If I told you then you'd know."

"That's kinda the point?"

"Naw, you can't know."

"Would it be rude to say you're the most frustrating person I've ever met in my entire life?"

"Naw, I get that I lot." He laughed, moving a few of his wooden pieces around. "Just remember that the Golden One has the answers, and play along when he comes back." I rolled my eyes and sighed, trying to find a good place to settle in for the day, knowing he wasn't about to elaborate.

The rest of the day was largely uneventful. No matter how hard I wriggled, I couldn't get my hands on that stone. I checked the bond regularly, finding it was alight with fury and pain, tempered to a false calm, the smallest sliver of panic in him. I tried to stay calm, tried to keep a cool head, tried to convey that I was alright. It wasn't until night fell that it became clear that wasn't the case.

"You're sure about this?" Percy said. I heard footsteps approaching the tent, footsteps I now knew to belong to Percy and Olaf.

"I'm sure. We have to move. I wanted to give her more time to think, but it's clear there's no way."

"Heartlock said we needed her."

"But he doesn't know anything else. Maybe we need her dead."

I felt my blood chill as I pulled on the restraints. They didn't budge. He was going to kill me. I felt panic rise, shaking in every part of my being as Percy slid inside, sword drawn.

Heartlock tried to get my attention but I didn't look to him until Percy did.

"Don't. Please, don't," I begged.

"Red light," Heartlock said, his voice but a whisper before looking to me. Percy's sword arced forward toward my head but stopped an inch from me, his eyes flashing with meaning. Play along. I forced myself to fall over in the direction he had arced his sword, making it look like a delayed drop from an initial blow. He stood over me, sword in hand, and lifted it, carefully cutting the rope.

"Please don't do this," I choked out.

"This is the only way," Heartlock said quietly, and Percy nodded before stabbing the spot in the sand beside my head. He leaned over me as he stabbed again and spoke swiftly, quietly.

"You need to lay still once he comes in for this to work. Hold your breath. The fewer movements I have to cover the more real it'll look."

"Your power is altering perception."

He nodded swiftly.

Olaf being unable to dispatch his enemies himself would be the only reason I survived. Slowly, he stood, placing a foot on my side, and pulled the sword swiftly from the sand. Heartlock gave a believable cry, burying his face in his hands as he turned away. These two were good.

"Done," Percy said loudly, and I held my breath as I heard the tent flap flutter, trying to keep from looking around as I lay limp. What was Percy making him see? My dead body for sure, but why? Why not just kill me?

"Excellent work. I…it was unavoidable?"

"Yes," Heartlock sobbed, and I heard my uncle give a shuddering sigh, as if trying to hold back a sob of his own.

"Bury her and her things in the desert," he said quickly as my lungs started to burn, my chest threatening to burst. He turned around and left just as quickly as he came.

Percy gave me a thumbs up and mouthed 'stay' before following Olaf. I nodded, sitting up and starting to take off those stupid gloves, dropping them to the ground once my hands were clear of them. It was nice to be able to move again and I slid the pocket off of the necklace Anza made for me, letting it rest against my skin, the sweet relief of singing stone washing over me.

Percy came back a moment later with a heavy pack over his shoulder. My pack. My axe hung from it and my bracelets dangled in one of his hands. He waited until the flap fell behind him before holding my bracelets out to me. I took them and slid them on.

"Why?" I asked quietly.

"I really don't know," he said, looking to Heartlock. "He's the only one that really knows anything, and half the time I think he's guessing."

"Am not," Heartlock chimed as Percy passed me my bag. "Beware The King who Barely Was, and stand with The Queen who Shouldn't Be."

"You two aren't staying, right?" I asked, knowing he meant Olaf and Saha. He had to mean them.

"You're the only one who leaves tonight.The Golden One knows the way, follow her lead."

Who could that possibly be?

"But—"

"He thinks you're dead. I'm literally going to just take you to the desert and point you in the right direction."

"We could all leave."

"What he says, goes."

"Why?"

"Do you question that Echalon you always have with you?"

"It never really goes well if I do."

"Well, it's kind of the same concept. Anytime someone questions him, shit hits the fan, and while I am about to take a shower, I don't like the idea of being covered in metaphorical shit, so for fuck's sake, listen?" Percy pleaded, and I sighed but nodded.

"He's not going to be near the tent. You need to go now if you don't want anyone to see you," Heartlock said and Percy led the way out. It wasn't until we were out of the dozens of rows of tents that I dared ask another question.

"Why doesn't he just tell us what's going on?"

"Because if he does, knowing might make us make a different choice, which would lead to other opposing choices. It could also lead to us struggling to make the 'right' choice, all to make sure we follow the so-called 'correct' path."

"Why keep me alive at all? And why the hell does he call me Chispa?" I asked as he led me to the top of a dune.

"Heartlock is a lot like a gardener. He knows what the outcome will be, what kind of plant is growing, but we're just the seeds. We hold all the potential but have no idea what's going to happen next. He's just doing his best to make sure we have everything we need to flourish, to guide us where we need to be."

"And where is that?"

He shrugged and started to head back.

"Hey, you didn't answer me about the Chispa thing!"

"He told me not to tell you! Honestly, it doesn't make sense to me either, and I know what it means! Head toward the sunrise and keep going," he said and I sighed, turning to look out at the rows and rows of sand dunes before me before taking a breath and stepping into the unknown.

27

"I swear, if I get any more sand in my pants, I'm going to lose my fucking mind!" I screamed up at the circling birds as the day stretched on. My canteen was still mostly full after a full night of walking, but daytime was upon me and that wouldn't last much longer. How long did I have to walk? How far was the camp? I had freedom at least, and Anza's angry desperation made one thing clear: he was searching for me. I just had to live long enough to see those gilded eyes one more time.

The heat pulled my energy away much faster than I realized, and the farther I walked, the heavier I felt. It wasn't until I spotted a dead tree that I settled down in its shade, praying I could rest enough to move once night fell.

The birds descended and I struck one with my axe before the others flew off, keeping their distance again. I felt my body scream at me as I sat and checked my brace. The different components felt tighter than usual, as if there was something wrong, but without Whisper, or even an adequate surface to work on, I could only pray Anza found me before it gave out.

I waited in the shadow of that tree for a mere few moments before I felt the fuzzy rumbling from below. Like the ground was blurry. I moved as the sand shifted quickly upward, running from whatever was rising up from the depths as quickly as I could as I felt tendrils snap at my legs.

A sickening crunch rocked through my body and pain engulfed me as my right leg gave out and blood stained the sand as I looked up at the massive creature now towering over me. Multiple limbs swayed in the sand, sending it rippling as it lifted its huge head up from what must have been a burrow. Rows of serrated teeth munched at the air as two tendrils lashed out from the edge of its lips on either side. The mangled tree I had been sitting under was nestled on its head, a decoy for unsuspecting prey.

I scrambled backwards, throwing a bracelet toward it as I struggled, sand inching its way into my brace as I moved, aiming carefully for where I hoped the brain was on this eyeless sans-colored-scales creature. My stone passed through its head as a tendril grabbed my now-broken leg and it collapsed. I inched backwards, getting out of the tendril's grasp and tried not to scream as every movement sent agony down my leg and up my spine. I had to do something. Fast.

Carefully, I unbuckled my pants and took off my brace, sliding inch by agonizing inch out of my pants to get a better look at my leg. Rolling my pant leg up wasn't possible. Even the idea hurt too badly. A bird fluttered down, not far from my injured leg, and I shooed it away with a hand.

"Get outta here, you little shit," I said, focusing on my leg as I drew a healing sigil. I focused first on my bleeding, and settled back knowing that if I kept going it would take more out of me. After a few moments, I focused myself on healing the bone as the bird hopped closer.

"Peck me, I fuckin dare yah," I snarled, and it hopped back a little. I quickly drew a larger sigil on my leg, focusing on the bone, trying not to scream as it knitted back together. That's all I had; healing sigils, a little water, and a direction.

I pulled myself up onto my feet, taking out a bandage to wrap my leg the best I could, trying to give it extra support before I tried it. It was tender, but it was better than having a broken leg.

"Alright, we can work with that. We can work with that, right?" I asked up at the birds before shaking my head. "You're losing your fucking mind," I grumbled to myself before heading back out into the expansive dunes.

My legs took turns threatening to give out, pain still trailing up one as I trudged forward.

It was less than an hour before I could feel the ferocious sunburn I was getting start pulling my skin tight, so I summoned a bracelet, flattening it and pushing it up into the sky to act as a makeshift umbrella, shielding me from the sun.

I grabbed the stone at my neck, remembering the promise Anza made to me in that hold, what felt like a lifetime ago. He would come for me, no matter what.

There wasn't another tree for miles, and after another hour, I was too exhausted to keep trucking in this sunlight. I sat down, using my stone to shield me from the sun's rays.

"Come on, just a little farther," I said, running my fingers over my cracked lips before I took a deep drink from my canteen. It was just under half gone now.

I waited until nightfall. The sun and dry heat had made my lungs feel like sandpaper. My clothes felt too heavy and my body didn't want to get up as the chill of night set in, but I could at least put the stone down. I slipped it back around my wrist and kept trudging, my feet aching with every step.

"I'd give up a kidney for a new pair of socks right about now, Anza," I said, focusing on moving forward. I couldn't stop. If I stopped, he might not find me. If I stopped, those birds might eat me. I could feel the sand and shifting blisters in my boots, the scrunch of my skin, the burn in my legs as I walked on until morning. I didn't drink, saving the water as long as I could as the cold set me rubbing sunburnt arms. I could feel the little blisters rising up on my skin from before I had put up my stone. Had it been enough?

Every breath was agony, and as the sun dawned, I felt my brace lock up and I fell. Sand rushed up to meet me and I tried to turn over to look at my brace but I couldn't. My body felt like dead weight. I pulled a bracelet from my wrist, trying to get it into a flat stone barrier so I could use it like the day before, but it wouldn't shape right. I pulled my water to me, barely able to move, and drank it. I couldn't get to my brace, couldn't turn over, and every inch I moved sent my skin screaming, the sun threatening to burn me alive.

I thought about Anza, the way he had cared so much about me, even before the Sky Fields. How he had covered my back in hundreds of situations. I could feel him now down the bond, growing more and more desperate. Did he know I was dying? I was dying.

I thought about Whisper and Abronoma. Their friendship was new but founded in knowledge and the pursuit of it. They were so smart and strong and capable and kind. Individually, they were amazing. Together, they were flirting with greatness.

He flew.

I thought about The Two. How they were ravenous in their pursuit of knowledge, how they worked in tandem with each other to all but terrify us every day. How would they be told their mother was dead?

I thought about my parents. How would they feel to know their only child died before they did? How would they feel about having to live with never having found me?

I thought about Saha and Sil. They had sounded like they made up before I was taken, sounded like things were good. What kind of strain would my death have on them?

I thought about Graz and Taryn; the future king and queen. I knew I wasn't going to see them with crowns on their heads even before this. Saha was Sil's age, and Photomyran lived far longer than us. She had a good century or two left, but still, I wished I could see them grow and thrive.

I thought about Baden. I barely knew the guy, but he looked and acted so much like Arlo. He was kind and fierce and bright.

I thought about Tamaj. Sweet, snarky, patient, careful, stubborn Tamaj. The way her sandy fur fell gray, that beaded and feathered earring of hers. She was a close friend to my parents, to Sil and Saha, to me and Anza and Whisper. Tamaj permeated every day with her presence. She'd been loyal to a fault and determined to survive, and she was dead.

The thought barely crossed my mind as I caught a glimpse of movement, a sandy brown color moving toward me, spattered with gray.

"Tam-aj?" I fought out as it slowly came closer. Its footsteps sounded like a Barbarza's.

"*Get up.*" I heard Tamaj's voice roar in my head from every direction. Then, before I could blink, I felt a soft mind touch mine, and a voice that sounded almost familiar, but not the same as Tamaj's, spoke.

"*Please be alive, please be alive.*" She skidded to a stop near me, but I couldn't move to her as she nuzzled her snout down under my head. Her eyes were the same color as Tamaj's, but her sandy brown coat held no grays and that look of raw, unbridled worry was enough to make it clear who this was.

I pulled up all of my strength and inched my hand closer to her, nearly blacking out from the process.

"*Oh my stars, you are alive!*" With that, she leaned in and grabbed the back of my shirt, flipping me onto my back so I was no longer face first in the sand. With my shirt and backpack strap, in her jaws she started to pull. I had no idea how long she dragged me before I heard him scream down the bond, desperate and angry and scared.

"*Come on, Mira, where are you?!*"

"*She has me, a Barbarza.*"

I felt relief wash over him as the Barbarza's voice rang out. "*I think I found her!*"

It hurt to breathe as I heard the footsteps running for me. She slowed to a stop, and there he was, wrapped in light clothes to keep the sun from slowly cooking him to death, those gilded brown eyes brimming with tears. He lifted sweet, cool water to my lips and I drank deeply, feeling it wash into every inch of my being, spilling through me in a way I had never known before.

"My brace jammed," I fought out, seeing my father behind him with a thin, light, cloth blanket.

Anza picked me up, holding me tightly against him.

"We'll fix it later. Let's get you outta here," he said and I rested my head on his shoulder, looking out to see if I could find Saha or Graz, my mother or Sil, looking for any more familiar faces. In this vast expanse of endless dunes, there was only Brian, Anza, their Barbarza friend, and me.

"Where's everyone else?" I fought out.

"Can you kneel, Zerah?" The Barbarza, Zerah, kneeled and he climbed on. "Thank you."

She nodded as my father scrambled on and shifted over us to drape the blanket over me as Zerah stood.

"They're not here. We left a second team of your mom and a few others behind, in case Saha tried to come stop us, or in case we didn't come back," my dad said.

"Why would Saha stop you?" Silence fell over the both of them as they shared a look and realization crashed into me.

Olaf had been telling the truth.

28

"Easy, easy," my mom said as I reached for her. The moment we were back in camp, we had been swarmed. Zerah was far faster than I had expected and now, carefully, Anza was passing me down to my mother.

I could feel her power wash over me like electricity as she healed my sunburn and legs, then she held me up long enough for Anza to get down so he could help me. He lifted me up again and I held my mom's hand tighter, trying not to cry. I spotted Saha at a distance, leaning heavily against Sil, and glared at her, trying not to tremble with fury.

She was going to leave me. She had used me. Like some kicked dog. Like a piece of trash in the street. She was going to *leave* me.

"Stop glaring, we'll burn that bridge when we get to it," my dad said gently as they ushered me into a nearby tent. The tent flap closed, obstructing my view of Saha.

Anza tucked me against him settling against the thick furs we had become accustomed to sleeping in. The aches in my body crept forward, the pain I'd endured becoming clear as I finally relaxed back against him. His hand gently rubbed my cheek as I felt a few tears slip out. He wiped them away without a word, eyes locked on the opening of our tent.

When Taryn slipped in with a bowl, I didn't expect my stomach to snarl. Meat and vegetables settled in the thick sauce steamed, the savory smell making my mouth water as I tried to sit up. Anza helped me upright as he took the bowl and handed it to me. I didn't hesitate to practically inhale each bite as quickly as I could, even though it burned at my throat. When was the last time I had eaten?

"Thank you," Anza said gently as Taryn nodded, resting a hand on my shoulder. Taryn could still be trusted, right? She had helped me, been my friend since I found my way to the castle. I wondered where Graz was.

"I'll let you guys rest," she said gently, slipping out of the tent.

After I was done eating, my father took the plate, my mom focusing her power on my leg.

"I'm gonna go get Whisper, alright?" Brian asked and I nodded. I wanted to see my daughter.

He slipped out of the tent as Anza offered me more water and I drank until I couldn't anymore before resting back against him.

"Thank you."

"You don't have to thank me."

"I almost, I'm sorry, I—"

"Hey…" he started, and I looked up from the top of the canteen to him. "You're going to be okay. We're okay. Take a second," he said, pulling me closer. I clung to him, burying my head in his shoulder, shaking with the pain and stress my body still held. His hand rested on my back, holding me tightly. "You're safe. We're safe. You're not there anymore, he can't hurt you here." With every sentence, I could feel the fear and tension slipping away, making it easier to relax into the furs again, but the rage still sat there as he wiped the last of my tears away and I got my breathing more under control. It was only a few more seconds before Whisper rushed in.

"Mom!" She scrambled onto the bed and hugged me.

I hugged her back, burying my face in her hair as I cradled her close to me.

"I'm okay. I know it looks rough, but I'm okay," I said.

"We thought…that in the aftermath you had…you had died," she said, trying to fight back the sobs.

"I'm alright, I'm alright."

"Dad knew you hadn't, he knew."

"Of course he did."

"Mom…Tamaj is—"

"I know, I saw." I held her tighter as her tears spilled over and Anza wrapped his arms around us both, resting his head on my forehead. I reached for Emai, who wrapped the three of us tightly in a hug, her cheeks already raw from her own tears and she sighed, almost in relief.

"Saha wasn't going to come for me."

"No."

"Why are we doing any of this at all then? Why not let him win?"

"Mira…" she said.

"He's right. She uses us. Just like every other pawn in this sick twisted game. She was ready to write me off. A necessary sacrifice. Why be loyal to her?"

"You don't have to be," Emai said, stroking my cheek as we all sat there. "Ask yourself where your loyalties lie."

"With my family," I said immediately.

Olaf was family too. He was right.

"What path will best serve your family? Your mate? Your children?" she asked, and I met her gaze. Anza and Whisper clung to me and I closed my eyes. I knew what my choice had to be, for them, but something whispered in the back of my brain, a seed, tucked deep in the recesses of my mind.

"I'll stay and fight beside her, for now."

"For the record," Emai said, "even Sil gave her a piece of her mind."

"Yeah?"

"Yeah."

"And when you're ready, you can use the Exit Clause, and you and your family can be safe. There's a little cabin in the mountains with your name on it," she said gently.

"Your cabin?"

"Our cabin," she clarified, and I couldn't help but think about using the Exit Clause. The only legal dividing line between Agrenon and other kingdoms. It gave all Endering of Agrenon the ability to walk, upon notifying Saha. It granted us certain allowances we could take with us too, specific goods such as a map, and money. That was the only real difference between us and Endering of other kingdoms. We were allowed to leave.

"I'd like that," I said.

"Me too," Anza agreed.

"It better be a good cabin," Whisper muttered.

"It's amazing," I said.

"Good."

And for a while, we sat like that, the four of us taking comfort in one another as we made half-baked plans for the future. I imagined all of us in that cabin again, in those deep mountains, safe from harm.

"What's Dad doing?" I asked quietly.

"Don't worry about that, sweetness. Rest," Emai said, gently running her thumb up and down my cheek.

I don't remember when I fell asleep, but I do remember waking up and seeing the back of Whisper's head as she rested comfortably beside me.

"You put Brian in danger," Saha said.

"He put himself in danger. She's his daughter. I wasn't going to stop him," Anza said, but he wasn't beside me, he was standing, hissing the words at Saha. When had she come in? When had he gotten up?

"And if you didn't come back? Emai would have went for you, then Sil."

"And then you'd have no Endering to protect you."

"It's not like that."

"Seems a lot like that."

"We needed to get moving. Legalia is already fighting against the beginnings of Korrewen's wrath. It was a calculated decision, a judgment call that could have won us the war, and your decision to traipse off into the desert cost us days. You disobeyed a direct order."

"I went to save my mate! That goes beyond any order you can give."

"Not when it's from your queen."

"Let me make this perfectly clear." The growl in Anza's voice sent a shiver down my spine as he stepped closer to her, an inch from her face now. "You are *nothing* compared to her."

Saha flinched away from the harsh words. "Is that what you think?"

"It's what I know. If she decides to let you burn, then you burn."

"And if she decides not to?"

"Then I tolerate you until she says otherwise."

They stared each other down for a moment before Saha broke eye contact and nodded, turning to slip out. Anza stood, waiting for a moment before he sighed.

"I didn't mean to wake you."

"You didn't," I croaked, and he poured me a glass of water, coming back to my side. "Thank you for defending me." The familiar buzz of electricity hummed in my blood as our fingers brushed as I accepted the cup from him and drank deeply.

"Rest?"

"Yeah, and Anza?"

"Yeah?"

"She doesn't burn, at least not yet."

"Do you have something in mind?"

"I do, but I have to work out some kinks. I'll let you know when I have more to work with."

"Alright, and for now?"

"For now, we fight for our world and our family. We keep living to fight another day,"

"I love you," he said, kissing my temple and settling in behind me.

"I love you too," I said before sighing and trying to get back to sleep, but as the night stretched on, I kept looking at that tent flap.

Anza, my father, and Zerah had technically committed treason. I couldn't help but lie awake, waiting for Saha and the rest of her army to march in here. It wasn't until the morning light brushed the canvas walls a soft shade of orange that I entertained the idea that their transgressions might be tolerated.

As morning crept in, I clung a little tighter to Anza while the sound of movement began outside.

"Something, something fight the sun?" Anza said, kissing my head.

"Yeah," I grumbled sleepily, and he kissed me gently.

"Get up slowly?"

"Can't we just lay here?"

"That's not going to stop your uncle," he said, but let me sit up slowly, not rushing me at all as I gathered my shoes, knowing the minute we left the tent we would be swept up in the preparation of moving on toward Legalia. It was only another moment, another breath, before I nodded and Anza helped me up.

While Whisper fixed my brace, tucking into the outside of the tent to do so, Anza helped me get dressed.

"Alright," I said as I finished dressing, Anza helping me stay upright as Whisper brought the fixed brace in.

Carefully, I slid it on and Anza took my hand, lifting it to kiss my knuckles before he led me out of the tent.

Abry spotted me almost immediately, rushing over to hug me tightly.

"Hey, kiddo."

"I'm really happy you're okay."

"I'm happy you're okay too," I said, hugging him back tightly. Graz kept his distance, but tried to approach thrice, only for Saha to scold him from afar. I couldn't hear what she said.

It didn't take long until we were ready to go, Zerah and Baden sticking close to Anza and me as Saha approached. Zerah lowered her head, baring her teeth as Baden took a step forward. They barely knew me, but it seemed that they had decided they knew enough. Saha stopped, looking at me.

"Easy, guys. Let her through." She needed assurance that I wasn't going to kill her. Of course she was going to talk to me.

Want me close?

No. Ease back. If she threatens me, I'll let you know.

If she threatens you, it's the last thing she'll ever do.

I nodded, waving her forward, and she stepped close, closer than I wanted her, her voice but a whisper.

"Are you alright?"

"I'm good."

"I'm sorry I didn't send anyone after you. We didn't have time and—"

"It's fine." I cut her off, shaking my head. "I get it, it's fine." I forced a smile, trying to put her at ease, and she nodded, pursing her lips again.

"Are you sure you're alright?"

"Yeah, but we need to get going, right?" I asked and she nodded, looking me over as if trying to see if there was a crack in my façade. I wanted to punch her in the jaw, but I held back as she gave me a brisk nod before turning and heading back to the front of the slowly forming formation. She gave Graz a nod and he quickly came to me.

"She wouldn't let me see you sooner," he said as I hugged him, and I sighed.

"Yeah, I know. I get it, she didn't know if I was compromised," I said, feeling Anza start to calm down the bond. Graz wasn't a threat.

"She's not gonna let us ride close, but I can have Taryn near you. She wants us to spread out so we can better protect the sides of the formation."

"Well, she's going to have a rude awakening if she thinks they're going to listen to her now," I said, nodding to where my family was gathering. My parents, Tamaj's children, Abry, Anza, Whisper; even Sil hung back, closer to us.

"Yeah, I figured. I'll figure it out, but I have something for you," he said, digging into his bag. "I know it's not much, and it's no replacement but…well, the blade smith was able to get this together and…" He let the sentence fall off, passing me a cloth bundle.

I knew almost immediately what it was upon holding it. Slowly, I unraveled it to find a throwing axe. Well crafted, matching my own in style and form, elegant and untouched by battle. At its hilt, a small leather insert held a bone dagger, and at the handle, wrapped in the leather, a single beaded and feathered earring. I felt my throat go tight. He passed Whisper and Anza both a cloth bundle as well and they opened them to reveal bone daggers. "May she be with you, even in death."

"Thanks, Graz," I choked out.

I didn't need to ask who he crafted these weapons from. It was exceptionally clear. I had them both with me. I grabbed the handle tight, finding it fit snug in my grip. He took a steadying breath before moving to get into formation again. I moved to Baden's side wordlessly.

"Can we ride with you?"

"I wouldn't have it any other way," he replied as Anza, Whisper, and I climbed on his back, encouraging my parents to clamber onto Zerah with Abry.

It was then that I noticed the woven pieces of leather strapped against Baden and Zerah. Both of them had a band that passed over a shoulder tucked close to them, with a single bone bead and a leather holster for a bone dagger. Well within reach of whomever was on their back. They had their mother with them.

I looked over, spotting Emai's new dagger hanging from a thick necklace, which rested against her chest. My father's was tucked into a new sheath that sat beside his swords, and as I looked up, even Sil had one tucked into her belt. I took a breath. She was with us. She would always be with us.

We started moving forward, toward Legalia. The moment Olaf saw me he would know that Percy and Heartlock had tricked him.

I hoped they got out sooner rather than later as I glared daggers into the back of Saha's head.

29

"I cannot believe we're taking the Coward's Pass. This is such an easy route," Zerah said, shaking her head.

"I think, considering what everyone's been through, easy is the point," Baden retorted as his sister all but danced past us.

"Ugh. You don't get it, the desert can be such a beautiful place if you're not moping about in the tree line," Zerah grumbled, snorting as she tossed her head toward trees, which twisted upward, reminding me of Joshua trees from Earth.

"Personally, I think I've had enough sun, Dune Queen," I teased as she looked out at the sand dunes to our right, mere meters away.

"I second that," Anza said.

"Same," resounded up around us.

"Fine," she grumbled as we kept moving forward.

"What is so beautiful out there anyway? The anatomical make up of sand?" Baden asked, nudging his sister's flank.

"I will have you know that sand has a distinct anatomical make up that—"

"It's little rocks. So many little rocks."

"I'm gonna little rock your ass."

"That doesn't even make sense."

"Remind you of anyone?" my dad asked Emai, and she managed a small smile.

Whisper was hard at work on a piece of metal plating with carefully pressed sigils scattered across it. Twisting and turning, they wove into each other, building a large scale spell on the piece of metal. She had barely started, working from one corner, with sketches of sigils across the whole piece. She pressed different sections down, constructing something magical I couldn't pick out. All I knew was that it looked like it was sturdy, something to be used again and again, but it wasn't anywhere near done yet.

I didn't dare question her, keeping my eyes linked firmly on Saha. Sil had caught up with her and I wondered what they were talking about. I rubbed my finger over the leather on Tamaj's axe, taking a breath as we started through the pass, passing over a row of thick bricks buried in the path that marked the border between Biena and Legalia.

"Welcome to Legalia," my mother said as Abry tested his wings from where he sat.

I took a breath.

We had taken so many blows. Every single portal had been ripped to shreds because of Olaf. We had to stop him.

And while I was furious that Saha had even entertained the idea of leaving me, she was right in her own way. By trying to find me, they had wasted time they could have used chasing him down. It still didn't make trying to leave me right. She still uses us. All of us.

I looked back and forth as we started through Legalia's territory. The front lines of the war that had raged for decades between the two sand-bound kingdoms was something Saha had spoken of regularly, but I didn't see a single troop. Not one person. Even in this heat, I would have expected to see a patrol, but there was nothing. A single building rose up in the distance, the only sign of life for as far as the eye could see.

We kept going and I heard Baden snort, shaking his head as he lifted it to the air.

"Whatcha got?" I asked as Zerah lifted her head. Several other Barbarza turned their heads as well, lifting them to the hot wind.

"Blood."

I bit my lip and took a breath. It wasn't long before we climbed the next dune and saw where the scent of blood was coming from. The space between the dune we rested on and the next was littered with bodies, Korrewenian and Legalian alike. The only differentiations were their outfits and the symbols on their arms. I held Whisper as she leaned closer to get a better look, kicking her feet out as if wanting to be let down.

"We're not getting closer to the dead bodies."

"But—"

"No."

"They could have cool stuff on them…" she grumbled.

"I promise, whatever they have on them isn't cool enough to get sick over," I insisted.

"I know how to handle a dead body," she said, rolling her eyes, but we kept going without any further protest.

"I know troops were headed this way but, this is…so much worse than I thought," Baden said as we started to pick our way past them. I saw Sil break from Saha, making her way back to my side.

"Something seem wrong here?" she asked, almost as if she knew something I didn't.

"We're at war. Death is gonna happen, right?"

"Look at their wounds," Sil said without looking down. I felt my stomach twist, but I looked, and the first body I saw sent a shiver down my spine. A Maraung woman, clad in Korrewen's colors, with a single hole in her forehead.

"You don't think…"

She nodded

"And if that's the case…"

"What's wrong?" Anza asked, looking down at the bodies.

"Nothing we can be sure of yet," I said quickly, and Sil gave me a stern look. "We shouldn't jump to conclusions. We don't know, but it's better to be safe than sorry," I said, and she nodded before going to Saha's side, likely to fill her in.

"Mira," Anza warned, his hands sliding onto my hips. "Please tell me."

It wasn't that I thought he couldn't handle it, Anza could handle anything. I hesitated because I was afraid that Sil was right, afraid of what it might mean for all of us.

"She thinks it's a gunshot wound."

"I don't know what that is," he said gently, encouraging me to continue.

"You know how we fight with swords and daggers and tactics and trebuchets and carts and strategy?"

"Right…"

"A gun is another tool, a means to an end, and a gunshot wound would mean someone capable of shooting—with deadly accuracy—is here. A gun is…devastation, faster than you can blink, its a device that makes me sending a rock through a brain look like child's play." He nodded slowly as I tried to convey the depth of what we just found ourselves in. "It's something from Earth, something no one here would ever be prepared for. If someone has any kind of gun, depending on the situation…"

"They can kill en masse from afar?"

"Like a much faster, more accurate, smaller arrow, and depending on the type of gun, they might be able to decimate battalions without so much as a blink," I said quietly. "And this" —I gestured out over the battlefield of corpses—"looks like the aftermath of a group of people with a lot of guns."

"That is…horrifying," he said as Whisper leaned back against us. I held her closer.

"Are they gonna use their guns against us?" she asked quietly.

"I don't know, but I need something thicker than sand if I'm gonna protect us."

"I might have an idea." Abry's voice was soft, quiet, and though he had clearly been gaining more confidence, he seemed more reserved at the proposition.

"What do you have in mind?"

"Well, deep down under the sand there might be bigger rocks, maybe."

"Probably. The problem is reaching them. I've never reached that far down before. I've reached down, sure, but there's a lot of sand here. It's all I can feel."

"I think if you give it a try, and keep trying, maybe you can reach it," he said, not meeting my eyes.

"I think it's worth a try," I agreed.

"Really?" he asked, as if unsure I would listen to him.

"Yeah, I'll give it a whirl here sometime."

"Really, really?"

"Yeah. If you've got theories to help me find the limit to my powers, I'll listen all damn day."

"Told you," Whisper almost sang as Abry's eyes lit up.

"Really?" he said happily.

"Really, really, kiddo. Any other ideas you're hiding in that big brain?" I asked.

"I have a few theories about another Endering but…I don't think she'd really be open to it."

"Sil?" There was no doubt in my mind.

"Yeah."

"Sil can be…snippy and temperamental. If you want to try, you can, but don't expect a positive response."

"It's just that Em says her downside is a lack of control but—"

"Abry, I know you have faith in others, but some people just want to burn," Brian said, my mother nodding her agreement.

"Finish your thought," Anza gently encouraged, and Abry sighed.

"I just…I can't believe that an Endering's power is outside of their scope of control. Why would they have it to begin with?" he pondered, looking up to where Sil was.

"Any ideas to what her downside might be if it's not that?" I asked, and he shook his head, eyes still locked on Sil.

"It makes her angry and sad. Though, there's more, I just know it."

"One miracle at a time," I said, reaching over to pat his shoulder as the group started picking up the pace.

30

"How far off is Legalia?" I asked.

"We should be there by morning, so long as the sands sway in our favor," Saha explained, and I nodded before falling back toward the rest of the group.

"The sands are a lot like the sea. They do what they want," Zerah said, snorting as she padded back.

"Yeah, we'll see how it goes."

"How can you be so relaxed talking to her? She would have left you if not for Anza."

"I'm not. Right now, she and I just have the same goal: keeping the worlds from falling apart. When that changes, well, that changes," I said before we stepped into earshot of the others.

I didn't need to be empathic to see the rising fur on her neck or hear her snort. Did she know Saha before this? Or had she just met a queen who had decided an Endering was worth nothing more than fodder? Either way, Zerah was not happy with her. I rubbed at her neck and the fur at her nape started to lay a little flatter, her irritation calming a little as we got back to the group.

"We're about to head out, are you ready?" I asked, and Anza nodded, pulling from a conversation he was having with Abry and Whisper. He helped Whisper onto Zerah's back with me before climbing up himself.

Her frame wasn't as stocky as Baden's, but Brian and Baden were locked in a conversation and I didn't mind switching. Honestly, I was just thankful they were letting us ride on their backs at all.

Together, we started forward, Zerah just one step ahead of Baden as we kept close.

I felt rage bubble up as Sil settled her pace beside Saha and started talking with her. The back and forth was heated, but not uncivil. I stayed close to my parents, Whisper leaning back to pass Anza something.

"This work?" she asked as I caught a glimpse of the piece of metal plating she'd been fiddling with for days now.

"What's that?" I asked.

"Just a little something we're working on with Abry," Anza said as he quickly tried to smother the panic down the bond.

"Oh, are you seriously not going to tell me?"

"It's a surprise," Whisper said firmly as Anza passed the plating back.

"It's perfect."

"Great."

"Better be a hell of a surprise," I said, casting Anza a look.

"It's nothing bad, I promise," he said, wrapping his arms around my waist. I leaned back against him.

"I can't wait to find out..." I said, trying to get it out of him, but Anza smirked and shook his head.

"Nice try. We're not saying anything," Abry pipped up, smirking from his spot on Baden's back.

"You little shit."

"In the flesh," he said, Emai and Brian holding back laughter as Zerah picked up the pace and put some distance between us.

"Why did you do that?" I laughed.

"There was too much audacity in one spot," she said, and I couldn't help but laugh as she carefully placed us closer to Graz

and Taryn, but just as we settled, I felt her tense, her head snapping around to look out at the night-dusted dunes.

"Something wrong?" I asked.

"I'm not sure," she said, and I went quiet, scanning the sands for something, anything that might be a danger. "I smell something" I turned, looking back to find almost every Barbarza lifting their nose to the wind.

"What is it?" I asked, scanning the dunes to try to find any whiff of a scent.

"Blood again."

I swallowed hard, Anza shifting slightly behind me as he tore his eyes across the landscape.

On edge, we pushed forward.

It wasn't long before Saha slowly signaled for us to stop. Zerah padded forward, bringing me to her side, and I felt a pit of ice well in my stomach as I looked down the sand dune.

Blood soaked the sand, staining it a deep, dark red, but there were no bodies. Not even a finger. I felt my stomach twist as I tried to imagine how many bodies it must have taken to cause this. A half dozen? More? What had done this? Where had they gone? Slowly, Sil came to my side atop her assigned Barbarza mount.

"I can't even find a scrap of clothing," I said as she settled beside me.

"Me either."

"Should we go down there?"

"Probably not," she said, but Zerah started forward anyway, pressing her nose close to the sand as she wove with carefully placed steps over the sand.

"Smell anything besides blood?" I asked and she snorted.

"There is something down there, something…oh no," Zerah said, starting to back pedal toward the group.

"What? What is it?"

"We need to mo—" Sil started, but stopped as a rumbling rattled below us and Zerah tensed.

"Scatter!" she shrieked just before sand erupted from below us, a large sand shark-like creature leaping up from directly below us. I saw sand scatter and clung to Whisper as she was almost thrown from Zerah's back as the Barbarza twisted in the air to right herself with just enough time to see we were airborne, thrown up, heading down into the jaws of a massive creature not unlike the one I had met alone in the desert. We were sand shark chow.

"Zerah!" I screamed as we descended, and she stretched her reach, landing her powerful haunches onto the creatures top lip, twisting her body as it tried to crunch us, narrowly missing us as Zerah pushed off, twisting her body away from it to land hard into the sand, her legs nearly collapsing beneath her.

I turned, taking one of my bracelets and throwing it firmly into the creature's brain, just as I had when I was alone in the desert, knowing that it would kill it. I watched as it shuddered, groaning before it collapsed onto the ground. Silence hung for a moment before I heard the screams rise up.

"Graz!"

"Brian!"

"Where's Baden?" Zerah panted, and I tore my eyes over the group. My mother was digging frantically at a pooling spot of sand, a few Barbarza moving to help her, and Sil was trying to help Saha and Taryn do the same at a different spot.

"Mom?!"

"Your dad and Baden got pulled in!" Emai said as Zerah immediately started to rush to her. I felt the panic rise as another voice pierced the air, desperate for salvation, for their partners and comrades to be saved. The buzzy, blurry desert lost at my finger tips as I slid from Zerah's back, I felt like I was in a fog.

My dad was under the sand, probably suffocating slowly, along Baden and Graz and what had to be at least a dozen other soldiers from our company and dozens of bodies from whatever had come before us.

I couldn't save them.

I felt the softest hand touch mine and turned to see Abry, as calm and unmovable as stone.

"Come on, you can do this."

"How?"

"On your knees, hands in the sand as deep as they can go."

I could do that. That was easy.

Carefully, he sat down with me as I shoved my hands deep into the cool and crisp sand. I could feel them struggling to move, struggling to breathe, as if just out of reach.

"Now what?"

"Where does your power come from?"

"What?"

"Where?!" he said, his dark eyes still locked on mine. "Focus on where."

I hadn't thought about it before, but I felt the humming symphony deep in my chest, tucked in the space just below my sternum. I focused on it and took a few deep breaths.

"Good. Now, relax."

I tried relaxing a little and felt my power slip outward, out and out around me. The more I relaxed the farther it went, reaching down until I found them. I could feel their slowing heartbeats as they scrambled to dig upward. Carefully, I solidified the sand beneath them.

"Slowly, so you don't bury anyone else," Abry prompted, and I carefully lifted them.

Cries of relief rang into the cool, twilight air as people started poking up out of the sand, the living rising with the dead the creature had left for later in the sand.

"You scared the shit out of me, Brian."

"Sorry, Lovey," I heard dad choke out.

"Can you breathe?"

"Are you alright?"

"Here, water."

"I swear to the stars, Baden, if you die on me I'm gonna bring you back to life so I can kill you my damn self!" Zerah snarled as I

watched her shove her brother. The shove quickly turned into a hug.

"I'll keep that in mind," Baden sighed, rolling his eyes.

"I'm fine, Mom," I heard Graz groan as Saha carefully checked his arms and legs for scratches.

"It's alright, Your Majesty, he's okay," Taryn said gently, trying to calm her.

"It's Saha to you," Saha said back, finally giving in. "Alright, alright, so long as you're sure you're alright."

"I'm okay."

I looked to where Anza and Whisper now stood, Anza hugging her tightly and rubbing her back as she hugged him, scared and shaking still.

"It's alright, Mom has them. They're alright."

"Good job," Abry said as I turned back to him, sliding my hands from the sand.

"How did you know how to do that?"

"It's something I'm working on. I think people hold their power in different places, and that if we learn to tap into those little wells of power, we can do way cooler things."

"Like make a mountain sing?"

"Sure, why not? We should all be able to see the scope of our own power, to control it and direct it. It's *our* power after all."

"But...how did you think of that? Like, I know Whisper said you were smart, but damn."

"Oh, it came to me when I was falling off that roof. My power sits along my shoulders, across my wings, and down my back, it's how I knew how to fly."

I couldn't help but hold that gaze, the gaze of both a young teen and an old man; eternal and wise and beyond comprehension. Then I blinked and he was standing up, rushing off to hug Whisper.

The rarest feeling settled on my shoulders, looking back at them as Anza welcomed him into the hug, and I couldn't help but smirk. I had to stop meeting the most astonishing people at knife point.

I pulled myself up onto my feet, hugging my family tightly before moving to my parents, who were still locked in an embrace. Zerah rested her head on her brother's as he panted, catching his breath.

I had saved them.

No, I didn't save them. I couldn't save them. Abry did. His knowledge did. His theory did. Him having faith in his own intellect saved them, I was just necessary to enact the plan.

"Hey, you can be in awe of him later?" Anza said quietly as we all started to collect ourselves and head back out over the dunes, leaving the bodies and near suffocation behind in the sand, Abry sitting happily with my parents as he tested his wings. I kept Whisper tucked against me and sighed.

"It almost feels like he is ethereal."

"I know," Anza said gently.

"It's how he knew how to fly…he just…knew."

"I keep telling you, he's amazing, and I know you have a bad habit of listening to me, but I need you to listen to me again," Whispers started. "That kid is going places."

"Yes, yes I think he is."

31

I clung to Anza for as long as the evening allowed after we woke, running my fingers through his hair and cherishing the way he still, even out here, smelled of the woods. I didn't want to get up, didn't want to go out and face what was likely the last few days that we had to change the world, but Olaf wouldn't stop, not on his own, and there was no one else to stop him.

Eventually, Taryn came to the door of our tent, but didn't open it, lingering outside.

"You two are going to have to get up eventually," she said, and Anza groaned, rolling over on top of me.

"Nooo!" he said dramatically, his voice muffled by the pillow. I couldn't help but laugh.

"We'll be out in a minute," I called to Taryn.

"You better," she said before I heard her step away.

"You don't want to get up either?" I asked Anza, and he wrapped his hands around me tightly.

"No, but we have to, don't we?"

"Kind of" I said, running my fingers through his hair again as he sighed.

"Alright, if you insist." We kissed, once, twice, then thrice before he got up and helped me to my feet.

We dressed quickly and slipped out of our tent to take it down, only for Zerah to nod to her back, hurrying us up. Whisper was already settled in the saddle.

"You two have a long night?" Whisper asked, raising an eyebrow.

"I don't know what you're talking about," I said, trying to ignore the fact that my face had just gone completely red.

"Riiiight," she said, rolling her eyes as we settled in the saddle as well.

"Let them be," Zerah said before trotting quickly to our place in the formation.

Anza just rested his hands against my hips, leaning his head on my shoulder for a moment before kissing the crook of my neck. He had missed me just as much as I had missed him. We couldn't fall. Not the two of us. The thought of life without Anza was sickening, a devastation I didn't even want to begin to fathom, one I had almost had to face several times over and would doubtlessly be called to face if Olaf succeeded. I tried not to think about it.

It wasn't long before Zerah lifted her head to the wind again.

"What is it?"

"More blood," she said, the other Barbarza getting antsy as we approached what must have been the source. We crested another hill to find a sea of bodies, Zerah bringing me up beside Sil again.

"See any gunshot wounds?" I asked, but she was already shaking her head.

"These are good old fashioned Otherworld warfare tactics at play," she said quietly and I nodded, trying not to feel too relieved. The blood-soaked sand was still unnerving, but at least we were safe from gunfire.

Though, as I started counting bodies, it became clear Legalia had not prepared for this confrontation. The Bienan Photomyran soldier that looked akin to a cactus hadn't made it to warn them in time.

"Movement," Saha said, and I turned to follow her gaze, spotting a trembling of faint light not far off. My panic only lasted a moment before a familiar voice rang out, making me cringe a little.

"You really are a sight for sore eyes." All at once, the trick of the light, what must have been a display of his power, dropped, and the dark-haired Chinese man, an Endering of Eynon who had flirted with me relentlessly, stood surrounded by six of his own soldiers only a dozen or so yards away. "We were hoping you'd show up."

"Buffer..." I greeted through nearly bared teeth.

"Mira, was it?"

I could feel Anza seething down the bond and reached over to rest a hand on his leg.

Easy.

I hate him, Anza countered.

Noted.

"It's a pleasure to see you again, Buffer," Saha said, drawing his attention away from the simmering tension radiating off Anzo and placing it squarely on the queen.

"I apologise, Your Majesty, your Endering was so radiant I confused her for the sun itself, and I am quite prone to sunstroke," he said, leaving my face a deep red as he bowed. Saha stifled a laugh.

"Charming as ever. What are you doing here?"

"Well, it looks like your friend is working his way through the other kingdoms, so we were sent to try to put a stop to him here," he said.

"Before he could cross the sea to Eynon."

"Perceptive as ever. I'm out here doing recon, looking for your butts—" Saha smothered a smirk as he suddenly seemed to realize he had just said that to another kingdom's ruler.

"Are you able to lead us to Legalia's castle safely?"

"I am. That bird you sent was a welcome warning, but a little too late, unfortunately. We've been expecting you since."

"How is it looking?" Saha asked as she reached a hand out, offering him a ride. He accepted it, grasping her hand at the wrist as she pulled him onto her Barbarza. It was only a moment before the soldiers he was with were also settled more comfortably in either wagons or riding with others.

"About as well as it could be. We've managed to hold the line until now, but it hasn't exactly been easy," he said before pointing us toward Legalia's castle. "Their Endering is pretty reluctant to do much, skittish too, but he means well."

"Didn't they have two Endering?" Saha asked and Buffer nodded.

"Only one now."

"Any chance you know what happened?"

"Unfortunately, Your Majesty, I have a bad habit of keeping my head attached to my body, so I do not."

I knew what happened. One got away. A russet-haired, ill-tempered beauty. But I was the only one who knew. I kept my mouth shut, but felt Anza's mind nudge mine. I shook my head slightly and leaned back against him.

It doesn't matter, I'll tell you later, I said down the bond and he nodded as we started over the next few hills.

It was only a matter of minutes before we crested a hill to see the towering castle in the distance. Built of heavy limestone, it soared into the air with dozens of towers and buttresses. I could see dozens of spots where shadow and stone twisted artistically, but couldn't make out the exact design from this angle.

The most notable thing was the sound. I was almost completely sure no one else could hear it, but it was a melody that spoke to my very soul.

Stone sings, it has since my power came to fruition, but that particular limestone was so old that I could hear the ancient hum from its base. There was much more to this castle than what met the eye.

Before it was the all-too-familiar sprawl of a bloodbath, led by a striking red banner.

I took a breath.

Legalia had been holding their own against the invading forces for long enough that they *had* to have made a dent by now. Between our army and the Eynon battalions that had presumably been sent along with their Endering, an unfamiliar feeling vaguely reminding me of hope blossomed in my chest.

We could win this.

We had to win this.

32

"Whisper," Saha called, and Zerah trotted forward.

I tried to ignore the tension in my throat as we got to her side. What could Saha want with my daughter at a time like this?

"Yes?" Whisper asked.

"In the last few battles, I've ignored your opinion on the grounds of my experience superseding anything you could possibly know. I was wrong to do that, and would greatly appreciate your input," she said, and I couldn't help the shock in me as Sil gave the smallest smile and nod from her place just out of Saha's line of sight. What had they talked about when I hadn't been right there?

"Oh..." Whisper started. "Well, right now they're distracted. If we could get a better view of the entire battlefield, we could better prepare."

"On it," Abry said.

"Hey, no," Brian said, my mother shaking her head.

"Do you have a better idea?" Abry asked, raising his eyebrows, and I sighed, knowing they were about to lose this battle.

"There has to be a better way. You aren't exactly well-practiced in flight yet."

"I can go up and adjust direction, it's just down that's the hard part."

"If you don't want to break your legs, down is the important part," Emai said.

"Anza had a method to help him land, we could do that again, and so long as he flies above the height an arrow can strike, it should be fine," Whisper argued.

My parents both looked nervous, but it was my dad who finally spoke.

"We could send Rivet with him, have him come back if he gets hurt?"

"Alright," my mother said before helping Abry down. They took turns hugging him as I climbed to the ground, Whisper slipping down after me.

"Fly high. It's going to be cold as fuck up there. If arrows get close—"

"Climb. I can do this," he said as they hugged.

"I know you can, Sunshine, just don't come in too hot when you're landing."

"Yeah, yeah," he said, beaming at the new nickname before turning to me. "Can I get a boost?"

"Thought you'd never ask, just hang tight," I said and he nodded before I carefully pulled a pillar of earth straight up from beneath him, going slowly so I didn't scare him. I had to dig deep to get high enough but he gave me a wave when I should stop and I stopped.

"Thats perfect!" He said, his smile reaching his eyes.

Saha shifted nervously and I quietly prayed to whatever might be listening for his safety as he reached the top. I saw him take a breath and look to the sky for a moment before throwing himself off. Like a sliver of the night sky, he ascended until he was but a speck in the distance.

"He better be okay," Emai said quietly.

"Do you doubt that I can lay and disarm traps?" Whisper asked.

"No."

"Or that Mira can move the stones and dirt?"

"Of course not."

"Then please, don't doubt Abry. He's got this."

"I don't doubt that he's got this," she said quietly.

"Then what is all this uncertainty?" Whisper prodded.

"Care," I said quietly. "It's the same worry I get when you slip out of sight. It's not that I doubt you, it's that I worry for you." Whisper turned to look up at me, an understanding smile on her face. "If I don't know where you are or if something's about to go wrong, I panic. We're a long way from him right now, which means he's a long way from help if something happens." I turned my eyes back to Abry, watching like a hawk as he surveyed the battleground.

"He better be okay," Whisper said, her hand finding mine. I squeezed her hand tightly, hoping to comfort her as we watched him.

It took time for him to carefully circle the battlefield. Twice, thin lines posted up, arrows trying to shoot him down, but they fell short. I finally exhaled when I noticed his form begin to grow larger as he made his way back toward us.

"He's coming back," Anza said, moving to a more open spot to help him land. I expected something to go wrong, anything, a stray arrow or a rift in the air or some bullshit, but Abry carefully drifted down to Anza, who helped him land just as he had done before.

"We really need to get you some landing gear," Whisper said.

"You have something in mind?" Abry asked, teeth chattering as he spread his wings, letting the heat of the sun-baked sand warm him.

"Maybe," Whisper said as Abry folded his wings.

"The battlefield is pretty thick on the right hand side, but the left and center are thin."

"Could we easily make a push for the castle walls, or at least get to Prince Quaren?" Whisper asked and Abry nodded.

"It looks like we could."

"Excellent, thank you Abronoma," Saha praised, smiling.

"Abry," he corrected, clearly preferring the nickname.

"Or Sunshine," I heard Baden whisper, smirking slightly, only for Abry to playfully glare at the Barbarza.

"We should split up into three teams and attack at different spots in the line, especially if we want to get to price Quaren. Where should we be aiming?" Whisper asked, looking to Buffer.

"Easy, just look for the purple flag," he said, pointing to a small purple flag tucked against a building. Directly in the thick of the fighting.

"That's not the weakest spot," Abry grumbled and Whisper nodded.

"I know, but we aren't all going to one spot. We have to split up to be most effective, and one thing we need to do is establish contact with Quaren," Whisper explained "Most of us head for the weak spot. Mom?"

"You want me to go to Quaren?" I asked, nodding already.

"You can clear a path more efficiently than anyone I know," she said.

"No worries, Moonbeam. I've got this."

"You'll have to lead Buffer there," Saha said.

Alright, maybe I didn't have this.

"Whats wrong, scared to be alone with me?" Buffer purred.

"She won't be alone with you," Anza nearly snarled, reaching for his necklace. I reached for mine as well and a flash of realization flitted through Buffer's eyes.

"Oh shit, my bad," he said, holding both hands up.

Easy…

I hate him so much.

He'll probably back down now, I said , trying to ease the tension as we started to organize to prepare for Whisper's plan. It was only another few moments before Zerah snorted, Buffer on his own Barbarza at our side.

"You two stay out of sight," I instructed, turning to look at Whisper and Abry.

When have they ever done what we asked? Anza said.

Never, but I can try.

"No promises," Whisper quipped as Abry nodded.

I rolled my eyes as I heard Saha yell, "Forward!"

We leapt forth, Zerah aiming for the thickest part of the fighting, not too far from Eynon's purple flag. I knew that Saha and the others would rush toward the weak spot Abry had pointed out. They could do a lot of damage from that vantage point.

With a small jump and a flash of paws, we pressed our way firmly into the fray. Anza kept her left flank clear as I focused on her right, lashing out with my axe as a Korrewenian soldier tried to lunge at us, catching them in the shoulder and sending them to the ground. We left them there to be trampled as Zerah pushed forward and I reached back, pulling a wall up from behind us. I had to cut a path, break up the thick of the fighting while the others attacked at the weak point. We could divide and conquer.

When a Barbarza from Korrewen approached on the left, I threw up the wall between us and them, keeping them from getting to us as we moved forward. It was only a moment later that I felt something slam into us from the right, though. I turned as Zeraah reared back on her hind legs, a far-too-vulnerable position, just to see a larger Barbarza close its teeth around her throat. Anza drove his sword into their shoulder but that didn't stop the strangled noise that came from Zerah. I tried to pivot, shifting my weight to lift my axe over Zerah, but as a voice roared through my mind, I knew I didn't need to.

"No one touches my sister!" Baden came from the left, closing his jaws around the throat of the Barbarza trying to kill Zerah. They released her, turning to try to take on Baden as he shoved them to the ground.

"Baden?!"

"Go!"

"But—"

"Go, Zer!" Zerah surged forward, leaving Baden to fight for the upper hand.

"I've got him, he'll be alright," Anza shouted, dropping from Zerah's back to the ground.

"Anza!"

"I'll be okay, keep going!" he called back, rushing toward Baden. I had to trust him, had to believe in him.

"They'll be okay," I said, trying to convince myself.

"They better be," Zerah said, continuing forward as I went back to protecting her flanks.

"He's a good brother. He's got your back," I said quietly.

"He's my only brother. We have to find them later, no matter what."

"We will," I said before slamming my axe into the head of another soldier.

The fighting thickened mere seconds later and I risked a glance back, seeing Buffer a few yards behind me, fighting with a soldier before a force, a shield bursting out from him, unseen to my eyes, threw them back into the fray.

I turned forward just in time for another soldier to leap from their Barbarza on a direct collision course with me. I turned, trying to land a blow as he crashed against me, shoving a knife cleanly into my chest. It grazed my ribs and I felt hot blood start to well at my lips as I tried to shove him off. Zerah sidestepped, trying to turn around to grab him, but he was out of reach. I reached for my side, trying to keep him from pulling the blade out, before a vine crept around his neck, and with a single, smooth motion, he was yanked away and thrown to the ground, left to die, suffocating as an Endering rushed forward.

Her features were similar to Buffer's and she didn't hesitate to clamber in an agile fashion to my side.

"Pull it out," she said as I caught my breath.

"If I pull it out before—"

She didn't hesitate to yank the knife out herself.

My lungs burned, my body shaking as shock started to set in.

She carefully pressed her fingers to the wound and drew a sigil. It was different than the healing sigil I was familiar with, but the same rushing feeling of stitching flesh came over me.

"Oh, thank fuck," I sighed as Zerah kept going.

"You're The Mountain?" she said, trying to stifle the softest giggle.

"I am, and you are?"

"They call me Ivy." The fact that she couldn't give her real name, just like Bats hadn't, just like Buffer hadn't, made me ache with anger, but I shoved it aside.

"Well, I'm really fucking grateful you just showed up. Can you help me get to Prince Quaren?" I asked.

"Considering my brother is taking his time? Sure," she said, casting a sly faux glare over her shoulder at Buffer.

"Hey! I am trying back here!"

"Try harder," she started before hurling what I assume was an insult in Mandarin at him.

I almost couldn't contain my laugh as he balked at her before she encouraged me to move more left, directing us toward the tent with the obnoxious purple flag. We pushed through the thick fighting as I cut down another enemy before seeing a large Barbarza rushing us.

"Oh, you've got to be kidding me," she snarled, trying to get more speed in an attempt to overwhelm him. Snapping jaws sounded as he nearly collided with us before I shoved a barrier up between Zerah and the enemy Barbarza, the twisting feeling of air—no, not air, power—rushed over me, making the hairs on my arm stand on end as Ivy reached out a hand, vines bounding up my wall before striking out at the unwitting Barbarza on the other side like thorn covered snakes. They stabbed and prodded as we swished past him, finally bounding the last few yards toward the tent Prince Quaren was in.

"Okay, that was cool," Buffer said as Ivy and I dismounted.

"Yeah, yeah, I know," Ivy said, flipping her hair as she adjusted her glasses.

I bit my lip, pulling my eyes from her to turn my attention to the tent before taking a breath and starting toward it. I stepped in, pushing the flap of the tent to one side to find five men in the room, the prince in the center.

It wasn't until then that I realized I was in a makeshift room with five men I didn't know, and the only thing I had going for me were two other Endering, who I also didn't really know, and Zerah, whom I had just left outside.

Prince Quaren looked up, flanked on two sides by advisors and guards.

"You're a bold one, aren't you? Barging in here without announcing yourself."

"S-sorry," I started before I felt Ivy step up to my side.

"Apologies for the intrusion, My Liege. The Mountain of Agrenon comes to our aid."

I couldn't take my eyes off those cold blue depths as he weighed his options.

"Is this true?" he asked me and I nodded. "I'm going to let you try that again, and this time, remember your manners."

I could kill him on the spot, deader than dead, but he was a prince, a crowned prince, and the backlash that would ensue would be catastrophic. He wasn't used to dealing with Endering that were allowed to do a majority of what they pleased. He could not fathom having an Endering who might not adhere perfectly to what he considered to be manners.

Manners. Ugh.

"My apologies, Your Highness," I started, giving a bow before speaking again. "Agrenon is here attacking the enemy at its weakest point on the battlefield. I have been sent to ensure their safe passage and to inform you of their arrival so you can adequately adjust for the moving temperament of the battlefield."

"Really?"

"Yes."

He pulled away from the table, his advisors and guards moving away from him as he strode over to look me in my eye. I could feel his foot come down, almost casually on mine, and I tried to step back, but he pressed down, pain lancing through my foot as he held me in place. I bit my tongue as he leaned in, his breath hot on my ear.

"Remind me to talk to Saha about your manners." I nodded, hearing my heartbeat in my ears before he stepped back, letting me go. "An attack at the weakest point in the battlefield may very well break the enemy line, a very welcome assist," he said as he turned his back on me, a clear dismissal.

I felt Buffer grab my wrist as he pulled me quickly from the tent.

I waited for them to lead me away before I spoke.

"What's his deal?"

"He…dosen't take kindly to how your queen handles her Endering."

"I don't take kindly to how he's a raging cunt," I grumbled, stretching my toes as we walked.

"Oh, I like her," Ivy said quietly as we slowly came to a stop.

I sighed, feeling Zerah come to my side as I looked out over the fighting.

"See Baden yet?" I asked, and she shook her head, but just as she stilled, the familiar Barbarza stumbled out of the fray, a little bloodied, bitten and scraped, but intact.

"You absolute asshole, making me worry like that!" she snapped.

"Oh yes, thank you so much for saving my ass, Baden. You are so very welcome, sister of mine."

I tried to shove their banter out of my mind and focus on where Saha and the rest of the army were making their way through the enemy soldiers toward the path I had cut with my stone wall. Several battalions were attacking at different points, but our strongest attack was on the weak point in the enemy line. We were gaining ground.

Now I just had to keep people off the walls.

"That was smooth as fuck," Buffer said.

"Fuck isn't smooth," Ivy retorted, and in that moment, I wondered how I had gotten paired with not one, but two pairs of bickering siblings.

"It is if you do it right."

"You're disgusting."

"Can I get some help here?" I said over my shoulder.

"Yeah, Buffer," Ivy said before reaching out, thick brambles racing down the top of the wall as Buffer rolled his eyes.

"Leave a path on the top so I can block them," he said.

"Already on it." I pulled out some stairs on our side and he climbed.

"*What can we do?*" Baden asked.

"You can go to the medical tent," I said, pointing at the tent beyond Prince Quaren's.

"*But—*"

"*No buts.*"

"*Hah, you said butt.*"

"*What are you, three?*"

"*I know you are but what am I?*"

"*A reckless pain in my—*"

I climbed the stairs, knowing Zerah wouldn't let Baden jump back into the fray. Fully balanced on the flat top I had made for Buffer, I watched him shove away those that would try to conquer the wall I had made. Looking past him, I could see the others rushing forward, coming to our aid.

I turned my attention downward, feeling someone's fingers touch the top of the wall. I threw a stone out, slamming it into the soldier, but not before he grabbed the end of my pants. We fell together, my hands reaching out for some sort of hold before crashing to the ground. My heart leapt into my throat as I looked up into the face of a lunging Barbarza.

I was on the wrong side of the wall.

33

"Get back here!" I twisted away, the Barbarza crashing against the wall at my back as I bolted. I heard its jaws snap behind me as it rushed after me. I would never be able to outrun it, even if my leg was in top shape, so I turned and tried to pull some stone up in time, but I was too late. A paw hit my shoulder and my head slammed back against the ground as he lunged toward my throat.

I didn't even register the child-like laughter until after I saw the Hazzal clamping its jaws around the Barbarza's throat, fear rushing through me at the sound. If it had been a fraction of a second later I would be dead. Another rushed out of the fray, and in a flurry of movement, three more rushed to overwhelm the Barbarza. I tried to scramble backwards, unable to get my footing for a moment, before a hand touched my shoulder, gently, softly. As I turned to look up, I felt relief wash over me as I met Nadder's slightly sunken-in gaze. He snatched back his hand a little before offering it again, almost as if he were forcing himself to do so.

"You're a sight for sore eyes," I said, reaching for his hand.

He helped me up, letting my hand go very quickly before sighing. "Believe me, lass, the feeling's mutual."

The Hazzal returned to his side.

"Your power?" I asked, gesturing to the Hazzal as he waved them away. They individually split, bolting to new targets.

"Yeah. Let's get you back over the wall?"

"That sounds great."

Nadder led me along the side of the wall and we carefully bashed and slashed our way through those that tried to stop us until the fighting thinned a little. I slid between him and the wall as he pulled his Hazzal into a loose formation around us, keeping himself between me and the wall. I opened it up just in time to see Anza get to the new opening.

"Anza!"

"There you are!" he said, rushing to hug me tightly.

"How'd you get inside the wall?"

"I saw it forming and knew it was you," he said as Nadder backed into the safer space. I closed the wall behind him, trapping the fighting outside of the wall.

"A barrier like this, around the enemy's line..." Nadder said quietly

"Yeah, I know. Priceless," I said, nodding as I pulled back from Anza, who kept his hand in mine.

I turned, looking for Saha and the others, watching them rush past, hurrying to back up the raging cunt that was the Prince of Eynon.

It was then I heard a scream wrapped in a roar that shook the ground, familiar and resounding. The battlefield already felt hotter as Grio targeted the line Olaf's forces had set up for, leveling medical tents and trebuchets with a single breath as Sil watched out for archers, diverting him as many reached for their arrows. The wind tossed her hair as she expertly moved with the dragon's very form.

"What the fuck is that?" Nadder hissed.

"Oh, that's my grandma," I said as we looked up at Grio climbing up into the sky, Sil upon his back, shifting her weight to his every movement as if she was just an extension of him. Or maybe he was an extension of her.

She directed him away from the projectiles and toward a thicker part of the fray to break up. I didn't think Nadder could look paler than he was, but the color still drained from his face.

"Just remember, we're on your side," I said, patting his shoulder as Anza and I started to follow the wall back toward the Eynon tent.

I scanned the flood of soldiers, many of which were bent over on their knees, throwing up directly onto the ground, and found my fathers eyes. He jerked his head backwards and I turned to see Emai with Whisper and Abry closer to the rear, my mother scanning the crowd for danger as another group of Agregonian soldiers—medics, actually—set up our own medical tent.

The kids had listened to us for once and stayed out of it, though I noted Whisper was holding what looked like a small pad and paper. I remembered her talent with magic from the day I had met her and wondered what she was planning. Had my parents encouraged them to stay safe by their side?

Regardless, I felt Anza's hand along my hip and I relaxed as my dad made his way to our side.

"Where are Zerah and Baden?"

"The medical tent. Baden got pretty beat up on the way in," I said, and for a moment, I worried for Ivy and Buffer. I hadn't seen either of them in the fray. When had they slipped away? Were they alright?

"Alright, make your way there, Saha is going to convene with Prince Quaren and we're going to go from there," my dad said and I nodded, Nadder keeping behind Anza and me.

As my father headed to follow our queen, I turned to look at Nadder, whose eyes were steady on the ground.

"Hey, you should come with us," I said. "The bulk of the fighting should calm down now that Agrenon is here."

He nodded but didn't meet my eyes.

Carefully, Anza and I picked our way back toward the medical tent, occasionally looking back to ensure that Emai, Whisper, and Abry were still nearby. My mother likely the only reason our own medical tent wasn't being targeted. No one wanted to flirt with the personification of death itself.

Saha slipped down from a Barbarza as we neared the tent, the sound of slaughter raging on as she came to my side, blood splattered on her petals, a gash on her cheek. She didn't hesitate to meet my eyes.

"How did your initial meeting with Quaren go?"

"He called me rude and stomped on my foot," I said and her glance turned to a glare.

"Is that so?" I didn't get to answer before she turned, gesturing for me to follow her. I felt Anza's hand on my hip again, trying to settle the spike of fear.

I can handle it.

I'm not worried about you handling anything. Quaren on the other hand…

I didn't answer him, focusing instead on keeping up with Saha as she burst into Prince CuntWaffle's tent.

"Saha it's so good to see—"

"You harmed my Endering."

"She barged in here and—"

"So you don't deny it?" Saha slammed her hands on the table he was working on, causing him to flinch back. I settled my shoulders back, sticking near the door, and folded my hands behind me, wringing at my wrists and the bracelets upon them.

"No. She was being—"

"I hold my tongue when you treat *your* Endering badly because it is not my place, but I assure you, Quaren, I will not tolerate the mistreatment of *my* Endering."

"Saha, you have four Endering. They need to know their place."

"Five. Believe me, they do. The world is on the brink of ruin.

Do you think it is a good idea to infuriate an Endering who can, and would, bury you without so much as a second thought?"

"You wouldn't let that happen."

"*Let* is an interesting word, isn't it?" Saha said. Quaren stared at her, neither of them blinking for what felt like an eternity, but it had to have only been a few heartbeats. I bit my tongue, keeping my eyes locked on Prince Quaren.

It was he who looked away from Saha and to me.

Saha had five Endering to his two. Two of whom could kill or seriously sicken at a touch. One defending the injured, the other dropping enemies to their very knees with illnesses that may or may not kill them, one who settled on the back of a dragon for funsies, using her fire to cut sections into the enemy line from the very air, one who commanded the skies, the perfect scout, leading us to the one spot we could do the most damage, and myself. I had sat with singing mountains. Mountains that, in the right mindset, I had no doubt I could crumble.

Why were we listening to queens and kings? They were not gods and we were power incarnate.

Let.

Saha had said it was an interesting word. She may not *let* me, but she knew something Quaren clearly didn't until just now: it wasn't a matter of *letting* me. It was a matter of stopping me.

"My apologies, Mountain. I was…out of line."

"Apology…accepted," I said simply as he looked away. We had bigger problems. I could bury him later.

"You are very lucky she is merciful, lest you have another far more dangerous battle before you," Saha said firmly, and he nodded.

"I don't think either of us could survive that."

"That we can agree on," she said, her temper settling as she cast a look at me, checking to see if I was really alright. I nodded and she flicked her hand. I could go. If I wanted.

I turned, stepping out of the small tent, leaving them to strategize for the morning.

She had almost left me. She had *wanted* to leave me. Was that display one that she had crafted to regain my loyalty, or was she actually trying to make up for the wrongs she had done? She had leapt in front of Sil before I was taken. She did care for us. She had a kingdom to save, a world to save. One Endering couldn't get in her way. She did care for me, but it was more than that though. She feared my wrath.

That went well. It was comical to watch, at least. Are you alright? I asked down the bond.

Yes. Getting the little light beams settled.

I knew immediately he meant Whisper and Abry, the Moon and the Sun.

Good, and the front?

Has your mother, father, and grandmother. Rest, please rest, he said, and I couldn't help but sigh as I felt the weight roll off my shoulders. They were safe. All of them.

I turned my attention to the medical tent, heading quickly toward the entrance to peek inside, finding a medic tending Baden's wounds while Zerah waited, looking more irritated by her brother with each passing moment. I didn't interrupt, slipping away and toward a more centralized location where people were settling into tents and a campfire crackled. I felt a lump in my throat rise as I took in those tucked against the campfire's edge.

"There is the Goddess of Earth and Stone herself."

"Cut it out, Buffer," Ivy chastised as one of Nadder's Hazzal came up to nudge my hand. I felt the fear well up in my chest, but shoved it away and petted the good boy's head.

You okay?

Yeah, Nadder's power is…terrifying.

They're not giving you trouble, right?

I looked them over, Nadder gesturing toward an empty seat as he pulled his cloak tighter around his thin form.

No, I don't think they're going to cause me any problems at all. I might be a moment though, I want to talk to them.

I'm here if you need me. You're…not alone with that Buffer?

No, I'm not alone with Buffer, I said, almost rolling my eyes as I padded toward the campfire surrounded by other Endering.

"Hey," I said, stopping just short of the small campfire.

"The great Mountain graces us with her presence," Buffer said before gesturing to one of the open seats available. Nadder turned, glancing around to ensure we were alone before turning back to the group and pulling his cloak closer to himself again.

"You okay?" I asked, and he nodded.

"Just a lot of people," he said, his eyes locked on his feet.

"You can feel them, can't you, with your power?"

"Yeah."

"Sorry, that must be pretty overwhelming."

He nodded but still didn't meet my eyes.

"Don't worry too much about Nadder here, he's tougher than he looks," Buffer said.

Ivy slapped his leg in response. "Be nice."

"I am being nice."

"You're being a…" She hesitated, looking to me before saying something I didn't catch in Mandarin. Buffer balked at her.

"Am not!"

"Are too."

"The enemy is out *there*, guys," I joked as Abry stepped out of the shadows and settled down near me, and they laughed. Even Nadder cracked a smile.

"Do you think we can win this?" Nadder asked quietly, the question drawing the silence over us like a blanket. We had to win this.

"I don't know," I said honestly.

"Of course we can," Abry said, tilting his head. "There's something else bothering you, isn't there?"

Nadder didn't answer for a long moment, instead looking to Abry, surveying him, as if assessing how much of a threat he could be before he spoke.

"I knew someone…I thought I'd…see her," he started, his voice dropping so low the crackle of the fire almost drowned it out. "Someone…who got out. She made me a promise, but I don't know, they probably killed her," he said, eyes locked on the fire. It took a moment for me to recognise who he was talking about.

"I have a feeling she made it."

"I don't know."

"I do." He looked up, meeting my eyes. "I have a feeling she made it," I repeated a little more firmly, keeping my eyes locked with his as realization fluttered into them. I couldn't tell him in any certain way, there were too many ears.

He closed his eyes and sighed, a weight on his shoulders lifting as he buried his head in his hands.

"It's…so hard to get away from them sometimes," Ivy said quietly, keeping her voice low, as if afraid to be heard. "Sometimes, if your downside plays against you, they use it to keep you trapped."

"But it's not all bad," Buffer piped up. "And we have plenty of time to change it."

"Change it?" I asked.

"Buffer has this grand idea that he can change the whole world."

"Imagine it, a world where Endering can go where they please, do what they want."

"Shh. They'll hear you," Nadder hissed, quickly stealing a glance into the shadows. We all looked out carefully, searching for eyes in the dark, and found nothing.

"It could be amazing though. We could make the world a much better place. Go where we're needed and wanted. Go where we want to go."

"The Sky Fields of Agrenon," Nadder said quietly.

"The Mountains between Korrewen and Agrenon."

"I've heard Eynon's so vibrant and bright, with plenty of big buildings and trees to drop off," Abry said quietly.

"What about you, Mira? Where would you go if you could go anywhere in the whole world?" Buffer asked, and I took a breath and closed my eyes.

"There's a safe spot, hidden deep in the mountains of Agrenon, where even the trees are afraid to approach. There's a home there, a home full of warm comfort, bright and safe and tucked away from everything dangerous and fearsome. If I could go anywhere and stay, I'd go there." They fell quiet as I spoke about my parents' cabin, and when I opened my eyes, I saw Abry and Buffer both nodding.

"That sounds amazing," Abry said.

"Yeah, it really does," Buffer agreed.

"It is. And once we're done with this shit, I'm going to go there," I said.

"Wait, you're going to leave Agrenon?"

"Yeah. Aren't you guys going to go see the mountains? The Sky Fields?"

"We...can't. They don't let us," Nadder whispered, and I felt my heart plummet. Olaf wasn't just doing this for himself. For me. He was doing this for them. For every Endering hiding in Agrenon, disguised as a Photomyran like Flit. For every Endering that shies from touch like Nadder. For every Endering with stars in their eyes like Abry and Buffer. For every Endering too shy to stand for themselves like Ivy. For every Endering caught in an impossible-to-escape spot like Bats. For every Endering.

"Part of me just wants this guy to do his thing," Buffer said. "Maybe we'd finally get a chance to make a break for it."

"If he succeeds, it brings every aspect of this world to its knees though. Nothing will function well. Entire ecosystems are already collapsing," Abry said tentatively.

"And if he succeeds, then the people you care about, those who aren't Endering, they are at risk too."

"There aren't very many of those," Ivy said quietly. "But I don't think I like the idea of…letting so many innocents die. Not if we can stop it."

"I don't like fighting to uphold an oppressive regime," Buffer grumbled.

"Me either," Nadder said, pulling his blanket tighter.

"It's an impossible situation," Abry agreed.

"At this point, we have to work as if we're hurt. If you have a wound on your head and a wound on your foot, what do you take care of first?" I asked them.

"The head wound," Ivy said, Buffer, Abry, and Nadder nodding their agreement. I could see the small smile meet Abry's eyes. He knew the connection I was about to make.

"The worlds falling together is a head wound, not a foot wound. We can't work toward finding a path to freedom in this world if there isn't a world left."

"I hate that you're right," Ivy said.

"But you *are* right," Buffer said. "I'm gonna see it in my life-time though, a free world."

"I hope so," I said as he turned his face to the sky.

Slowly, each of us, even Nadder, looked up to those blazing stars above us. I wanted to tell Buffer he was right, that we could just let Olaf win, but if we didn't at least put up a fight, all the loss of life that came after would be just as much our fault as Olaf's.

That little seed in the back of my mind took a feeble breath. Buffer believes. Olaf believes. One day, I was going to see it. Endering at home in their own kingdoms. Abry deserved to be free, Nadder and Flit and Buffer and Ivy and Percy and Heartlock and Bats and the other Endering inside Biena and every Endering to come after them, they all deserved to be free to choose their own path. To take their names back.

I stared at the stars in silence with them for a long time before Nadder spoke.

"I'm...I'm gonna head to sleep."

"Hey, try to actually get some rest?" Buffer asked.

"I think I will tonight," Nadder said, flashing a look to me, the relief still in his eyes as he looked away before getting up and trudging quietly toward his own tent.

"We should probably turn in too, brother, before the prince notices we're gone."

"I'll just tell him I was flirting with Mira. He loves it when I flirt with women," Buffer said, shrugging as they got up together.

"Careful what you wish for, brother. I don't think the Mountain would appreciate it."

"Just tell him I'm stuck up and turned you down again," I said and Buffer lifted his hand, covering his heart and gasping as if he'd just been struck with an arrow.

"You pain me, beloved. Won't you return my devoti—" Ivy jabbed him in his side again before leading the way back toward their tents. "I'm coming, I'm coming," Buffer said, giving the rest of us a wave before heading off.

"If Anza was here, he'd be soooo jealous," Abry laughed.

"Yeah, that Buffer is pretty slick, isn't he?" I asked as we got up.

"He's a hopeless romantic, but at least he has spirit," Abry said as we walked together toward our tents.

"He has something, for sure. I don't know if it's spirit or just an extra dose of audacity, but the hopefulness thing is...nice."

"One of us has to be hopeful."

"Yeah, and I just don't have the strength for that right now," I said.

"Are you kidding me? You're one of the strongest people I know!" he said.

"Please, if I was so strong, we wouldn't be losing all the damn time."

"There you go again. Beating yourself up isn't going to help us win. And besides, winning wouldn't be winning if we didn't lose once in a while," he said as we got back to our tents. I watched as he ducked inside, quietly hoped he was right, and slipped into the tent to find Anza lying down already.

I tried to sneak into bed, moving the blankets carefully, only for him to roll over and pull me tight to him.

"There you are."

"Hey. Sorry, I didn't mean to wake you up."

"You didn't wake me, I was waiting for that Endering to try something."

"I don't think he will now."

"Me either, and he didn't seem like he was really trying to approach you. It felt like a façade."

"Then why'd you get so jealous?"

"I wasn't jealous." I almost laughed as he protested. "I wasn't," he insisted.

"You know that whole feeling thing does still go both ways," I reminded him, resting my hands on his, rubbing the back of his hand with my thumb.

"Okay, maybe I was a little jealous."

"You know I only have eyes for you, right?"

"Yes, and I would never doubt you, I just, I can't put my finger on it. I hate him."

"No reason?"

"Besides the hitting on you thing?"

"Yeah, besides that."

He thought for a long moment.

"He has a punchable face."

I shook my head, shifting as he moved slightly to the side so I could rest my cheek on his shoulder.

"Well, you're going to need to refrain from punching for the time being. Prince Quaren probably won't like a soldier of Agrenon beating the shit out of one of his Endering."

"Fine, but I don't have to like it," he said, kissing my cheek.

"I guess that's as good as I could hope for."

"Yeah it is," he said as I laughed, kissing my cheek again before we settled down beside each other, exhaustion settling in as we slid into sleep.

35

"Mom, get up!"

I jolted up at Whisper's voice, feeling my heart leap into my throat. The day hadn't fully broken yet, but I could already hear it; the heartbreaking roar rattling the camp. Anza started to get up beside me.

"What is it?"

"They attacked at first light."

"Where? The med tent? The castle gates?"

"Grio, they attacked Grio."

"Grio?" Why would they attack the dragon? He was liable to eat them. Then it hit me. They weren't attacking the dragon. Sil had used him just yesterday to cut through the enemy line. He was a tremendous threat. Killing a dragon was a suicidal attempt, but not killing him would lose them this war, and without him, they would ground his rider.

"Where's Sil?"

Whisper didn't give me an answer. She didn't need to. The crackling of fire was enough of a response. The beating of wings rose as, together, we tore out of the tent, watching the bloodied dragon rise, fire lashing out as Sil raced along the top of the wall toward him as arrows were loosed.

"Grio!" she shrieked, Saha leading a charge alongside my wall toward where Grio was struggling to rise into the sky. I couldn't see Graz, but Taryn bolted across the small space to me.

"He's here."

My blood rushed as cold as ice. He had tried to get to his mother before. Tried to kill Saha before. He was trying to separate them. The flower and her fire. He was baiting Sil and she was falling for it.

"What's the plan?" I asked Taryn, but she just looked at me, those wide eyes unsure of what step to take next. "Hey, where's Graz?"

"In with Prince Quaren, Saha didn't want him to—"

"Stay with him, keep him safe. You can do that, right?" I asked, but she was already nodding. She was a member of the Queen's Guard, protecting the royal family was second nature. She turned, rushing toward the tent as I started toward the wall, Anza and Whisper hot on my heels.

"For once, can you please just stay here?" Anza all but begged as I felt his worry spike. Sil wasn't someone to be played with, and though we had our differences, I could feel the threat in the air, like a tension that was about to break, like a glowing ember threatening to ignite, and I was worried for her.

"But—"

"Please."

I let them discuss, throwing up a set of stairs at the base of the wall and beginning to climb. After a moment, I looked back just long enough to see just Anza following me before turning my attention to the dragon, who was still trying to take off, only for him to crash back against the ground.

Hundreds of tendrils were scattered around his body, ropes and people en masse trying to hold him down. A small dark form wove between the ropes, dipping down toward Grio just long enough to pull arrows from him. I had no doubt it was Abry, but he was only one person, a child in the thick of smoke. How long could he last?

Surely, with the two of them it wouldn't be enough to keep him grounded right?

As I bolted along the wall, the rising light glistened red across his wings, the softest glow of light below him, light as dark and red as the light on his wings. I realized then that it was magic holding him down, not just the arrows and ropes. An Endering, likely The Siren or Olaf, had literally grounded him. He wasn't able to fly. Seeing Sil start to stagger to a stop at the edge of the wall, I reached out, throwing down stairs for her. She glanced back at me, meeting my eyes, her gaze frantic.

"Go!"

She flinched and whirled, rushing down the steps toward the badly injured dragon.

For a moment, I wondered where my parents were. My mother would be drained from healing wounds of this magnitude, but it was possible. I could do something with the healing sigils for sure, but we had to get him safe first. I had to get in range.

I reached out, feeling the depth and breadth of my power rushing toward him, knowing Anza was keeping me safe from behind. I slid past the last of the ramparts of the castle and something screamed in me to look to my left. As my eyes spared a glance at the small window there, I saw him, his dark tangle of curls and deep eyes. He went white and before I could take another step, I felt the blast of ice push me from the wall.

"Mira!" Anza lunged as I fell, almost falling over the wall as he grabbed my hand. I looked up, seeing Olaf looking out at us as I dangled. He turned his attention to Anza.

"No…"

He leveled his hand at my mate.

I drew my power closer to me and reached out to the tower, trying to stop him.

We unleashed our powers at the same time.

Ice bursted through Anza's shoulder as his arm went limp

and I watched his balance shift as I slammed up a wall in the space the window held, blocking Olaf's line of sight as we fell.

I grabbed on to my power tighter, running it up the insides of the tower, all while keeping my eyes on Anza as we fell, my stomach churning at the way he was clutching his shoulder. We had known this was a possibility—it felt like death was breathing down our necks at all times—but in that moment, unsure if we would make it, unsure if my mate was even breathing, I lashed my power outward. In a single, swift moment, the tower whined, shaking as, brick by brick, the limestone burst into sand.

The ground met us without mercy, my brace rattling as I tried to catch myself, my arms and legs screaming. I tried to stand, but couldn't, leaving my gaze to fall upon Anza, who wasn't moving.

"Anza?"

Nothing.

Anza?

Nothing.

I tried to pull myself up again. I had to get to him, had to do something, but as I tried, darkness swam at the edge of my vision, my body shaking as I felt my nose dribble blood onto the sand. I realized with startling surety that we were on the wrong side of the wall, and we had drawn attention. A lashing vine rang out, streaking past where we lay as a Barbarza rushed by. Boots hit the sand.

"Buffer!"

"I've got them! Go!" I couldn't sit up, my body screaming with pain as I looked up at Buffer, taking note of the shimmer of his barriers as they slipped into place, forming a semi circle around the three of us as enemies closed in.

"Buffer..." I fought out.

"It's alright, I've got you, both of you, it's—"

I watched, unable to do anything as the arrow embedded itself in his neck.

"No!" I fought out as he reached for his neck, his blood spattering the ground.

I scanned the crowd for Ivy, for Emai, or Brian, or Abry, or Sil, anyone, *anyone* who could save him, anyone who could save *us*, but found no one. Slowly, agony ripping through every inch of my body, I managed to inch to him, pulling his head into my lap. His dark-brown eyes met mine and he reached up to touch my cheek.

"Hang on, okay?" I said, trying the healing sigil, but I couldn't focus through the rattling pain.

"Don't let them…"

"Please hang on, Buffer."

His barriers dropped and I became vaguely aware of the approaching enemy onslaught.

"Don't let them—" He coughed, blood spattering my face as he tried to fight his body to get his words out.

"Don't let them what?"

"Take…my name…"

"What's your name? Your real name?" I asked, fighting the tears as even then, he managed the smallest smile.

"Yuze."

"Yuze."

He smiled a little wider, tears streaking down the sides of his face. How long had it been since someone had said his name?

"I won't let them. I promise."

His breath was already leaving him and all I could do was watch, bearing witness as the light left his eyes, enemies approaching from every angle.

I felt my power surge, trembling on the ends of my fingers as a feeling, unbridled and pure, spilled over me.

Rage.

Losing him while Anza lay dying beside me was crushing me; lying helpless and unable to save them was too much.

All he ever wanted was his freedom. His name.

I looked up to those who dared try to approach us and unleashed myself upon them.

36

Draw another healing sigil.

Feel the magic die at my fingertips.

I can't focus.

I can't save them.

Another spike of stone shoots up, grazing the boot of someone I don't recognise.

"Whoa, easy Mira."

"Don't go close to her, I don't even think she sees us."

I recognise those voices. Yes, I know them. I can't bring myself to turn to them. I had pulled together enough strength to witness Yuze. To pull Anza to me. I could still feel the bond. I could still feel the rise and fall of his chest.

Draw another healing sigil.

Feel the magic die at my fingertips.

I can't focus.

I can't save them.

"Follow behind me." Whisper.

"Alright…we have to get to your father." Emai.

I looked up.

Spires of earth rose all around me, in every direction as far as I could see, a single bubble of safety in the area surrounding

Anza, Yuze, and me. In the distance, a single glint of gray-white light caught my eye and I saw my mother tuck herself behind my daughter, Whisper leading the way to us.

"Mom?" Whisper said.

"Moonbeam?"

"It's okay…it's alright, we're coming."

"They killed him."

"Dad?" Her voice broke and I shook my head. I could still feel Anza down the bond and the pain fluttered in me as relief filled her gaze. My mother stepped forward, past her, approaching slowly, hands up. Steady.

"He didn't deserve it."

"I know," she said, stepping closer.

I drew another useless healing sigil against Anza's shoulder.

"Ivy…Ivy doesn't know yet."

"I know."

"It's not fair."

"I know." She was at my side now. Gently, she touched my face before reaching past me to Anza. I felt the bond grow stronger and heard his cough and groan. I leaned my head forward, resting it on her shoulder as Anza started to come to, trying to steady myself.

"You protected them so well," Emai said, Whisper coming to me as well. I brushed the hair from Yuze's face.

"It wasn't enough."

"You did your best."

"It's never enough."

"If we don't move them…" Whisper didn't finish her sentence, but my mother moved both her hands to my cheeks, lifting my face up, making me look at her.

"Grio has fallen, Mira. Sil…she's set everything ablaze in her grief. We need to move."

They needed me. I had to get up, for them. My family was my reason, my reason to keep fighting. Sil was family, Grio was part of her, and she was part of him, and he had fallen. She already had a difficult time wrangling her temper and I knew better than most how sharp her emotions could be. This would tip her over an edge we couldn't afford her sliding over. I needed to get up.

I *shouldn't*.

I didn't *want* to.

Even if I had wanted to, I shouldn't have been able to.

But I *needed* to.

They needed me to.

My resolve snapped into place all at once.

"Okay."

"Okay?" my mother asked and I nodded, reaching for Anza, who had just started to lift his head.

"We've gotta get up now."

Together, we struggled to our feet and I watched as my mother scooped up Yuze's body.

"Promise me you'll get him to the med tent."

"There's no saving him."

"I know." I fought the tears back, trying not to let them take me. I was needed. Fire could be combated with stone. I was needed. I couldn't truly break now.

"Mira…" Anza said, clutching his chest, his own eyes threatening tears.

"Sorry, sorry," I said as he shook his head.

"Don't apologize," he said gently, rubbing at his shoulder.

"I'm gonna have to take that off to fix it," Whisper said and I nodded, Anza letting me lean on him as she took the brace off.

"Go with Emai. Get that fixed up for me?" I asked her, and she gave me a suspicious look. "Please, Whisper."

"Fine," she said.

"Go," Anza encouraged her as Emai met my eyes again.

"What is it?"

"Saha and Abronoma…"

There was no need for her to elaborate; she had lost track of them.

"I'll find them," I said before looking to Whisper, then back to her.

She gave me a nod, a quiet understanding that she would tend to Whisper.

Without another word, they turned and I dropped the thousands of spikes rising up beyond us. Anza allowed me to continue leaning on him, and as we turned, I felt my stomach lurch.

There, in the distance, Grio lay with thousands of arrows sticking out from him. The magic that had held him in place was gone, the red light having vanished. His side did not rise or fall against the hot air of the battlefield, regardless of the fire that licked at everything between us and him. Thousands of men and women lay crisp and unidentifiable in his wake and a crescent moon almost looked like it rested its back on his scales, the thin spattering of white light reflecting off the pooling blood that dripped from his now-lifeless form.

I couldn't see Sil in the fray, but I could hear her. The agony tore through the very air and I felt a lump rise in my throat.

What had her dragon meant to her? We knew so little about him. We had no idea where she had found him, or what their bond was like, but dark marks of the razed ground all around him were enough to see how hard he had fought to get away from the magic that had held him there. Was the fire an aftermath of him fighting for his life? Or was it Sil?

"It's alright, I've got you."

"Are you alright with me leaning on you the whole way?"

"As if you need to ask," he said, his hand moving across my back to my hip, holding me to him. I expected him to be worried about Yuze and how I had felt when he died; the bubbling, unbridled need to keep Yuze alive and the crushing grief that accompanied my failure. He did seem to sense that I needed him to be careful as he held me to him, though.

"Okay...into the fire we go," I said, waving a hand out,

turning over the stone before us to make a path toward the corpse of the dragon.

We walked together, the fire licking up around the edges of the path I had created, knowing that there was only so long we could last in the raging smoke and ash. It was only a moment before my throat was full of smoke and Anza reached over to pull my shirt up over my nose before doing the same for himself.

"We can do this," he said, and I nodded, pushing forward, forging more of a path with every anguished footstep.

We kept going like that until movement could be seen to the right, familiar but frantic, a splash of green, heavily wilted and singed as she moved toward the dragon.

"Sah!" I called, waving a hand. Her head turned toward the sound of my voice, and when she spotted us, she adjusted course.

I opened the pathway more as she reached us, trembling. I could see each of her petals and leaves were limp at her side, twirling as they wilted. She didn't have enough oxygen.

"This fire is too much for you. You should go back," Anza said.

"Sil's fire has never been too much for me. I'm getting to her no matter what."

Anza opened his mouth to argue, but I could see the tears in those crystalline eyes. She wasn't leaving. Even if it meant she let the flames take her.

That's when I heard one of the deepest, most feral screams I had ever heard. One of anguish, wrapped in agony.

"Was that...?"

"Sil," I said, recognising the voice.

Wordlessly, we quickly pressed forward as the flames licked at the pathway I'd made, shaking as the screaming grew louder, stronger.

As Sil came into view, an ache burned forward in my chest. She was on her knees at Grio's head, running her hands across his scales, trying to clear the blood from his face. A single spear poked out of one of his eyes, likely the killing blow to his brain. Thousands of spears, arrows, and swords were caught in his massive form, but that's not what made me shudder. It was the look in my grandmother's eyes. Devastation. Real, true devastation.

"Not again. Please, not again," she begged, Saha quickly stepping away from Anza and me, hitting her knees at Sil's side before reaching out and taking her face in her hands.

"Sil..."

"No."

"Sil!"

She finally looked at Saha, tears leaving clean streaks through the ash on her face.

"Saha?"

"It's okay, Little Flame. It's okay."

I hung back with Anza, trying not to look at Grio's body as a dash of night bolted for us, fleet footed as ever. I waved him to me and Abry sidestepped a rising patch of flame to get to us. Anza reached out to pull him closer and I used my other arm to hug him tightly. His feathers were slightly singed and he smelled of smoke, but otherwise, he was unscathed.

"What are you doing out here?" I asked.

"I saw the flames. I knew I was right. Her downside isn't lack of control, I just had to see it to know for certain."

"Her downside?"

"Her fire is connected directly to her emotions. She can't stop it and start it on her own, it's just raw, unbridled, emotion"

"So we're trapped in this?" I asked, but as the words fell from my lips, I saw the flames start to snuff out.

"I've got you, I've got you," Saha said as the two of them held each other, Sil's face buried directly into Saha's shoulder as slowly, the fires started to wink out, and as they did, Saha met my eyes and held them. She needed something from me.

She looked to Sil's leg and that's when I saw the pooling

blood that had, moments before, been hidden by the flames and smoke.

"Oh, shit!" I tried to step forward, but Anza caught me as I nearly fell at the quick movement, and together, we moved to their side.

Sil flinched, looking up to see who was approaching.

"Easy…easy," I said, reaching down to her leg. I could see the bone popping out of the front of where her kneecap should be, and carefully, I drew a healing sigil as she buried her head into Saha again.

Thankfully, now that I was more focused, the magic knitted together her leg as she clung to Saha for comfort.

I turned my gaze to the destruction around us. I had been warned by so many people about Sil's capabilities, how horrific her power could be, but nothing could have prepared me for the smell of burning bodies or the sight of the charred remains of the enemy piled in every direction. Her grief, much like my own, had been insurmountable.

"We need to go now, my love," Saha prompted.

"I can't," Sil said.

"You can," Saha urged, her voice soft as silk as she got Sil to pull back. They met each other's eyes for a moment as something passed between them. "We can do this, together."

"Together?"

"Together."

"Okay."

Sil shuddered, but Saha helped her to her feet. It took another moment to lead her away from Grio, but gradually, Saha managed to get her to leave his side. Abry stuck close to Anza and I, and gradually, we moved back toward where what was left of both armies continued to fight. Soldiers from both sides were scattered across the battlefield in the chaos from the flames. There was no direction, no leadership, seemingly from both sides. No one had the upper hand that she could discern.

We needed to refocus on the portal or they were going to win.

37

"We need to split up. I have to get Sil to the medical tent," Saha said.

"I can't walk far without my brace. We get to the tent together, then we split up," I countered and Saha nodded. "I might have taken Olaf out."

"What?" she asked as we picked our way through the sea of burnt bodies.

"I brought a tower down on top of him. I don't know if he made it."

"Hopefully, he didn't, but he's not the only one we have to look out for."

"The Siren."

"Right," she said, Anza still supporting my side and pulling his shirt up over his nose as we made our way through the thick of the debris.

I looked to Sil, but she didn't look at me, her eyes distant. She wasn't with us.

We quickly covered the few yards to the medical tent. It was painfully obvious that the chaos was too much for the soldiers to make heads or tails of where they were supposed to be.

"There you are," Emai said as we approached the medical tent, rushing forward to Sil and Saha.

"Can you take her? I can't keep this up," Saha said, her legs visibly shaking.

"Yeah, of course. I've got her," Emai said. Sil didn't react as they moved her to my mother's side. Carefully, Emai led her into the tent, Anza leading me through right behind them.

"Mom!" Whisper cried, leaping to her feet with my repaired brace in her hands.

"Are you alright?" Anza immediately asked as I opened my mouth to ask her the same thing.

"I'm okay. Here." She passed me the brace before looking to Abry, who was quiet now. "Hey, hey." Anza helped me sit. It wasn't until I was sat down that I realized Abry was fighting back tears. Whisper hugged him and he buried his head in her shoulder.

"There were so many people…"

"I know. It's going to be alright, I've got you," she said as Anza took my brace to help me put it on.

We exchanged a glance. We didn't need words. They were just kids. Fucking kids. Caught in this mess. We should have sent them with the Echalon, should have fought harder for them to go. I didn't blame Whisper for wanting to stay with us. I didn't blame Abry for being afraid of my father, or for wanting to stick close to my mother, but damn. This was too much for them.

"Hey, we're going to be alright," Emai said after settling Sil down on a cot, moving to Abry and Whisper. Abry almost immediately relaxed a little and wiped away the tears threatening to fall, but the tension was still there.

My mother's eyes met mine and I looked quickly to the kids, then back up to meet her gaze. She gave me the smallest nod, blinking once, slowly. A simple unspoken agreement. She had them. They were safest with her.

"We need to go," Saha said quickly.

"No, you need to stay right here," I said, Anza helping me to my feet. I tested my leg to make sure it would hold me.

"But—"

"You were deprived of oxygen out there. You and I both know you need to take a minute."

"How did you—"

"Your leaves. You might be queen, but that title won't do you any good dead," I said, and Saha pursed her lips.

"We've got it," Anza assured her.

"Your father isn't far from the castle entrance. You should be able to meet up with him," my mom said, and I nodded, though I wasn't sure how she could know such a thing.

"Be safe, Mom. Love you," I said, hugging her gently as she moved over to me. I almost felt her melt as I called her mom. "Keep them safe," I whispered into her ear.

"No one would dare even entertain the idea of harming them as an option," she said quickly before Whisper slipped away from Abry to hug Anza and I tightly. We hugged her back, Anza pressing a kiss into the top of her head.

"You better come back."

"We will," Anza promised, and she nodded, stepping back. I rubbed her back a little as she stepped away, and together, Anza and I slid out of the tent.

I had no idea where Baden or Zerah were, but we turned our attention to the castle doors as I took out Tamaj's axe. If Olaf was alive, I wanted it to be her axe that I sank into his head. Anza led the way into the fray and I kept close as we moved, spotting someone lunge for him, sending a single spike through their body, stopping them as we kept going.

My stomach began to turn as we approached the castle doors.

"Dad!" I called out, knowing in my gut that my stomach twisting was his doing. The feeling immediately subsided as the castle doors came into view. My father had his back against the doors, a sea of soldiers at his feet, collapsed, exhausted from vomiting and shitting themselves thanks to a sea of illness that had progressed so quickly, death would have been merciful.

"The doors were open when I got here. I think he might be inside but I'm not sure."

"Got it, I think I crushed him, but we're not sure" I said as we approached, Anza pulling his shirt up over his mouth and nose again.

"Let us in, we'll find him, dead or alive," Anza said, and my dad looked at him, then at me, and back again. Something passed between them, wordlessly, and he stepped aside just enough for us to sneak past him, opening the door to Legalia's castle.

The inside was enormous, with cathedral ceilings and ivory-colored statues tucked into alcoves that resembled kings and queens of the past. As we looked around the echoing space, our footsteps bouncing off the walls, I found we were alone. Anza's hand found mine and I laced my fingers tight in his.

"There," he said, gesturing to a sign by a door tucked into the farthest left corner. The sign was written in Maraung and simply directed us to the portal room. How convenient.

We quickly approached, slipping through the door, his sword drawn as he led the way. I shook my wrists, checking for my bracelets as we stepped into the wide open room. Heads turned and I felt my heart drop.

He was there with the Siren.

Five other people sat around a circle, gagged and bound: a Barbarza child who couldn't have been more than five, eyes wild with fear as her voice screamed in my head along with the others; a Photomyran man, beaten within an inch of his life, his chest barely rising and falling; a Maraung woman on her knees, eyes closed, as if praying, accepting her fate; an Ecalon child, about the same age as The Two.

I could see it in his eyes. He knew what was about to happen. Had Olaf taken Echalon with him from Korrewen's cells? The ground was already alight with magic and Olaf was tucked over the edge of the sigil, hands placed on it firmly, his eyes, ice blue, locking on mine.

"Go, go!" Anza said as we bolted forward.

I rushed for the Echalon who was closest to me as he tried to roll from the sigil circle, but a song met my ears and my legs froze in place. The Siren. She lunged for Anza as I summoned my power, reaching past the song and into the ground. Anza sidestepped back, giving her room before landing a kick firmly into her ribs. I couldn't physically move closer until the air rushed out of her lungs, but I still had my power. I felt her affect over me drop as I pulled the Echalon to the side just an inch, breaking the sigil.

"You bitch!" Olaf snarled as the Siren turned her focus completely to Anza. She couldn't take us both.

"Careful!" I said as Anza slipped something into his ears, not looking away from her as she squared up to him. Olaf kept his eyes on me.

"You almost buried me."

"Yeah, the almost part of that kinda sucks," I said as he carefully stepped toward me. I couldn't look away to check on Anza. He would rush me. I trusted Anza. My mother wasn't far. We would be okay.

"Focus," the Siren snapped at Olaf as I stepped forward. He glanced at her, giving me an opening. I flung forward a bracelet, shifting it into a dagger. I aimed right for his throat.

A single spike of ice stopped it in its tracks.

"*Tsk tsk*," he said before ice burst up from below. I fumbled back, Anza scrambling backward as well, before I reached through the floor, grabbing at the stones and throwing them up in an attempt to stab through Olaf. I could see Anza in my peripheral, the Siren at the end of his sword.

She shifted forward, letting his sword cut her cheek.

"Careful, Claire," Olaf said without taking his eyes from me.

"Aww, what? Did you get yourself a girlfriend?" I needed to get the Echalon free. Just one person being removed from this spell might make it worthless. Sure he wasn't in line with the spell right now, but he wasn't free. I needed to get him out of here. I sent a spike of stone up near him. Near his hands. Keep taunting him, keep him going.

"You're a little too predictable, Mira," he said, almost laughing as the Echalon tried to reach for the stone. Ice covered it, making the sharp-edged stone smooth and slick.

I lunged for Olaf, and he dove for me as I lifted my axe, slamming it down toward his shoulder. He tried to block it with ice, but it shattered as I cut through it, driving Tamaj's axe down on his shoulder. Hot blood roared forward as I tore my axe free, his fist finding the place just below my sternum and driving my breath from my lungs.

I tried to catch myself, but felt the ice bolt down my left leg, locking my brace in place as I caught sight of Anza slamming Claire down a few yards away. It was already dripping from the heat, he was trying to buy himself time. The ice melting and refreezing. She was scrappy, but without her power's effect, Anza had the upper hand. Olaf grabbed at his shoulder, pressing a hand into the wound, ice building up over it, forming as quickly as it melted in the desert heat. How long could he keep refreezing the water? He had to have a limit, a downside, but what was it?

"I might be predictable, but I bite a little harder than I used to," I snapped before sending out spikes of stone, trying to slam them up through his body.

He was quick though, side stepping them before pivoting and pulling the Echalon back into place, ice rising to form the edge of the sigil he had crafted.

I tried to reach out, tried to crumble the stone into sand beneath his sacrifices, but as I did, he slammed both his hands down into the crumbling stone. The sigil barely existed. Barely stood sound. But barely was all he needed. I couldn't move, couldn't rush him, couldn't stop him as a force knocked me back and the crumbling floor and the towering walls vanished.

My vision went white.

38

"…any minute now and she should—" I opened my eyes, looking up into the stormy eyes of my mother. "There you are."

"Mom?"

"It's alright, you're alright." I tried to sit up, just for her to press me firmly into the cot I was on. "Don't."

"Anza?"

"He's okay," she said, nodding to my right. I turned my head, realizing suddenly how much my head and neck hurt.

"You probably should try to move a little slower than that," Emai said as I took in Anza's form.

His face was bruised badly on his left side, and a thick wrap of bandages covered his shoulder. His eyes were closed, unconscious, and who knew what other wounds there were beneath the thin blanket that covered him? But his chest rose and fell. The bond still hummed quietly.

"The portal?" I asked, looking back to my mother. She closed her eyes and sighed. "We were right there. I turned the floor into sand, there's no way…there's no fucking way."

"I'm sorry."

"Is he at least dead? He's got to be dead, right?" I hoped.

"The room collapsed inward when he destroyed the portal.

We don't know, but…if he survived you dropping that tower on him and you survived…" She reasoned.

"It's likely he knew it'd fall inward. He'd need to escape, he'd have a plan" I grumbled as she nodded, opening her eyes to look at me again.

"How are you feeling?"

"Like death warmed over. Where are the others?"

"Your father, Zerah, and Baden are all helping look for survivors in the rubble of the portal room."

"They won't find anyone." The people Olaf and his Siren, Claire, had brought with them had been a price to pay. They were gone. I knew it in my soul. I hadn't been able to save them. Any of them. My father had warned me that larger spells had higher prices, that sometimes spells had to be spread out over multiple people. This had to be the biggest spell someone could think of. One that required surrendering lives. No wonder Sil got antsy around magic.

"Saha? Sil?"

"Together. Sil is…mourning, Saha hasn't left her side."

"Graz and Taryn?"

"They've taken to tending to the injured and regrouping the rest of the army." That was Saha's job, but with Sil on the verge of potentially burning the entire encampment alive, even I knew she needed to focus on my grandmother. I took a breath and finally asked the one question I actually wanted the answer to.

"Whisper and Abry?"

"Safe," she said before sidestepping to come around the other side of the bed, revealing the two back to back on an empty cot nearby, asleep. "They've been helping me tend to the wounded as well."

"I'm surprised they didn't run into that fight."

"It took a lot of reasoning to keep them here. Whisper almost did, but Abry convinced her to stay."

"Good. Mom?"

"Hmm?"

"Thank you."

She nodded and brushed my hair from my face. "I'm gonna tell you something that you didn't ask."

"Okay?"

"Your father was the one who pulled you both out." I felt the irritation spike a little but shoved the thought to the back of my mind. "Anza was over you, covering your body with his own," she said gently. "He kept you from a worse fate."

"You did say he was worthy," I said quietly, looking to the still-unconscious Anza.

"Yeah, but I think your father believes it now, finding him trying to save you and all."

"That makes sense," I said quietly.

"It's alright if you don't like him. You know that right?"

"Dad?"

"Yes. He does not seem to mind, so long as you're alright."

"Good. Because I don't like him."

"Mira…"

I bit my lip, not meeting her eyes. "He's…fine."

"Mira."

"Fine, I don't hate him, or whatever," I said, blinking hard to stop the stinging in my eyes.

"I knew it."

"Don't tell him?"

"I won't say a word," she said, trying to smother a smirk.

"Promise?"

"Promise."

"Mira?" I heard Anza say, and I turned back to look at him.

"Hey, you. I thought we agreed no more almost dying."

"That goes for both of us. Oh, I'm not great," he said, trying to sit up. "How are you?"

"Also not great," I said, watching him rub his face.

"You'll be fine," Emai said as she went back to his side. "This is not the worst thing I've dealt with."

"Yeah, we're not broken."

"Anymore…" I grumbled, leaning back hard into the cot.

I watched my mother open her mouth to say something, only for a shriek to shatter the small fragments of peace and banter we had.

Ivy.

I closed my eyes, trying not to let the tears slip out as Anza quietly whispered down the bond.

You did all you could. You did.

It wasn't enough.

"You stop that now." I flinched at Quaren's voice as Ivy yelped, and almost immediately, I felt my feet hit the floor.

"Mira, don't get up," my mom said.

I got up, my leg almost giving out as I clung to the edge of a counter, limping to the main room just in time to hear Prince Quaren again as Ivy cradled her face at her dead brother's bedside.

"You knew walking into this that there was a chance you both wouldn't get out alive."

I don't know how I managed to find the strength to cross the room, but I did. He finally looked up at me as I grabbed him by the collar. I almost fell as I pinned him against the wall, but he didn't need to know that.

"Mira, stop!" Saha's voice rang. I hadn't heard her before pinning him to the wall, but she pushed through the front entrance. She wasn't fast enough. I punched him firmly in the stomach. He nearly bent over into me, eyes looking to Saha, as if begging her to stop me.

"You ever hurt her again and I'll make sure your father needs a new heir," I snarled, relishing the fear in his eyes. "I will rip your spine out your front without hesitation and watch as your kingdom crumbles." Someone grabbed my arms, dragging me backward. "I'll drop your whole fucking kingdom into the sea! I'll fucking kill you!"

"Hey. Hey!" I whirled, meeting the eyes of my father. "I know. It's alright, I know," he said quietly as he pulled me behind a curtain again, letting me lean on him a little as I shook.

I couldn't help but slam my fists into his chest. He just nodded.

"It's alright, get it out."

I hit him again, and again, and again.

"Brian…" my mother warned, but he shook his head at her.

I hit him again.

And again.

It wasn't until the sixth time that I finally could scream, and he reached up to hold me as I sobbed. Yuze hadn't deserved this. Ivy didn't deserve this. We didn't deserve this. Olaf was right. He had almost always been right. I wanted to kill Quaren. Wanted to rip out his eyes and force feed them to him. I wanted to end him. To end this agony. Why did any of this matter? Korrewen, Agrenon, Biena, and now Legalia. Eynon's portal was the last one standing and the son of a bitch had a head start. . We were losing.

That little Echalon boy's eyes haunted me as I shook, my father's support the only reason I didn't drop. I heard a few hushed but harsh words exchanged between Quaren and Saha, but I couldn't make them out as I felt Anza's hand on my back.

"Come here," he said, and I turned from my father to him.

"You alright?" my mom asked my dad.

"That was nothing."

I let Anza lead me back out into the main area, and I was happy to find that Quaren was no longer in the room. Anza helped me to Ivy's side as she cried silently, trembling.

"It's okay, let it out," I said to her, wiping my own tears away.

"He'll—"

"I wasn't bluffing," I said, interrupting her, and she met my eyes. "Let it out."

She crumbled, loosing the agony that even a moment ago she had been holding back in fear of retaliation. There were so many people in here, witnessing her grief. It felt wrong. She wasn't even being allowed to grieve in private.

"Hey, help me get everyone out of here?" Anza asked my father, who nodded, and the room quickly emptied as if someone set it on fire, leaving just me, Ivy, and Yuze.

"Do you want me to go?"

"No…yes…no…stay?"

I nodded, smothering my own sobs as I rubbed her back, trying to help soothe her the best I could as she mourned over the loss of her brother. I hadn't really known Yuze. All I had known was that he was blisteringly confident and that he cared for his sister. He had been kind to me, even in rejection, even throughout everything that had happened so far. All I knew was that he didn't deserve this. No one deserved this.

I pushed the growing rage back again and sat with Ivy until she couldn't cry anymore. Until she just stared at her brother's face, trembling. It was Anza who came back in, a thick blanket in hand.

Saha and Graz need to talk to you.

I don't care how much trouble I'm in, I said.

I don't think you are, I just think they need a word about what we're going to do next, he said.

Sit with her? I asked

Of course.

"I'm gonna be right back, alright? Can Anza sit with you?"

Ivy nodded, swallowing hard, as if her own voice was untrustworthy.

I stepped away as Anza stepped closer, gently wrapping her in the thick blanket as the night cooled the world around us.

Carefully, I stepped out of the tent, still feeling unstable, just in time for my mother to come back to my side. The welcome feeling of electricity ran through me as she started to heal the remainder of my wounds.

"Thanks."

"You don't have to thank me for this."

"Whisper and Abry?" I asked.

"Sleeping still. They've been through a lot lately, I can't blame them."

"Just surprised they slept through that. We're going to win this, right? For them?"

"I don't know," she admitted, reaching up to brush the hair from my face. "But we're going to try."

"Right," I said, and she took my hand.

I let her lead me to the tent Saha and Graz were in. I half expected Prince Twat Waffle to be in there, but he wasn't. Just Saha, Graz, and Titanus, stood around a table. Tucked into herself in a chair, Sil sat, eyes fixated on a wall. My dad sat beside her, rubbing her back. Her eyes were puffy, but filled with rage. She didn't look up, but the tent felt like a sauna.

"Whats the plan?"

"Well, first we need to get to Eynon. Olaf is going to have to cross the sea to get there," Saha said.

"If you stick me on a boat with Pickle Dick, I swear I'll throw him overboard," I said firmly.

"Oh, no, we have agreed to keep you away from him the best we can, so you dont end up incurring the wrath of an entire nation,"

"I will, too," I grumbled, crossing my arms.

"We'll have to arrange for transportation, which is where I need you to help me."

"Me? I don't think a rock boat is a good idea."

"Not thinking about a rock boat," Saha said simply, "but I do need you to help cover my ass while I do what I have to to get the boats."

"How sketchy is this going to be?"

"Very."

"Fantastic."

39

"You know those are pirate ships, right?" I asked, Anza keeping a single hand on the handle of his blade as we moved closer to the bobbing ships in the harbor.

I was surprised how close we had been to the ocean. A short traipse on Zerah's back had led us to a flourishing harbor tucked into a bend in the sands.

"Yes," Saha said simply.

"This is a bad idea," Sil grumbled. I could feel the heat roaring from her from where she stood beside me. Even I knew she was still upset with herself.

"Just don't interfere," Saha said.

"What if they try to hurt us?" Anza asked.

"Don't interfere," Saha said more firmly.

I bit my lip as we approached one of the largest ships, getting hungry glances from some of the docked crew. Saha ignored them, coming to a stop at the edge of the dock, as if ready to board the biggest ship there.

"Can I help you, tremble vine?" The voice had come from my left, but I hadn't heard anyone approach. A slender Photomyra danced past me, making Saha stop abruptly to let her pass before stepping up onto the edge of the ship.

"Ah, as punctual as ever, Leeze," Saha said, flashing her a smile.

"It's a gift," Leeze said.

I watched Anza, who was looking them up and down in turn, as if there was something he couldn't quite place.

What is it?

Banter, familiarity, almost as if they've known each other for decades. I can't quite place it.

"How do we know she'll help us? Or if her captain will come to our aid?" Sil hissed in Saha's ear.

"Firstly, Little Flame, I think I can convince her to help you," Leeze started, "and secondly, I cannot *wait* to see your face when you realize who the fuck I am!" Leeze said, flipping her short green hair. Her blooms, a blue so dark they were almost black, sat neatly along the back of her head. Leeze turned her attention to Saha. "You need my help."

"I do."

"Does it have anything to do with the spicy air? Because we're getting packed up to get away from it," Leeze said.

"I'm afraid there is no getting away from it," Saha started before explaining what Olaf was doing.

"You always had terrible judgment," Leeze said.

"Do not," Saha protested, gently swatting Leeze's shoulder.

"You so do, but alas, I'll help you."

"And what would you require for payment?" Saha asked as Leeze put down her arm load of supplies before taking a steady breath and looking Sil over.

"Don't tell her," Leeze said.

"Deal."

"Seriously, I've never met her before," Sil said firmly.

"You're going to have to think long and hard about this one, my love," Saha said, gently patting Sil's shoulder as Leeze welcomed us on board.

"This still feels like a bad idea," I grumbled as realization flashed down the bond. "Figure it out?"

"Oh yeah."

"Wanna share?"

"Oh no, this is too funny to share."

"Anza…" I said, rolling my eyes at him.

"Yeah, kid, share with the class," Sil pressed, clearly unsure of the young Photomyran.

"I don't like you, and I don't share secrets," he said, his shoulders relaxing as we boarded the ship. I opened my mouth to protest again but was nearly bowled over by a small Barbarza.

"*Oh, so sorry,*" she said as she crashed into me.

"It's alright, no harm done," I said as she stepped forward. Anza helped me regain my balance and she danced back a few steps.

"*I really am sorry, I should have been watching my step. We just aren't usually open to visitors and —*"

"Yana, please stop apologising, my love," Leeze called back over her shoulder from where she strode across the boat, already several yards ahead of us.

"*Right, right, sorry,*" Yana said.

"It's okay," I insisted as she nodded, quickly stepping past us, rushing toward a rope that seemed to shove a pole, which swung erratically.

"Where is the captain?" Sil asked quietly, Saha flashing her a coy look as Leeze bounded up the stairs.

"You can meet the captain once you guess who I am."

"Well, you've said your name is Leeze."

"Oh, come on, you can do better than that," Leeze said.

I reached for Anza's hand, feeling his fingers intertwine with mine as Sil looked Leeze over again.

"I don't—"

"She's—"

"Sah, don't."

"I'm not, I was just going to give her a hint," Saha said.

Leeze hesitated before nodding.

"She's an older friend. Remember dark blooms, fleet footed,

annoyingly charismatic," Saha said, rolling her eyes before looking to Leeze fondly. I watched Sil's eyes steady on Leeze's face as Saha gave her clues, her eyes widening as slowly. The realization must have hit her.

"No fucking way."

"Hi there, Candlelight," Leeze said, giving Saha a wink before someone passed her a large black cap with a blue feather in it. She slipped it into place on her head as she made her way to the wheel of the ship.

"Prepare to shove off!" she yelled, and a chorus of voices answered her.

"Yes, Captain!"

It was mere moments before we were pulling away from the shore.

"I still don't know who she is," I said quietly to Anza, feeling my stomach start to pitch.

"Take a long hard look at them. Leeze is shorter, sure, but the frame of their faces, the way she holds her shoulders, the steadiness of her step," he prompted as Saha padded to Leeze's side. When I looked at one of them, I missed it, but seeing them there, side by side, the idea came to mind.

"No fucking way."

"Saha was the eldest of two. An heir and a spare."

"She has a sister?"

"She seems to, yes. One that loves to taunt your grandmother."

"And you were going to keep that from me?" I said, playfully slapping his shoulder.

His smile reached those gilded eyes as he laughed, bracing me as the boat started forward, away from the dock and toward where the rest of the army lay in wait, several others breaking off to follow. It was then that I noticed the black flower on the deep green flag, which rose on each of the ships. Leeze didn't have a single ship, she had a fleet. One we desperately needed.

My stomach pitched again and I reached for him.

"Oh no," I said.

"What's wrong?" he asked as the salt and speed paired with the rocking made my stomach flip, and I scrambled to the nearest edge of the ship.

It wasn't until after I was done tossing the remnants of my last meal overboard that Anza quietly said, "It might be a good idea to sit down."

***

"Is she gonna be alright?"

I didn't have the energy to tell Graz I was, in fact, right there.

"Eh maybe?" Anza said.

"There are no rocks anywhere. This sucks," I said before resting my head against the edge of the banister I clung to.

"At least Abronoma is having a good time," Graz said, and I chanced a look upward at Abry in the crow's nest high above us.

"Hey, Abry!" Anza yelled.

"Yeah?!" he called back, looking down at us.

"Open your wings a little!"

"Is that a good idea?!"

"Just a little!" Anza said, nodding, and I watched as Abry cracked his wings open just a little. Bathed in sunlight with the wind in his feathers, I couldn't even begin to imagine how good it must feel. Abry's laughter rose as he opened his wings more, careful not to curl them so he wasn't snatched upward by the rushing speed of the ocean breeze.

"Oh. My. Goooood!" he yelled into the wind.

"I feel sick," Whisper grumbled, tucking in beside me and dangling her feet over the edge just as I was, resting her head on a banister.

"Join the club," I said, offering her a weak smile.

"I didn't think you could look so green," she said, and I closed my eyes, reaching over to rub her back.

I could hear the rushing of the ocean below us and I looked

up for another moment just in time to see Leeze climbing up a rope to untie a sail manually. I risked a glance across the rest of the ship, watching the other members of the crew, spotting Yana chatting happily with Baden and Zerah. They had been nearly inseparable since we all boarded, save for a few moments when she split away to tend to something that must have been important.

I flinched as someone dropped from the sky, a flash of green rushing past as Leeze swung around to land on her feet at the front of the ship.

Anza sat down beside me.

"Are you two going to be alright? Can I do anything?" he asked.

"I don't think so, just gotta ride it out," I said, taking deep breaths as I tried to steady my stomach. I wanted to be back on solid ground, back where my power sang to me from all around me. The soft hum of my bracelets was the only proof of my power here. "Can you check and make sure Sil and Saha are alright? I'm supposed to help Taryn and Graz spar but I don't think I can stand up," I said.

"I'm on it." He gave me a kiss on the temple and headed over to Sil and Saha, who were chatting near the front of the ship.

"At least Dad's not seasick."

"Lucky," I grumbled.

It had already been two days of sea travel and I thought I would have gotten over the salty, fishy smell and the constant rocking, but my supposed 'sea legs' didn't exist and my stomach still hated me. Pair that with the fact Prince Twat Waffle wanted to go on a different ship, probably so I couldn't keep an eye on Ivy, and Legalia's leader, who had been painfully absent, hadn't let Nadder come with us to Eynon, and the whole situation was less than ideal.

I sighed deeply, trying to get my stomach to settle again.

"Uh, guys?"

I didn't want to look up to Abry in the crows nest. I just clung to the banister and pinched my eyes closed.

"Enemy ship off the starboard bow!"

I immediately turned to look, and sure enough, there was a ship in the distance flying a distinctive red flag.

"Ready for defensive maneuvers!" Leeze called, her voice booming around the ship.

"Heard!" resounded around the ship and I fought my way to my feet.

Anza found his way to us, helping Whisper up as I tried to settle my stomach. Surprisingly, I kept my feet as we rushed toward Olaf's ship.

I hoped that maybe we could sink it here, stop him, sever any ties he may have with this world. It would be easy right? A small hole in the right place? He'd go down with the ship. Ice lashed out, crafting spikes that bolted out toward our ship, just in the right place for the rocking ocean to send the spikes careening at an angle against our ship.

The last thing I saw before my feet swept out from under me was a sheet of unyielding ice, then there was nothing but water.

40

I didn't know which way was up, but I could hear cannon fire. As I tried to swim, a bubble escaped my mouth, the breath I barely held burned in my lungs as I locked my eyes on the bubble, chasing it upward, up toward what I now recognised as the surface of the water.

I barely got my head up and caught a breath before a wave crashed into me, sending me spinning. I fought upward again, and this time, as soon as I reached the surface, a flash of green plopped beside me, clinging to a rope. Leeze snatched me up out of the water with a jarring tug and I was yanked right back onto the ship and into the chaos.

"We need to get over! Now!" Yana snapped, the soft spoken, kind hearted Barbarza gone in the frantic need to keep the ship afloat. Two other Photomyran leapt over, snatching up people from the sea.

"You good?" Leeze asked.

"Yeah, I think so…Whisper, Abry?"

"One of the crew is pulling your daughter out of the sea now, bird brain is up there still, but I have a crew to lead," she said before quickly leaving my side.

"I need you to get these people back on the ship now!" Leeze snapped.

Cannons boomed, the percussive force of the blast close enough to feel in my chest, and a cannonball clipped the banister along the edge of the ship, singing as it passed me.

I found my footing and followed after Leeze.

"The next volley will sink us if we don't back up!"

"Don't back up," I said quickly, meeting Leeze's eyes.

"If they tear through us, everyone here is dead. You, your parents, your mate, your daughter, your queen, everyone. We might be able to get to another ship, but that's quite the risk."

"I can do this," I said, holding her eyes. Her hesitation only lasted a second.

"Okay, do what you have to," she said before rushing back to the wheel, turning us to keep chasing Olaf's ship.

I took a breath, deep and firm, allowing the clunking sounds of the world around us to wash through me.

The sea hated me. But the cannons were not the sea. The cannonballs were not the sea. They were *mine*.

They were out of range for now, but it would only be a moment before they rushed into my range, singing, vibrant and beautiful. I slammed them downward as hard as I possibly could, driving them into the sea and under the boat. The tension in the air tipped and I could feel the hope start to creep in. We could do this. If I could keep this big-ass boat afloat.

Leeze's commands rushed onward as the boat rushed forward, and it was another few minutes before the next volley sang out, I slammed them down into the ocean again before the ship got in range of Olaf's. People rushed to ropes and pulled forward planks of wood to help cross to his boat, but before they got the chance, a blast of sea water formed into ice that froze our ship in place.

"Motherfucker," Leeze hissed as Sil scrambled to the edge, the other boats in our fleet slowing as Olaf started to make his escape.

"I've got this," Sil said.

"Quickly, Candlelight!" Leeze said as Sil turned her attention to the frozen patch of sea. I turned my attention to Olaf's boat. I was able to move cannonballs down into the sea. Metal manipulation was within my ability.

"Not so fast, asshole" I growled, reaching my power across the ship, grabbing everything metal I could possibly get ahold of. Cannons, cannonballs, nails, fastenings, swords, rigging and so much more sang at my command. Sil started working on the frozen patch of sea, but in one fell swoop, I pulled. All at once, the ship started to come undone.

"Mira," Sil gasped, astonished.

"Just get us unfrozen," I barked as holes tore through the side of the ship. Chaos erupted from their boat as we snatched back boards we had been about to cross in our effort to board their ship. I couldn't focus on any one person, on any one need, I kept my focus on the aspects of their boat I could tear away, and before I knew it, they were sinking, fast.

"Whoo!"

"Yeah, Mira!"

"Drown, you bastard!" Voices I couldn't place rose up around me as I pulled their ship apart at every nail and hinge, tearing it to pieces with triumph ringing in my chest before another voice rang out.

"Hey!" I heard as I dropped their cannons into the ocean and looked up, causing my power to falter just long enough to see the arching ice rise from the ocean. Was that a boat? Stiff sails rose up out of the water, ice crafted rigging, as slowly, a boat made completely of ice rose up and out of the salt water, Olaf, at its helm and glaring daggers at me.

"What's the matter? Did I inconvenience you?!" I called as his crew mates scrambled on board. A volley of our own cannons slammed through his newly crafted ship, just for him to repair it immediately.

"I've almost got this!" Sil said, but Olaf lashed out, blasting more ice into the side of our boat as he turned, pulling away from us once again.

The ice moved with us, firmly attached to the boat. Between that and the waves, there was no doubt that it would capsize us in the right situation. Sil focused on melting the ice, careful to keep her flames from the wooden boat as I turned to look for Whisper, spotting my father wrapping another thick towel around her as she chattered, clinging to his arm.

"It's alright, I've got you," he said gently as she met my eyes, and I moved quickly to their side.

"Are you okay?"

"Yeah, I sank so fast. That was scary."

"I'm sorry it wasn't me pulling you out," I said as she reached for me.

"They told me you were in the water too, other side of the boat. You couldn't have gotten to me."

"It's my job to protect you."

"You can't do the impossible." I bit my lip as she gave me a thousand excuses, but the reality of it was that I *could* do the impossible. I could do wild and wonderful things. I just hadn't been able to save my daughter. How could I have been so careless, so shortsighted? I could have made her go back to Agrenon. I should have.

She would have just come along anyway. She did *just come along anyway,* Anza said gently, starting toward us.

I didn't know what he had been doing, but he was soaked and his hands were red, aching. I just nodded as he wrapped himself around us, the pitching boat still threatening to toss us all as Sil broke the ice. It felt like the world was spinning, as if any moment would throw us back into the salty ocean and drown us all. I should have made her stay. I should have made her.

Let.

She wouldn't let me.

I released a breath as the boat settled on calmer waters.

"We need a plan. Like, an actual plan," Whisper said quickly, shaking as she clung to us.

"I think I have an idea." I hadn't seen Graz clinging to a railing not far from us, but there he was, trying and thankfully managing to keep his footing.

"Anything is better than this."

"Alright, we have to get my mom and Prince Quaren together, Sil and Titanys too, they'll be able to let us know if it's ass."

"I'm sure your plan is not ass."

"Again, better than no plan."

"I'll get them together," Leeze said.

"Means I gotta be on the same boat as Sergeant Twat Waffle."

"It's…Prince…Twat Waffle?"

"The prince of getting his dick cut off if he looks at me wrong," I grumbled.

"Believe me, I'd love to gut him too, but that is a fight for a different day," Anza said gently, kissing my forehead.

"What's the worst they could do, drown me?"

"Mira…"

"Fine," I grumbled. "But he better not be a prick."

"I think he's scared enough of you to behave."

"Better be," I said, clinging to Whisper as Leeze signaled for one of her other boats to get closer. She swung to the other ship, a piece of rigging knocked loose in the battle presenting itself as the perfect mode of transportation, and returned in a shockingly short amount of time with a pale Prince Quaren in her grasp.

"There has to be a better way to traverse from boat to boat," he complained.

"Probably, not as fun though" Leeze said as Saha, Sil, my parents, and Titanys started to find their footing, gathering around to hear Graz's plan as Titanys laid out a map for us to reference.

"Olaf is heading on what seems to be a straight path from Legalia to Eynon. If he stays on this heading, he'll have to walk on land through most of Eynon to get to the capital farther up," Graz said, carefully showing what he meant on the map. "If we stop pursuing him and bolt up the coast here, we can get to the capital first and mount a defense."

"We would have the upper hand," Saha said quietly, Quaren already nodding.

"It's a sound plan. It relies on him going up through the length of Eynon on land though. If he skirts around the peninsula and up the side, then inward from the other side, it would give him more time to lose us and a strong shot at the capital," Titanys said.

"But even then, we'd beat him right?" Sil asked and Titanys nodded.

"To the capital? We would."

"Either way, if he goes around Eynon and cuts in, or if he storms the capital by land, we stand a chance. *If* we head straight there from here," Graz said, and I nodded, watching as he met Saha's eyes. He held her gaze, filled with bright pride, as she nodded before looking to Quaren.

"What do you think?"

"I think the kid's got a decent idea. Let's hope it works," he said, nodding.

"Whisper?" Saha asked.

"If we don't do this, we might as well sink ourselves while we're ahead," my daughter said flippantly.

"Great. Let's get moving," Leeze barked, and in a matter of moments, with a few adjustments to the ships and the fleet, we were heading toward Eynon's capital—and the last remaining portal—as I hoped that Graz was right.

This whole time we had been chasing Olaf, trying to stop him, right on his heels, or making up time to try to save all that we loved. We just had to beat him to Eynon's capital, to the portal. Every moment of this war against him had felt like trying to scramble up a stone wall.

It was his turn to scramble.

41

"How are you doing?" Anza asked as the night crept in, Whisper asleep in her hammock as we tried to settle down below deck.

"Still green around the gills, if you know what I mean," I said, and he managed a weak smile.

"I meant about almost drowning."

"I didn't almost—" I had almost drowned. Shit, Whisper had almost drowned.

"Hey, hey, you're alright. She's alright. Breathe."

"What even really happened?" I asked as his hands grazed my arms, rougher than usual. I grabbed up his hands, seeing the sores on the back of his knuckles and along the inside of his palms.

"I'm fine. Olaf tossed the ship, Leeze was already going after you, and Whisper was in the water."

"You had to choose."

"There wasn't a choice. She was sinking faster than you and the Photomyran on the end of the line needed someone to anchor his rope so he could get back to the ship. I couldn't save both of you…I'm sorry."

"Don't you dare apologize for saving our daughter," I said

gently before kissing his knuckles as music drifted down from above us on the ship deck.

"I just couldn't be—"

"Anza, it's okay. We're alive. If you had jumped in to save me and Whisper had died—"

"Don't."

"Then stop beating yourself up. You did the right thing." He didn't believe me. I could feel his guilt eating down the bond. I couldn't convince him otherwise as he blinked the start of tears away. "Lets go up on deck," I suggested, gently weaving the magic of the healing sigil against his beaten up hands.

"I don't know—"

"You need a distraction," I said, and he took a moment to weigh the decision before sighing and nodding.

I led him back up to the main deck, watching our step as our friends, family, and crew lined the ship's edge, some people dancing in pairs together in the middle as music lit the boat alight with joy.

"What exactly are we celebrating?" I asked Graz, who just looked at me and smirked.

"Not dying, apparently."

"What's with that look?" I asked.

"You're up to something."

"Let's just say the last few weeks have left me...inspired. And I just got some news."

"What kind of news?"

"News that makes you think of the future," he said before reaching into his pocket and sneakily showing us a pair of artfully crafted rings. I felt my heart skip a beat.

"Saha gave you her blessing?"

"Different news, but yes, thank the stars," he said, laughing nervously.

"Hey, breathe, you can do this," Anza said, and Graz nodded, taking a deep breath.

"I can do this."

He wasn't that scared little Photomyran boy anymore, something was alight within him. I scanned the crowd for Taryn, spotting her leaned against the side of the ship not far away. She wasn't singing or clapping or anything, unlike the rest of the crew. She was seemingly lost in thought.

"When are you going to ask her?" Anza asked.

"In a little bit, I'm gathering my courage."

"Don't gather too long now. It's gonna be scary whenever you decide to do it," I said, smirking as Anza took my hand and pulled me toward the impromptu dance floor.

Once we know she says yes, do you want to get their room ready with me? Like they did for us?

Absolutely, I responded as he began to lead me in a quick-footed dance. I noticed my parents on the makeshift dance floor as well, and as their dance ended, I watched as Sil tenderly held a hand out to Saha, which she accepted, and my grandmother led my queen out onto the dance floor.

Anza tapped my shoulder and I followed his gaze to Graz, who nodded at us. He was ready.

We finished up our dance with the song and slipped back to the side of the boat, not far from Graz, before he started to pick his way through the front of the crowd toward Taryn. I felt Anza's hand meet mine as Graz offered his hand to Taryn, who only hesitated for a moment, her mind still wandering as she took it. My heart slammed in my chest as he led her out into the quick-footed dance—one I had caught them dancing in the dead of night beneath the glow of the full moon far from Saha's sight every single month.

She seemed to snap out of it as the dance began. It wasn't a full moon; she knew something was up.

"Here we go," Anza whispered as the dance floor started to clear. Taryn and Graz were soon the only two left.

"What are you up to?" Taryn said quietly.

"You'll see soon enough."

"We didn't really get to talk about that thing, from earlier."

"Later."

"Graz."

"Trust me?" Graz asked as Taryn sighed and nodded, the music climbing as he spun her around. "Remember, when you saved me the first time?"

"You had been caught in Olaf's room late at night, sneaking about. They didn't see you clearly enough to identify you though."

"And you pulled me into that secret tunnel."

"And you followed me to meet Narin. I couldn't ever forget."

"And the space was so small. You held your hand over my mouth and just looked into my eyes," Graz said, smirking.

"Begging you to stay silent."

"I never got to tell you. You didn't have to ask me with your eyes to stay quiet. I already liked you then, and there, in that space. I don't think I *could* have uttered a single word." Taryn didn't have a response for him now as he spun her away from him, let go of her hand, and took a knee as she spun to a stop. "From that moment, and every moment after that, it's been so hard to breathe in your presence, so I beg you, never let me take a steady breath again?" he asked as he dipped his head, hands resting out to each side, much like Anza had.

Taryn's hands slowly moved to cover her mouth as she realized all at once what was actually happening and she fought back tears before moving forward to settle before him, taking his face in her hands and meeting his eyes as they sought her out.

"As you give, so do I. You're not scared of being short of breath?"

"Suffocate me for all I care," Graz managed to get out before they pulled each other into a kiss.

Applause resounded throughout the crew as Anza and I started to sneak toward their room below deck. Music and dancing started up again as Graz brought out the rings and we slipped into the nearest shadow. I barely heard Saha behind us.

"To Prince Grazham Bloodthorne and Princess Taryneer Bloodthorne!"

"To the future of Agrenon!" sounded back before the sounds muffled below deck.

Together, we slipped into their room and I swiftly neatened the bed as Anza wrangled some small candles, arranging them carefully on shallow dishes to ensure there was no risk of burning the ship down. I laid out several blankets and carefully refilled a water pitcher as Anza swept.

That was all we had time for, slipping out as we heard the soft, familiar footfalls of the two Photomyran turning in for bed as we slipped out of their room. I managed to shove Anza behind a crate, ducking down so they didn't see us. I heard them gasp as they closed the door behind them, Anza starting to go red as we heard them make it to their bed.

We quietly got back to our feet, sneaking as quickly as we could away from their room and back to our own.

"I wonder what he could have meant by 'looking to the future.'"

"We probably won't know, and it won't matter if there isn't a future to grasp."

"I think there's a future there. It may look different, and it might be frightening, the wind might pry at us all, and the night might be terrifying, but this life is also weird, and wild, and wonderful, and I'm happy they get to live in it. I'm happy *you* get to live in it," he said as we closed the door to our own room.

"Weird?"

"And wild," he said gently.

"And wonderful."

"Wonderful."

"I think you're right."

"Of course I am," he said before kissing me gently. "Now, let's get some rest. Those two are going to be late tomorrow morning."

I couldn't help but smother the laugh that fought up my

throat as I noted Whisper was still asleep, and he led me lovingly to bed, full of hope, and faith, and wonder.

"Ow! What the fuck?" I managed as the boat shifted, pitching Anza and I to the floor. He twisted as he fell, catching himself on top of me before protecting me from something that tumbled on top of us.

"Are you alright?"

"Yeah, what was that?"

"I don't know," Anza said, and as we sat up, I felt my heart sink when I heard the sound of rushing water.

Even in the dark of the night, I could see the trickle that had begun to seep under the door. By the time we jumped to our feet, our room was flooded up to our ankles and panic had set in.

We were sinking.

42

"Everybody to the deck!" I couldn't tell who the scream was from, but it was definitely not someone I recognized as Anza shook Whisper awake and I fought our way out of our room, water rushing in as the door opened.

"I can't find Abry." My heart shot into my throat at the words and I spun to find my mother, my father searching a nearby bedroom, her arm limp from a wound I couldn't fully see in the dark.

"What?" Whisper asked, panic in her voice.

"He's not in his room?" Anza asked before I could speak.

"No, if he's stuck down here—"

"We'll find him if he's down here. He might already be up on the deck. Go check?" I said just as quickly, and she nodded as I turned to Whisper.

"Go with her."

"But—"

"If he's up there, he'll be scared. The storm's windy as fuck. Go," I said, and she sighed but nodded. Anza and I rushed past her, my father slipping out and reaching for me. I took his hand. "Get mom and Whisper out of here, we're okay."

He met my eyes for what felt like an eternity.

"I trust you. Both of you."

"I trust you too, now get her and Whisper above deck," I said, and it was only a breath before he was rushing after my mother. Anza and I instinctively split up, the water rushing in quickly as we tore through rooms.

"Abry!"

"Abronoma!"

"Help, my wing's pinned!"

I rushed to the room his voice had come from, shoving the door open and finding Abry pinned against a wall by a crate.

"What the hell are you even in here for?" I asked, rushing to try to help him.

"Later," Anza prompted as he rushed in behind me.

He was right, the water was rising faster and faster. Together, we heaved against the crate pinning Abry's wing to the wall and he slipped out just as the water rushed over his head. I pulled him up, helping him keep his head above water, but we needed to move. We were all swimming by the time we reached the door.

"Go, Abry. Go," Anza prompted as Abronoma slipped out of the room, swimming toward the stairs that led up to the deck.

"Where are you guys? Whisper has an idea," I heard Zerah say in my mind.

"Zerah says Whisper's got an idea," I said out loud, the water still filling the hold around us.

"In Whisper we trust," Abry said, and we kept swimming until the water rushed over our heads, each of us dragging in one last gasping breath before ducking and swimming to the stairs and rushing up.

I felt a hand grab my shoulder as my dad lugged me up out of the water, Sil pulling up Abry before going back to grab Anza's hand once Abry was safe.

"We need to do this now!" I heard Whisper say as I coughed. Before I'd finished, she was there before me, taking my face in her hands.

"I've whipped up a spell. It's complex and it's gonna need all of the Endering on this ship to make it work. It's a combination of a water expulsion spell and an amplification of power, it just needs a source to amplify."

"One that can rebuild a ship."

Fire and Death. Plague and Flight. They couldn't do it. It had to be me.

"What do I need to do?"

"Once the spell takes effect, the water will be pushed out through the holes in the ship. You'll receive a temporary amplification of power from everyone else involved. It'll be draining, but if you put that power into moving and manipulating the cannonballs into patches—"

"We'd stay afloat."

"Right."

"That's too risky," Sil said. "That much power would kill someone,"

"You really think I'd just let my mom die?" Whisper snapped back. "It's a delicate balance for sure, but it's possible."

"We don't have time to argue, we're doing it!" I said firmly, my parents finishing up the sigil on the deck.

Carefully, we got into position, Sil holding back, standing away from the group. Abry, Emai, Brain, and I carefully settled our hands on the sigil. My father, to my right, caught my eye.

"You need to release the energy as it flows into you. Sil's not stressed for no reason, you *have* to."

"I will," I said, nodding as my mother looked to Sil.

"We need you to do this. I know you're not into magic, but without you, she might die. We're not just sharing our power with her, we're sharing the backlash too."

"I can't."

"Yes you can, you just have to put your hands on the sigil and breathe. Just let it happen, the magic will do the work." Tears slipped down Sil's face, but she swallowed hard and padded quickly to Emai's side, resting her hands on the sigil as she shook.

"You can do this," my dad said.

"The last time—" Sil started, but he cut her off.

"This isn't then. We're okay." As he spoke, Sil met my eyes.

"I've got this. *We've* got this," I said as her tears kept spilling and she blinked hard.

Banishing them, she nodded as we all breathed in unison, summoning the magic forth. It felt vibrant, electric and beautiful as it danced through the sigil to me.

I had torn metal from a boat sure, but molding it, manipulating it into another form, was something I had never even tried, but it was our only option to save the main fleet ship with minimal casualties.

I pushed the power outward, willing the water out of the holes in the boat. The ship physically shifted, moving to a less-sunken position in the ocean as I searched for and found the cannonballs. I pulled at them, feeling the magic welling even more within me, starting to rip and tear at my seams as I pushed. Carefully, I tried to manipulate one, my heart thundering in my chest as I pulled at it.

It didn't budge.

"Come on."

"Mira?"

"Won't move," I managed through teeth I didn't realize were gritted, my body tense as I tried to contain and force the magic where it was needed.

"Look at me." I looked up into my mother's eyes as she demanded my attention. "Magic is not something to be resisted, it is something to be experienced and directed. You are fighting with it, trying to make it do one thing or another. That's what the sigil is for. That's what intention is for. It is here to be used. Use it, but don't force it. It should not be this difficult. We are all here to bear the backlash with you."

"How do I do that?"

"Relax, and let it flow through you."

"And if I can't?"

I saw Sil look to Emai, panic in her eyes. She knew what would happen if I couldn't.

"You have to."

I swallowed hard, panic starting to rise in me before I felt the soft brush of peace laced with fear down the bond. Anza breathed, settling his emotions and helping anchor me in the moment.

I focused on the cannonballs, noticing my muscles start to relax. Carefully, I tried again, finding each of the cannonballs becoming as easy to manipulate as clay. Smoothing them out and into the holes in the ship, I pushed, inching the flattened masses of metal into any cracks and crevices I could find. I didn't know if it was enough, if it was good enough, if *I* was good enough, but I kept going, patching the holes I could now see through the darkness.

The tension and pain waned, transforming into pure, unadulterated bliss.

I was magic. Magic was me.

I felt the power crackle to a halt, like a flame that had lost contact with air, smothering itself, and I almost couldn't catch myself as the kick back rattled through the now-dying spell sigil. I saw my parents, Sil, and Abry all flinch as exhaustion settled in my bones; my vision starting to swim and fade as Anza instinctively propped me up. My arms and legs felt like lead and blood trickled from my nose spattering onto the wood of the ship. A chill settled over me and as I looked to them I had a feeling that though their slumped shoulders and ragged sighs suggested they shared the weight I was still getting the worst of it as my stomach threatened to toss.

There was no doubt in my mind anymore; if I had done this alone, it would have killed me.

"Good job. You did it. You did it," Anza said, moving to my side to gently help me up.

I couldn't feel my power singing, I couldn't feel any magic at all, I was just so tired.

"What even caused that?" Sil asked quietly.

"You don't want to know," Leeze grumbled as she ordered the ship to keep going.

"I kinda wanna know," Whisper said quietly.

"The sea is full of creatures that don't like to be trifled with. We just happened to be in the wrong place at the right time. We keep moving and pray it doesn't find us," she said, signaling to the fleet to keep a tight formation.

Gradually, we all began filtering back below deck and carefully started putting our things back in order.

Once we were mostly finished with that, I made my way into the room Abry had been in and found the well-crafted metal plate he and Whisper had been taking turns working on, now filled with tiny, intricate sigils and markings.

Abry stopped and met my eyes as I stepped into the hallway. I raised my eyebrows at him.

"This yours?"

"Maybe?" I held it out to him and he took it.

"Wanna tell me what it is yet?"

"No, I really shouldn't."

"Gonna blow anything up?" I asked as we walked back toward the deck.

"No, no explosions."

"No one's going to have their bones yoinked from their body?"

"No. Where did that come from?" he laughed.

"I don't know, man, you kids have been hella sneaky with this thing."

"If you really must know, it's for Anza "

"For Anza?"

"He's…not happy he can't help as much as you and us other Endering can."

"Now I just have more questions than answers."

"I don't know anything."

"Abry…"

"I didn't see anything either."

"Hey!"

"In fact, I'm pretty sure I can't land straight cause I'm partially blind," he said, earning himself an eye roll from me.

"Fine, I'll leave it alone."

"Thank you."

"But it better be cool."

"It will be," he promised as Whisper met us at the bottom of the stairs, taking both our hands.

"Hurry!"

"What now?"

"I have to talk to you guys. I've wrangled a couple other people too."

"About what?" I asked, letting her pull us into a side room. I looked up, finding said group of people looking back at me. Emai, Brian, Anza, Taryn, Baden, and Zerah were scattered about the room, waiting for us.

"Do you remember when we sent the other Echalon back to Agrenon and I sent that letter to The Two?"

"Yeah?"

"I didn't just ask them to take care of the Echalon. I might have…done something else."

"Whisper, what did you do?"

"Something Saha would probably call treason," she started, the little seed in the back of my head drawing breath as we all leaned in to hear what exactly she had done.

43

"Land!"

"Thank fuck," Whisper said, and I almost laughed as we rushed to the edge of the boat, spotting the docks in the distance. Thankfully, the last few days had been nothing but keeping the ship together and flirting with sea sickness, but the stones were moments away.

Leeze's fleet was still carefully docking and settling their anchors when we scrambled off the boat. I caught a glimpse of Prince Prissy Pants shaking his head as he called to Saha.

"Do all your Endering run around unchecked?"

"Let," she responded simply, and his smirk disappeared.

Ivy stuck close to him, her eyes still unfocused, but she seemed unscathed from the trip. I tried to catch her gaze, tried to push the promise of a future to her, but she didn't meet my gaze. She didn't know what we had done in the dark of that ship.

"Emai!" Brian declared as my parents rushed to the ocean side, my mother splashing my father as he rushed after her. He hefted her up over his shoulder before he began to spin, their laughter contagious for a moment as Anza stopped beside Whisper and I, Zerah and Baden padding behind us to get off the boat.

"That's what love looks like," Zerah said.

"You wouldn't know love if it cracked you in the muzzle," Baden retorted.

"Oh, and you're just suuuuuch a ladies' man."

"Everyone, all the ladies, just falling over me."

"I haven't even seen one lady look in your general direction."

"That, my dear sister, is a lie."

"Scowls don't count."

"They do not scowl!" Baden protested before getting gently booped on the muzzle with Zerah's tail as she danced away.

Anza's hand found mine.

"They are pretty amazing." His tone and the way his eyes shone expressed perfectly his awe and happiness, but there was a tiny nugget of guilt and pain inside of him.

"Hey, so are you…" He glanced at me, giving me a small smile.

"I'm alright."

"You're amazing just as you are."

"Yeah, Dad," Whisper said, reaching down to splash water up at him.

"You little shit," he said, scooping her up.

Her laughter rang out of her as he stepped off the dock into the now waist-deep water, both of them laughing as they splashed each other as we carefully made our way to the beach while the ships offloaded both nations' armies.

Saha hugged Leeze, who hugged her back tightly.

"Don't fuck this up," Leeze said, rubbing her sister's back slightly before they stepped away from each other.

"No promises," Saha said, drawing a laugh from Leeze before they parted ways.

I begrudgingly followed Saha across the beach to meet up with Prince Jerk Face and Ivy. The monarchs agreed that he would lead us, seeing as he was most familiar with this kingdom.

"Come on, Pouty McPout Face," Zerah said, nudging my

shoulder as she tossed her head, encouraging me to get on her back.

"I'm not pouting."

"Oh okay, I totally believe you," she said, rolling her eyes. Her smug smile made the grief in my chest ache, but I shoved it away and swatted playfully at her ear as I climbed on, Anza and Whisper climbing up with me as we began our trek along the shore line. My parents were both soaked and Abry's wings fanned out behind Baden as he trotted along the sand, occasionally glancing inland toward the trees, as if longing for them.

We hadn't even made it a hundred yards from the water before I saw Ivy lagging behind Prince Shit Head.

"Hey, Zer, can we catch up to Ivy?"

"Sure," she said, increasing her pace to just shy of a trot.

"Easy," Anza said, shooting me a knowing look. Yuze's death hadn't been that long ago. She'd still be feeling it.

"Hey, how are you?" I asked as Zerah got to her side.

"I'm alright. It's just so quiet without him."

"Tell us about him?" Anza asked, and I looked back at him, surprised. He had been so jealous and abrasive when it came to Yuze, but as I watched Ivy's small smile bloom, I felt his guilt eating down the bond. He hated himself for how he'd responded to Yuze. He felt bad for not understanding him, for being harsh. He wished he could take it back.

"He was always true to himself, even when they didn't like it. When we were…" She hesitated a moment, glancing around to make sure we wouldn't be overheard, but Whisper was keeping an eye out to make sure our conversation was private without needing to be prompted. "Punished, he would crack jokes. It made them target him, but that also meant they went easy on me. He snuck snacks off of trays at parties and gave them to me too."

"A good guy," I said quietly.

"The best brother." Her voice sounded tight as she blinked away tears.

"We'll make sure he's remembered."

"By his name?"

"By his name," Anza said, nodding.

We sat in relative silence after that, comfortable and calm. I wanted to tell her everything, everything about the plan, about what Whisper had set into motion, but I knew that this was not the place. Even if Quaren, Saha, and Graz were far enough away there was no chance of them hearing it, word would get back to them, which would ruin it. Sil and Graz stuck close to Saha, but I didn't expect her to look back to me. My heart leapt into my throat.

Relax, she doesn't know.

What if she does?

She doesn't, I swear. She probably just wants to talk.

"Hey Zerah, can we—"

"Oh yeah, sorry, sorry."

"Don't be sorry, you didn't know."

Tamaj had always been on the lookout for Saha's glances. She had known the queen far better than I did, but Zerah was still learning, and at my prompting, she bounced forward to bring us side by side with the queen.

"Are you alright?" Saha asked.

"I'm fine."

"Mira, I wanted to give you some time after Olaf took you, to let you process and come to terms with everything but—"

"I really don't want to talk about it."

"I just need to know you're with me."

"But I'm not," I started, and she flinched, swallowing hard. "I'll fight for you, for Agrenon, for balance in the kingdoms, but once this war is done, I'm using the Exit Clause. My family is already in danger and I don't like what I've seen."

"Mira, I really didn't want to leave you behind," she said very quietly.

"It's not about that, though it is part of it. I just...I need time. I don't know if I'll come back, or when, if I do. Mom said you made a similar agreement with her." I could feel Anza's tension down the bond. He was ready to snap at her if she had so much as a single harsh word to say to me.

"I did, I do." She took a breath to steady herself. "I would be lying if I said I wasn't disappointed, but you must do what is best for you and your family. I'll make sure you have everything you need. Just let me know when."

"Of course," I said as she nodded.

"I am sorry. I've made many mistakes as queen and I can't take them back, but I do try to learn from them."

"And what have you learned from this one?"

"To never leave an Endering behind," she said simply, and we both fell to silence.

Was this the right move? It was the move I had to make, but was it one I was making because Olaf was in my head, or was this something I was doing of my own volition?

I felt Anza's hand on my waist, tucking his fingers into my belt loop like he had a thousand times before. He could sense me spiraling. I took a few steadying breaths and leaned back against him, knowing that if we were going to succeed, we needed to both have level heads.

We were going to Eynon to stop Olaf. We *needed* to stop him.

With a portal intact, we could carry out our plans and finally put an end to all this. If he were to get to that last portal before we did, the devastation that he would rain across the worlds could never be undone.

I hadn't told Saha or Graz, or anyone, really, about the influx of Endering that would occur. It was something Whisper had already calculated for, but the last thing someone in charge of a nation in the Otherworld needed to hear was that there would be more Endering.

Would they let Olaf finish his work if they knew? Would they willingly let the portals fall if it meant getting access to more power?

I felt Anza nudge my hip. Spiraling again.

Zerah pulled back, falling back toward where Baden was, and Abry stood on his tiptoes, offering out the gauntlet he had been working on.

"Done, I think," he said, and Anza reached back, gently taking it from him.

"It looks awesome."

"Thanks. Whisper, can you check my work?"

"Sure. I know it's good work, but just for peace of mind, right?"

"Yeah, this kind of magic is new to me," Abry admitted, settling back down behind my father.

"What kind of magic are you used to?"

"Spoken magic. It's different from Sigil magic in that it doesn't last as long. Nice to have in a pinch, but not reliable for long term," he explained, shrugging.

"I'd love to hear more about it," Whisper said. "After I check this out, of course."

"Of course." Abry laughed and I took a breath. It was refreshing to be around them both at once. They played off each other's strengths and weaknesses well.

I looked to the trees to my right, taking a moment to bask in the calm, knowing that we were walking toward a kingdom preparing for war. Toward a fight we might just have the strength to win.

One we couldn't risk losing.

44

I didn't know why I expected a fight as we grew closer to Eynon's capital, but there wasn't one.

Quaren and Ivy easily led us to the capital city and right through the massive gates in the wall surrounding it.

Unlike Agrenon, there were no large walls separating the city from the castle. The beautiful stone ramparts rose up, and the city within was neatly designed around an open concept. The military ring flowed into the merchant ring easily. The low buildings sprawled out from the castle, the bridges and roads large and welcoming, wide open and easy to traverse. There were dozens of pathways that could get one where they were going.

The entire city was beautifully designed, right down to the light posts and walking stones that had been carved with depictions of fish and monstrous water creatures. It was clearly a place made for the people, not for battle.

I bit my lip, unsure of the open concept in a fight.

Eynon didn't historically take sides, and while their army was large and their forces mighty, they hadn't actually had to use them in a very, very long time. Eynon was the Otherworld's Switzerland, just bigger.

I took a breath, trying to stick close to my parents as we rode into the heart of the city, climbing a set of stairs that led to the luscious gardens of the castle. The large doors reminded me of Agrenon's castle in a way, artfully designed with depictions of the native flora. It was quite the sight to behold.

Slowly, Quaren led us to a stop and Saha and Sil dismounted, Saha looking back to me. We were about to go meet Quaren's parents. The idea made my stomach churn.

"I'll be back," I said, Anza grabbing my chin to kiss me.

"Don't murder."

"Aww, but murder is the best part," I said sarcastically before he kissed me again. "Fine, no murder."

"I love you."

"I love you, too. See you in a sec."

He nodded, his hands lingering in mine for a moment before I slipped away from him to Saha's side, leaving Whisper on Zerah's back.

"Ready?" I asked Saha, and she nodded.

"We have a good rapport built so it shouldn't be hard to get everything in order."

"Awesome, I hate it."

"I know, sorry," she said as we started up the stairs after Quaren and Ivy. "Please, just hold your tongue? I'm begging you."

"Yeah, I figured that'd be important," I grumbled as we slipped into the massive throne room.

Elevated on a set of stairs, a throne of wood rose up, just as intricately carved as the doors. Seated on the throne was a single elderly man, a crown neatly nestled on his wavy gray hair.

Quaren and Ivy bowed, and I remembered I was supposed to bow too, managing to correct myself quickly. The only one not required to bow was Saha, but she did regardless.

"The Flower of the North," he said as she rose, the rest of us rising only after he waved a hand to release us from the bow.

"It's nice to see you again, old friend."

"You know you could leave the old part out of it, right?"

Saha smiled, nodding slightly as she blinked. "Bad habits."

"The worst," he laughed. "You're ready for this?"

"I hope so. Shall we talk strategy?" she asked as he nodded.

"Feel free to invite your heir, I'd be delighted to meet him," he said, waving for Quaren to stay. Ivy fell back, taking my hand to encourage me to do the same.

"Ivy, take the rest of the evening to show Mira around. We'll update you as needed." Ivy nodded before looking to me, almost begging me to keep my mouth shut. I gave her a nod and let her lead me down a long hallway to the left of the entrance.

"Where are we going, exactly?" I asked as we got out of earshot of the royals. I noted the guards down the hallway at regular intervals and figured I shouldn't speak too freely.

"The portal room is down this way," she said.

"Lots of guards."

"They're not for you."

"They're for you, aren't they?"

"Can't have us getting away," she said before she took a steadying breath. "Me, can't have *me* getting away."

"It's gonna be alright."

"How?" she asked as we got to the end of the hall, the doorway opening as we stepped in.

The portal was surrounded by guards who stood at attention as she came in.

"I can't say here, but I need you to trust me and be ready when it comes."

"When what comes?" she asked.

I wish I could just tell her, but there were too many ears.

"You'll know." Fuck, I sound like Heartlock. "For right now though, we try to stop Olaf."

"We can do this?"

"We can do this," I assured her, and she nodded, taking a steadying breath as we looked around the portal room.

It was beautiful. Icy blue pillars towered above us, depictions of sea beasts, all teeth and tentacles and power, twisted up them, just a shade darker than the pillars themselves. Each support came to rest at the base oft an arching cathedral-style ceiling, a deeper blue making the tallest parts look like the night sky. Behind the well-protected portal was a set of dual staircases, which curved up to a second floor.

"Is that where you stay? Up there?"

"Yeah, fancy cages." she said quietly.

"Like bedrooms?"

"With bars."

"I'm sorry."

"It's not like that in Agrenon?"

"No."

"There are stories of Agrenon," she said quietly, as if trying to choose her words carefully. "Of how Endering are treated…"

"Differently?"

"Better."

"It's true," I said, but the words hurt coming out, as if I was lying to her. I was just as much of a dog of my nation as she was. The lack of a leash didn't change that harsh reality.

"Well, live it up over there for me when this is all over?"

"I will," I said as she started to lead me back toward the main space. It took time, showing me the ins and outs of the rest of the castle, and as we finished, Saha waved me over.

"We've just got word of an army marching north. It has to be him. We need to talk with Titanys and the others."

I nodded, Ivy already starting to head back to Quaren. I wanted to give her a hug, promise her it would be okay, tell her everything, but I couldn't. I had to turn with Saha and slip back out of the castle.

Heading back to where our troops were preparing with Eynon's army, I was surprised to see Whisper chatting with Sil and hung back to listen in on their conversation.

"Yeah, you really were being a shit," Whisper said.

"Honestly, it's one of my best traits."

"That's really not a good thing."

"Oh, I am aware," Sil laughed. "I really am sorry for giving you such a hard time."

"I forgive you, but you should maybe talk to my parents about it. I think it's a good idea to get this out of their minds, get things settled before we walk into battle, you know?"

"I think that's a good idea too," I said, finally approaching. I nudged Anza down the bond and he stepped away from where he was helping a Barbarza get out of the straps of a cart they had been pulling to come over. He was tense, ready to tell my grandmother exactly what was on his mind. "What were you saying?"

She took a breath and gave Whisper a look, but our daughter just smiled brightly back at her.

"I…wanted to apologise. I'm sorry for implying this little shit isn't your daughter," Sil started before looking to me. "I'm proud of the woman you've become. I can tell, even after all this, you two will go on to do great things. And I'm sorry that I failed you."

"And Emai." Anza prompted.

"And I'm sorry I didn't tell you about Emai."

"Why didn't you tell me?"

"Mira—"

"I just want to know why," I said, and Sil took another breath.

"When your parents were younger, they were even more careless with their lives than they are now. They chased magic with everything they were. One day, we heard an explosion in the library, and when we went to go see what it was, they were both on the brink of death. Magic is dangerous, and I tried to forbid them from using it. Forbidding teenagers though…never goes well."

I gave Whisper a look.

"Whaaaat?" she said, shrugging.

"It came out later that it was Emai's idea. Her recklessness almost got them both killed and I didn't want you to step into this world slinging magic that might kill you, following in her footsteps just to be like her."

"It's why you hesitated on the boat. You're afraid of magic."

"I'm afraid of what I can *lose* to magic, to the spirit of recklessness. She can see death, literally, she knows when it's near. Because of that, her recklessness is less dangerous. She knows she won't die. We don't have that luxury,"

"It was still shitty."

"I'm not asking your forgiveness. I don't need it to be sorry for what I've done."

Well, shit.

"It's a good thing you got it anyway. Just…don't do any more of that brand of fuckery, deal?"

"Deal."

"Anza?" Sil asked gently.

"I've let my anger get the best of me more than I'd like to admit these past few months. It hasn't gotten me anywhere. If Mira says you're forgiven, then you're forgiven. Now, let's go get ready to take on your least favorite son," he said, and Sil forced a smile, nodding.

"Thank you."

"Now that that emotional garbage is out of the way, I need you two. We need to find wherever my damn grandma ran off to, too. I have an idea." The glimmer in Whisper's eye should worry me.

"Oh great, an Echalon with an idea," Sil said playfully.

"In Whisper we trust," Anza and I said together, knowing full well our daughter was about to give us an edge over Olaf.

One that we desperately needed.

45

"You did not!" My father exclaimed as we looked out over the edge of the walls that surrounded Eyncn, waiting in the darkness for Olaf's attack.

"I did!" Anza laughed, punching him on the arm.

"You were all but frozen. How the hell did you even get to your feet with a dragon licking at your heels? That's impossible!"

"I had some help," Anza admitted. "But the shield was my idea and without it we would have burned for sure."

I let him have the moment, knowing that he often minimized his own accomplishments when he compared them to mine. He marveled at me for sure, loved me without conditions, but too often he felt he wasn't enough. I could feel it from him; he needed this.

"Em told me you were worthy, but damn, a Maraung in a snowstorm is a terrible idea! Frostbite?"

"Oh yeah!"

"How'd you get rid of it in that weather?"

"Um…"

Time to save them both that explanation.

"Hey, Dad, did you see what Whisper thought up? She saw it in old history books of Earth."

"The Czech hedgehogs? Yes, wonderful little inventions that will make it hard for carts and trebuchets. She really is a magnificent little girl, and honestly she's quite terrifying."

"This is the first time we've had the luxury of preparing instead of just reacting to an attack in progress. She's in her element," I said

"Give her a year or two and she'll be talking about how she can bring down the kingdoms and rattle the wonders of the world."

Anza and I shared a glance.

Thanks for saving me there.

No problem.

"We're pretty proud of her, I just wi—" I didn't get to complete my sentence before a stone slammed into the wall right beside my father. We all scrambled back, mere inches from death.

"Oh, it seems he has arrived," Brian said nonchalantly. I flattened the stone, giving us space to get back to the tower stairs that led downward. We rushed forward, Anza and my father leading the way as massive rocks rained down around us.

My magic instinctually reached for the singing stones as they hurtled toward us, crushing them to powder before they could find their marks, but there was no way for me to stop all of them. There were just too many.

"I thought they couldn't get trebuchets close enough," Anza said.

"It seems he wants to pull out all the stops. The hedgehogs only slow them down, they can't actually stop them."

"That's not something anyone has ever said."

"It's not?" Anza asked.

"No!" I insisted as we slid to a stop at the bottom of the stairs, flinching as the wall shuddered.

"We have to get them to stop."

"Mira, we need to find Emai!"

I turned toward the sound of Sil's voice. "What for? The wall's gonna drop if we don't reinforce it!"

"Kaboom," Sil said simply.

"Yes!" Brian declared, rushing off in search of my mother.

"What's 'kaboom'?" Anza asked.

"I have absolutely no idea," I admitted.

Thankfully, we didn't have to wait long because it was only a second before my parents were back.

"Tell her, tell her, tell her," my dad said, so excitedly that he was almost jumping for joy. Sil shook her head and laughed.

"Kaboom."

"Yes," my mother immediately said.

"But," Sil said, holding up a finger before pointing at me, "contained and launched on a trebuchet."

"You are a fucking genius!" my mother said, tears coming to her eyes as she closed the few steps between her and Sil to shake my grandmother's shoulders.

"Will someone explain to me what kaboom is?" I said, trying not to shout as Emai took my hand, pulling me toward one of the trebuchets.

"Find Abry and Whisper!" I called to Anza.

"On it!" he shouted back to me, rushing off to wrangle the kids. Sil was right behind us as we got to the trebuchet.

"Okay, okay. We need you to put a really big rock on here, with thin walls, it has to be hollow."

"This better be good," I said.

"Oooooh, you have no idea," Sil said.

It was strange how giddy the two were over this, but I carefully did as they asked and formed a perfectly round, hollow ball with thin walls.

"Em," Sil said before looking to me, "make a tiny hole, one large enough for her to put her hand in, and get ready to close it."

"Alright," I said, making the adjustment she asked for. My

mother flattened her hand against the hole and I saw smoke tremble at her fingertips, filling the inside of the ball with the ashy smoke she could, and *had,* left behind when she destroyed someone's being.

That's when it clicked.

"We're gonna fling this at them, but then what? What does it do?"

"Well, yes—" Emai began before Sil cut her off.

"We're going to light it on fire first," Sil said, lifting her hand up to spark a small flame at the end of her fingers.

"Put that away until we're ready," Emai said firmly before looking at me. "It's full. I'm gonna pull my hand out," she said, and I nodded, sliding the small piece of stone back over the opening as she did so, effectively creating a massive, flaming, flying bomb that could probably reduce anything it touched to ashes.

I stepped back, unsure of the agony that this could bring as Sil carefully tied a rope around the stone.

"Ready?" Sil asked.

"As ready as I can be," I said. "Let's send it."

I nodded as Sil lit the rope aflame and we all quickly stood back as she cut the rope holding the launch scoop down, flinging the dangerous ball up and over the wall toward our assailants.

I climbed the stairs, peeking my head up over the wall just in time to see it crash into Korrewen's army. My mother's smoke erupted once Sil's fire caught hold of it, sending bodies flying.

"We need more of those," my mom said flippantly.

"Oh yeah, yep," I said as we rushed back to the trebuchets.

I quickly made more hollow balls, as Titanys rushed toward us.

"Mountain! We need the walls reinforced!" he yelled.

"I'm gonna need to get closer to the castle to do that all at once, unless there's a specific place," I said, and he nodded.

I left Em and Sil with closing mechanisms built into several empty stone shells, allowing them to fill and launch them at their leisure.

"This way!"

I followed him, knowing he'd take me to a better vantage point. He quickly led me to the steps of the castle and I carefully reached my power out, pulling stone up and over the existing walls on the outside, lining them with a layer about a foot thick of fresh stone in order to help reinforce them.

"Good job," Titanys said, and I took a breath, taking a minute to survey the battlefield.

Hundreds of soldiers and guards were fighting outside, and hundreds more stood at the ready just inside the gate. There hadn't been a sighting of Olaf yet, nothing that indicated he was there.

If I saw him, he was as good as dead.

I took a breath, reminding myself he was the last person standing between myself and a tiny quaint cabin with my mate and my kids.

Panic lashed down the bond.

He's inside the walls! Anza yelled down the bond, and I felt my heart drop. How had he gotten in?

Where are you? I'm coming! He didn't respond, panic and fear alight as pain soaked into the thread between us. I followed my instincts, rushing toward where I thought he might be, the bond leading the way back into the castle. I froze, feeling cold as ice when I saw the pretty ballroom that had been left soaked in the blood of dozens of guards.

I steeled myself, turning toward the hallway that led to the portal. That was his goal, undoubtedly what he wanted. I had to stop him. Em and Sil were distracted. Saha was planning with Quaren and Graz to keep him out and they had no idea he was already in the castle, already at the portal. There was no time to warn them, no time to ask for help.

I rushed down the hallway, side stepping the dead guards and nearly tripping on what looked like a loose manhole in the floor. I stole a glance down into the sewers. *The sewers!* We hadn't thought of the sewer system. I pushed past the loose manhole and into the portal room, freezing at what I found.

Anza shielded Whisper with his body, a spike of ice through his shoulder as several others tried for his legs, one arm raised up over his head to protect them, the gauntlet glimmering with the magic Abry had imbued it with as it created a familiar force field over their heads as icicles crept down the ceiling toward them. He couldn't cover their legs and their heads, and his force field was protecting them from the ice creeping downward, threatening to spear them from above.

The force field immediately reminded me of Yuze.

"Mom!" Whisper shrieked as she reached out from behind Anza, who just nodded, trying to keep himself together to ensure our daughter survived. I took a step toward him, but Olaf stepped in the path between myself and my family. It was then that I noticed he already had the sigil complete and his sacrifices were already unconscious at their places.

"There you are. Took you long enough."

46

"You fucker," I snarled, twisting Tamaj's axe as I started toward him, reaching out a hand to throw my power to aid Anza, smashing through the icicles that had him pinned.

"In the flesh," he said as I lashed my axe at him. He side-stepped as the ground grew slick beneath my feet, but I stayed upright.

"Where's your little girlfriend?" I taunted, keeping Anza in my periphery, watching as he and Whisper tried to free his feet from Olaf's icy grip.

"She's on light duty." He shrugged.

"Poor baby," I hissed, righting myself as I sidestepped off the patch of ice he had manifested beneath me.

This was far from a fair fight and he knew it, but I lunged anyway, hoping that he'd be forced to sidestep away from the sigil. I kept after him and he raised an eyebrow, icing over my shoes. I purposefully slid, using his ice and my slight momentum to crash against him, digging my blade into his shoulder.

"You're gonna have to try harder than that to kill me," he snarled as blood dripped down the axe head. I shoved my hand forward, willing one of my bracelets into a spear in an attempt to run him through, but he swatted my hand away and shoved me back. I staggered, catching myself, only to feel a spike of ice graze my left knee.

"You missed," I said, smirking.

"Did I?" he asked as I tried to take a step toward him but couldn't move. I glanced down just long enough to see my brace caught up in an ice spike. "Interesting that you seem to think you're being noble. Stopping me is, in fact, the opposite of nobility."

"Oh yeah, killing friends and family for your own sick twisted game is totally noble," I said sarcastically.

"No game, just an attempt to free us from our oppressors," he said, carefully crafting an elegant sword of ice as he started toward me again. I didn't have time for this banter. If he killed me, he would kill them. Spikes were already starting to inch up against Anza and Whisper again.

"By destroying everything?"

"If I must. And I must, I assure you. Radical change is a necessary evil," he said. He was trying to distract me. "Don't pretend that you haven't thought of it, haven't seen it; the way the other kingdoms treat their Endering. The way Saha barks commands. She is just like them. You are nothing more than a pawn to her, and you are just like me," he snarled.

I lashed my power outward, raising a spike of earth in an attempt to skewer him straight up through his body, but he stepped back a single step. The spike slashed up his face and blood welled around his eye as I tried to break free of the ice at my brace.

"I'm nothing like you!" I hissed.

"Sure about that?" he hissed back as he lunged just as I got my leg free. I slammed the blunt side of my axe head against his skull, sending him sprawling to the ground, his sword clattering down as I started toward him.

"Positive," I said, stalking toward him. As my feet started to slide beneath me, I tensed my legs, adjusting my stance to the ice now below me. "What was it you told me? You have to do better than that?"

He didn't speak, carefully scrambling to his feet as I approached.

"Mira!" Anza said, and I quickly stole a glance over my shoulder, seeing the spikes growing more quickly, starting to press back into his flesh. I had to get them out of here. It was then I was slammed back, Olaf's hand suddenly against my throat, pinning me against a wall. I clawed at Olaf's wrist, fighting for a breath as he started to crush my windpipe. I felt the pain spike in my side as Anza tried to move, tried desperately to get past Olaf's icicles so he could get to me.

Don't die, please don't die on me, he begged, raw terror racing down the bond as my vision began to blur. He couldn't get free, couldn't get to me. I tried to focus on my power, but as I clawed at his wrist, the panic inside me kept me from focusing.

"You have been a thorn in my side for the last ti—"

I fell to the ground as his grip was ripped from my throat, taking a gasping breath as I desperately looked up, my throat aching from the pressure that had been applied, just in time to see Brian kick Olaf firmly between the legs before he took to punching him repeatedly in the face. I couldn't count how many punches he got in as my vision swam back to me, but I did notice him turn just enough to glance back at me, to check and see if I was alright.

Olaf took that opportunity to throw him off, the two getting to their feet as I felt the crackle of power surge through the room. I looked to my husband and daughter and tried to crawl toward them, my body screaming from the movement after the lack of air.

"Why can't you stand with me like you used to? For years we were on the same team!" Olaf snapped.

"You kept me from my daughter her whole life. You almost killed my wife for trying to save me. You kept me in a cage! You don't deserve *anyone* to stand with!" Brian yelled, his voice chilling me to my core as they rushed each other.

I could hear them scuffling as I watched Anza and Whisper, trying to crawl to them. Anza's legs shook as she tried to break the base off of one of the icicles in an effort to buy them time. I crawled an inch closer as I watched Anza's eyes move from me to where Brian fought Olaf out of sight, only to feel devastation rush down the bond. I turned just in time to see Olaf plunge his sword upward, into my fathers chest.

"No!" I screamed as the sword tore through him, hot blood spattering on the white-blue floor as Olaf shoved him off the blade. He immediately moved toward the sigil.

I forced myself back to my feet, urging myself forward to stand, raising a hand toward him as he spotted me, shaking as the tears welled in my eyes. How far was my mom? Could she get here? Did she even know? Could I stop him? Would I be fast enough?

"You wouldn't be able to save them," he said, his own hand lifting to where my family was pinned. "Not if you stop me. You wouldn't have time."

"If I skewer you—"

"I kill them."

"And if I go to them—"

"I go to the sigil" he said.

Could I move fast enough to kill him before he killed my family? They were what I was fighting for, what I had always fought for.

"You won't be fast enough," he said, as if he could read my mind.

I felt the tears creep over the edges of my eyes as the deep-red blood spilled from my father, his breaths shuddering to a stop. My chest felt like it was folding in on itself. I couldn't take a breath and I couldn't tear my eyes from Olaf.

"Don't do this," I begged him, shaking as I watched him.

"Choose!" I felt my entire body shudder. There wasn't a choice.

I ran to my family.

He ran to the sigil.

I felt the blast of power as I reached Anza's side, slamming us against the wall with the force of a speeding train. I kept my body between the blast and Whisper, desperate to keep her safe.

My legs didn't want to respond as I tried to get back up. Rubble crumbled down around us as we both tucked our heads and pulled Whisper between us, using our bodies to shield her shaking, terrified form. My head burst with pain as a piece of the roof crashed into us from above.

Anza's gauntlet could only do so much.

It felt like an eternity before I could move again, and it was my mother's scream that roused me from the daze I sat in.

Looking up, Olaf's absence was the first thing I noticed. Emai was on her knees at my father's head, desperately trying to push his life back into him. How long had it been? I felt the tears slide down my face faster and found myself unable to catch a steady breath.

"Please, please." I hadn't even realized I said the words out loud. She couldn't hear me.

"No, no no, don't leave me like this!" she shrieked, Sil frozen at the sight of the demolished portal room.

"Stars," Whisper muttered, and I looked to her.

Her eyes were locked upward, and as I turned my face to the sky peeking in through the ruinous building, I realized she was right. The stars shone down on us.

The wrong stars.

"We failed."